CLAWHAVEN CLIFF

Genre: Historical Fiction /Family Saga

APPRECIATION

To Caroline, Carol and Ann for your invaluable input and support.
To the support of good friends within the local writing groups and
local library.

i

CLAWHAVEN CLIFF

Published at Ingram Spark
by Elizabeth Rimmington. 2025.
Queensland
Australia

Copyright 2025 © Elizabeth Rimmington
National Library of Australia
State Library of Queensland

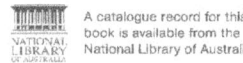 A catalogue record for this
book is available from the
National Library of Australia

978-0-6454944-3-3 (Print)
978-0-6454944-4-0 (Epub)

≈

Disclaimer

This novel is a work of fiction. While some of the names, characters and business places mentioned may have existed, their interaction with the story characters is pure fiction. All incidents are either the products of the author's imagination or have been used in a fictitious manner. The opinions expressed or beliefs held are those of the characters and should not be assumed to be the opinions or beliefs of the author.

CLAWHAVEN CLIFF

Written by Elizabeth Rimmington

Previous Books by Elizabeth Rimmington:

Shadow of the Northern Orchid
Shadows on the Goldfields Track
Shadows Across Cape York
Burdekin Heartbeats
Rhylla's Secret
Chill of Blame

Elizabeth Rimmington
Elizabeth is an Australian author living in a rural area of South-East Queensland. During a career in nursing followed by several years driving a taxi cab, Elizabeth has met many and varied people from all walks of life. A storehouse of memories from which to plunder and develop story characters able to infiltrate the reader's heart by osmosis. Their laughter, their heartbreak and their pain will fill the booklover's soul with happiness, tears, fear and empathy.

Visit Elizabeth Rimmington at her website
www.elizabethrimmington.com.au
Find her on Facebook – elizabethrimmington.author

CLAWHAVEN CLIFF

PROLOGUE

Townsville - Queensland

1921

"Oh, bother it," Florence Mayford Treloar growled. She plopped back from her knees to rest on her buttocks with her back against the three sturdy drawers built into the end of the right-angled polished timber desk. Perspiration trickled down her face. She felt its dampness between her breasts. Even at seven o'clock in the morning, the summer heat and humidity of North Queensland seeped into every corner.

Once more on her hands and knees, she peered through the gloom under the desk trying to identify the obstruction preventing another large cardboard box of books from fitting snugly into place.

"Damn, damn, damn!" The curses felt good and sinful upon her tongue but did nothing to release the blockage. She was ten years of age – fourteen years ago – when she first heard the word 'damn.' The gardener-handyman's apologies followed loud and fast when he noticed her wide-eyed stare from where she stood rooted to the spot at the corner of the shed. No doubt, Mr. Jimmy Braydon still issued forth similar curses, when the need arose, but not before checking his surroundings with more care, she warranted.

"Miss Florence, if your mother heard you swear like that, she would be most displeased. You know it is not lady-like to curse." The housekeeper's grey straggly eyebrows almost met in the middle of Mrs. Braydon's forehead, above the twinkling dark eyes. "It always worried Mrs Odette knowing you mixed with all sorts when working at the hospital. She only agreed to your training as a nurse because it seemed a noble deed to help the war effort, but now it is 1921 and the war is over. It is time to reapply our standards."

Florence struggled to keep the grin from her face. Her downcast gaze swept across the office floor. She knew full well Mrs. Braydon hid inside the large hall cupboard to vent the frustrations of her day in a low rumbling grumble. The amusement was short-lived upon her lips as her thoughts turned to her recently buried mother.

"Oh, Mrs. Braydon, if only my mother was here to scold me. I miss her so much."

"Yes, darling, it will take a time before the pain will subside, particularly because it came hard on the heels of the loss of your Aunt Bridie." Rosa Braydon blinked her eyelids rapidly as she tucked a grey recalcitrant hair under a hair clip and moved over to rest her hand upon the young woman's shoulder. "Now, tell me, what on earth do you think you are doing there? We have a housemaid and the handyman to do the heavy chores."

Moisture glistened in Florence's blue eyes. She swallowed before speaking.

"I am trying to fit this box of books under the desk here, but something is jammed at the back."

"Another box of books? Shouldn't they go into the library?"

"When Mr. Braydon builds the new shelves for my nursing books, I will unload them in there, but until then, I thought I could hide them out of the way in here." Florence gave a random shove with her foot but nothing moved. "I will have to drag everything out and restack things."

"Just because you have graduated, doesn't mean you won't need your books for reference, I shouldn't think, Miss Florence."

"No, you are right, Mrs. Braydon, and I do plan to have them easy to access when the bookshelves are finished."

"I'll have a word with Mr. Braydon today on your behalf, dear. In the meantime, I'll send Ethel-May to help you."

Florence and Ethel-May dragged each overfull archive box out, to be placed in the middle of the room. Sneezing and sniffling accompanied the latent dust stirred up in the process. As far as Florence knew, many of the boxes had never seen daylight since her mother, Odette Treloar with her Aunt Bridie Mayford, first arrived in Australia from England in late 1896. For a moment, Florence allowed her mind to reflect on the father of whom her mother never spoke. She rolled over, wiped her nose, and sat up. Many years ago, she had learnt such idle ponderings were just a waste of time. Any questions asked were answered with a snap.

"Only you and I, child, and your Auntie Bridie; there is no father. We will do just fine."

"Are you alright there, Miss Florence?" The freckled-faced woman with her brown hair tied back and wearing a white starched and ironed apron to cover her navy dress hanging to just above her ankles spoke.

"Yes, Ethel-May, it's all this dust. My nose is running like a tap." Florence dabbed her handkerchief to remove the errant tears before wiping her nose.

The two women discovered under the desk at the very back, what appeared to be a small case jammed sideways absorbing a large area for a small item. A groan of frustration and impatience rolled up from Florence's prostrate body stretched out upon the floor. There was nothing else for it. *That case must be evicted – preferably into the next garbage collection.* As this thought flashed inside her head, a screech of guilt followed it to the surface of her mind. *Oh, dear, if Mother were still alive, she would rate such talk a sacrilege.*

Florence's finger marks lay deep in the dust as she hauled the case out into the light streaming through the wide gap between the window drapes. She recalled one of the few times she ever saw her mother crying. She had been sorting through this miniature suitcase's contents when it happened. At the time, Florence promised herself to investigate the music case at her earliest opportunity. Well, it had been nine months since they buried her mother's frail body and still this small case and its contents remained an unresolved mystery.

The newly proclaimed lady-of-the-house, Miss Florence, with the housemaid Ethel-May, sat back to examine this well-worn leather case all of sixteen inches by twelve inches and five inches deep. Rust coated the thin metal locks on either side of the leather handle worn smooth with the touch of many hands. Florence's fingers failed to unjam the catches. Were they locked or just rusted? She lifted the case and felt the weight within. A sharp shake revealed no clue to the contents other than papers of some kind, perhaps. On the tail of those thoughts, she asked herself, why would these papers be stored in this special container and not relegated to plain archive boxes like all the other files stored away by her mother and her Aunt Bridie?

As she addressed her mind to the problem of opening the rusted locks, the chimes of the large hall clock announced it was time for her to bathe and dress, if she was to be on time for her shift at the Townsville Hospital.

As Florence travelled the short distance to the hospital in the small, horse-drawn, open carriage pulled by the bay horse and driven by Mr. Braydon, she pondered on the music case discovered earlier.

Three days later, Florence found the time to further investigate her mystery leather case. She was pleased to see evidence of Ethel-May's hand in the scrubbed and polished office room. Not a skerrick of dust remained on the floor or the storage boxes – not even on the stubborn leather music case.

With little hope of success, Florence once more strained to open the locks on either side of the leather handle. Suffocating a mumbled curse, which would have horrified her mother, Florence jumped up and strode down to the 'bitta this and that' drawer in the vegetable room. In this drawer, Mr. Braydon kept a few simple tools used frequently within the house. She took out a small hammer and a solid looking screwdriver. Her grey eyes flashed with determination.

Once the rusty locks were gouged out from their foundations, Florence flipped back the lid of the mystery case. She sneezed as the musty smell of old paper wafted up into her face. A sigh of disappointment fell from her lips. On top of the contents lay sheets of old music with tattered edging and pencil marks scrawled across every page. When she noticed the name *David Lewis* written in a bold hand across the top left-hand corner of each of the six musical scores and *Bridie Mayford* printed in neat letters beneath, Florence vaguely recalled Aunt Bridie having mentioned a man named David. She sat for some moments in deep thought. *Did this man mean something special to Aunt Bridie?* Florence removed the pages with reverence and lay them on the polished floor beside the small music case – its mouth wide open to reveal further treasures within.

A pink ribbon holding ten letters all addressed to Miss Odette Mayford next drew Florence's gaze. Smudged, dirt-stained fingerprints covered the envelopes. With care, she removed the friable paper of the first letter. She read the words, *My Dearest Detta*. Florence's heart pounded. Her gaze raced to the bottom line to read, *From your true and faithful love, Peter Treloar*. Waves of excitement washed through her body like the ocean waves running up and down the hot sands. Was she to learn the answers to all the questions her mother had avoided addressing throughout her life? At a young age, Florence learnt just how determined her mother could be – and the lengths she took to guard her privacy. To keep the peace over the years, Florence contained her curiosity concerning their lives. Was this man her father? With trembling hands, Florence replaced the letter into the envelope, re-tied the bow on the bundle of letters and set them aside on the desk to read later at her leisure.

A single envelope stained with what may have been dried tears next drew her attention. The name *Bridie Mayford* had been scrawled across the front along with an address to a place called Clawhaven Manor, West Sussex, England. Inside was a single page with words loud in the dark scrawled print. *"DON'T BOTHER COMING HOME. YOU ARE A DISGRACE TO THE FAMILY."*

Florence leant back against the desk drawers to ponder what Aunt Bridie could have done to deserve this warning. Arriving at no solution she delved back into the treasure chest.

Two small drawstring bags decorated with stump-work embroidery – one a red rose and the other an English red robin – were next to be examined. In the first, she found an amethyst brooch which Florence recognized as one Aunt Bridie often wore to church. In the second, nestled the gold locket which seldom left Aunt Bridie's neck. Aunt Bridie often told her it could not be opened, but Florence discovered today that this was not so. A perfect miniature painting of a man's head – his blue eyes and distinctive red hair – rested inside. In the same embroidered bag lay a golden tie pin shaped like a ship's anchor enclosed inside a golden heart. The last object she found was a wide gold band.

Wrapped in aged silk cloth, two sheets of glass with smoothed edges secured by gold clasps held a sketch of two soldiers – young men dressed in British Cavalry uniforms. One a Captain and the other a Lieutenant.

A bulky brown envelope, when opened, contained official documents belonging to a woman named Mrs. Beca Lewis who lived in Wales. Briefly, Florence pondered the connection of this woman to the music lover David Lewis. A quick scan of the other pages revealed an old property deed in the name of David Lewis for a house in Sussex, England.

Another large brown solicitor's envelope included papers of ownership for this house near the seafront at Townsville, in the name of Bridie Mayford. Florence knew this was the house in which she was born. A second paper registered the transfer of this ownership to Odette Treloar, after Aunt Bridie's death nearly three years ago. Less than twelve months had passed since Florence had sat in the solicitor's office to hear Mr. Livingstone Jr read her mother's will. Her tears flowed again as they had the day when she signed for the transfer of this same property into her name.

Wills and testaments of Aunt Bridie, her mother and one for Peter Treloar, were also removed from the case to lie with the collection gathering on her desktop. On the bottom, in a stout cardboard box two inches square, Florence discovered two small rings, one a plain gold band and the second a gold band with a modest diamond surrounded by small amethysts. On closer inspection, she read the words *Detta - Peter*. The thrill, like an electric current throughout her limbs, accompanied her tears which blurred the words.

A hard-covered book opened to reveal a journal started by her mother in 1896. The entries commenced when Aunt Bridie and her mother were on board the ship coming to Australia late in that year. The entries were erratic and sporadic – sometimes little more than a word or two, to jog a memory perhaps. Other entries were expanded prose written as the mood took the author, maybe. Florence's heart beat faster at the possibilities of what she might find between the pages.

The ticking of the clock in the hall sounded loud inside the office. She really must not waste any more time, she was due on duty within the hour. The temptation was not to be denied. As she flicked through page after page, between the hard covers of her mother's neat handwriting, her heart and soul became swamped in tears.

PART ONE

BRIDGETTE MAYFORD

(BRIDIE)

CHAPTER ONE

Entrance into the World

1856

Athena Mayford's strength was fading fast. For almost two long days she had struggled to deliver her fourth child into the world. Her mother, Anna Wellington, sponged the perspiration from her face, including the dried trickle of blood on her cheek which followed the rupture of fine blood vessels in her right eye.

"One last push, Mrs. Mayford," Physician Grimley encouraged, as he watched the hands of the midwife gentle the head of the almost-born child. With restless hands, the doctor stroked his thick dark moustache.

Athena's deep growl vibrated through the bed, as she gathered the remnants of her strength. She refused to scream despite the agony resident within every muscle of her body. She did not want to frighten her three children: George, the oldest at four years of age, Maxwell, the middle son aged three years, and Toby her two-year-old. She trusted Nanny to keep them well away in the south wing of their home, but she feared the sound may carry, even to there, if she gave full voice to her pain and frustrations. Besides, stoicism had been a large element in her upbringing.

She bore down with what little muscle power remained and a limp, bloodied child landed in the open hands of the midwife.

"Well done," the doctor offered automatically, while he watched the nurse wipe the nose and mouth of the quiet infant. She massaged the baby's feet, slapped the baby's bottom and began rubbing the tiny chest vigorously. Almost ready to give up all hope of life, the nurse grinned widely when a loud bawl of protest burst from the small open mouth. The nurse and the doctor exchanged a brief look of relief before the doctor glanced back to the patient. Horror in his expression drew the attention of the nurse, whose gaze also turned. A river of blood flowed out onto the already stained sheets.

Physician Grimley watched the life ebb rapidly from the face of his patient. The skin of her beautiful face paled to a blue-grey and the flesh became flaccid. He turned to Athena's mother, who did not miss the tell-tale signs of her daughter's death.

"I am so sorry, Mrs. Wellington," the doctor's face whitened also at this unwanted, but not unknown, complication of a long-drawn-out childbirth. "I am sorry," the doctor repeated. "Mrs. Mayford has haemorrhaged as a result of the torturous delivery she has undergone."

Anna Wellington sat unmoving. The colour drained from her drawn and tired face. Inside her head, she screamed, though her voice remained silent. *What sort of vindictive God are you to take my daughter? What have I done to deserve this? Have I not given you enough with my two sons in battle and now you steal my only daughter? Am I to be grateful that you have allowed me to be with her at this time – something I never had the chance to do with either son? One child each year! Well, I have no more, are you satisfied?* Anna's fingers clenched and unclenched on her lap. She reached over and held Athena's lifeless hand. A whimper fell from her lips.

Sometime later, with the patient sponged and dressed in clean clothes and lying on clean sheets with her blond hair brushed over the pillow, the doctor left to speak to the husband, Mr. Douglas Mayford. Doctor Grimley chewed on his top lip as his stomach churned at this task ahead. Mr. Mayford was a man known throughout London to have a quick temper. The knock sounded dull on the heavy timber door of the man's office.

Inside the room, Douglas Mayford frowned. He looked up. After only a brief second his face cleared. He jumped up and opened the door.

"Aah, Grimley, you're here. Has my Athena eventually rid herself of this latest brat? Come on in. You'll take a drink with me then to wet the new arrival's head, will you? A boy, I hope. They are much more valuable to the business, are they not?" His chuckle was little more than a clearing of his throat.

The physician followed Mr. Mayford two steps into the room before he drew on his courage and spoke.

"Mr. Mayford, I am sorry it is not all good news that I bring, sir."

"Oh, dear, a girl then. Never mind, Athena will be pleased. I know she has been yearning for a girl to design in her own image, or whatever it is girls do."

The doctor stared at the man. "Mr. Mayford, yes, Mrs. Mayford gave birth to a baby girl, but this is not what I am trying to tell you."

"Oh dear, the babe did not make it. Well, my wife will be most upset I am sure, but then there will be others to divert her attention, no doubt. We must make allowances. Women are rather emotional about this sort of thing."

"That is not what I am here to say …."

"Well spit it out, man. I haven't all day to spend on another noisy brat in the house." Douglas Mayford returned to his desk.

The doctor's voice sharpened. "Mr. Mayford, I am trying to tell you that it was your wife, Mrs. Mayford, who did not survive her ordeal. It has been a long, drawn-out childbirth after all and she has succumbed."

The colour drained from Douglas Mayford's face. He gasped and placed one hand firmly on each of the doctor's shoulders.

"What are you saying? Good grief, man, what exactly are you saying? My Athena ...," the bluster fell from him like air from a holed balloon. "She's not ...?"

"Yes, Mr. Mayford, sir, that is what I am saying. Mrs. Mayford has given her life for her baby."

Douglas Mayford felt his body shrink in upon itself. He felt the pain of a blunderbuss exploding inside his heart. The weight of a large boulder dragged at his chest. He felt the tremble in his legs and feared they were about to let him down. His grip on the doctor's shoulders tightened.

This cannot be true. Not my Athena – my beautiful Athena – the only person in my life I have ever loved.

He stumbled backwards until he felt the pressure of the office desk against the back of his legs.

"Thank you, Doctor. I will see her for myself." Douglas Mayford pushed off from the desk in the direction of the birthing room.

Grimley hurried in the man's wake. His legs were no match for Douglas's long stride down the hallways.

Douglas threw the doors open and stood red-faced and gasping, taking in the sight of his wife lying with the fresh pink bed-spread drawn up tight against her chin accentuating the pallor of her skin. Not a word passed his lips for long seconds. He waved his arms expressing his desire for everyone to clear the room. The midwife and the maid tiptoed along the wall and out through the doorway, the nurse with her small Gladstone bag and the maid almost hidden behind the roll of soiled linen she juggled in her arms. Douglas sat on the vacated chair by Athena's side and held her hand. He made no attempt to see the child responsible for stealing his precious Athena's life. When the babe gave a squall, he turned towards the sound.

"Take the brat away. Take it away, Anna," he never even turned his head, "I never want to lay eyes on it again." Douglas commanded his mother-in-law.

Anna Wellington swept up the infant in the long shawl and departed towards the guest rooms on the lower floor of the South Wing. Her tears fell, not only for herself and her husband but for Douglas. She knew he was a hard man, but she was aware that he loved their daughter Athena with his whole being. The thought of the child growing up without at least her father's love filled Anna with a feeling of deep sorrow.

After the burial of Athena Mayford in 1856 following the birth of her daughter Bridgette, Anna Wellington departed the city with the small baby in her arms. On the opposite seat in the carriage, Nanny Granville, a middle-aged woman with warm grey eyes, sat straight-backed watching the passing scenery outside the window of the vehicle, while taking in the sad figure of Mrs. Wellington, whose tears were barely held at bay. Nanny Granville knew she should insist on relieving the woman of the burden of the baby, but in her wisdom, she appreciated the woman's need to hold her own daughter vicariously through the child. They travelled to Clawhaven Manor on the coast almost two days carriage ride southwest of London. The baby's three brothers George, Max and Toby remained in the care of a nanny and a tutor at the well-staffed London home with their father.

CHAPTER TWO

Bridie's Childhood

1861-1873

The name Bridgette quickly became truncated to Bridie. As she grew older, the child was allowed the freedom enjoyed by country children. She loved her quiet but determined grandmother with her streaks of greying hair, and the fingers that brought the piano keyboard to life. Bridie doted on her Grandpa Wellington, the gentle man forever pushing his reading glasses up higher onto his nose. A man who spent many hours each day buried in the books of his extensive library. His broad smile at her every question, followed by patient answers, stimulated her interest in his world of books.

On the sunnier days, Grandmama often asked the kitchen staff to prepare a picnic basket that the gardener/handyman named Baines carried to the shingle beach. Unless Nanny Granville was on her half-day off, she joined the small group. On this spring day at their granddaughter's fifth birthday, as with every picnic day, Bridie's laughter and squeals bounced off the waves lapping the shore, when she ran up and down the high tide mark searching for the best driftwood for a fire. Baines lifted his soft cap from his head and ran his fingers through the thinning hair. He scratched his forehead and mumbled, "I've said it before and I'll say it again, where does the lass get all her energy?"

"I don't know, Baines, but if you ever find out, I'll be happy to share," Grandpa Wellington laughed as he smoothed his wife's cushion on one of the two sea-carved chairs worn out of a pair of large boulders. He moved across to the matching seat, wiggled into the familiar hollows and watched as Baines lit the fire to boil the kettle. "Did I ever tell you, Baines, nothing tastes as good as tea made on the water boiled over a campfire of debris from the sea?"

Anna Wellington interrupted with a laugh. "I think I can say with confidence – you have told us that at every picnic we have ever had here on the beach."

"That will be quite a few now, Mrs. Wellington. Young Miss Bridie reminds me so much of her mother at that age. Miss Athena would be so proud if she were here now."

Both William and Anna Wellington sat in silence enjoying, yet mourning, the memories of their only daughter. It was Anna who spoke first.

"Yes, Baines. Except for the dark curls, Bridie is the very image of her mother when she was five years of age. Maybe she is a little more boisterous though, or am I slowing down and cannot keep up as I used to?"

"We all miss her too, Mrs. Wellington."

Anna blinked her tears away and swallowed those at the back of her throat.

"Thank you, Baines. Now, is the kettle boiling yet? I am perishing for a cup of tea."

"Only another moment, Mrs. Wellington."

As Baines tossed a handful of leaves into the boiling water, the three at the picnic site looked up to see Bridie tearing along the beach waving something above her head. Held by the strong tie, her hat flapped from side to side at the back of her neck. Bright pink ribbons streamed out behind. The shingles crunched as she landed in a heap at her grandfather's feet.

"Look, Grandpa, I found a treasure the smugglers must have left behind." In the palm of her hand, she held a large, smooth, shiny, black stone polished by time, the waves and the seabed.

"That certainly looks to be a valuable piece of smuggler's treasure, little one," William Wellington agreed, as he took up the stone to give it a close examination.

Bridie retrieved the black treasure from her grandpa's hand and took it to her grandmother for inspection. After Anna turned the stone over several times in the palm of her hand, she nodded her head with the wisdom of the elderly.

"I'd suggest you keep this in a safe place, young Bridie."

Not content with the enthusiasm of the audience so far, Bridie ran to show the handyman.

"Look, Mr. Baines, do you think this is a smuggler's treasure?"

"Surely it is, Miss Bridie. Now, you be careful and do not stray too far. My grandmother used to tell me of how her father was stolen from the family when he was about your age. He was taken away to work on the smugglers' ships."

Bridie's blue eyes widened. "Oooh, did he turn into a smuggler too?"

"I guess he did, child, but Granny was never going to admit it."

Anna and William exchanged amused glances at the sight of the awe in the face of their granddaughter.

"I think it might be wise not to stray out of our sight, Bridie, dear." Her grandmama advised.

"When I grow big, I'm going to be a smuggler, I think." Bridie stared off into the dreamland only she could imagine. "I will bring all my treasure back to you and Grandpa, I will. This will be my very first …," Bridie's frown indicated her struggle to recall the word she wanted, "… instalment." Her grin of pride and satisfaction widened the smiles on each of the faces of the three adults.

17

"Come, Bridie, will you join Grandpa and me in a cup of tea and fairy cake?"

After serving the Wellingtons and Miss Bridie, Baines sat over near the fireplace drinking from his chipped pannikin.

"I love this place the best in the world, Grandmama. I'd like to stay here forever more," Bridie spoke her thoughts aloud.

"I think it might be a bit unpleasant in the winter when the snows arrive, Bridie."

Bridie fell into a silence, while she pondered her grandmother's words. She accepted another small cake with pink icing.

"Life with Bridie is truly a constant challenge for the pair of us, Anna. Just keeping ahead of her imagination is a struggle." The smiles flew between the grandparents like bluebirds darting between favourite nesting sites.

1863

After some discussion, Anna and William had decided their granddaughter should have a small birthday party on her seventh birthday. When they sat down to plan who and how many children were to be invited, they discovered very few of their friends had children of Bridie's age. Eventually, they settled on the few children from the estate cottages. Sadly, their plans went askew when, as Anna sat writing the invitations for hand delivery, the mailman presented them with news from London. In his usual autocratic manner, Douglas Mayford announced his planned visit the very day in question.

"Oh dear, William, I am so glad we have not told Bridie of our plans for her party. I would not have liked to disappoint her."

"If I know our Bridie, she might feel a little relief. I am afraid she takes after me in that respect. She craves the company of her books and the horses more than she does that of her peers."

"That's as may be, but she really should be encouraged to mix more with others her own age."

"Anna, my love, Bridie is content with the company of you and me. Call me selfish if you will, but for that, I am eternally grateful."

Anna scowled at her husband. "William, we cannot deny her the opportunities we have had."

"Oh, Anna, I know you are right." William smiled and reached over to stroke his wife's hair. "I think Bridie will be more upset at the arrival of her father and her brothers. My guess is, we will hardly see her during their stay. You can be sure she will find a cubbyhole and barely come out to meet them."

On the day of Bridie's seventh birthday, she shared her birthday cake with her brothers, where they ate in the small room adjacent to the adults' dining room, under the supervision of Nanny Granville. Bridie's wide dark gaze followed the boys' quiet antics as they sat around the table, but her mouth remained closed as she listened to their conversation.

As soon as possible after being released from their company, Bridie waved goodbye to Nanny Granville who left in the spring cart, with Sanders in charge of the horse. Today was her half-day off and she had promised to clean the local church at the Clawhaven Cliff Village.

Bridie went exploring through the grounds of Clawhaven Manor by herself – to escape the presence of the man she knew to be her father. His visits were rare, this was the second time that she remembered. To the small girl such a loud, arrogant man terrified her. She only felt brave, when she stood between her grandparents waving the man goodbye, as his carriage disappeared along the driveway.

This afternoon's trek in the grounds was no different from many others – at least to start with…. Her feet led her to the family vault. At the edge of the tree line, the child cast a glance left and right. It fascinated her to think of all her forebears lying inside this stone-hewn building little bigger than a large room. She imagined all their ghosts sitting around talking and comparing the caskets their relatives had chosen for their burials. Did these wispy remains wander around seeking a crack or gap through which they might shimmy into the world outside? Her fingers trailed along the rough surface of the outside wall as she followed the path around the circumference of the building. Today she knew there was little chance of gaining an entrance. Even on her highest tiptoe, she had several more inches to grow before her fingers reached the large bolt in the top of the door. Grandpa usually made short work of the door-opening process.

"Oh," she gasped when the large wooden door seemed to flinch at her touch. Bridie noticed the bolt had not been pushed home into the door frame. She stopped and pressed hard below the knob of the large heavy bolt. The door opened a fraction. She strained to exert every ounce of her slim body against it. The timber scrunched on the stone floor and the hinges squeaked. The gap extended enough to allow her entry into the dimly lit, dusty room.

Fear threatened to release a scream from her throat, but fear of her father's displeasure on finding her in this out-of-bounds building hushed her voice. His arrival with her three older brothers two days ago had set the usually peaceful household into disarray. She recalled the conversation overheard between her grandparents, while she was hiding in the linen cupboard on the top hallway landing.

"Douglas and the boys will be returning to the city the day after tomorrow," Grandmama had said.

"Can't say I'll be sorry to see the back of those wild tear-a-ways," Grandpa commented. "They make more noise than a herd of cattle bellowing at milking time."

Inside the room, Bridie's blue-eyed gaze cast about seeking any ghosts sitting on the lids of the coffins reaching out from the edge of the walls, or for those other spectres that may be floating along with the dust motes on the thin streams of light drifting in through the narrow grillwork along the top of the walls. Bridie's curiosity swallowed her initial fear. Her first task was to close the door. She retained the presence of mind to realize anyone walking outside might notice it unlatched.

Her hands froze on the timber at the noise of approaching voices. She recognized the sound of her three brothers arguing. Once again, she resented their presence here at Clawhaven and, like Grandpa, looked forward to their return to their London residence.

Her light footsteps took her to the back wall, where she hunched down between the end of one coffin and a statue of an angel with a hand outstretched, palm upwards. Bridie held her breath for as long as she could. Her little heart pounded inside her chest wall. It almost deafened her to the boys' voices.

"How many times have you got to be told, Toby? Your job is to cover up all evidence. If we get caught, Max and I will seek revenge. How did you not remember to collect our tobacco pouch?"

Bridie knew that was George, her eldest brother – the blond-haired one. Not dark-haired like their father or herself. He was four years older than her and thought he was all grown up.

"Sorry, George, I forgot. Anyway, Max was last through the door."

"That does not count. The youngest tidies up behind the others." Max reported the rules of the trio.

"Now toughen up, both of you. If you plan to work on Father's ships one day, you'll have to toughen up and smarten up." A short silence followed until George continued, "Now pick up the pouch, pull that door shut and slip the bolt before the gardener sees this door open and wonders why."

In the shadows, Bridie dithered. She wanted to call out and tell them not to leave her here with the ghosts, but she feared her eldest brother as much as she feared any ghosts or her father. The bolt slid into place with a solid clunk. Tears washed her eyes as the room darkened leaving only the faint glow through the grill panels above her head. She jumped up planning to go and bang on the door and call her brothers back. Pain blinded her for a moment when her head smacked into the stone angel's hand. She fell back to her knees. More tears threatened until a soft swish sound caught her attention. The angel was turning away from her. It took some moments for Bridie to realize a panel in the wall that held the angel was turning.

The secret door paused leaving ample space for Bridie to walk past the angel into a narrow room. Similar high grill panels to those in the first room allowed a little light in on two sides of this small space leading to steps descending into a dark hole. Bridie's total absorption in this new environment deafened her to the slight "swoosh" as the angel returned to her original position. When she realized her dilemma, Bridie's fingers, hands and forearms bled as she pushed, shoved and scraped, trying to lure the angel back, all to no avail.

Instinct urged her to scream towards the grillwork in the hope one of the gardeners or maybe a farm hand was outside, but it was the fear of an angry father that sat her down in the dust to think. She ran her tongue over her wounds and padded them with one of her petticoats. An idea triggered her legs into action. Bridie stood and gently ran her fingers over the surface of the wall. Down near her right foot, her fingers touched a hidden lever – almost invisible to the naked eye. It took all her strength, but she pushed it until once again the secret door swished quietly open. She jumped back out into the room of the dead. After several moments, the door shut behind her.

Her gaze flashed once more around the room hoping not to find any ghosts out and about. Bridie remembered there was no way out in this direction, with the door now locked. If she had looked more closely at the door, she would have seen the slot high up and level with the bolt outside. A steel bar attached to the bolt enabled someone inside to move the outside bolt back and forth. Even if Bridie had noticed this convenience, it would not have helped her. She was too short to reach up high enough. Bridie held her breath again for ever so long. She felt the urge to cry once more, but the words of her grandfather settled her nerves.

Fear is a good thing if we use it to plan and think. Don't let it paralyse you, little Bridie.

Sitting in the dust on the floor, Bridie rubbed at the lump on the back of her head.

"Oh, Grandpa, I cannot get out of here except by the secret door, and I am frightened of where the secret doorway may take me. Does the devil use that dark hole with the steps? Does he come and take away the dead who have been naughty?"

She recalled more of what her grandfather often told her when she was frightened of anything.

I want you to always remember this. If you cross your middle finger over the pointy finger of your left hand, I will be inside your head giving you courage, whenever you may need it.

Her eyelids drooped and her head lay upon her folded arm. Bridie Mayford slept.

When she awoke to find her situation unchanged, she stood up and spoke quietly into the dim light.

"Grandpa, if I hold my fingers crossed as you showed me, will you come with me into the dark hole?" she whispered.

Inside her head, she was sure she heard Grandpa say, *Yes, Bridie, my dear.*

Bridie lifted her left hand, folded her middle finger over the pointy finger and pressed them tightly. With her other hand, she took hold of the angel's hand and tried to move it. It felt stiff. She pushed sharp and hard. It was when she twisted it, the forearm rolled sideways and the angel's secret doorway swished open. Bridie's feet faltered as she tentatively moved into the chamber beyond. She pressed her folded fingers tighter together and took a deep breath, as the secret door shut behind her.

"Are you there, Grandpa?"

She heard the answer clearly inside her head. *Yes, Bridie.*

In the dim light, on a ledge, Bridie noticed several candles; three were a dirty brown colour, but two were white and new looking. Two small candle holders lay near them. By their side sat a tinder box and a sharp-edged stone. Grandpa often lit the candle in his office using a similar tinder box and stone. The young girl found the chore of lighting a candle in this way not as easy as Grandpa made it seem, especially as she had to keep the two fingers of her left hand folded. Eventually, a candle flickered into a flame and Bridie sat it into a holder. The glow from the flame revealed the worn stone steps leading down into the depths beyond.

Bridie's heart quailed. She heard again Grandpa's voice inside her head, and bravely moved her foot down onto the first step. She heard another of her grandfather's oft-repeated words of advice. *The first step on any journey is always the hardest.*

Holding the candle high, she took one step at a time. A cold chill sent goosebumps up her arms. When she lowered the candle, its small flame held little warmth. Bridie stumbled at the bottom step when the dark hole became a dark tunnel in front of her. The candle wavered – the light flickered. Her sharp cry echoed down through the emptiness. Bridie swallowed and removed the errant tears from her cheeks with the back of her left hand.

It was the mass of darkness all around her compared to the small perimeter of her candlelight, which held Bridie's feet still for several more moments.

"Are you there, Grandpa?" she whispered.

The voice seemed to come loud in her ear. *Yes, Bridie, walk on.*

One foot after another, Bridie plodded forward. The tunnel seemed to go on forever. None of the children in the story books Grandmama read to her each evening encountered such a long, dark, black tunnel as this one. She squealed and jumped back against the solid wall when a T-piece opened in the tunnel. Bridie felt safer remaining in the long, straight tunnel she felt a connection to, rather than veering off into this new direction.

After an aeon of time, or so it felt to a little girl only just turned seven years old, her feet tripped on the bottom step of a staircase leading upwards. The candle holder dropped from her hand and the candle, now dripping with streams of melted wax, fell onto the step. Being careful not to burn her fingers, she reclaimed the candle holding it sideways to allow the melted hot wax to drip out onto the stairs. Once the holder was retrieved and the candle reinstated into its assigned place, Bridie's weary legs climbed up and up until she spied a faint light in the wall, which revealed the end of the tunnel at another small enclosed chamber.

Feeling a little wiser after her adventures this day, Bridie rested the holder, with its flickering flame, on a ledge. Stretching up from tippy toes she put an eye to the glowing hole. She recognized her grandfather's office. Late afternoon sunlight streamed in through his open windows. Grandpa sat stretched out in his comfy chair in the corner snoring softly.

Bridie wanted to call out to him, but what if someone else was in the room, where she could not see – someone like her father? She sat back and chewed at her fingernails. The sound of a door banging back against the wall and her Grandmama's laugh sent Bridie back onto tiptoes to spy into the office.

"So, here you are, William, my lad. You told me you were going to be busy with the accounts this afternoon and could not help me entertain our son-in-law and our grandsons. Here I find you sound asleep."

"Anna, you are a perfect treasure. Did I ever tell you that?"

"Only when you want to wriggle out of something, my dear." She smiled.

"I could not face those monsters a moment longer. It is a shame they never had a mother's hand to soften their natures."

"I am sure our Athena would have loved them fiercely if she was still alive."

William Wellington rose from his chair and stretched. "Ah well, we all miss our Athena. Talking of which, have you seen Bridie? I have not seen her since Nanny Granville left for the village after lunch."

"No, that is why I came here to talk with you. The staff have not seen her since then either. Perhaps you might need to go and search her favourite haunts. No doubt she has fallen asleep somewhere. It will be nearly time for her dinner."

"Of course, Anna, my love. I will make a magic spell and spirit her back from wherever she is."

Grandmama and Grandpa Wellington both jumped at the sound of a familiar voice talking from the wall beside the bookshelves.

"Grandpa, how do I make this secret panel open?"

"Good heavens, William, that sounds like our Bridie. Where is she?"

William walked over to the bookshelves and spoke into the small hole disguised within the ornate panelling.

"Are you alright, Bridie, dear?"

26

"Yes, Grandpa, but I cannot find a lever here to get into there."

"Can you reach high up on the wall to the strip of square timber?"

"I can only just touch it with my fingertips."

"Well, try to push it upwards."

Bridie grunted and groaned to no avail. She began to jump upwards with her hands outstretched until suddenly the panel opened leaving her in a heap on the office floor. Grandpa bent and reached into the chamber, where he snuffed out the candle, and left it and the holder on the ledge.

Bridie did not notice the panel return to its position as she was enfolded into her grandmother's arms.

"You have had an adventurous day then, my young lady?" Grandpa commented with a wry smile. "You really must collect me to share your adventures, when they are as dangerous as this may have been."

"Oh, Grandpa, you were with me all the way. When I was frightened, I folded my fingers like you said and you were in my ear all the way like you promised." Bridie lifted her left hand which still held the folded fingers wedged into place. "Ouch," she groaned as she pulled them apart.

The three people in the room jumped back in a line at the sound of Douglas Mayford's voice from the doorway.

"So, there you are, lass. I've been looking for you." He raked his hands through his thick dark curls so like Bridie's.

"I am here, Father," Bridie whispered.

"Speak up, child, speak up. Now we are all together, I wish to inform you, Colonel and Anna, I must return to London with the boys tomorrow at first light. I will increase your allowance for Bridie's upbringing and select a tutor in London to further her education. I presume you can put him up somewhere. We do not want her to grow up into a complete rustic, do we? Who knows, she may make a very

27

suitable catch, when she is older and can thus contribute to the family coffers."

If he noticed the brief flash of disgust in the faces of his hosts, he did not reveal it in his demeanour of arrogance.

It was Anna who caught her breath and spoke first. "Douglas, you may not realize, but it is usual for a girl child to have a governess, not a male tutor."

Douglas frowned. It was seldom anyone had challenged one of his decisions. He shook his head.

"That's as may be, but I know this fellow, and his qualifications are exemplary. I will remind him of his responsibilities. He will heed my instructions."

"As you wish, Douglas." It was William who accepted the responsibility while he vowed never to leave his precious granddaughter alone with any male tutor.

After the evening meal which was consumed with the minimum of conversation, the boys disappeared into their bedroom while Bridie sat between her grandparents in the parlour. They and her father shared a drink and a discussion on the latest news of the expansion of England's railway network. An errant sigh of relief escaped Anna's lips when Douglas rose to leave.

"I will say good night, Colonel, and Anna. A good sleep will be appreciated. I'll see to the boys before I retire." Douglas turned on his heel and departed along the corridor towards the guestrooms.

Bridie, Grandmama and Grandpa stood staring at the open doorway long after Douglas Mayford left their sight.

"What did my father mean this afternoon when he said that I am a suitable catch, Grandmama?"

Anna Wellington drew Bridie into a tighter embrace. She smoothed the line across her granddaughter's forehead and swept the errant strands of dark hair behind her ears. She kissed the top of her head. Grandmama released Bridie from her hold and sat in the nearest deep chair pulling her onto her lap.

She asked, "How did you know about the secret tunnel, my girl?"

By the time the story was told, Bridie's eyelids drooped.

"Damn those boys, they're more trouble than they are worth," Grandpa grumbled.

"Hush, William, boys will be boys, you know."

"It looks like this little girl has the imagination to get into scrapes too," he smiled and continued, "Come on now, my little Bridie, I will carry you off to bed, my dear. Tomorrow, I will show you how to maintain all the secret openings in the tunnel, by lubricating them with the Kaylak grease"

"Have you still got that old recipe, William?"

"Yes, my dear Anna, of course. It is written in the oldest ledger in this office. Tomorrow, I'll find it and show Bridie. Whoever wrote it knew what he was talking about. The Kaylak does not glug up like most lubricants. I may as well show our Bridie how to care for the candles and tinderboxes too."

Later in the evening, Douglas Mayford pulled the door to his sons' bedroom closed with the greatest of care. The hallway carpet muffled his cautious footsteps as he made his way down the stairs leading to the back doorway. Once outside, his pace increased. The half-moon guided him directly towards the stand of oak trees just west of the family vault. His gaze searched for whom he waited, or for others who he did not want to meet. After five minutes his body relaxed and he drew out his pipe.

"Do you have to advertise to the world that you are meeting me? The smell of your pipe will drift for miles." The man known to the Wellingtons as Sanders spoke softly.

Douglas jumped as Sanders stepped out from behind a tree.

"Don't be uppity with me, Sanders. Just remember who pays you the ample bonus you receive each month."

"Yes, sir, of course," the twisted smirk on Sanders' face went unseen in the dark shadows of the trees.

"What have you got to tell me, man? Hurry it up, I've had a long day and I want to get some sleep before I face the return journey tomorrow."

"To be honest, Douglas, there is really nothing to report. Other than the preacher once a week and the delivery of groceries or farm supplies, seldom does a stranger set foot on this place. As far as that young lass is concerned, she is hardly ever seen without one or other or both of her grandparents. I believe she spends most of her time in the library with her grandfather or playing the piano with her grandmother." Sanders smothered a cough and continued, "When will I be able to come back to London? This is stifling me out here in the country."

"You will stay here whilst ever I need you here. Remember, I know lots about you that you don't want to be shared around. Just you keep your nose to the ground here."

Sanders shrugged and turned on his heel. He disappeared into the shadows.

Every morning, after her breakfast and a quick walk to the beach, Bridie and her grandfather retreated to the library where Mr. Bacon sat on one side of the large table with the day's lesson books spread out in immaculate tidiness. Grandpa Wellington sat at the far end of the table with several books of interest scattered around him like good friends. Bridie climbed up onto the large chair at the opposite end of the table with her tutor on her right.

Bridie turned to her grandfather. She tried to speak, but emotion stole her words. Eventually, she formed her thoughts.

"Oh, Grandpa, did you see that? Is that how all calves are born? I want to see every calf born here from now on. Oh, did that hurt the baby? Did it hurt the cow?" William was trying to sort out the questions when he noticed the child deep in thought staring at her feet.

"Are you alright, my dear?"

Bridie looked up into William's eyes. She took a little time to present her question.

"Grandpa, is that how people babies are born?"

"Yes, pretty much the same."

"Is that why my mother died, when I was born? Did I hurt my mother?"

Confusion filled William's face. His expression spoke volumes. He wished Anna was here to get him out of this mess. He took Bridie's hand in his own.

"Your mother was my beloved daughter, and I know she wanted more than anything to deliver you into the world – a healthy baby girl. Remember what Grandmama always told you. Your mother is in heaven looking down upon you with nothing but love. I think God took her to heaven because he wanted her by his side. He knew that with us, you would be loved beyond measure."

1869

Bridie's eyelids snapped open. Her gaze flew to the large painted sign hanging from her mirror. A sign, that changed this day of every year, but the theme remained the same. Large pink rose petals interlaced by a twist of green vine to the yellow blossoms of daffodils framed the words.

HAPPY THIRTEENTH BIRTHDAY
TO OUR BEAUTIFUL BRIDIE.

She threw back the covers and jumped out of bed. Her nightgown landed in a heap on top of her pillow. Her rush came to an abrupt halt at the chair. Her day clothes were missing. Every night before retiring, she diligently placed her clothes ready for the following day, but this morning they were not to be seen. A long slim cardboard box with a pink ribbon rested across the seat. Her eyes gleamed as she hugged her cooling body and stared at this surprise. Bridie reached out to untie the ribbon. Trembling hands lifted the lid and discovered a forest of tissue paper. Her instinct was to toss it all aside, but the tidiness instilled in her by her grandmama had her remove each sheet of paper and fold it in half – maybe not as neatly as she should have. A gasp of pleasure filled the room. A new set of outdoor clothes lay waiting for her inspection. With reverence, she lifted out the long-sleeved pale blue blouse. The material felt soft and smooth against her cheek – each button carved to the shape of the head of a horse. She pushed her arms through the sleeves and secured each button with care. An intricate ruffle of lace sat against her neck above the top button. Next came a smart navy jacket that curved nicely around her budding breasts. Bridie's hands reached down to lift the navy skirt out by the waist.

"Oh," she grunted as she held it up. Something looked strange. It had been sewn like two long skirts on a single waist. After a pause to make sense of this new design, she placed her legs into each skirt and secured the waistband button.

Bridie stood in front of the mirror. Who was this lady standing staring back at her? Slowly her smile widened. Grandmama and Mrs Potter the dressmaker had been very creative this year.

"Happy birthday, Bridie. Do you like it?"

Bridie spun around to see her grandmother watching from the doorway. She twirled back and smoothed down her skirts.

"It fits perfectly, Grandmama, but why has it got the two legs in separate skirts?"

"That is a divided skirt to wear when riding horses – especially if you do not want to ride side-saddle."

"What a good idea, but I don't have a horse to go riding, do I?"

"Perhaps if you stop asking questions and finish dressing you can run down to the stable. I think you will find Grandpa, with his present, waiting for you there."

"What should I wear upon my feet?"

Anna Wellington's smile overflowed with indulgence as she absorbed the sight of this young woman before her. She felt as though Athena was back with her again and yet not so – Bridie was a developing woman in her own right and with her individual personality.

"You will find your new boots at the back door, dear."

Wearing her new dark riding boots with the small heels, Bridie flew across the track to the stable. She found Grandpa leaning against the rail of the outside yard talking to Mr. Axel the farm manager.

"Good morning, my child," William's grin could not be contained. "Happy birthday." The sweep of his hand encompassed the small railed paddock in which a three-year-old grey filly trotted with grace from one side to the other.

"Good morning and a happy birthday, Miss Mayford," the farm manager extended his greetings also.

"Thank you, Mr. Axel," Bridie replied before she threw herself into her grandfather's embrace. "And thank you, Grandpa. Oh, thank you so much. Is this horse my present? She is beautiful."

"She has been reserved for you since her birth. We had to send her over to the other farm to keep your curious nose from sniffing her out and asking questions."

"What is her name?"

"You will have to decide, Bridie. Mr. Axel has the papers here prepared in all but her name for you to complete and then she will be registered in the thoroughbred register."

The three stood leaning on the rail watching the filly exploring the limits of her paddock.

"She is regal in her bearing. I think she will have to have a royal name of some kind. Was she born here, Grandpa?"

"Yes, Bridie, she is the second filly out of Winnie's Joy and sired by our very own Royal Charles."

"Can I name her Wellington Royal?" Bridie paused. "I can call her Welly then."

The two men shared their glances. "That will be lovely, Bridie."

"Has she been broken in? When can I ride her?"

It was Mr. Axel who answered the question. "She has spent twelve months in the training program and has been a star pupil, but I would advise that you only go riding when you have myself or one of the stable hands with you for a few months yet."

"A good bit of advice there, Bridie," William turned to the farm manager. "Thank you."

"And before you ask, Miss Bridie, Sanders is our best rider having had experience in the 12th Royal Lancers. He is available to lead you on your first ride now if you wish. He will also provide lessons each morning for an hour before breakfast." Mr. Axel turned to speak to William. "Sanders has been with us for eight years now, Colonel. He knows his place. He can be trusted to behave around your granddaughter."

William nodded his head.

"Thank you so much, thank you, Mr. Axel," Bridie's eyes flashed as she turned to her grandfather. "Will that be alright with Grandmama, do you think?"

"You can ask her yourself. I see she could not miss this moment." Both William and Bridie turned to watch Anna's approach.

Bridie ran to her grandmother's side. Slim arms slipped around the older woman's shoulders.

"Thank you, thank you, come and meet Wellington Royal, Grandmama. He is my very own horse. I will not have to share the horse I ride with the farm hands anymore."

Anna smiled at the excitement she saw in Bridie's sparkling blue eyes.

Bridie's days kept her busy from daybreak until her bedtime at nine o'clock at night. Even then it was left to Grandmama to call an end to the day. Daylight found Bridie feeding and brushing the grey filly in the cool of the misty mornings. Her apologies filled the dining room after her ride when her grumbling tummy announced her arrival at the breakfast table.

"How is Wellington Royal this morning, Bridie?" Became the daily greeting from one or the other of her grandparents.

After two weeks of lessons riding Welly on the end of a rope, either circling Sanders in the railed yard or following behind him as he rode Mr. Axel's horse Sea Spray, Sanders removed the lead rope between himself and Welly.

Bridie's grin brought a smile to the usually deadpan face of Sanders. A nervous tremor ran through her body to be reined in as she took control of her mount. She sat up straighter and held a little tighter to the leather reins. Bridie pushed her weight down onto her feet in the stirrups. Welly paused in response to her sudden change of attention, but walked on when called by Sanders. They negotiated the narrow track down to the shingle beach where the horse's hooves went ker-runch ker-runch on the small pebbles. The sea breeze whistled around Bridie's face and lifted the hair from her neck. The crash of the waves on the shore sent a shiver down Welly's back. The horse hinted at a nervous shyness, but Bridie gentled her with a soft voice and tender strokes along the smooth grey coat.

Sanders led them to a bridle path further up the beach near the tree-line, before starting into a trot. Bridie sucked in a sharp breath; her pulse raced. She matched his pace. Once the pair were into a canter, Bridie wished they could ride like this to the end of the earth. The wind dragged tears from her eyes – tears of joyful emotion.

Bridie's laughter echoed off the waves every morning to the beat of the horses' hooves as they raced along the waterfront. This became a regular part of their daily ride. Sanders would never have admitted it to anyone, but pride, a feeling he had lost long ago, threatened to take up residence in his soul. His admiration developed for this young girl who, if she failed in any endeavour, gritted her teeth and had another go.

He woke every morning in anticipation of seeing Bridie's excited smile. He returned to his small room each night dreading to discover word from her father demanding a meeting. Sanders knew Douglas Mayford's ambitions were all for himself and not for his daughter.

Bridie's laughter rose above the dancing pair as they glided around the piano room, where Anna sat playing a fast waltz. Her grandfather spun her so fast that it seemed the room became a blur. Her hairpins gave up the unequal task of maintaining order within the dark curls and dropped to the floor between the twirling feet. The dark locks swept down her back. Squeals of delight exploded through the open windows along with the music accompaniment. Mr. Baines wore a smile on his face as he pottered around the rose bed outside.

"Enough, enough!" Through his laughter, the colonel begged for a reprieve.

Anna's fingers halted over the ivories. "You are both going to be too ill to eat your lunch." Anna's smile took any heat out of her words. "You will show them in London how it is done, Bridie, my dearest."

"I am not going to London, Grandmama. I will never go to London."

"But one day you will want to be presented to royalty. It will make your father so proud."

Bridie slid onto the piano stool beside her grandmother.

"I have no reason to want to make my father proud. He has done nothing to make me proud."

"Hush, child, that is not a nice thing to say."

Bridie's mouth opened to say more but closed with a snap. She loved her Grandmama so much. She did not want to upset her anymore.

"Grandmama, I will play now. Let me see you and Grandpa dance."

"I think Grandpa may have had enough, dear."

Bridie's blue eyes begged her grandfather's permission.

William grinned at his wife. "Are you game, my sweet Anna?"

"Yes, William, but only if it is a slow waltz."

"That is all I have left in me, a slow waltz." He turned towards Bridie. "A very slow one, my girl. You have nearly brought me to my knees."

Bridie's fingers caressed the keyboard and began one of her favourites – the recent piece by Johann Strauss, The Blue Danube.

After three rounds of the room, William guided Anna out through the doorway and into the hall.

"What do you think, William? Has our Bridie's dancing improved?"

"In leaps and bounds, my sweet. I think she has worn me right out."

≈

Bridie only vaguely recalled meeting her brothers George, Max and Toby, when she was seven years of age. She hardly registered later, in 1869, when Anna Wellington informed her that her two siblings Max and Toby had gone to sea on one of the ships in their father's fleet – Toby, the youngest as a cabin boy for the captain, and the older boy Max, as a ship's hand. George, the eldest boy, never went to sea. Douglas demanded he learn the company business in London.

It was the sorrow seen in the face of her grandmother as she spoke, and the stony face of her grandfather at the time, which alerted Bridie to the possibility this was not particularly good news.

She peeped out from hooded eyes to watch as her grandmother struggled to hold back her tears. Bridie's gaze became fixed on the sheet of paper trembling within the bony fingers.

"William, they are little more than children. If Douglas is concerned so much for the company, wouldn't it be preferable if they continued their education into university?" Anna's voice softened to a little more than a whisper. "If our Athena were still alive today, she would never have agreed to this."

"No doubt, Athena would have been able to talk sense into the man, but since her passing, there is no reasoning with Douglas."

The memory eased into Bridie's head of the three boys at the vault when she hid inside on the day that she first discovered the tunnel.

She hesitated to speak, but could not bear to see the sadness in her grandmother's expression.

"Grandmama, I remember the boys talking about going to sea on their visit here when I was seven years old. The boys knew then they were going to sea. In fact, the way George spoke, they wanted to go to sea."

"They were little more than babes in the woods then, Bridie." Anna shook her head and sat up straighter. "It is not our place to say anything, I suppose. I will pray tonight to keep them safe."

1871

It was the evening before Bridie's fifteenth birthday. Anna Wellington brushed her greying locks one hundred strokes, a practice she had kept up since a young girl. William sat upon the end of their bed and admired his wife.

Anna looked at his reflection in her mirror. "William, have you thought about what I mentioned this morning? Bridie is fast growing into a beautiful young woman. I think she should have a suitable chaperon with her when she goes riding each day. I know the chap Sanders has behaved as a perfect gentleman to date, but he is a man after all."

"Yes, my love, I have thought of little else all day. With sixty-two years to my name, I am not too sure if I have the stamina to keep up with our little grasshopper. On the other hand, the exercise might be good for me."

"Well, I was thinking about the Braydon sisters who have started the riding school on their deceased father's farm. I was talking to the older one, Eleanor, after church last Sunday. Eleanor was saying she and Teresa, her sister, would welcome the extra work."

"Exactly how long have you been planning all this, my little schemer?"

"It has been bothering me for a while, I must admit. It is only a two-mile ride through the shortcut from the Braydon farm. I have not asked how much money she might expect for her time."

"Well, you sort it all out, and in the meantime, I'll sacrifice my life and aching muscles for our granddaughter."

The next morning, Bridie rushed up to greet her grandfather when he arrived at the stable.

"Oh, Grandpa, this is a wonderful surprise." Her gaze examined William. "You are wearing riding clothes. Will you be joining Sanders and me on our ride this morning?"

"If you think you can slow down a little for an old man, dear, there will just be you and I. Sanders has an auction to attend today."

Neither William nor Bridie noticed Sanders standing in the shadows with a speculative look in his eyes.

"Try to keep up, Grandpa. I'll show you the best ride along the beach."

William grinned as he mumbled to himself. "Don't think you can teach an old dog new tricks young lady." He settled his bony bottom in a more comfortable position on the saddle and called to her, "I'm right behind you, Missy."

Today Bridie took her companion-on-horseback over her favourite run past their picnic area, around the point, into the bay, across the stream and then along the straight run up to the nest of huge boulders below the old cottage on Clawhaven Cliff.

The horses' chests heaved when they were reined in. They threw their heads into the air and snorted.

"I always wanted Sanders to take me out into the water to see what is on the other side of those big rocks, but he said we would have to swim the horses. He thought it might be too deep for me."

"I am glad he had enough sense not to let you go out there. If I remember rightly, there is a deep hole chewed out by the waters being sucked into the caves within the rocks at high tide." Before Bridie had a chance to offer her assurances about her skills as a fish, William offered an alternative suggestion. "There is a path up the cliff and around the rocks."

"Sanders said the cottage on Clawhaven Cliff is vacant. It has been for years."

"Yes, so I understand. It will take someone special to take on that old place. It is a lonely corner of the world."

"Can we go today?"

"I think not, child, I know your grandmother expects us back early for your birthday breakfast."

"We can take the track back through the Braydon's place and make it home in time for the bell."

"You have been learning about our countryside, I see."

"Oh, yes, Sanders knows all the hidden shortcuts."

The two explorers returned in ample time to clean up and arrive at the breakfast table before the cook rang the bell.

After breakfast had been eaten, during which time Bridie shared the news on her latest adventure with her grandfather, Anna handed a small jewellery box to Bridie.

"This is a little gift from your grandfather and myself, dear."

Her fine fingers trembled with excitement as Bridie opened the little box to reveal an amethyst brooch.

"Oh, Grandmama, this is exquisite. Thank you, Grandpa."

"Bridie, darling, that was my mother's favourite brooch. Look, it matches your eyes to perfection," Grandmama smiled. "Here, let me fix it to your jacket."

"Thank you, both." With the brooch secured, Bridie rose from the breakfast table to walk around to plant a firm kiss on her grandmother's and grandfather's cheeks. "I'll treasure it forever."

From then on, Mr. Axel ensured Sanders had plenty to do in other areas of the property away from the manor. Either Eleanor or Teresa Braydon arrived at 06:30 a.m. each morning, except on Sundays, to accompany Bridie on her explorations of the countryside riding her precious horse, Welly.

When Bridie skidded to a halt at the library doorway at ten a.m. sharp, Mondays to Fridays, only the top of her tutor's head was visible above the pile of books set up in front of him. This was the workload for her day.

At the far end of the table, Grandpa Wellington usually looked up from his books with a wide grin and a roll of his eyes. Bridie always threw him a grin in return.

Saturday mornings were all her own. If the Braydon sister riding as her chaperon had the time, the morning was spent on Welly's back exploring the beachfront and new countryside.

1872

Bridie's feet tripped down the staircase. She paused. Something was different. It took some moments before she realized what bothered her. At this time of evening, the music from her grandmother's piano usually filled every nook and cranny, but today a hush lay upon the manor. She hurried down the remainder of the stairs and made her way to the music room. Bridie paused again at the open doorway.

Grandmama sat with her back to the keyboard, while she spoke quietly to Grandpa.

"This wedding is in a few weeks, William. George is still only twenty years of age. What does he know about life – or her for that matter? If I recall, Beatrice Collingwood was one of the debutantes who came out just this last season." Anna held a large invitation card in her hand.

"I am sad to say, I doubt if Douglas cares too much about either of their ages. Her family will contribute much to the company coffers, I should imagine."

"Possibly so, but if Angelina Perkins knows anything, she tells me George has the young lady in a delicate condition and she may be confined before the end of this year."

"Trust Angelina to have something to contribute."

"Well, it certainly has been a brief engagement when the wedding invitations follow only two months behind the engagement notice. The wedding is September the twentieth, which is only three weeks away."

William Wellington looked up and chuckled. He noticed Bridie at the doorway.

"What is going on, Grandpa?"

"Your grandmother has received the invitation for your brother George's wedding."

Anna held the card up briefly but did not offer to show it to her granddaughter to read. The words at the bottom may have been hurtful to Bridie.

I think it best if young Bridie does not come up to London stood out in Douglas's determined sloping pen stroke.

"I hope my father does not expect me to attend, I hardly know my brother let alone anyone else," Bridie put in quickly, stirring a sigh of relief from her grandmother. "Anyway, you will need me to look after things here because you and Grandpa must go to represent my mother's family."

Her words brought another chuckle from William. He turned to Anna and spoke.

"Bridie sounds just like her mother, don't you think, Anna, dear? She has us all organized in a single sentence."

"Of course, if that is what you want, Bridie." There was nothing left for Anna Wellington to say.

Having been given such short notice, Anna knew the option of designing and sewing a new dress was beyond possibility. She accepted that one of her previous and least used frocks was her only choice. Bridie helped her sort through the large collection.

The days flew by. After an early breakfast, Anna and William settled back into the coach seat exhausted before the two-day journey to the city even began. Sanders sat atop the driver's seat in control of the four matching brown horses. Bridie stood at the entrance of the manor and waved them on their way.

Her horse riding had been deferred to this afternoon. Bridie made her way to the library, where the tutor sat flicking through the stacks of books in front of him. Bridie sighed as she settled into her studies.

If Bridie gave any thought to the presence of her grandmother's senior chambermaid sitting in her grandfather's chair in the corner of the room with her fancy-work basket at her side and a crochet hook, which twisted and turned at great speed in her knobbly fingers, she gave no voice to her curiosity.

If Bridie noticed the frequent glances of annoyance cast towards the woman by the tutor, again, she gave no voice to her curiosity.

≈

On the first of the five evenings in September, when the Colonel and Mrs. Wellington were away in London at their grandson's wedding, Mrs. Coburn the housekeeper assumed Bridie had gone for a late afternoon ride with one of the Braydon family as chaperons. The thoughts of Mr. Axel in the stable travelled along the same path when he noticed Welly not in the stable on his return from the far farm. Bridie appeared just after he rode in himself.

"Did you have a nice ride, Miss Bridie?"

"Yes, thank you, Mr. Axel. It is a beautiful evening, is it not? I must fly now or Mrs Coburn will be cross if I am late for dinner."

Bridie rushed Welly into her stall, filled the feed bag and checked the water drum was full. To deter any detailed conversation with Mr. Axel, she sang all the while as she brushed the horse's dusty coat.

A similar enthusiasm greeted Mrs. Coburn at the dinner table. Before the housekeeper questioned her on the afternoon's activities, Bridie enthused over her meal and the things she must do later before retiring.

She did not want to share her excitement at an unsupervised ride, nor the thrill of an illicit entrance into the cottage on Clawhaven Cliff. This was something to be savoured alone, as she lay on her bed bathed in the moonlight through the large windows.

With no one present to distract her, Bridie secured Welly's bridle rein to the branch of a fallen tree beside the cliff path. Her light footfalls took her around the perimeter of the deserted cottage. Dust almost covered the windows of the house on the inland approach. This thwarted her view of the contents of the rooms. The width of the ground floor of the house on the inland side was made up of two large doors. Bridie gave them a shake, but they must have been bolted from the inside. Timber shutters protected the windows of the house facing the sea. It surprised her to find the smaller door on that side of the house unsecured. Her hand turned the knob. With some effort, she forced the door inwards. Bridie's head turned left and right sharply. She feared anyone in the vicinity might have heard the heavy timber, as it grated with a loud screech, across the stone floor. She stood still, waiting for her heart rate to settle and her breathing to steady.

She examined her surroundings. Bridie discovered she stood in an entrance area, which led off into a kitchen on the left, and a store room with large heavy shelves, on her right. The kitchen held a small table in the middle of the room and an open-fire cooking place at the end. A large cookpot hung from a steel tripod above long-cooled ashes. Opposite the fireplace, a half wall opened out into a stable enclosed with the large doors noticed earlier.

Bridie felt her breath catch. A tingling sensation raced back and forth over her fingers and hands. Something like a presence lightened her body. A joyful sensation swelled inside her chest. She felt the urge to laugh but had no idea why. Instinct convinced her there was nothing to fear as she stood in the room dimly lit with thin streams of sunlight through the shutters. She savoured this awareness.

Moving through the half-door, her feet crunched on the small shingle pebbles on the floor of the stable section. Of their own volition, Bridie's legs ascended the narrow set of stairs winding to the top floor. Old timbers creaked at her every step. Tree branches scratched across the roof. In what light broke through the smudged windows on the three sides of the large room at the top of her climb, she discovered a smaller room – a bedroom perhaps, by the look of the wardrobe squished into the back wall. She also found an old iron bedstead with little wire attached to the frame.

The deepening shadows alerted Bridie to the passing of time. She must hurry home before her absence was discovered. On her way out, she noticed amongst the bushes clinging to the rough cliff top, a lavatory that provided a view of the sea to any user of the amenity.

As she lay in bed with a cool breeze rustling the soft drapes near her head, Bridie recalled her adventure only hours before. Her

48

imagination pondered on what sort of person or people might want to live in the little cottage on Clawhaven Cliff. She wondered at her strange reaction inside the walls. Had she been inside the dwelling before – if so, then when? Had her mother loved the cottage and spent time in there when she was a young girl? Maybe it was her presence she felt this afternoon. Was it some sort of premonition of something in her future? Sleep stole away her mind's wanderings.

Eleanor from the Braydon farm arrived early each of the following mornings to accompany Bridie on her riding excursions leaving no opportunity to explore the cottage further. The remaining hours in the day were filled with her studies provided by the tutor, in the presence of the senior chambermaid, and with her piano practice. On the few occasions, when time hung on her hands, she set out on walks to the stables and the dairy. She questioned Mr. Axel on any difficulties encountered in running the farm. The manager looked down upon the sixteen-year-old with a glint of amusement in his eyes. He took the inquisition all in good heart and smiled as he answered her astute questions.

After the return of her grandparents from London, Bridie noticed Sanders out exercising a young horse.

"Good morning, Miss Bridie," he called. He nodded his head in greeting to Miss Braydon.

"Good morning, Mr. Sanders. That is a beautiful animal you have there." Bridie responded.

"Yes, Miss, it is another by Royal Charles." Sanders slid off the back of his mount and kept pace with Bridie.

"Did you enjoy your sojourn in London, Mr. Sanders?"

"London is too busy for me, I'm afraid. I find I like the quiet country life much better."

"Yes, Grandmama and Grandpa expressed the same sentiments last evening, when they arrived home."

On the periphery of Bridie's thoughts, it seemed no sooner had her brother been married than her grandparents were talking about the imminent arrival of a child.

"It is a pity the baby was not due in the spring. I doubt if we will get to see the newborn until then," Anna moaned to William.

"The farmers are all expecting heavier than usual snowfalls this year, so I think you may be right, my love," William added.

The snow held many people captive in their homes. Smoke from house fires hovered low, held by the dull skies and frequent snowfalls. The men milking the cows leant in close to the side of the animals seeking their body heat. They rubbed their hands vigorously between milking each beast.

The mail lay for days at the Clawhaven Cliff Village Post Office. It was several weeks before news of the birth of George and Beatrice's son Edward, on the 12th of December 1872, reached the manor.

1873

With the weather warming up, Bridie resumed her early rides on Welly. On the morning of Bridie's seventeenth birthday, a young lad turned up at daybreak at the back door of the kitchen.

"Mum said she and Auntie Eleanor can't be coming today. I will ride wid Miss Bridie if she wants. I be a purty good rider." The boy stood with his cap in one hand and the other hand outstretched with a note, "It be fer the Colonel and Mrs. Wellington," he explained to Mrs. Ogilvie, the cook.

Bridie arrived at the kitchen door with her hair flying out behind her and her cap and riding crop in her hand. She pulled to a halt at the back door looking for her young chaperon.

"Where is he, Mrs. Ogilvie?"

"Over under the tree eating a bit of toast and jam. He ain't much primer-looking than a sparrer." The cook passed across a piece of toast for Bridie and one for her horse."

When the lad appeared from around the large trunk of the tree, Bridie stopped in her tracks. She stared.

"I's Jimmy Braydon, Miss Bridie." He even bowed. "I can teach you anything you want, and I can show you lots of new places you've never seen."

"How old are you, Jimmy Braydon?"

The boy stretched himself up higher. "I's twelve, Miss, and I only short because good things come in small packages."

"Oh, is that so? Well, good morning, Jimmy Braydon. Come on then, where is your mount? We will go and test just how many places you can show me, that I have not seen before." The lad's grin matched Bridie's own.

Once again, Bridie found herself staring in astonishment. Jimmy Braydon led a brown horse out from behind the tree. The animal was at least seventeen hands high.

"This'ns name's Flyer," the boy introduced his steed to Bridie. "He's unaccountable clever and fast."

"Jimmy, how are you going to mount that horse? He is twice your height."

"My Ma says no problem is insurmountable." Jimmy's left arm reached its limit as he held the shortened rein and the horse's mane. With a shuffle of his feet and an enormous jump, his right foot curved over the saddle, while his right arm scrabbled to drag him further up the near side of the horse and into the seat with his feet slipping into the stirrups hanging from short leathers on either side.

"I am impressed, Jimmy."

Once Bridie claimed her mount from the stable, Welly and Flyer set off at a trot. The riders laughed out loud in anticipation of the freedom of a ride in the countryside.

Jimmy did indeed know several paths through the forests and around farm boundaries, which Bridie had never encountered. Two new, almost hidden, animal tracks led down to the beach on the far side of the rocks near the cottage on Clawhaven Cliff. Bridie committed them all to memory. At the bottom of one of these trails, Bridie pulled her horse to a standstill. Music came soft upon her ears – beautiful music, haunting music.

"Jimmy, am I imagining it or can you hear that music also?" She asked her riding companion who drew his horse up beside her.

"Yeah, it's the new bloke, a fella with red hair, he is. He be livin' at the cottage now. He only turned up this past week wid a horse, a dray, a few boxes and a large piano."

"Who is he? What is he doing here at the cottage?"

"Dunno, no one's be knowin' not even Mrs. Featherstone at the Post Office, I don' reckon."

"Oh," Bridie said no more. She did not want to interrupt the flow of music as it swooped and fluttered along with the birds through the leaves of the trees down the rise.

The pair sat still and quiet straining their ears. Even their horses appeared hypnotized. They neither stamped their feet nor fidgeted with impatience.

Jimmy looked up towards the warming sun. He whispered, "Miss, it's time we be makin' our way back to the manor. Your folks will be worritin' where we be. Ma said I was not to let you stay out too late."

Bridie looked across at Jimmy whose horse's superior height brought their heads almost level.

"You're right, Jimmy, I do not know where the morning has got to." With reluctance, she edged her horse around and they turned for home. When no amount of effort and imagination could any longer bring the sound of the music to her ears, she asked, "Which one of the Braydon sisters is your mum?"

"Teresa," Jimmy stared ahead between the points of the horse's ears as he spoke the following words. "Dad, he be kilt in the mines up north when I was a wee bairn."

"I am sorry, Jimmy. If he were alive today, he would be so proud of his son."

"You reckon, Miss?"

"Yes, Jimmy, I do reckon, very much." Bridie smiled.

That evening, after her piano lessons with her grandmother, Bridie used her impressive persuasive skills to convince her grandparents that Jimmy would be a fine companion every morning before his school lessons now that the workload of the sisters Braydon had increased.

If Bridie had been asked, she could not have said why she did not tell her grandparents of the new tenant at the cottage on Clawhaven Cliff. She lay in bed that night once again holding close the feelings of intimacy and passion the musician's outpourings from his fingertips on the keyboard instilled in her very soul. Even her grandmother's considerable skills as a pianist fell short in comparison.

It was not until she entered the library the next morning that Bridie remembered her grandfather's words last evening as she climbed the stairs.

"Bridie, your brother's wife Beatrice has had a baby boy. Your grandmama and I will travel down to London to welcome the newcomer – maybe later when the snows have cleared – when they are ready to christen the child, perhaps."

A warm feeling of anticipation ran through her veins. The unknown red-haired musician's music whispered in her mind.

Anna and Colonel William Wellington did not get to London until May 1873, for the christening of their great-grandson Edward – nephew to Bridie. Once more Bridie remained home in the care of the staff of Clawhaven Manor. Two days after her grandparents departed, Jimmy Braydon's horse turned lame while riding chaperon with Bridie. Bridie insisted he walk the horse home through the shortcuts. She assured the lad she would go directly home herself, past the cottage on the cliff and along the beachfront – a route they travelled almost every day.

On the cliff path near the cottage, the music drifted out through the open stable doors luring Bridie from her promise to go straight home. She nudged Welly into the shelter of the thicket of trees and dismounted. Gradually her body sank to rest on a fallen log with her back against a tree. She allowed the music to flow over her like a silken blanket. Her eyes closed.

Neither Welly's warning snort nor the soft pawing of the ground disturbed her dreams. It was the deep chuckle and warm voice that snapped her eyes wide open.

"Well, I must get used to it, I suppose. You're not the first one to fall asleep while listening to my music."

Bridie scrambled upright, full of apologies. Her breath caught in her throat at the sight of the handsome face with its strong jawline surrounded by a halo of red hair. The pounding in her chest stole her voice for several moments.

"Oh no, sir, it is wonderful music. I thought my grandmama played the best music in the world, but I think yours is even better." Bridie struggled to remember her manners and not stare at the gentleman. She felt as if his blue gaze pierced her body right through to her soul. "My name is Bridie Mayford. I live at Clawhaven Manor with my grandparents."

"So, Miss Bridie Mayford of Clawhaven Manor, what are you doing running free like a wild animal and without a chaperon?" His cheeky grin enticed Bridie's own smile out of hiding.

"My chaperon's horse took lame and he has gone home. I said I'd take this shortcut to the manor." Bridie brushed the dust from her skirt. "I heard the music and only stopped for a minute to listen."

"Can I offer you a cup of tea?"

Horror filled her expression. "Good heavens, what is the time? I'll be late for my lessons and the tutor is such a grouch at the best of times." Welly threw up her head as Bridie rushed to untie the reins. "I'm sorry I cannot take tea. I will have to fly." She landed as light as a feather into the saddle and swung Welly's head around. "You never said what your name was, sir."

"David – David Lewis." The warm lips chuckled. "You will return for tea one day when you lose your chaperon again?"

Bridie laughed out loud herself, as Welly began a steady trot down the narrow path.

"Keep the kettle hot," wafted out behind her.

When Anna Wellington and the Colonel arrived home at dusk to be greeted with overwhelming enthusiasm by Bridie, her eyes alight with fire and excitement, Anna suspected she and William might not be the only cause for their granddaughter's happiness. She mentally ticked off a reminder to investigate this phenomenon further.

William felt his feet almost stumble as his granddaughter threw herself into his arms in welcome. He turned to his wife.

"Maybe we should go to London more often if we are to receive a greeting of such fervour on our return."

"Hmmm," Anna smiled gently.

Later in their familiar bed as they settled beside each other on the well-known bumps in the mattress, William asked, "Anna, did I detect a hesitation in your response to Bridie's welcome?"

"Something is different, did you not feel it? I am not sure if we warrant such enthusiasm and anticipation."

"What are you saying?"

"She behaved like a girl in love."

"How can that be? She has not had a chance to meet anyone new. Are you sure you are not imagining this, Anna?"

"Cast your mind back to when Athena met Douglas, William."

"Oh, good heavens, this cannot be so – Bridie is only a baby."

"Bridie is seventeen years old – only a year younger than Athena was when she and Douglas became engaged."

"That is hard to believe. How fast the years have gone."

Eleanor Braydon played chaperon the following morning. Her program for their morning's adventure was a little different from what Bridie had wished for.

"Miss Bridie, I'm hoping you won't mind coming back to the riding school to cast your eye over our jumps that we have set out for the more advanced riders."

Bridie released a silent sigh. "Of course, Mrs. Braydon. It will be my pleasure. You do realise I have no experience in jumping a horse, don't you?"

Eleanor swung around in her saddle. "Is that so, young Miss Bridie? I find that surprising as you seem to manage splendidly when out in the countryside."

"Thank you, and I will be grateful for any advice you have to offer."

Both women enjoyed the morning exercise. Eleanor admired Bridie's natural talent and Bridie felt great satisfaction for the skills she acquired within the short hour over the jumps.

It was Jimmy on Flyer who delivered Bridie home to the manor on his way to the village school.

Later in the day, when she approached the music room doorway for the lesson with her grandmother, Bridie paused to let the music seep into her soul. Her heart tripped over itself and her breathing became erratic as the melody of a different tune returned to her subconscious. She felt the flush on her cheeks, as she approached the piano and her grandmother.

"Are you well, Bridie, my dear? You look as though you have a fever."

Bridie felt the flush deepen as she stuttered her answer.

"I am fine, Grandmama. I ran up and down the stairs to put the books for my homework reading into my room."

Anna smiled a soft smile, but her thoughts were not so convinced.

"What is it you have been told about running and rushing about, young lady?"

"Ladies never rush about. It is unbecoming."

"That is correct, dear. Grace is always essential in a lady." Anna's smile widened. "Do you enjoy your music, my dear?"

"Oh, yes, Grandmama. I so much want to play the piano like ... er ... you, one day." Bridie's breathless speech attracted Anna's attention further.

"Perhaps you might like to come with me to one of the operas in London this year?"

Bridie lifted her head, her eyes wide. "Oh no, Grandmama, I do not want to go to London," she fiddled with the music scores she held in her hand. "I am enjoying the music we have right here." Bridie's thoughts ran directly to the music from the cottage on the cliff. She felt her face heat further with the memory of yesterday morning's interlude and her guilt at not wanting to share the moment with anyone, not even her grandmother. Bridie's inherent honesty sent the words bubbling from her lips, "Besides, we have a musician living in the cottage on Clawhaven Cliff now."

Anna Wellington's head lifted a fraction. She gazed at Bridie's bright eyes and flushed face.

"Oh, and you have heard this musician, have you, dear?"

Bridie stumbled over her words. "I … er … yes, Grandmama. His music could be heard when we passed by on the cliff track. Oh, Grandmama, his music poured forth from the cottage like liquid gold."

Anna's eyebrows lifted. She decided a chat with Mrs. Featherstone at the Post Office might not go astray, if she wanted to hear more about this musician in the cottage on the cliff, whose music flowed like liquid gold, no less.

It was Sanders who sat on the coach seat as it pulled up at the front of the manor at ten on the following morning. Anna Wellington held a basket over her right forearm as she descended the few steps at the front of the building on William's arm. Sanders hastened down to open the coach door.

"Good morning, Ma'am, lovely day for an outing."

"Good morning to you too, Sanders. Yes, the sunshine is quite pleasant."

"Where do you wish to make your first stop, Ma'am?"

"I think Mrs. Hawkin's Tea Shop, thanks Sanders."

When Anna walked inside, she was pleased to see Gladys Berrington seating herself near the window. She smiled at her friend's greeting.

"Good morning, Anna, this is a lovely surprise. Come and join me. We don't often see you here on a Tuesday?"

"I need to visit the post office to post a letter and a gift to my great-grandson. I know he is only a baby, but it just felt right to get it away as soon as possible."

"Sounds like you are captivated by the lad."

"Babies are always such a delight. Now what have you been up to these days? I missed you last week at church. We went up to London for the christening."

Delighted as she was to meet Gladys, her mind was not on their conversation, but more on her forthcoming visit to the Clawhaven Cliff Village postmistress and what knowledge she might plumb from her store of gossip.

When she did arrive at the post office, there were no other customers in the shop and Mrs. Featherstone was ready to chat.

"I hear you have a new neighbour in the cottage on Clawhaven Cliff, Mrs. Wellington, a musician no less, I believe."

"Oh, is that so, Mrs. Featherstone, and where does he hail from, do you think?"

"His name is David Lewis, I believe – or that is what he signed the register as. A small parcel was waiting here for him from a Mrs. Beca Lewis, who he said was his mother in Wales. He has moved here for his health, I understand." Mrs. Featherstone's eyes sparkled. It was a thrill to have someone as important as Mrs. Wellington to show an interest in her.

Anna, on the other hand, hid her disgust towards the gossipmonger and the guilt she felt inside herself for encouraging the woman. She smiled at all she had learnt in these first few seconds.

"How sad for the poor man having to move away from his family. What on earth would be so debilitating to warrant such a thing? If he is aging, it would be more difficult, I should think."

"Oh no, Mrs. Wellington, he is only a young man – no more than thirty years old, I would think. A handsome man too. He plays the piano, so Farmer Jenkens says – very well too, he says." Mrs. Featherstone snapped a quick breath before going on. "He was poorly as a child and the church taught him the music, I think. He didn't actually say, but it sounds like that to me."

Anna did not blink as she stared at her informant. "Oh, that is tragic. His wife will be devastated, no doubt."

"No, he isn't married – or so he said. He said it was a blessing he had no one dependant on him."

Anna returned to the manor to hear raised voices coming from William's office downstairs next to the library.

"Colonel, I really must protest. It is not the place of women to be taught mathematics and accounting."

"Mr. Bacon, you will pardon me, but I strongly disagree. This is not the seventeenth or even the eighteenth century when women were treated with such disdain. We are approaching the end of the nineteenth century and women are proving their intelligence every day. Can you deny Bridie already has above-average mathematical knowledge?"

"That is by the by, Colonel. I am sure her father would never agree to her joining you and the accountant when he comes to check the books each month. He pays me to see to her education."

Anna found Bridie frozen to the spot just outside the open doorway of the office. She took Bridie's hand in her own as the vitriolic discussion continued inside.

"He pays you?" Anna could almost hear William sucking in a deep breath. "Then explain to me how come the sum of your stipend comes from my account each month?" Anna held her breath waiting for the tutor's reply, but only silence filled the air until William broke in once again. "If I am not mistaken, we house and feed you as well, do we not?"

"That is so, Colonel, but it was Mr. Mayford who hired me and I must endeavour to meet the trust he placed in me to educate his daughter."

Anna heard William's snort of disgust – a sure sign he was becoming overly excited.

"A man cannot serve two masters, Mr. Bacon. You will be well advised to remember that. Now will you leave this room and send Bridie in? She will spend the afternoon here, with myself and the accountant when he arrives."

The tutor swept past Anna and Bridie in high dudgeon with little more than a muttering, which may have been an apology or it may not.

Anna hurried to William's side to soothe her husband's flustered state. Bridie hesitated. She went to turn away, but her grandfather's choked call drew her forwards.

"Come in, Bridie. I apologize for that ruckus. Come in and sit down, my child."

When the atmosphere in the office returned to its usual peace and quiet, Anna retired to her bedroom to refresh herself before lunch. William turned to his granddaughter.

"Bridie, is there anything you want to turn your mind to other than the accounting?"

"No, Grandpa, I am looking forward to learning with you and Mr. Langford. I have enjoyed all Tutor Bacon taught me in English and Latin and even the German languages. The poetry, theology, geography and history certainly caught my interest, but numbers have always fascinated me." She hesitated. A frown lay upon her brow as she considered the wisdom in asking her next question. Bridie took a deep breath and spoke, "There are two other things I would really like to learn and I know you have the skills. Will you share with me what you know about archery and how to fire a gun?"

William Wellington burst out laughing. "I'm awfully glad you never mentioned those to Tutor Bacon. He would have gone apoplectic." He scratched his head. "Even your grandmother may struggle with that idea. I know she has plans for turning you into a young lady." William laughed again as Bridie screwed up her face. "You cannot go on living like a wild animal, my girl. Your position in this world delivers many responsibilities, I am afraid."

"Yes, Grandpa." Bridie rolled her eyes.

With a soft chuckle, William stood up. "I will talk to your grandmama about the arrow and gun business, but I cannot promise you anything." He moved his chair back. "I will go first and begin the long process of appeasing your tutor. Or at least sending him off with a respectable reference."

Sanders brought the two brown horses hauling the carriage to a gentle stop in front of the manor. At the bottom of the entrance steps, Anna and the Colonel stood on either side of Bridie watching Tutor Bacon descend the stairs with his portmanteau in his hand.

William moved across to shake the man's hand and wish him well in his future as the head of the new local government school.

Displaying limited grace, the man shook hands and thanked the Colonel for his kind wishes. Tutor Bacon then walked over to say goodbye to Mrs. Wellington and his former student. With a rigid back and a severe expression, he turned and boarded the coach. William closed the door behind him with a sharp slam.

Anna found Bridie sitting out near the orchard. Several books were scattered across the table in front of her.

"Hello, dear, I thought I might find you here on such a lovely day."

"It is a glorious day, Grandmama. I felt it a shame to be wasted in the stuffy library."

"The men will be picking the fruit very soon, I should think." Anna settled into a chair on the opposite side of the table.

"Mrs. Ogilvie will be baking her wonderful fruit pies again," Bridie grinned.

"You have to admit she makes a wonderful fruit pie," Anna leant forward towards her granddaughter. "Bridie it is not pies I wish to speak to you about this morning."

"Oh, is everything alright, Grandmama?"

"Yes, dear, it is about a conversation I was having with my friend, Gladys Berrington, recently. She is going to London for the next season to present her granddaughter, Martha. Mrs. Berrington offered to have you join them."

"To join them? What does she mean?"

"She wanted to know if you would like to be presented at the next season in London. Of course, I would have to get your father's permission, I suppose. He may expect you to stay with the family in London at Blue Seas House. But this will not be too much of an inconvenience I should think."

Bridie sat in silence for some moments watching the birds scratching for worms in the ground under the trees.

"Grandmama, this will mean going to all the important social events in London, won't it? It is where the young women meet men who might want to marry them, is it not?"

"It introduces you into respectable society, dear."

This time Bridie's silence continued for such a long time that Anna became worried.

"Are you alright, Bridie?"

"Yes, Grandmama, but I really do not want to go to London for any reason. My father did not want me when I was born, so why should I want to have anything to do with him?"

It was Anna who sat back in a prolonged silence. Sorrow and pain lay heavy on her heart. Why had she not realized how Bridie felt about her situation?

Bridie spoke first. "Even if I went to the London season and met a man I liked, my father would have none of it. I recall, when I was only very young, he made it clear he would see me marry for the good of the company." Her lips tightened and her fists clenched on the table. "I intend never to marry, no matter what he says."

Anna gasped. "Oh, Bridie, dear, never say never."

CHAPTER THREE

Romance

1874 – 1876

The spring sunshine and clear skies looked down upon the coach with Sanders in the driving seat as they progressed along the turnaround at the front of the church, on this Sunday in the middle of May. An explosion of music roared through the open windows of the prayer house to swirl and hurl around the villagers gathering for the Sunday service. Today, the passion within the composition of exultation, praise and joy touched every soul present. All heads turned towards the music.

If Anna had not been endeavouring to avoid the attention of Tutor Bacon hovering around the outskirts of the gathering, she may have observed the rising flush upon Bridie's face. Bridie recognised the composition of Johann Sebastian Bach played by David Lewis. When out riding with Jimmy Braydon who had been promoted to her regular groom, they often stopped in the shade near the cliff to listen to David Lewis practising his music. With fewer classes demanding her time, Bridie summoned her young groom to accompany her on regular occasions along the narrow animal track above the shingle beach as far as the cottage. More than once, the pianist delivered a jug of water and two glasses for their refreshment, to where they sat on a log at the edge of the thicket, listening to the music as it floated and soared through the open doorway.

Anna Wellington looked askance at her husband, "Has Mrs. Barnes had a magical cure to her arthritic fingers or have we a new organist today?"

"Mrs. Barnes on her best days never delivered music like that," the Colonel replied as he stood listening. "Perhaps we should make our way inside. We might discover the answer to your question, my dear."

Following Colonel Wellington's example, several of the villagers made their way through the front doors of the church. Instead of the usual mumble of voices awaiting the presence of the preacher in the pulpit, a hush fell over the congregation as they absorbed works, now by Handel, from the supple fingers of this new organist.

When the final chord vibrated on the light breeze, the last few stragglers moved inside. The parishioners trod softly as if not wishing to desecrate the space, which had so recently captured such beauty of sound for far too few minutes.

Bridie led her grandparents into their usual pew but slid along the seat a little further on than where they usually sat. She sought an uninterrupted view, between the pillars and the pulpit, of David Lewis at the keyboard. When the musician looked directly at her and he smiled, she gasped and dropped her gaze to the gloves upon her hands. Anna missed the exchange, but it did not go unnoticed by Tutor Bacon, from where he sat three seats to the back of Bridie and a little to her right. Another interested observer was Sanders, the coachman, who sat with the other workers along the side wall to her left.

In Bridie's mind, the service was over all too soon. Normally she became fidgety by the time the Rector had his fill of saving his congregation. Her gaze wandered from the line of sight betwixt the pillars and the pulpit to the perfectly stitched seams of the white gloves covering her trembling hands.

Later, as the carriage turned for home, Bridie almost fell off the seat when Anna Wellington informed her and William, that there was going to be another for lunch today. She had invited the musician David Lewis to join them in their repast.

"He will follow close behind on his own horse," Anna smiled gently at the bright pink flush upon Bridie's face. Anna's next announcement sent Bridie's stomach into the gyrations of a butter churn.

"I am thinking this man may be able to teach you more than I can on the piano, Bridie. What do you think, William?"

Grandpa's eyes twinkled as he looked upon the top of the folds of blue material making up a delicate hat worn on Bridie's bent head.

"Anna, you know I have always said no one can outclass your musical skills, but I will admit this fellow has a special talent, which may be of benefit to our dear Bridie."

While the parlour maid served the plates of steaming roast lamb with mint sauce and vegetables to the family and their guest, Bridie attempted to follow the conversation between her grandparents and David Lewis. His smiling eyes and handsome face stifled the voices leaving only the earlier soaring music of the church organ, swirling around inside her head.

After her grandpa finished saying grace, Bridie found it almost impossible to eat. She nibbled at her food.

"I'm sorry to hear that, Mr. Lewis," the voice of Anna Wellington registered. *Sorry to hear what?* The words blared inside Bridie's mind. Her glance lifted.

"Your mother must have been devastated after losing your father only a short time before."

Bridie struggled to catch up with the conversation. She raised her eyes only to look directly at the glance thrown her way by David Lewis before he answered Anna's comment.

"The neighbour took on the work at our farm on a share-farmer basis. Our local Rector supported Mother as much as he could, of course. He and the Bishop were responsible for sending me to continue my music studies in London, within the church system. I was able to earn a small amount of money to send back to her when I obtained paid work on the keyboard."

"What then brought you to our neck of the woods, Mr. Lewis?" It was William who posed the question.

"My condition deteriorated and the physician recommended I move to the southern coast, or even to another country with a warmer climate. I had no desire to live any further from what was left of my family, so emigration was out of the question. Again, with the help of the church, here I am in the cottage on the cliff as the locals call it."

Anna did not miss the interaction between her silent granddaughter – an unusual event in itself – and their guest. She noted how Bridie pushed the food around her plate and barely swallowed a morsel. This was the girl who always arrived at the table with a hearty appetite. Anna's sharp eyes caught the glances that passed between Bridie and their guest.

When the meal was over, Colonel Wellington led David Lewis, with Anna and Bridie bringing up the rear, out into the garden. The discussion revolved around Clawhaven Manor. William spoke in detail of his forebears and their acquisition of this property.

"When our granddaughter joined us here as a squawking infant, watching her interest develop was like reliving my love of this land all over again." William turned to his wife. "Anna, we have listened to Mr. Lewis on the organ this morning. I think you should now wave the flag for Clawhaven and demonstrate your musical skills, my dear. Shall we go inside?"

After a moment of modest protestations, Anna led the others into the music room and took her place at the piano. Her fingers danced up and down a few scales to warm up before she began some of her favourite compositions. After half an hour, David walked across to stand beside the keyboard.

"May I sit beside you and make a duet of this piece, Mrs. Wellington?"

Anna smiled and shifted across the seat to her right. David's fingers on the base notes stalked the soprano melody from Anna's agile digits, as they flittered across the high notes carrying the tune. David thrilled the audience with his adaptions to the composition.

It was the arrival of the parlour maid as she moved quietly around the room collecting the glasses and cups, which drew the interlude to a conclusion.

David jumped up. "Oh, I'm sorry, I never know when to stop once I start on the keyboard. Forgive me, I've overstayed my welcome."

"No such thing, lad," William reassured his guest. "It has been a privilege and a pleasure to listen to you," William nodded his head towards his wife, "To both of you."

"Thank you, sir. Now, I really must away or my horse will give up on me and head home on its own."

Everyone proceeded to the front portico from where they waved David on his way.

"A truly delightful gentleman, don't you think so, Anna?" The colonel nodded to the departing guest.

"A very polite man and a marvellous musician, I must say."

The words washed over Bridie like a fragrant summer breeze.

It was later the same evening, when Anna Wellington slipped into Bridie's bedroom to say goodnight, that she delivered the warning to her granddaughter.

"Darling, Bridie, I know your heart yearns for David Lewis, but it sounds as if his physical health may be a precursor for heartache and sorrow."

"But, Grandmama, he looks in the peak of health. As long as he remains living here, he will be alright, won't he?"

"Who knows what our God has chosen for any of us? Mr. Lewis and his family have already been dealt a load of tragedy, with little future ahead. I know a man who plays the piano as he can should never go hungry, but you need to think seriously if you have dreams of a husband and children. You need to think of any possible offspring. I fear David may have only a very limited future." Anna leant down and kissed Bridie's forehead. "I am sorry, darling."

Bridie could not answer her grandmama as the tears poured from her eyes and choked the words in her throat.

When time permitted, and with Jimmy in tow, Bridie often ventured forth to listen to David's music drifting out on the warming breezes across the sea. The summer arrived in full strength and the wildflowers sprinkled the grasses above the beach.

Bridie sat beside her grandmother reading in the drawing room when Mrs. Coburn arrived with the newly delivered mail. She watched her grandmother flick through the letters sorting those addressed to Grandpa on one side of the small table in front of her. Bridie noticed as she stroked the three envelopes left in her hands. She wondered at the sigh as Grandmama read the writing on the larger envelope. It was tossed aside as if of no importance. She lifted each of the two others to her face and inhaled the fragrance of the paper. Another sigh escaped into the room as she reluctantly put them onto the table and reclaimed the large envelope.

"This will be from your father if I am not mistaken. Perhaps I should leave it for your grandfather to look at, but I know he will hide it under whatever pile of papers he has on his desk." Anna spoke softly – as if more to herself than to Bridie.

With a slim blade, she slit the larger envelope open. The paper rustled as Anna spread it flat. Holding it up to the light she began to peruse the news.

Bridie looked up sharply when her grandmother gave a short cry and jumped up.

"Oh, that cannot be, that cannot be." The colour drained from her face. She turned left and right about the room as if seeking another option to this current news.

"Bridie," Anna's voice came out barely audible. She tried again. "Bridie," louder this time.

"Yes, Grandmama, what is it? Should I get Grandpa?"

"Yes, my child, get your grandfather," Anna managed to squeak around the stranglehold the shock had on the muscles of her throat.

Bridie beat a hasty exit from the room and across the hall to the office. "Grandpa, Grandpa," she knew better than to yell. She swung through the doorway to find her grandpa sitting in the old armchair in the corner catching forty winks.

He struggled to his feet. "Bridie, my dear, whatever is the matter?"

"Grandpa, you must come right now; something is wrong with Grandmama. It was the letter, you see."

William did not wait to find out what letter Bridie might be referring to. His aged legs threatened to give up under him as he strode from the office. Bridie followed hard on his heels. William froze at the drawing-room doorway at the sight of his Anna standing with her mouth open holding a letter out for him to see. He rushed over and urged her back into her seat. He gently removed the letter and retired to the neighbouring chair where he sat to read.

Bridie remained alert at the doorway. She controlled her impatience at the time taken for Grandpa to absorb the contents of the tainted letter.

When his old fingers lowered the paper to his knees, he reached over and clasped Anna's outstretched arm.

"Can it be true?" she asked.

Bridie bit her lip. If she drew attention to herself in such a pregnant moment, it might invite a diversionary tactic such as being directed to her room.

But William's mind was otherwise taken aback at the news. "Anna, my love, I am afraid it must be true. Douglas says the ship went down eight weeks ago and they have no indication of anyone having been rescued. It would seem he has lost his two younger boys. That will be a large blow to his aspirations."

"I think it will be a blow to his heart, surely, William."

Only Bridie heard William's almost silent words. "If he has a heart at all."

Anna's sorrow disallowed any such words to register within her brain.

William gently shook her fingers. "Douglas says he is having a memorial service in London next month for his boys, and for the families of others who have lost loved ones on the ship."

"Max and Toby were only babies, why did he send them to sea in the first place?" It was as if Anna did not hear his words.

"Anna, the boys have been crossing the oceans for the last five years – time enough to make men of any young lads. Max was only a month away from his twenty-first birthday and Toby was nineteen years old."

"It is too terrible. I am glad our Athena never had to witness this." Anna sucked in a deep sob. "What about all those others on board the ship? The letter says no survivors were found. How tragic for all those other families too."

"You will come to the memorial with me, won't you, Anna?"

"Of course, William." Anna appeared to only just realise Bridie was still in the room. "Bridie, I am sorry you have heard the news of your brothers' loss like this."

"Do not fuss yourself, Grandmama. It is always sad to hear of anyone dying, particularly when they are young, but I never really knew my brothers. It all feels surreal somehow. Do you mind if I stay and look after Clawhaven while you and Grandpa go to London for the memorial?"

"That is to be held next month. We will make a decision when it grows closer to the time, my dear."

Bridie waved goodbye to her grandparents who were sitting inside the carriage with Sanders in the driving seat. After the carriage disappeared at the bend in the track on their way to their grandsons' memorial service in London, Bridie collected her large outdoor hat with its blue scarf tie and secured it to her head. Despite her empathy for her grandparents' sorrow, she felt little on a personal level for the loss of her once-met brothers. Her smile brightened as her feet led her to the narrow animal path above the high-tide mark leading towards the cottage on the cliff. A path decidedly more pronounced since the frequent use she gave it in these past months.

At the sight of David standing at the top of the cliff path waiting for her, Bridie laughed and started into a run removing her hat as she did so. It waved out behind the hand holding the ties. She threw herself into his arms. His lips on hers united them in their love and trust. As they turned towards the cottage, David pulled her closer and asked the question uppermost in his mind.

"Have you thought about what I said to you the other day, my love? I do not wish to commit you to a married life caring for an invalid and yet…."

"David, my dearest, I have thought of little else." Bridie dropped her face into his neck. She smelt the sea salt on his skin.

David lifted her head and looked into her eyes. "And …?" he asked. "Do you really understand the possible consequences?"

"Yes, my love, I do. I also know that you are my whole world and I want to share all of you in what little time you … we, have left." Lifting David's hand into her own, she guided him into the cottage. She closed the door behind them and threw her hat onto the stool near the door. Her arms slipped around his neck drawing him even closer. "I love you beyond everything else," she whispered.

Inside the entrance room of the cottage, the kiss deepened. David's hand reached up and released the buttons of Bridie's bodice at her throat. His lips traced her neck and the swell of her breasts drawing a groan from deep down inside her. Bridie's nimble fingers unbuttoned the remaining front of the delicate materials to expose her naked chest.

"Oh, my darling," David stopped to admire.

Bridie's fingers released the clips at her waist. Her skirt slithered to a heap on the floor at her feet along with her underwear. She stepped out of it before applying her supple fingers to aid in the removal of David's shirt and trousers. Bridie's experience watching the farm animals opened her mind to what was about to happen, but she never had any inkling of the tumultuous feelings now stirring and clashing inside her inner core. Her hands wanted to touch and hold all of David at the same time. They faltered for a moment. As light as the touch of a warm summer breeze her fingers ran lightly over his chest, they found their way to his waist. She sucked in a noisy breath as her fingers discovered the promise of his desire. Her eyes flew open.

David looked up to see the anxiety mixed with love and desire in her eyes.

"What are you afraid of, my dearest?"

"Oh, my love, what if I cannot please you?"

"You please me on many levels, dearest Bridie. I will be gentle, my darling. You only have to say stop, if you want me to." He dropped soft kisses onto her lips.

Of its own volition, a groan initiated in the depths of her insides, rolled out of her mouth as David's sensitive fingers twirled her nipples and ran around her breasts. As inquisitive as an explorer of unchartered territories, his hands ran back and forth across her abdomen before instinct guided them to discover the hidden cave below.

"David, I will never say, stop. Please don't stop." Bridie felt unable to breathe with her heart pounding in her chest. The echo of it in her head drowned all memories of the lessons received on decorum and modest behaviour.

He lifted the edge of her bottom onto the kitchen table, scattering the plates and cutlery as he did so. Bridie's gasp turned into a giggle. When their bodies united, David's mouth covered her own – his kiss deep and sweet. A brief whimper escaped Bridie's lips only to be driven out by the deepening moans from both as their bodies began to move in unison. When she did not think she could survive this exquisite pleasure anymore, she threw her head back. With a soft low growl, she discovered her body had further pleasures to thrill her. The spasms within her core overwhelmed Bridie.

Perspiration ran freely over their skin as they clung to each other in love and satisfaction. David began to lick the salty moisture from her nipples which stirred the senses deep within her core to life once more. The sound of David's excitement and pleasure triggered Bridie's spasms again.

"My love, my Bridie, you are beyond all my dreams."

"David, my darling, my only desire."

The late afternoon sunshine through the windows found the pair of lovers lying on the bed upstairs still holding their naked bodies close.

"Come, my love, it is getting late. You must return to the manor before you are missed." David stood up and smiled down at her. He took her hands and lifted her into his arms.

"Oh, David, I do not ever want to let you go. I have never felt so comfortable in my own skin."

"It is getting late, my love. We do not want your grandparents to confine you to the manor, now do we?" He kissed her forehead and began to help her dress. With gentle hands on her shoulders, he turned her around.

Bridie alternated between walking and running along the path almost two miles to the manor. Her heart soared like the sea hawk swooping low over the waves. Where the path turned to lead through the orchard and into the garden of her home, she paused and drew a piece of fruit from a tree. Bridie savoured the juice. Some trickled down her chin. Guilt niggled at her conscience as she slipped quietly up the back staircase to arrive undiscovered in her room.

After she sponged her body in the basin of water on her washstand, Bridie changed into a fresh muslin dress and clean silk stockings. She brushed her hair and held it in place with a pink ribbon to match her frock. She grinned at the lady in the reflection.

"Soap, perfume and clean clothes, an amazing camouflage, but you cannot fool me. I know a sinful woman is hiding inside there.

However, I am sure God did not mean anything so beautiful to be sinful."

She ran her hands down either side of her body – along the route taken by David's fingers earlier. Her skin tingled. She felt an echo of her earlier sensations deep within her. Her head swung to the door at the sound of the sharp knock.

"Miss Bridie, are you there?"

Bridie opened the door to the housekeeper. "Yes, Mrs. Coburn, can I help you?"

"Yes, Miss Bridie, I thought you might like your dinner served on the back porch, given it is such a mild evening."

"Oh yes, Mrs. Coburn, that sounds delightful. I will be right down."

Along with the stream of early sunshine, Jimmy Braydon knocked on the kitchen door.

"Did you be wettin' the bed, young Jimmy Braydon? I'm not too sure if the mistress be astir yet."

At that moment, Bridie's head hung out from her window above. "Give me five minutes, Jimmy."

"You'd best be comin' in and havin' a piece of toast. You be needin' some fat on those bones young man," the cook, Mrs. Ogilvie, instructed with a roll of her eyes and a smile.

Later, as Welly and Flyer headed along the bridle path above the beach, Bridie's mind was still in the cottage with her lover when Jimmy spoke.

"We 'ad Tutor Bacon scrougin' aroun' our house late yesterday."

With only half her attention on the conversation, Bridie asked, "What on earth would he be doing at your place? I hope you have not been in any trouble at school, Jimmy."

Jimmy laughed. "No, I don' goes to school no more. I work full time on our farm now."

"Oh, sorry, I forgot. So, what did he have on his mind?"

"Poxy rogue fancies my Ma, I'm thinkin'," Jimmy grinned. "I reckon Ma'll send him on his way."

"Your mother is a handsome woman, Jimmy. A school teacher might be an advantageous husband."

"I'll break 'is legs first. That man's not a nice person."

Bridie's curiosity was fully aroused. "What do you have against him?"

"'Ee be a lecher, Miss. Mary Piper says the man always be rubbin' 'isself on her back, in class." Jimmy's face turned scarlet. "Sorry, Miss, I ought not be sayin' that word in front of a lady."

"Maybe not, Jimmy, but nor is a lecher nice in the classroom; especially if it is the school teacher." She turned in the saddle to look Jimmy in the eye. "I have to admit he never gave me any trouble when at the manor, but then Grandpa was always in the same room with us."

"Unaccountable spiteful sod too. Bad-mouthed the Colonel one day, but Aunt sorted 'im."

"Good for her," Bridie laughed. "I don't think Grandpa would give the tutor's opinion any weight."

"Be wary of 'im, Miss Bridie, mayhap your father rescued 'im from a bad situation in London, I understand."

"What sort of situation, Jimmy?"

"I've no idea, only it be the talk in the town."

"Oh dear, I wonder why he stayed in this area." Bridie did not waste another thought on Tutor Bacon as they approached the cliff path that led past the cottage.

She felt the flutter of her heart. Her hands trembled. Her breath deserted her.

"Look, Miss Bridie, there be the music man wavin' at the doorway," Jimmy stood in his stirrups. "Mornin' to yer, Mr. Lewis, sir."

"Morning, Jimmy. Morning, Miss Mayford," the musician called with a grin.

Bridie felt the heat in her face, but a glance in Jimmy's direction assured her his attention was taken with the man at the cottage doorway.

"I'll be comin' over this afternoon, Mr. Lewis, to chop that wood fer yer," Jimmy called.

"Thanks, lad, I'll appreciate that." His grin widened as he waved again at the riders.

Bridie did not hear the coach arrive home from London. She had not long returned from another walk along the beach to the cottage on Clawhaven Cliff. When she heard the knock on her bedroom door she shoved her dirty laundry into the basket for the morning's collection.

She smiled at the sound of her grandfather's voice and skipped over to open the door. Bridie threw her arms around his neck.

"You are my favourite Grandpa."

William gave a rueful laugh. "I am your only grandpa." His usual response to such a comment from Bridie.

Bridie giggled. "Mrs. Coburn hasn't sounded the dinner bell yet, has she?"

"No, child, she has not, but it won't be long before she has it clanging throughout the hallways." William stood back and admired his eighteen-year-old granddaughter. *Where have the years gone,* he found himself thinking – a phrase he used too much these days. "Was that you, I heard clattering up the back staircase earlier, young lady?"

Bridie lifted her head in surprise. She thought she had been so quiet. Her basic honesty quelled the initial tale she was going to tell, but at least she had the grace to bite her lower lip in contrition as she edited the full truth.

"Yes, Grandpa, I was late coming in and knew I would have to hurry to change. The osprey hawks are back nesting in the forest near the shingle beach. They held me mesmerized as they soared and swooped and skimmed across the waves. I wish you were there with me to see them."

"Your mother always kept a watch out for the return of the hawks on that beach, too."

Bridie retied her hair ribbon and stood in silence for long moments looking at her grandpa's reflection in her mirror.

"What happened to my other grandpa – my father's father?"

William paused in thought before speaking. "I guess you are old enough now to know the truth." Again, he paused to gather his thoughts. "Grandpa Mayford died in a duel when your father was not even twenty-one years of age. Some say he was caught cheating at the gambling tables. He was never much of a businessman. He preferred the social side of life, I understand. Douglas, being the only son, had to put all his aspirations aside and rescue the family business that teetered on the brink of insolvency." William gazed up to the ceiling pondering how much to tell Bridie. "Douglas's marriage to our Athena brought him a face-saving dowry, but, as is not often the case, their relationship was a good and solid one. However much I may disagree with Douglas, I know for a fact he loved your mother and she loved him implicitly."

It was Bridie's turn to stand in silence absorbing all she had been told.

"Is that why my father hates me so – because she died when I was born?"

"Oh, Bridie, dear, he does not hate you. Douglas sees so much of Athena in you. When you cover your hair, you are the spitting image of her. It breaks his heart."

"But you and Grandmama were her parents and yet you do not hate me just because I look like her."

"No, that is correct, but we know the complete Bridie. You may look the spitting image of Athena at times, but the pair of you could not be more different. You are more forthright, whereas Athena was more docile. Our daughter never applied herself to her classes, other than languages – she did excel at those classes." He smiled in reminiscence. "Things like politics and mathematics never held her interest for more than two minutes." William threw his arms into the air. "I could go on for ages listing the differences in you both, but we loved your mother for what she was, and we love you just as much for what you are. I feel sorry because Douglas has missed out on so much not having known you."

"Why is he always such a grouch?"

William Wellington stood in silence looking down at his granddaughter. "Bridie, your father was not always like that. When he was a young man, he was very popular with his peers – full of fun and kindness. His horsemanship was seldom outclassed. He had every intention of joining the British Cavalry, but his father's death put paid to that." William reached over and hugged Bridie. "It was like the world crashed down upon his shoulders. I feel sorry also for your brothers, George, and when they were alive, Max and Toby. Your father was determined they should be schooled in everything about the business so they would not experience what he went through if something untoward happened to him. It made him a hard man."

≈

Anna and William were talking in the library when a sharp knock on the door sounded. Mrs. Coburn's voice called urgently.

"Mrs. Wellington, Colonel, are you there?"

"Yes, Mrs. Coburn, please come in."

At first glance, Anna noticed the stress on her housekeeper's face.

"Whatever is the matter, Mrs. Coburn?"

"It is Mr. Mayford, Mrs. Wellington, his coach has just this minute pulled into our driveway."

"This is a surprise to me, Mrs. Coburn. Will you greet him at the door and send him into the parlour, please?"

"Yes, Mrs. Wellington, right away."

Anna turned to her husband. "Oh, bother, what is he here for now? What on earth can be so urgent to have him travel down through the winter snows?"

"Well, we will never find out sitting here." The Colonel helped his wife to her feet.

"Do you think it might be what we were talking about only last night?"

"Bridie? Yes, but not necessarily what we were talking about. I am more concerned he plans to have her betrothed to someone totally unsuitable – someone advantageous to the company."

"Either of the subjects, our discussion or this objectionable idea, will cause an uproar that does not bear thinking about." The pair made their way across the hall to find their son-in-law ensconced in a comfortable chair enjoying a large drink of William's favourite whiskey. William and Anna shared a glance before they walked into the room.

"Good morning, Douglas, this is a pleasant surprise," William mumbled as he made himself comfortable in his favourite chair.

"'Morning, William, Anna, this is not a social call, I am sorry to say. I am here to find out what is going on with my daughter."

The shared glance between William and Anna spoke volumes. *What trouble is he stirring up now?*

"You have me flummoxed there, old man. I have no idea what you are talking about," William replied through tight lips.

Anna rang the small bell on the table beside her chair. Within seconds Mrs. Coburn swept into the room.

"Yes, Mrs. Wellington, is there anything I can get you?"

"Is Bridie back from her walk yet, Mrs. Coburn?"

"I have not heard her foot on the stair yet, Mrs. Wellington. Will I ask the handyman to fetch her?"

"Yes please, if you will. Once you have done that, I think a pot of tea might not go astray. Maybe you could send the maid in to stir up the coals in the fire, here. There is certainly a chill in the air today."

"Right away, Mrs. Wellington."

Mrs. Coburn's first port of call was the kitchen to let Mrs. Ogilvie know to prepare a tray and to give the maid her instructions regarding the fireplace. From there she glanced into the library before climbing the staircase leading to Bridie's room to check if the girl had indeed returned.

Bridie was turning to close her door when Mrs. Coburn arrived at her elbow.

"Oh, you startled me, Mrs. Coburn," she watched the woman now trying to catch her breath.

"Why you are quite flushed. Is everything alright?"

"It's your father arrived, Miss Bridie, he's in the parlour. The Colonel asks you to attend."

Bridie felt her heart sink to her toes. "I'll go right away, thanks, Mrs. Coburn."

Once inside the parlour, Bridie had little chance to make a formal greeting to her sire before he jumped up to accost her. She watched the flashing eyes and deepening flush on his face as he spoke.

"What's this I hear about your behaviour, girl? I expect better from my daughter than this gossip amongst the local commoners." His eyes flashed.

Bridie lifted her head. She felt her mouth dry beneath her tongue. She took a deep breath. After one false start, she spoke, her voice quiet but every bit as belligerent as her father's tone.

"If you will excuse me, Father, I think I may go out and come in again. You might like to make a pleasant greeting before you stand there berating me on my behaviour, as related from any village gossip you may have gleaned from one or other of your paid lackeys."

"What nonsensical rubbish – paid lackeys indeed!"

Anna and William exchanged worried glances. This was a Bridie they had never seen before. This was a Bridie, the daughter of Douglas Mayford – never afraid to broach the lion's den. Most concerning though was the changing hue of their son-in-law's face turning from a vivid red colour to the palest white within seconds.

"Now, Douglas, please, can we all sit down and talk like intelligent adults?" William rose to his feet. He turned to his granddaughter. "Please, lass, take a seat. Can I get you a cup of tea?"

"Thank you, Grandpa, but I think it might choke me at the moment."

While the glares of father and daughter scorched the air between the sparring pair, Anna stood and poured the tea for everyone.

"Sit, Bridie," she commanded as she rested the cup and saucer on the side table at Bridie's right hand.

Bridie sat, her back straight and stiff. Her gaze softened a fraction.

"Thank you, Grandmama."

With a grace of long standing, Anna reclaimed her seat.

"Now, Douglas would you tell us what this is all about?"

Douglas sipped at his tea before he took a deep breath and spoke in a more controlled voice. He turned to his daughter.

"I understand you have been paying too much attention to an organist at the church – visiting him at his abode even."

Questioning glances passed between William and Anna before they looked at their granddaughter whose gaze clashed with her father's stare across the room.

William went to speak, but Bridie reached out to lay a gentle hand on her grandfather's arm. She turned her head to answer her father.

"We are blessed to have a talented musician who offers his time to our church here in these bucolic lands, Father. And yes, when I am out riding with my groom, we often pause to listen to the man practising his music in the cottage on Clawhaven Cliff." Bridie sucked in a quick breath. Her heart thudded inside her chest. She held her hands on her lap to cover their tremble, but her gaze remained defiant.

Once more the reddened hue infused the face of Douglas Mayford. He spoke to William.

"William, I understand you have had this fellow here at the manor for Sunday lunch frequently. Surely you can see this is not the company my daughter should be exposed to."

William swallowed his tea almost choking as he did so. He coughed several times. His eyes narrowed.

"Douglas, are you telling me we cannot decide whom we may invite into our home? And, for your information, David Lewis is a gentleman who knows how to behave when he is in company." William fired off a scathing look in Douglas's direction. "We have brought up a daughter before, Douglas. Are you saying you were not satisfied with the quality of our Athena?"

It was Douglas's turn to almost choke on his drink. "No, of course not, William. Athena was everything a man could have wanted in a wife." Emotion held his tongue for several moments. It vacuumed the flush from his face. "I do not want Bridie to be the subject of the village gossips. She is twenty years old this year and I am in the process of negotiating a suitable marriage for her, and we cannot have loose gossip spoil this opportunity."

William turned to his wife. Consternation was reflected in both their faces. It was Bridie who stirred herself again. Her head lifted. The blazing eyes targeted her father once again.

"And do I have a say in this selection of a marriage partner, Father?"

"You are a woman now, Bridie, it is your duty to make a suitable marriage." Douglas snapped in her direction.

"Is that for your benefit or my benefit, Father?"

"You do not want to marry a pauper, girl. You will want someone who can support you and your offspring into the future."

"And someone who will infuse the coffers of your shipping company with investment contributions, no doubt."

"That is the way of the world. With the education you have been given, surely you can see this?"

"All I can see is a life not worth living – spending day in and day out with someone who repels me in every way. This is not the dark ages, Father," Bridie dragged the word out leaving it to teeter on the edge of disrespect. "We are nearing the end of the nineteenth century. Women are learning to make their own decisions about everything in their lives."

"Bah, that is a load of nonsense. Where will the world be if women go around making decisions of any kind? That is a man's prerogative. It takes a steady mind, not an empty space full of emotional tantrums, to make life's decisions." He shook his head in disbelief at the idea that this was not understood universally. He glanced over to William for support, but only saw the man's admiration in the look he had for Bridie. Douglas growled as he swung his attention back to his daughter, "I will be staying at the auberge in the town tonight. Tomorrow, you will accompany me to London where you will meet this man who will be your husband." He was not blind to the defiance in his daughter's face nor to the fact she opened her mouth to speak. "And before you say anything else, you may as well be prepared to stay in London until your marriage. George is doing most of the day-to-day running of the company and I can apply myself to this task of having you settled before I am too old."

Bridie gasped as if she had been punched in the stomach. She turned to her grandparents, but they sat as stunned as herself.

"Father, have you heard of the saying, you can lead a horse to water, but you cannot make him drink?" She dragged in a ragged breath. "You may haul me off to the altar, but while ever I have breath in my body I will say 'No!' when asked if I take this man, etc."

"We'll see about that, young lady."

"Things are changing, Father. This is not the Dark Ages. Women are gaining their rights. They achieved the Married Women's Property Act six years ago in 1870. The female suffrage is gaining momentum every year. Their Women's Disabilities Removal Bill might have been defeated in 1871, but it has been debated in the House of Commons four times since. It will not go away."

"Tsssh, just a lot of rabble-rousing women and their followers."

"You will find it will continue to be debated while ever it continues to have the majority of Members of Parliament supporting it, as it has now. Government support will come, and in the not-too-distant future I would think"

"It's all a storm in a teacup – you'll see."

"A very big storm in a very big cup then, Father. There is every chance that in my lifetime, I will get to see women be given the right to vote, just you wait and see."

"What rot have you been teaching this girl, William?"

"Sorry, Douglas but this information is in all the current newspapers and other articles. They are lucid points and most probable achievements for the future."

Douglas jumped to his feet. He stumbled. His mouth opened and shut. His face turned a purplish-red hue again.

"I'll see you locked up first," he fired across at Bridie.

From her seat in the corner, Anna's usually placid voice cut across the venom in the air.

"Bridie, remember, 'Grace above everything.' You owe your father an apology." Before Bridie could respond, Anna swung her gaze towards the other sparring partner. "Now, Douglas, do you really think this is what your Athena wanted for her daughter, a life of unhappiness without fulfilment?"

Douglas sank back into his chair. His smouldering eyes cast down towards the carpet on the floor.

Bridie surprised everyone when she stood as if to walk out, but then swung around to move across the room to her father.

"I am sorry I cannot please you, Father, but I will not marry anyone if I cannot marry someone of my choosing."

"You need to remember I am your father and it is my responsibility to make decisions for the whole family." Douglas stood. "I do not take kindly to being defied."

"I am sorry you feel that way, Father. Now, if everyone will excuse me, I must go and tend to my horse." Bridie swept out of the room.

"I will be here no later than ten in the morning. I expect you to be ready."

Bridie's answer was either non-existent or soft enough not to be heard.

The three remaining people seated in the room sat in silence. Their gaze followed the path of Bridie's exit for some time until Anna turned to Douglas.

"Douglas, you do realize your daughter has a strength and determination our Athena never had. This may stand her in good stead as she matures, but she will need gentle guidance on how to use this trait in the meantime. Why is it that you need Bridie's co-operation to further the company? Surely George and Beatrice are capable of this?"

Douglas rubbed at the pain behind his eyes. He sighed a loud sigh.

"George has begged me not to tell anyone, but I think, perhaps you should be told. Since Edward's birth, Beatrice seems to be having difficulty completing a pregnancy. After three miscarriages, she did eventually have a child last year, a girl. It seems Beatrice's mind has slipped since this birth. I am told it was due to the miasmas within the birthing chamber."

Douglas sucked in a noisy breath before going on, "You may have noticed, when you were down there for Edward's christening, George defers too much to Beatrice's whims. She has refused to have anything to do with this baby and it and the wet nurse have been shut in the west wing of the house since its birth. Beatrice has retreated into her own rooms, which are decorated like some sort of nunnery or church, according to George. She never comes out at all. It is not natural, I tell you."

Shock silenced both Anna and William. It was Douglas who spoke again.

"If the shipping company is to remain alive, we need to have someone producing people strong enough to build it up. Their son Edward is four years old now but I must admit concern. He might have a determination but to be honest, I do not think he has the character and temperament to carry the company forward." Douglas rubbed at the pain behind his eyes again and gave a rueful grimace. "I can see Bridie certainly has the strength and determination needed." Douglas pressed his fingers into the temporal lobes on either side of his eyes.

"Douglas, are you alright?" Anna asked.

"I am not too sure. The doctor tells me to slow down and relax more or I will end up having an apoplectic fit. If that happens, I worry that George will have no one to support him."

When the carriage carrying Douglas to the town trundled off down the driveway, Anna turned to her husband.

"I do not like the look of Douglas. He seems decidedly unwell."

"I am sure it will be just overwork and getting all het up about things, my love."

"You may be right, but do you remember Granny Wellington when she had the apoplectic fit before she died? She spent two days rubbing her eyes and head like he did this afternoon."

"Yes, I remember that. Well, our worrying will not make aught difference. He should learn to calm down."

"By the sound of things, Beatrice is causing Douglas a large headache. George may have been the elder boy, but I always said it was Max who should have taken over the company. I feel rather hurt that we were never told of George and Beatrice having had a daughter. What is going to happen to the mite being locked away from everything and everyone? I find it hard to understand Beatrice. What kind of mother can do that to her baby? Is there nothing we can do to help the child?"

"Sadly, it is the parents' responsibility, Anna. We can hardly interfere as much as we might want to. Now can we guess where our Bridie has gone to soothe her ruffled feathers?"

"I do hope we have not made her too smart for her own good, William."

William smiled. "Her knowledge will stand her in good stead one day – once she has learnt not to go off half-cocked." William pulled his coat close about him and kissed his wife on the forehead. "I will go over to the stable and bring her home. The night is closing in and it promises maybe more snow in the morning."

In the stable, Bridie's tears streamed down her cheeks as she shared her anger, fear and frustration with Welly.

"I'm not going, Welly. Perhaps I should run away tonight." She shivered as a cold breeze whisked through the building. "Where can I go? It is nearly the middle of winter. I will freeze to death." The idea of running away to join her lover in the cottage on the cliff filtered through her mind but was short-lived. David was no match for her father. David's health would never survive a sustained effort from her father to get his own way. The idea dribbled away.

"What about Grandmama and Grandpa? It cannot do them any good to see us knocking heads. If only my mother was alive. But then hers was a marriage planned by others. Grandmama said she loved my father, though. She would know what I should do." Bridie's arm gave several strong sweeps with the brush across Welly's withers.

Alec Bacon-Dowd, secretary to Douglas Mayford, emerged from the carriage just as Douglas was bidding farewell to his parents-in-law. He noticed at first glance that Douglas suffered one of his too-frequent headaches. He held the carriage door, while Douglas stepped in and almost fell back into the seat with a groan.

Alec climbed in and threw the rug over his employer's knees. He knocked on the roof of the carriage to let the driver know to make headway towards the inn, where they had rooms for the night.

"You, alright there, Boss?"

"No, I am not alright. My accursed head is about to explode."

Alec knew Douglas better than anyone knew the man. Since they were boys in short pants the pair had shared adventures and idle days, one way or another. They regularly bent the rules to breaking point. Taking Douglas's small sailboat down the stream from his home and into the river Thames, against the Mayford parents' specific instructions never to do so, was one of their favourite escapades. When Alec's father lost his fortune to poor investment and gambling, it was Douglas who ensured Alec had permanent employment.

Once Alec helped Douglas up the staircase and into his bedroom, he was surprised when Douglas demanded he take notes for a letter.

"What now, Boss? You need to rest. Remember what the sawbones told you."

"Devil's blood, if I wanted a nagging wife, I'd go find one. Will you just do as I say?"

Alec bit his lip and moved to the desk against the wall. He prepared to write as Douglas began to dictate.

Dear Anna and William.

Circumstances demand I return to London post haste. I will not be able to take Bridie with me tomorrow. Hopefully, by the time I return to do so, she may be in a better frame of mind.

Your son-in-law,

Douglas Mayford.

"Now, when you go downstairs, I want you to have the innkeeper send that note on to the Wellingtons tonight, if possible, or at least first thing in the morning. Give him a few coins for his trouble."

"You not coming down to dine, Boss? Can I bring something up for you?"

"No, I am going to call it a night. You can give me a drop of that laudanum the doctor in London prescribed. Hopefully, the pain will ease and I will get to sleep."

Two days later, when the Mayford coach pulled up in London at the front door of Blue Seas House, the home in which Douglas's children were born, Alec jumped out. With the assistance of the coach driver, he almost carried Douglas inside the building and to his rooms in the east wing. The man was almost comatose. Alec commanded the driver to help loosen Douglas's clothes and remove his boots and waistcoat.

"Boss, I'm going to fetch the doctor. We'll be right back." Worry filled Alec's hazel eyes.

Douglas mumbled a few incoherent words, but Alec was leaping down the stairs two at a time dragging the coachman along with him.

When the physician, guided by Alec, entered Douglas's bedroom, he paused at the sight of his patient lying there with his eyes shut, saliva trickling from each side of his mouth and a dark mottled hue to his face. At first glance, he assumed his need here was long gone. His fingers reached out and felt the feeble, slow pulse.

"It seems to me, Mr. Bacon-Dowd, that Mr. Mayford has had another apoplectic seizure. How long has he been unwell this time."

Bacon-Dowd scratched his head and spoke. "He complained of a severe headache the night before last when we were down in Sussex. He insisted we come straight home the next morning."

"It sounds like he has not listened to a word of the advice I've been giving him lately to slow down and reduce his alcohol intake. We can only hope that it has been a small turn again this time."

"I do not know anything about that, sir. He has been down visiting the family."

CHAPTER FOUR

Manipulation

1877

Bridie's eyes sparkled. Her footsteps fell light upon the staircase as she hurried up to her room. She threw her riding clothes onto the chair. As she poured water from the jug into the basin on the washstand, she grinned at the memory of her morning's visit to David Lewis. She shivered, not only at the coolness in the early spring air but at the recollection of her body's responses to their love-making. She hugged herself and felt again the echo of the throbbing music David's fingers and kisses enticed from her deepest core.

Once washed and dressed, she stood at her window lost in her daydreaming. The not-so-gentle clang of the breakfast bell stirred her from the thoughts of her upcoming twenty-first birthday in a few short weeks. The shadow of her father's threats faded as she dreamed her dreams.

At the top of the stairs, she greeted her grandparents as they began their descent to the dining room.

Steam rose from the bowls of porridge. A jug of fresh cow's milk stood in the middle of the table.

"Thank you," Bridie said, as she sat on the chair held for her by William, after seeing his wife seated.

After the empty porridge plates were removed by a soft-footed parlour maid, they each addressed themselves to their usual breakfast.

95

Grandpa and Bridie always faced up to a full breakfast of bacon, eggs and toast.

"A productive day requires a decent meal," Grandpa commented as he did almost every day.

Grandmama preferred two soft-boiled eggs and toast.

When Bridie and the Colonel proceeded to the library, Anna disappeared into the morning room where she took up her sketching pad from the cupboard near the front window and began work on her latest creative challenge.

Mrs. Coburn entered the room and placed the silver platter holding the morning mail lying in perfect symmetry upon the side table.

Anna lay down her drawing pad and reached over to sort the items, as usual. In a few short minutes, she had one pile of envelopes waiting for the attention of her husband. These were mostly bills to pay or replies from a wide variety of sources to his multiple queries on diverse subjects that interested him. The second pile was letters from friends and family or invitations to social events of which she accepted very few.

She recognized the handwriting on the envelope from Blue Seas House as that of Douglas's secretary, Alec Bacon-Dowd. The thought of this man suddenly triggered a curious coincidence to register in her mind. She had always been aware of both parties, but it never entered her thoughts that there might be a connection between the two men. *Oh well, I guess we have seldom had correspondence from Douglas written in his secretary's hand unless it was strictly business*, she consoled herself at her slowing mind. *I wonder if there is a connection between Alec Bacon-Dowd and our previous Tutor Bacon.* A furrow added to the age lines on her forehead as she pondered. *It was Douglas who sent the tutor to us at the time.* Anna sat tapping the envelope on the table while she considered the possibilities.

With a shrug of her shoulders, she took up her knife and slit the envelope to remove the short note.

Dear Colonel and Mrs. Wellington
As you will be aware, due to ill health, Mr. Mayford returned from Sussex to London four months ago. The doctor has been treating him for apoplexy since and he has shown wondrous signs of improving, but this past week Mr. Mayford has had another turn and is quite unwell.
He has made it clear he wishes me to request his daughter to come to Blue Seas House and supervise his nursing care.
He will send his carriage to transport her, as soon as she is able to do so.
Yours sincerely
Bacon-Dowd
Secretary to Mr. Douglas Mayford

Anna sat staring out through the window, not really seeing the mist still hanging over the creek behind the stable. Her thoughts raced through her head in all directions.

Poor Douglas, he was always his own worst enemy. He always used the most devious pathway when wanting his own way. Is this also a ruse to lure Bridie to London and pressure her into marrying the investor he mentioned on his last visit? And what about Bridie? She does seem to be enchanted with our organist. Will she be willing to answer what might be her father's last request?

I will talk to William first, I think.

With that plan of action in the forefront of her mind, she rose and made her way to the library. Anna paused at the large polished timber door with her hand on the shiny brass knob.

What if Bridie is in here with her grandfather? I do not want to be too obvious.

Anna need not have worried on that account. Bridie had left to talk to Mr. Axel, about the progress of the treatment for the lameness in Welly's near-side foreleg.

Anna opened the door and entered. She showed William the letter written on behalf of their son-in-law.

"Do you think this is genuine, William?"

"I cannot be sure – he certainly did not look very well that afternoon he left here."

"But this secretary says he improved and has since relapsed. This is not uncommon in apoplexy as far as I am aware. I do wonder though, if he has had a severe turn then how is he able to communicate?"

"Why not send a letter directly to his physician and find out exactly what the situation is, my dear?"

"William, I think that is a wonderful idea. I do not want to send Bridie up there if it is only a trap to manipulate her into his great plan of things."

"Bridie is no one's fool, but she is young and without experience in the deceitful ways of the world."

"I will write to the physician this minute. I have his address here, somewhere. They still have the same family doctor who treated Athena, as far as I am aware. Dr. Grimley, if I remember correctly."

"We will not say a word to Bridie until we learn the full picture, Anna. It might be a good idea to have Mr. Axel send a stable hand to the post office, as soon as you have the letter completed."

"Yes, William, of course."

Anna turned back towards William before she opened the door.

"What will we do about Bridie's twenty-first birthday? She is adamant she does not want a party."

"Then, we will just have a quiet dinner together," William paused in thought before speaking again. "She might like to have her friend, David Lewis, attend."

"He is such a nice, well-mannered man. I will ask her."

Five days passed before the envelope, with the address scrawled across the front of it, arrived. It was marked with the Oxford stamp.

William and Anna sat reading the weekly papers in the music room, where the breeze through the front windows cooled the heat of the day.

Anna passed the letter across to her husband. She asked, "Where's Bridie at the moment?"

"She took Welly for a run to test out the animal's foreleg. She said she was going to ask David Lewis if he would join her for her birthday dinner tomorrow evening."

William tore the envelope open and smoothed out the single page. He read the letter aloud.

Dear Colonel and Mrs. Wellington.

I understand your concern about your son-in-law's health, particularly as his daughter is under your care. You may be aware; Mr. Mayford has indeed experienced several small apoplexy turns over the past two years but this last one, ten days ago, was the worst to date. He has been left with a slight weakness in his right arm and leg as well as an occasional slurring of his speech. His mobility is slow and achieved with assistance. He has two nurses who care for him around the clock. I am sure the presence of his daughter will brighten his spirits and it will not be too onerous a task for her services as a nurse.

Yours sincerely

B.M. Grimley. Physician

"We will need to talk to Bridie," Anna spoke after some moments in contemplation.

"Yes, it is for her to decide. The man has done little for her to date. She cannot be blamed if she wants nothing more to do with him."

The three met in the dining room for lunch. Anna noted the rise of colour in Bridie's face and her sparkling eyes. She gave a soft gasp at the realization that Bridie and David may already have moved towards a complete relationship. A frown marred her forehead. Her heart thumped. She felt regret like a painful ache in her chest. Why had she not spoken more fully to her granddaughter long before this? The answer flew into her head. She had not wanted to acknowledge that her baby girl was growing up – no, was grown up. If the look on Bridie's face was anything to go by, she was already a complete woman. Anna stifled a groan. *Oh, dear, this is devastating.*

Anna sucked in a sharp breath at this thought. She found herself pushing food around her plate. She smiled a grateful smile when William opened the conversation with a discussion on the changes required in the police organization within the country, particularly in London. After their fruit and custard, it was William again who broached the subject of Douglas Mayford.

"Bridie, a letter arrived this morning from your father's physician. Well, it was Douglas's secretary who wrote to us on his behalf first, but we inquired from his doctor for more details." William read aloud the letter from the secretary followed by the letter from the doctor.

Bridie sat taking this all in for long moments. Eventually, she spoke.

"I killed my mother and now am I to be responsible for my father's death too?"

Anna and William responded in unison. "Absolutely not."

William went on, "Douglas Mayford has always chosen to ignore the doctor's advice and must now pay the price. You are under no pressure to go up there to help him if you do not want to." He wiped his chin with the table napkin. "If, on the other hand, you want to go to visit London for a few weeks then of course we will help you do this. You will be twenty-one in two days so he cannot apply pressure on you to do what you do not wish."

"I will not go before my birthday dinner. David accepted my invitation to join us – sorry I forgot to mention this earlier."

Anna smiled although an anxious shadow lay hidden in the depths of her eyes.

"I will let Mrs. Coburn and Cook know." Anna reached across the table and placed her hand over Bridie's, "Maybe we can talk of this in the drawing room later this afternoon before you go out again."

"Of course, Grandmama. I will send an acceptance to my father this afternoon also." Bridie's head lifted sharply. "Grandmama remember we spoke some time ago about George's girl, Odette? While I am in London, I would like to ask George if he will allow me to bring the child here to Clawhaven rather than think of her locked away in London. Would you and Grandpa agree to have her here?"

"We would love to have her here, Bridie, but I am afraid it is up to George and Beatrice to make decisions on the child's upbringing"

While the driver secured her portmanteau on the roof of the carriage, Bridie spoke to her grandparents at the front of the manor.

"Bridie, you will remember to ask Beatrice if you can visit with the little girl, won't you?"

"Of course, Grandmama. It is possibly the most important reason for this visit to London." Bridie held her grandmother's hands in her own. "Now, if Beatrice says we can bring the child here to stay, or even for a visit, are you and Grandpa happy with that?"

"Oh, yes, Bridie, we really must try to do what we can for the little girl. I will have the maids clean out the nursery – just in case you are successful."

Bridie leant over and hugged Anna before moving over to kiss her grandfather on the cheek.

"Take care, both of you."

When Bridie stepped into her father's carriage, she leant back into the luxurious comfort. Her gaze scanned her surroundings. She noticed the two bottles in the recess of the wall. According to the labels, one held whiskey and the other held gin. Her rueful grin accompanied her thoughts. *I guess the physician never ordered those for medication.* Beside the drinks were two crystal glasses. As the carriage rolled down the driveway, she felt her stomach churn. When they turned onto the London Road, the sensation of nausea repeated itself. Bridie swallowed hard.

Bridie assumed this indisposition was due to her cowardice. She admonished herself. *There is no reason to feel afraid. I am now twenty-one years of age. There is little he can say to make me do his bidding. I must remember, my father is unwell. I should feel sorry for the man.* Bridie began to relax until another worry nibbled on the edge of her mind. *What if this sick feeling is not just the worry about meeting my father again? It has occurred each morning for the past three days.*

Bridie's reading within her grandpa's library covered a large variety of subjects including medicine which fascinated her. Her gloved hand rushed to cover her mouth. She swallowed again, twice. Her reticule tumbled to the floor when Bridie jumped up. She threw back the curtain across the window in the door and with one hand firmly on her hat, she leant her head outside. Vomit sprayed forth to trail briefly like a ship's pennant in the wind.

The voice of the coachman called from his seat above, "Don't be worrying, Miss, it's just the swaying of the carriage making you feel a bit sick. It will pass in a few hours when you get used to the motion."

Her stomach contracted twice more before it settled. Weakness overcame her as she shuffled back into her seat. Bridie brushed the residue of her stomach contents off her gloves as best she could before she removed them. She lay them on the opposite seat in the sunshine pouring through the uncurtained window.

Bridie rolled her tongue around the sour taste in her mouth. Thirst tormented her until the labelled bottles caught her attention again. She pulled a face at the thought of whiskey and selected the bottle of gin. A trembling hand poured a small measure into a glass. Her first sip was a tentative gesture. She swilled the second sip around her mouth and swallowed. Her third sip disappeared rather fast. Bridie relaxed back against the upholstery. She shut her eyes, but her mind did not settle to rest.

What if I am pregnant? A thrill of excitement and anticipation swirled inside her. Her lips broke into a grin. Both were quickly dampened when commonsense arrived like a tsunami wave. *Oh dear, how am I going to tell Grandmama and Grandpa?* The swirl of excitement became an eddy of worry. *What is David going to say? Even though he always said he did not want to burden me with marriage to a man in poor health and limited life expectancy, I know he always wished we could be wed. Once he becomes accustomed to the idea, he will be proud to have a son or daughter.*

When this episode repeated itself the morning of the second day riding in the coach, Bridie knew pregnancy was a distinct possibility. Coach travelling and horse riding never bothered her before. Her arms wrapped around her tummy like a protective shield. She spent the remainder of the journey to London savouring her secret. Occasionally, a shadow cast itself upon her mind's meanderings. What if David was not as pleased as she was?

On her arrival at Blue Seas House late Tuesday morning, it was the butler, Evans, who gave her a brief tour, before he took her to her room. Bridie's gaze kept drifting to the long oily slick of dark brown hair he had swept across his head to cover the thinning patch on top.

"Your father will send for you later today, Miss Mayford. Lunch will be served in the dining room in fifteen minutes. There will be only yourself lunching in today."

Bridie retired to her room to repair her hair, face and dress. She was in two minds about whether to attend a lonely and strange dining room on her own, but the need to put something back into her tummy won out. When she arrived downstairs, the sight of the large room, which seemed to be filled with shiny timber, acres of pristine white cloth, and sparkling glassware, almost overwhelmed her.

"Welcome," the voice at her elbow made Bridie jump. "I am the housekeeper. Mrs. Larkins is my name. Please make yourself comfortable and I will have the maid bring your lunch."

When Bridie turned to meet the speaker, she found her gaze dropping to the head of grey, frizzed hair at the level of her own chin. The woman appeared as wide as she was tall.

It was four o'clock in the afternoon when her father summoned her to his rooms. A young maid, dressed in a dark grey dress with a white collar, guided her through an intricate network of corridors. She left Bridie standing for some moments drawing deep breaths at her father's door. Bridie sighed, took her courage in both hands and knocked.

She jumped back when a middle-aged woman, with her hair tied back in a knot at the nape of her neck and wearing a starched blue-coloured nurse's uniform, pulled the door open. Bridie was hard-pressed not to smile as she imagined what Jimmy Braydon's comment might be if meeting this woman. *Be keepin' her away from the dairy, Miss, she'll turn all the milk sour.*

The tight line of the woman's mouth barely moved as she invited Bridie inside the room.

"Miss Bridie, I presume. Please come in, your father awaits you." She stepped aside to allow Bridie to enter but did not leave until she tossed this last command. "See that Mr. Mayford does not excite himself, Miss. I will return at five o'clock with his dinner."

Bridie stepped back to allow her to pass before swinging around when her father spoke.

"You took your time coming."

Her face revealed the surprise she felt at the sight of her father in his invalid chair.

"Don't look so surprised, girl. What did you expect to find – me on my deathbed?"

Bridie struggled to bring herself under control. "Not exactly, Father, but you are speaking quite well. I understood this last turn left you with a slur in your speech."

"You can be assured I am still able to issue commands when required."

"Yes, I can see you are that." Bridie felt the flush in her face and stammered as she went to rephrase her unedited words. "I mean … that must be a positive sign, is it not?"

"Someone must oversee things around here or the company will fall apart. Now, getting down to business, have you considered the proposal I mentioned when we last spoke."

Bridie gasped at the suddenness of his attack.

"Don't look so shocked, girl. One would get nowhere fast if we fiddled while Rome burnt." He wriggled his bottom around on the chair seeking comfort. "First things first, what is this I hear about you and that worthless musician? According to reports you are no better than a street woman visiting the man alone at his cottage unchaperoned."

Bridie gasped again. It felt as if she had been kicked in the stomach by a horse. While she stood attempting to reclaim her voice, her father took advantage of her silence.

"You bring shame upon your family name. You bring shame upon your mother's name." Spittle flew from the wrinkled lips.

It was fury, not shame, which almost overwhelmed Bridie. She drew herself up, her eyes narrowed. She spoke with slow determination.

"You are spying on us at Clawhaven Manor? I may be no more than a harlot in your opinion, but where does a spymaster lie in reputable society?"

"Have you no respect for your father?"

"I have never had a father. Anyway, one must earn respect. It is not just handed out willy-nilly."

"Remember, girl, it was your father who allowed you to live with your grandparents all these years. Are you telling me I did the wrong thing?"

"As far as I can see things, Father," Bridie dragged the word out, "you virtually gave me away. You blamed me for my mother's death. You can hardly bear to look at me because I look so like my mother." Bridie's mouth snapped closed at the sight of the moisture glistening in her father's eyes. "I am sorry, Father."

"Bridie, all I want is the best for you. You need to look for someone with more prospects in life than a man who can do no more than tinkle a few keys on a piano."

Compassion smothered the fury in Bridie's heart.

"Father, I agree with you. Prospects are important in a woman's life, but you were lucky enough to know true love. You must understand life without love is like a rose without petals," Bridie stumbled for words, "Like a rainbow without colours or a land without song," she finished.

It was Douglas's turn to stop. He shook his head. "That is all very well for your dreams, but life is not a dream. It is real and it is hard, and you need to be hard to survive."

"I truly am sorry that my mother's death has made you so unfeeling."

"Bah, you just remember your duty to this family." Douglas wriggled again in the chair. "I have Mr. Cruickshank coming for dinner Thursday evening. You will need to entertain him at the table with George. You won't get Beatrice to the table – she never leaves her rooms. I will join you in the drawing room after the meal."

Bridie was in two minds to tell her father that he and his Mr. Cruickshank could eat together because she would be going home to Clawhaven Manor, but her grandfather's words of advice came to mind. "It costs nothing to stop and listen to a proposal. You can always say, no."

Yes, I can, she thought and held her tongue. *I am twenty-one and will please myself.*

After Bridie left his office, Douglas Mayford sat in deep thought. When the nurse arrived, he snapped at her.

"I did not call for you yet, get out until I call."

"Mr. Mayford, I am your nurse and it is my job to see you have your medication."

"Leave it on the table and go. I have work to do." He struggled to guide the wheels of his invalid chair about, to face the office desk.

"Can I help you with that, sir?"

"Go, I said."

As the door shut with a sharp click, Douglas dragged the writing tablet towards himself and took up his pen with one of its shiny new nibs – the gift from Athena on their very last wedding anniversary. Shaky fingers stroked the handle. He pushed the sentimental thoughts from his mind, dipped the nib in the inkwell and began to write. The first page contained instructions to his secretary.

Alec,

If my daughter does not promise herself to Mr. Cruickshank and if my health deteriorates in the immediate future, I want you to post this letter to my daughter.

He tore the page from the pad and folded it in half. He printed MR. BACON-DOWD on the front. Taking up his pad again he began to write on the following page.

Bridie Mayford – once my daughter.

You have seen fit not to support your family in your chase after a useless musician. If my staff are to be believed, you are pregnant too. As head of the family, I do not wish to support you any further.

"DON'T BOTHER COMING HOME. YOU ARE A DISGRACE TO THE FAMILY."

Douglas signed the letter, placed it into an envelope addressed it to Bridie Mayford, Clawhaven Manor, Sussex and added his seal. The slight tremor in his hand increased to a violent shake, as he pressed upon his family crest stamp.

Bridie found herself alone in the huge dining room for her meal that evening. It was Mrs. Larkin who delivered the message.

"Mr. George sends his apologies. He has been called out on urgent business, Miss."

When sister and brother eventually crossed paths for a lunch of cold cuts and freshly baked bread on Wednesday, Bridie opened the conversation.

"So, George, we meet at last. Seems hard to believe we are brother and sister and do not know each other."

"We did meet at Clawhaven Manor when you were only a small tot. My brothers were alive then."

After his few words, George sat in deep silence which Bridie tried to understand.

Is George still in mourning for Max and Toby?

"You were close, were you – you and your brothers?"

"Not really, I suppose. Our father had me spend all my free time learning the company business. Max and Toby had an easier life as children. I did not envy them working on Father's ships later though. He runs the ships with as few men as possible, from what I can see."

Silence reclaimed the diners as their thoughts pondered on this statement.

"Is the company so short of money? Is that why Father wants me to marry this Mr. Cruickshank?"

George concentrated on his next mouthful of food. Bridie wondered if he was avoiding the question.

"Bridie, it is our duty as his children to do as our father wishes. My son will inherit what our father has built and, because of that, I will remain here to do my best to ensure his inheritance will be worthwhile."

It was Bridie's turn to focus on the meal and let her mind ponder her brother's words. She expected little support on that front. She changed the subject.

"Edward is away at boarding school, I understand."

"Yes, Beatrice is not a strong woman, and cannot give him the attention a growing boy needs." George ran a thick layer of butter over the bread on his plate.

"And young Odette, who looks after her? She must be at least two years of age now."

George looked deep into Bridie's eyes. "Beatrice believes she has provided me with an heir and the girl will be her responsibility."

"Oh, I was hoping to meet Beatrice and Odette on this trip. Do you think Beatrice will see me?"

"You will not get to meet Odette. She is confined with her nurse to the west wing. As far as I am aware even Beatrice never visits her daughter."

Bridie's fork clattered onto her plate. She gathered it up and began eating again.

"George, would it help if I spoke with Beatrice do you think? The child might enjoy time in the country perhaps, and Beatrice need not be subject to the gossipmongering I am sure you have in the city."

"Beatrice will make any decision relating to her daughter. I do not like your chances of gaining an audience, I might add." George wiped his lips with the starched table napkin lying near his plate. "I must beg you not to upset Beatrice in any way though. She can cause a dreadful ruckus throughout the household when she is having a bad day."

Bridie raised her eyebrows. "Of course, George."

"Excuse me, Bridie, but I must get back to the office. I have several meetings this afternoon."

"Yes, George. Thank you."

Bridie's evening meal on Wednesday, her second day at Blue Seas House, was another lonely affair.

The butler informed her, "The nurse serves Mr. Mayford his meals in his rooms, and Mr. George has had to go out to an unexpected business meeting."

Bridie smiled her thanks and picked at the food on her plate, while her mind considered her discussion with George earlier in the day.

On Thursday morning, Bridie found herself alone at the breakfast table. This pleased her somewhat as she had things to plan for today. Two things remained unresolved in her mind. First, she wished to gain an audience with Beatrice to discuss Odette's future. After her talk with George yesterday, she knew she had little support from that quarter. He did not seem to care if his daughter might be better off living at Clawhaven Manor than locked up in the wing of this house here in London. Maybe he just cared more for a quiet life. The second item on her list was to find out how to order a carriage to take her home. She envisaged a rushed exit after her dinner with the mysterious Mr. Cruickshank this evening.

While waiting for a more respectable time to call on her sister-in-law, Bridie perused the meagre contents of her father's library. The dinner this evening with George and the unknown Mr. Cruickshank loomed before her like a form of torture. Several possible items for discussion with her brother caused a distraction for her, while she scanned through some of the London papers lying on the library table.

The hall clock chimed eleven deep notes. After three false starts, Bridie eventually found her way to Beatrice's retreat on the top floor of the east wing. She gave a timid knock.

An elderly woman opened the door. "Mrs. Mayford does not receive visitors, Miss." The arthritic hands began to close the door.

Bridie held it firm. "I am sorry, I am not a visitor. I am Beatrice's sister-in-law and I have never had the opportunity to be introduced. Please, may I stay for just a minute or two?"

The head of snow-white hair above the face of a hundred lines turned to her mistress. Beatrice's hazel eyes stared at this new arrival. Curiosity filled her gaze. She gave an slight nod of her head.

The door opened further. Bridie bit down hard on a gasp when she entered the room. It was as described to her – a cross between a nunnery and a place of worship. Bridie walked softly to where Beatrice sat in a deep chair in the corner. Tartan rugs covered her legs. A crocheted shawl covered her shoulders.

Bridie curtsied and spoke to Beatrice. "I am pleased to meet you at last, Beatrice. I am George's sister, Bridie Mayford. May I say that shawl is exquisite? Did you crochet it yourself?"

Beatrice took little notice of the polite small talk. Her mouth opened slowly. Her words came out thick as if not used too often.

"Good morning, Bridie Mayford. You are here from Clawhaven Manor, I believe."

Bridie smiled and nodded, but before she could reply, Beatrice went on speaking.

"I believe you are here to be told you must marry the wealthy Mr. Cruickshank."

"Oh dear, Beatrice, I am sorry, but I am unable to do so."

The mouth opened slowly again, this time to deliver a startling cackle.

Bridie's head lifted almost snapping her neck.

"You did not approve of this arrangement, Beatrice?"

"No, I did not. I know what it is like to be parcelled around like wrapped meat ready to be cooked for dinner."

It was Bridie who opened her mouth and did not shut it for some time.

"I am sorry, did this happen to you too?"

"Yes, I promised myself to the church, but my father was having none of it."

"Is that why you have hidden your baby Odette away? Is that so her father cannot use her as a commodity too?"

"No, I do not think so. It was more to make George think I am losing my mind so he will leave me alone." Beatrice smoothed the rugs over her knees. "I gave him a son and heir. I have done my duty."

"How old is Edward, now?"

"He is five years of age – and as mean as they come."

Bridie felt her eyebrows rise. She mentally commanded herself to control her features.

"He is just like Douglas Mayford if I am any judge of character."

"Oh...," Bridie responded lamely. "Would it advance your purpose if I were to take Odette back to Clawhaven Manor with me?"

Beatrice's gaze dropped to her lap. Bridie had thought she may have pushed her case too early until the woman spoke again.

"Why would you want to do that? I understand you are with child yourself so another young child might be a handful."

Bridie bit her lip. She could not speak. *How does Beatrice know this? I only just discovered it myself.*

"Do not be surprised, Bridie. In a house this size, gossip is flung around like orders. It was the coachman who told the butler, who passed it on to me."

"I have yet to tell the father."

"Will he be pleased do you think?"

"Yes, he will be pleased. He is a good man."

"Where will Odette fit in with all this?"

"Odette will take my place in the hearts of my grandparents. They are wonderful people. I will be her aunt and will care for her as if she were my own. We have a home well-staffed to manage."

Again, Beatrice sat in silence. "Let me think on this for a day or so."

Bridie almost groaned at the thought of having to remain here for two or more days longer than she wanted.

"May I see the little girl?"

Beatrice's fingers trembled as she stroked the stitch of her shawl.

"I will arrange for you to visit her this afternoon. A staff member will take you to the west wing."

"Thank you, Beatrice. I will wait in my room."

Thursday lunchtime and Bridie ate alone in the dining room once again. The butler informed her that George was having lunch with his father.

"How is Mr. Mayford today?" she asked the man serving the platters. "He did not look too well when we spoke on Tuesday night."

"As usual, the master is trying to do too much."

A slight breeze drifted in through the window, beside which, Bridie sat at a small desk of polished mahogany writing notes in her journal. The novel she had been reading lay, where she had tossed it on the pillow of her bed earlier, when her brain found it impossible to concentrate on the story plot, along with all the issues she must consider here in real life.

She jumped at the sound of the soft knock on her door. Bridie opened the door to find the same maid she met this morning in Beatrice's room. Her head of white hair was now covered with a smart maid's cap. Unruly wisps of hair stuck out the side.

"Mrs. Beatrice asked will you follow me? She will not be coming to the west wing, Miss."

Bridie picked up her shawl from off the end of her bed and followed the maid whose fast step belied the age of the woman.

Bridie discovered the west wing was not attached to the main building at all. As they exited through a side door the maid paused to catch her breath. Bridie did the same.

"Mrs. Beatrice said you are to stay with the child no longer than half an hour. I will collect you then and take you to Mrs. Beatrice."

"Thank you, I am sorry I do not know your name," Bridie replied.

"I'm just called Ally."

"Thank you, Ally."

When Bridie knocked on the red door with the black knob, it was opened immediately by a woman leaning towards plump, who wiped her hands on the apron she wore. Bridie estimated her age to be in her late twenties, but it was the warm smile on her round face that drew Bridie to her.

"Come in, Miss, we sure don' see too many vis'tors 'ere. My name is Mary."

"Good afternoon, Mary. May I see Odette now?"

"Of course, the wee princess 'as been beside 'erself she 'as, Getting a vis'tor an all."

Mary led Bridie to a large room redesigned as a playroom. Bridie's feet stopped at the doorway. Inside, a small child of two years stood watching. Her blond hair hung in ringlets from two pink ribbons on either side of her head. Her unadorned white smock hung down past her knees. White stockings covered her legs. A pair of the tiniest shoes Bridie had ever seen poked out from below the hem of the dress. Serious eyes as blue as the spring violets analysed the visitor. She turned to focus on Mary for a time as if to ensure her nurse was within arms' length. Her little feet moved one step at a time as she approached Bridie still waiting at the doorway.

Within three feet of Bridie, the child stopped and passed another gaze Mary's way as if seeking approval.

"Yes, baby, say h-h-hello to our guest," Mary reassured her. Mary stammered over the letter 'H' having been told to use it in front of the child.

The child curtsied. "Hello, my name is Odette," she lisped.

Tears welled in Bridie's eyes. She curtsied in return. "Hello, Odette, I am your Aunt Bridie and I am so pleased to meet you at last."

Odette rushed up to Bridie and wrapped her arms around her long skirt with the layers of petticoats beneath. The child clung on as if never to let go. A little hand crept up to take Bridie's finger and lead her to the armchair in the middle of the room.

"Sit," the small voice instructed. When satisfied with Bridie's obeyance, Odette toddled over to the row of shelves at the edge of the room and selected a book which she brought back and handed to her aunt now sitting in the comfortable chair. Odette leant in against Bridie's legs. Her small hand reached out to show Bridie how to open the book. "Please," she lisped.

Bridie glanced up at Mary who nodded with a smile.

It seemed only a fleeting time later when the sharp knock sounded on the door. Bridie felt a deep pang of loss as she reached down and kissed her niece on the top of her curls.

"I am sorry, Odette, but I must go." She felt the tears threaten. She imagined the baby inside her own body. "May I come again, if your mother will allow it?"

The large violet eyes stared up at her. Bridie realized the toddler did not understand. She hugged her, blinking back the tears as she did so.

Bridie followed Ally through the torturous route back to Beatrice's room. Her sister-in-law sat at her escritoire writing on a large pad. She glanced up.

"I understand your meeting with Odette went well."

Bridie gasped. *How does she know that?*

Beatrice almost smiled at Bridie's expression of surprise. "In a house full of undercurrents like this one, it is not surprising how gossip flourishes."

Bridie offered a weak, "Oh," in reply.

"You would still like to offer Odette a home at Clawhaven Manor?"

Bridie paused to select her words. "Beatrice, it is a wonderful place of freedom, of learning, of love. It would be an honour to have her there."

"You have your meeting with the wealthy Mr. Cruickshank this evening. What are you going to reply to his proposal?"

Bridie felt her optimism squashed. Was Beatrice a part of the plot to have her comply with her father's demands?

"I am sorry, but I will not agree to a marriage with the gentleman. I am twenty-one and have the right to refuse."

"Do not apologize to me, Bridie. I only wish I had been able to refuse my marriage. Pray, keep my daughter safe from the manipulators who would have her life shattered by powerful men."

Bridie's mind wrestled with this new impression of Beatrice she was now seeing. Her voice deserted her. She nodded her head.

"A carriage will arrive here at six o'clock in the morning. There is a road in through the back way near the west wing. Ally will wake you in ample time and lead you to the rendezvous. Mary and the child will meet you at the carriage – you will take Mary with you, will you not?"

"If she is willing, of course. Odette will adjust more easily with Mary's familiar face."

"The coachman will stop at an inn on the south side of London, where you will be given breakfast."

"Beatrice, I cannot thank you enough. I promise to take good care of your daughter. But what about you?"

Beatrice sneered. "I doubt if either George or Douglas will notice the child is gone – not even that nosey Bacon-Dowd fellow, most likely. Do not worry about me, Bridie. I have my faith to keep me safe." Beatrice gave a soft cough. "Now go, sister." She reached her hand out to Bridie who took it in a soft clasp.

"Thank you and be safe."

"God be with you."

Bridie felt her head spinning as she made her way back to her room. A cold hand clenched her heart. What if this was all a weird plot to trick her; that no one in this household planned on letting the small child out of their control?

Bridie had only enough time to wash, change into a fresh dress, and brush and pin up her hair before the gong for the evening meal sounded.

At the dining room doorway, Bridie paused to take a deep breath and straighten her shoulders. She jumped at the voice behind her.

"Go on in, Bridie." It was George. A tall man stood at his elbow.

Bridie entered the room and stepped sideways to allow her brother and his guest to join her. A waiter appeared. The wine sparkled in the glasses on the tray in his hands.

George moved up to remove a glass, which he handed to Bridie. He then took two more glasses and passed one to the tall dark-haired man at his side.

"Sister, may I introduce you to Stewart Cruickshank." George turned to the man and spoke again, "Stewart please meet my sister, Bridgette."

Bridie's eyes opened wide. The paunchy, bald man dribbling at the mouth with skin full of pockmarks of her imaginings disappeared.

Her gaze travelled from the well-groomed head of thick black hair with only a hint of grey at the temples, to the tanned face with a few laughter lines around the eyes. Without any control, her gaze continued past his broad shoulders threatening the stitch of his coat and down to narrow hips. She felt the laughter bubbling inside her, but the reprimand her grandmama would deliver, if present, dampened the temptation.

Her errant thoughts showed less control. *At least Father has chosen an attractive man and with a weighty bank balance, I am assuming.*

The gentleman bowed low to Bridie. Appreciation filled his smile.

"Where has Douglas Mayford been hiding you?" He turned to George. "George, how on earth did you end up with a beautiful sister like this?"

George chuckled. "Except for the dark hair, Bridie is the image of our mother, lucky for her."

Small talk followed as the three shared a little personal information and goals in their lives.

When they sat down at the table to the meal of roast beef and vegetables, Bridie felt nervous flutters in her tummy. She lightened the anxiety within herself by imagining it was not nervous flutters she felt, but her little baby telling her to be strong. Across from her, George and Mr. Cruickshank spoke of their separate experiences at Oxford and a little about the shipping business. Occasionally, one or the other turned to include Bridie in their conversation. When not eating, Bridie kept her gaze on her lap and her responses to the minimum.

After the meal, the men took their glasses of port and joined Bridie in the parlour room. The conversation turned to George's hopes for the company in the future. Bridie's studies with the accountant at Clawhaven Manor enabled her to follow the conversation without difficulty. She even put forth a suggestion of her own, which it seemed George was going to override, but Stewart Cruickshank was quick to acknowledge its merit. When the conversation turned to current political issues, including the disturbances the Women's Rights activists were stirring in the community, again Bridie was not backward in presenting her thoughts. Admiration filled the visitor's gaze. Surprise silenced George.

"I see you have not foregone your education out there in the rustic community, sister," he eventually commented.

"Father and Grandpa between them ensured I was never short on lessons. I guarantee Grandpa's library may shame many bigger cities' book collections."

They were interrupted by the sound of the door opening when Douglas arrived pushed on his invalid chair by the nurse. He accepted a glass of port avoiding the look of disdain in the face that Jimmy Braydon would say turned milk sour. Bridie's lips twitched.

"I am glad you two have met," he nodded to Bridie and Stewart Cruickshank. Never being a man to waste words or time he ploughed right in. "Bridie, as I mentioned the other day, Mr. Cruickshank is considering investing in our family company. He mentioned he has been away in the colonies for some years and is looking to meet a suitable wife here in London. I have told him he has no further to look than right here in our family."

The three others in the room gasped at the forthright speech. Bridie felt the flush bright on her face. Her gaze flicked up into Stewart's eyes and down again when she read the embarrassment he felt. Even George, who had witnessed his father's brusque ways all of his life, could hardly speak.

"Father, I think some tact would go a long way in this situation?" he commented drily.

Bridie stood up and put her glass on the table. She held her head high and faced her father.

"I think I made it quite plain when we spoke on Tuesday evening, I am not for sale, Father." She turned to address Stewart Cruickshank. "Thank you, Mr. Cruickshank, and to you, Father, for this opportunity, but I am sorry I must refuse. I have other plans for my future. Now, if you will please excuse me, it is time I retired, I am not used to late nights." Bridie turned to speak to her father again, "I will fetch the nurse to see you back to your room, Father."

She nodded to Mr. Cruickshank, "I am sorry, sir, you have been brought here under false pretences."

Bridie turned and swept out of the room, pulling the door closed softly behind her. She found Nurse Bates waiting outside in the corridor.

"My father has been a little disappointed in his plans tonight. I would suggest he may need extra medication to settle him."

No sooner had the nurse disappeared through the doorway than Bridie felt her legs wobble beneath her. She felt the tears well in her eyes. Her back sagged against the hallway wall. Bridie closed her eyes and tried to pull herself together. The quiet voice at her elbow brought her to attention. She had not heard the door near her open and close.

"I am sorry too, Miss Mayford. Please forgive my presumptuousness."

Bridie sucked the air into her lungs. It took her some seconds to find her voice.

"Apology accepted, Mr. Cruickshank. I know it is not your fault. I have only ever met my father a handful of times, but I know him to be a man who will manipulate people to suit his own schemes. There is one thing I would like to say to you though. Whatever you might think of us, you would be well advised to listen to George's financial plan for the company. It sounds simple, but you will find it is forward-thinking. If Father would only let him have a free hand, he could turn the company around in six months to a year."

"You sound like a well-educated woman, Miss Mayford."

"That will be thanks mostly to my maternal grandparents." Bridie smiled. "I have lived with them in Sussex all my life."

"They have done a marvellous job of your upbringing, I must say." A smile danced in Stewart Cruickshanks brown eyes. He ran his strong hands through his unfashionably unoiled hair. He gazed into Bridie's eyes. "Miss Mayford if we were to meet in other circumstances would you consider permitting me to visit you in Sussex?"

Bridie could not have said her heart did not do a little dance of its own at these words. She returned his gaze and explained.

"Mr. Cruickshank, I am honoured by your suggestion, but I am promised to another – a man whom I love very much. As you can guess, my father disapproves of David's status in life, but now I am of age his opinion holds little weight in my plans. It will be the man who has treated me as a daughter all my life, who will be asked to give me away."

"Good luck then, Miss Bridie Mayford. I wish you well."

"And you too, Mr. Stewart Cruickshank. May you meet a wonderful woman who will treasure you for life. I think you are a handsome and lovely man."

Stewart lifted Bridie's wrist to kiss the back of her hand. "I will take your advice and contact George to hear his plan." He grinned, "Now can you help me find my way out of this maze of corridors?"

"Of course, but it may be the blind leading the blind."

When Douglas watched Stewart Cruickshank follow Bridie from the room, he realized his intricate plan was disintegrating. He had thought he was tying the last knots to this deal of marrying his daughter off to a serious investor. He felt the shock of Bridie's final words hit him like a blow. Embarrassment darkened his face and squeezed his heart. Pain knifed him through the chest. His head felt as if it was about to explode.

Bridie tossed and turned in her bed for several hours. A soft hint of morning light eased through the gap she had left in the curtains. The hall clock outside chimed five o'clock. She threw back the covers and slipped her legs over the edge of the bed. After using the commode placed near the bedside, Bridie splashed water from the ewer standing on the wash table into the basin. She held the bar of soap to her face and breathed in the smell of roses. Using the fresh cloth provided, she freshened up before drawing on her travelling clothes. She brushed her hair and secured it up with her pins while peering through the dim light into the looking glass. Two long pins affixed her travelling hat on top.

With the toiletries and night clothes added to the contents of her travelling bag, she shut the lid and snapped the catch with a sharp click. At the sound of a soft knock, Bridie opened the door quietly to find Beatrice's maid, Ally, waiting.

"You ready, Miss Mayford?"

"Yes, thank you." Bridie took up her reticule and went to lift the large portmanteau, but Ally stepped in and lifted it as if it were only a featherweight. Bridie gasped at the strength of the older woman.

"Come quickly, it will be light soon."

Bridie followed on the heels of the maid through the twisted corridors until they exited the building. Ally sheltered the large bag within the shrubbery of the garden and indicated for Bridie to follow it into hiding.

"I will run and give Mary a hand. Keep hidden and keep quiet."

Bridie heard the muffled clop clop of the horse's hooves on the soft ground as it approached. She feared the creaking of the carriage timbers seemed loud enough to wake the household. In the far distance, a town clock struck six chimes. The carriage pulled up and a man Bridie had never seen before jumped down. He held the door open.

"Quickly, Miss, in wid you. I'll be gettin' your luggage."

Bridie felt some apprehension, but the accent similar to Jimmy Braydon's offered her some comfort.

"Where are Mary and Odette?" She asked with hesitation.

"We'll follow this track and pick 'em up at the back door of the west wing."

Bridie did not realize she was holding her breath until the figure of Ally appeared at the doorway. She exhaled in relief. Mary entered the carriage with a sleeping Odette in her arms. The coachman was heard above loading several cases onto the roof of the vehicle. Ally passed a large bulging travelling bag on a long strap into the carriage. She wished them all a safe journey, before slipping away into the foggy morning.

"Can I put my shawl on the seat to lay the infant on, Mary?"

"Not just yet, Miss Mayford, thank you. If the babe wakes up on the seat, she might not know where she is and cry with fright. I'll keep her in my arms for a bit yet."

"Mary, I will be happy if you call me Bridie."

"Oh, Miss, that would never do. I'll be happy to call you Miss Bridie if that should please you."

"As you wish, Mary."

Only the fall of the horses' hooves and the creaking of leathers and timbers filled the carriage as Bridie and Mary each dwelled on their own thoughts. After nearly two hours, it was the sound of the driver's voice calling the horses to whoa as they came to a halt which brought both women upright in their seats. Bridie's eyes opened to find an unsmiling Odette staring at her face. She marvelled at the beauty of those violet eyes.

The feet of the coachman landed with a thud outside their carriage door.

"We be at the inn where we can be gettin' some food. It should be nearin' eight of the clock," he advised. He pointed to an outhouse against the back wall of the enclosed yard. "That be the ladies' conveniences," he pointed. "We don' want to be tarryin' 'ere too long. We have a lot of miles to cover before our overnight stop."

Bridie nodded her agreement and with weak legs, she descended to the ground. She turned to take the child from Mary's arms to allow her an easier exit. Without a murmur, the child acceded to this arrangement. The small head turned left and right, her large eyes taking everything in.

"Do you smell the air, Odette? That is the smell of the countryside." Bridie drew a noisy deep breath to aid in her explanation.

The proprietor of the inn greeted her guests and led them to a room where they could freshen up. She served them a breakfast of porridge and milk.

"Would you like a full breakfast or just tea and toast to follow?"

"Just the tea and toast for me," Bridie offered. Her stomach still felt a little unsettled. She turned to her travelling companions. "What would you and Odette like, Mary?"

"I will welcome the tea and toast, and I think a glass of that lovely fresh cow's milk for Odette will be suitable."

Bridie opened her reticule and paid the landlady the amount requested for their meals, and for the coachman's meal also, along with a small extra to say thanks.

In a short while, the carriage bowled along the country road heading for the south-west coast. The little feet of Odette encased in her tiny shoes wore a path between one door window and the other. Excitement filled her expression along with bouts of frustration when she did not have the words to tell Mary what she had seen. She lifted Bridie's hand to gain her attention when a line of cows, with their young calves, walked along the animal track inside a farmer's fence line. She clapped her hands in glee. She knelt on the seat for a better view to watch six racehorses-in-training running around a large circular track.

"The wee lass has never been outside the west wing, Miss Bridie. Everything is new for h-h-her."

"When we get to Clawhaven Manor, she will see all the cows and calves and horses and foals she wants. In fact, as soon as she can sit a horse, we will get a small one for her to learn to ride." Bridie smiled at the memories of her own childhood. "The beach is only a short walk through the orchard. It is a marvellous place to run and play in the shallows. We will have picnics there like Grandmama and Grandpa and Mr. Baines had with me."

"It all sounds marvellous, even overwhelming, after two years locked up."

"I am sorry my family has put you both through such an experience. It is my vow to ensure you will have as much freedom as you want at Clawhaven Manor."

"What will your grandparents say to us arriving without any warning?"

"From the moment we heard Odette and her nurse were locked away by themselves, Grandmama and Grandpa have been trying to think of ways in which we could rescue you both."

"The Colonel and Mrs. Wellington must be exceptional people."

"Oh, yes, they are, Mary. They have given me a wonderful life at Clawhaven, and I hope I can do the same for Odette."

After a comfortable night at an inn only a few hour's journey away from their destination, it was eleven in the morning when the coach pulled up at the front door of Clawhaven Manor. Mary helped Odette outside, while Bridie went to talk to the coachman to see if he was suitably compensated.

"Miss Beatrice has paid me admirably thank you, Miss Mayford."

"Well, take these two sovereigns with my thanks," Bridie offered.

Mrs. Coburn, with the handyman in tow, arrived to greet the travellers. When Bridie informed her that Mary and Odette were going to be permanent fixtures at Clawhaven Manor, Mrs. Coburn disappeared to inform the Wellingtons of the new arrivals and to have the upstairs maid prepare the rooms.

While the handyman helped the coachman lift down the luggage and place it on the step, Bridie watched fascinated at Odette's response to her new surroundings. The child walked around in circles as if trying to decide what to see first. When Furball, the cook's grey ratter-cat, strolled by, her little legs took her right back into Mary's arms. Odette wiggled down again when she watched the cat rub itself against Bridie's legs. Her small fingers stroked the soft fur. She looked up at Mary in disbelief. Grandpa and Grandmama Wellington stepped out onto the porch to welcome them home. Bridie left decorum somewhere behind and hugged her grandparents hard.

"I have missed you both so much."

Her grandfather grinned. "We will have to send you away more often, lass."

"Were you able to talk to George and Beatrice about young Odette?" Grandmama asked anxiously. Her frown turned to a smile when young Odette toddled over to her great-grandmother and wrapped her arms around Anna's skirts. The child's gaze lifted to meet the smiling face above. Odette then wobbled over to her great-grandfather and hugged his legs also. He bent down and swung the child up into his arms.

"Welcome, Odette, what a beautiful child you are. I am your grandpa. Can you say, Grandpa?"

After some consideration, the word "Pa" came out distinctly.

William carried the infant over to Anna. "This is your grandmama. Can you say Grandmama?"

"Gran," followed her moment of thought.

"That's near enough at this age, I think," Anna smiled and turned to Mary.

Bridie stepped up to make the introduction before she went on to ask, "Grandmama, can Odette sleep in with Mary for a while? Mary says Odette has always slept in the same room with her and it might take a while for her to build the confidence to move into the nursery next door."

William and Anna burst out laughing. "You have this all worked out, my dear. Yes, I have already given Mrs. Coburn those very same tentative instructions," Anna replied with a smile. "And we have sorted through the old toys in the nursery also."

Everyone turned to move inside. Odette threw an anxious gaze Mary's way, but when she found her nurse following close behind, she sat higher in her Pa's arms and laughed loudly, just like she had heard William and Anna do moments before.

"That child has seldom laughed before in her life," Mary's voice held disbelief.

With that, everyone present laughed loudly including the toddler, Odette.

"Come in. There will be a light lunch set out for us shortly," Anna led the way.

Odette continued happily in William's arms throwing glances back to Mary to ensure she was not too far away.

Anna organized the placement of everyone in the dining room.

"I will sit Odette near you, Mary. You can supervise her food requirements."

"Mrs. Wellington, should we not sit away from the adults?"

"I would prefer Odette to eat with us being a part of this family, and as her nurse, I think it very fitting you join us."

"With respect, Mrs. Wellington, that may only work at lunchtime because Odette's inbuilt time clock may not fit the adults, when it comes to breakfast and dinner."

"Forgive me, Mary, of course. It has been so long since I had a little one to consider. I will leave those two meals in your hands then. The children's dining room is next door. Please let the housekeeper, Mrs. Coburn, or the cook, Mrs. Ogilvie, know your requirements."

Odette quickly became a darling to everyone at Clawhaven Manor.

CHAPTER FIVE

Heartache

1877-1878

The morning sun marched across the bed unnoticed by the two lovers. It was only after the yearnings of their recent abstinence during Bridie's sojourn in London were sated, that Bridie jumped up.

"Good heavens, it is late. I must fly."

"Must you go already, my love?" David reached over and grasped her escaping hand. "We could run away to sea together, you know," he grinned, "on a wooden raft."

Bridie jumped back onto the bed and kissed him soundly.

"Now don't you worry about the little one inside you, Bridie, my darling. We will be married as soon as you wish."

Bridie planted another prolonged kiss on his warm lips.

With her modesty and decorum restored, Bridie ran outside to where Welly remained tied to the hitching post near the back door. She gathered up the reins, threw her leg over the saddle and nudged the horse into a brisk walk down the cliff track. Once on flat land, the horse responded to the heel in her side with enthusiasm. The pair flew along the bridle path near the forest with the crash of the waves at high tide in their ears.

David stood on the large flat rock at the top of the cliff watching and waving as Bridie made it safely to the beach and headed towards her home.

"Look after our baby, my darling," he whispered.

Neither David nor Bridie noticed the glint of the hazel eyes watching from the protection of the thick shrubs near the cottage.

As Mr. Featherstone disappeared around the first bend in the Clawhaven road on his way to his next mail delivery address, Anna dropped into her chair in the parlour and stared at the envelope addressed to Bridie in Douglas Mayford's hand. In her heart, she felt sure this could only be bad news.

At that moment, William walked into the room.

"Anna, my dear, why the frown?"

Anna tapped the envelope with her well-groomed nails.

"William this is a letter to Bridie from her father. Knowing the man, I am sure he is not about to apologize. Do you think I should open it first? I may be able to soften any blow he is about to drop upon her."

"I am sure our Bridie will handle whatever her father might have to say, but if you feel worried about it, I am also sure Bridie will understand."

"Yes, I think I shall." As she picked up the letter opener and slit the paper, Anna's thoughts rested on their granddaughter. On many occasions during Bridie's life, Anna had witnessed the shadows of doubt and insecurity reflected in the eyes of the child, and then the woman, when she agonized over the lack of parental love displayed by her father. Anna gasped when the wording on the short note was revealed.

Bridie Mayford – once my daughter.
You have seen fit not to support your family in your chase after a useless musician. If my staff are to be believed, you are pregnant too. As head of the family, I do not wish to support you any further.

"DON'T BOTHER COMING HOME. YOU ARE A DISGRACE TO THE FAMILY."

At the sound of Anna's strangled cry, William turned from the window.

"Whatever is the matter, Anna?"

Tears glistened on her eyelashes as Anna passed the note to her husband. She remained silent while William read the note, not once, but twice.

"Why? What has Bridie done to deserve such a communique?"

"I suppose this is in retaliation because Bridie refused the hand of Douglas's chosen husband for her."

Anna sat in a silence that extended for a long period.

"What is on your mind, Anna?"

"Douglas obviously believes Bridie is pregnant?"

"What on earth are you saying? Is Bridie pregnant?"

"She has not said anything, but I have been thinking it may be possible."

It was William's turn to remain silent. He plopped into a chair his head falling back on the headrest. He stared at the ceiling.

"Oh dear, Anna, if you are correct, this will set the local tongues wagging. How will we cope with that, my love?"

Anna took her lace handkerchief and patted her eyes before she answered.

"Whatever Bridie has or has not done; we will love her with all our hearts. We will weather the storm."

"That's my girl, Anna." William reached over and held Anna's hand in his own. "Bridie is a strong-willed woman with a comprehensive education. She knows what she could be letting herself in for. I presume the father, if indeed there is a baby, will be that of David Lewis."

"She is besotted with the man ...," Anna sat staring out the window for a moment, "and he with her, I am sure."

"I agree with you there. I have always felt that the only reason why he has never married her before this is because he is worried about his questionable health prospects."

The lunchtime gong rang through the halls of the manor.

A knowing glance passed between Anna and William when Bridie arrived at the lunch table in a rush. Both their thoughts were on the letter which had arrived in the mail this morning.

"Sorry I am late, everyone. It was so beautiful outside today the time got away from me." Bridie reached over and kissed the top of Odette's head. "Hello, Poppet, what have you been up to today?"

"We are just about to say grace, Bridie. Maybe you can say it today. Your penance for being late," William raised his eyebrows.

"Yes, Grandpa, of course."

Bridie bent her head and took a deep breath. Her thoughts clashed with each other. The words of a grace refused to surface. It took another deep breath before the words came out of their own accord.

"For these and all thy Blessings, oh Lord, we thank Thee."

Grandpa's eyebrows rose further. "Short and sweet today, Bridie."

A flush coloured Bridie's cheeks. She lowered her gaze again, knowing full well she had been remiss in her tardiness.

Later, as Bridie and her grandparents sat in the library, Anna withdrew the letter from her knitting basket.

"Bridie, I am sorry, this letter was addressed to you, but suspecting it might cause you grief, I opened it." Anna held the envelope across to Bridie. "As you can see it is your father's writing, but it seems as if it was written in a moving carriage."

Bridie scrutinized the address written in an unsteady hand. "I noticed his hands did tremble a lot when I was up there."

Bridie paused before lifting the flap. She wondered what bitter words her father might have for her now.

She hardly registered the first sentence but the capital letters on the last sentence appeared to shout at her: *"DON'T BOTHER COMING HOME. YOU ARE A DISGRACE TO THE FAMILY."* Bridie lay the paper on her lap and continued to gaze at it unseeing.

Anna reached across and rested her hand on Bridie's arm.

"Darling this must hurt, but remember he is an unwell man and I am sure after all the turns he has had in the past year, he will not be thinking very clearly."

"Grandmama, I am not surprised. No doubt he sees me as an unfit daughter – after all, I refused to cooperate with his plans for my future."

The following three weeks were filled with family obligations which had kept Bridie away from the cottage, except when with Jimmy Braydon on their morning rides. The sight of David's smile as he leant nonchalantly against the frame of his doorway and the toss of his casual salute, set her heart racing. Even Welly felt Bridie's excitement and showed it in a tendency to prance with impatience. After no more than a brief greeting, Jimmy led Bridie off once more.

David sat on the flat rock at the top of the cliff near his cottage listening to the music of the sea crashing upon the shore below. Such a pastime often held him mesmerized as he studied how he might emulate in his musical compositions the whisper of breezes on a calm day, the whistle of winds rising, and the pounding of the waves. Even in the middle of a gale, he wandered out to listen and remember the music rising and falling – thumping and sighing.

Tonight, the deepening dusk settled around him while the rising moon peeped over the horizon. Inside his head a new musical composition flowed and swooped, it dived and drifted on a tinkling top key. In the forefront of his mind, Bridie's blue eyes framed by her dark curls smiled approval at his efforts. The cough of a fox nearby and the hoot of owls and chirrups of other nocturnal birds in the forest barely registered.

David did not hear the soft footfall behind him. He did not see the wooden cudgel raised in the shadows. Instinct drew him to his feet. He turned his head. David felt his feet slip on the rock. The last thing to catch his eye before he fell from his precarious position was a sudden shadow at the corner of his eye as he spun around. The weapon that had been aimed at the back of his head caught David square between the eyes. He did not feel the pain as he toppled out and into the sea one hundred feet below. He did not struggle in the swirling current of the high tide in front of the caves at the bottom of the cliff. His body tossed, it turned and it rolled with the crashing waves. Blood stained the water around David's lifeless body. Eventually, the sea spat him out on the beach fifty yards east of where he entered the water.

The figure on the top of the cliff watched until the body drifted out of sight, then turned and ran off into the thicket.

Jimmy's laughter echoed along the seafront as he and Bridie galloped beside the forest through the cooler air of an approaching autumn morning.

"You must be feeding that mare fresh oats, Miss Bridie, to have her gallop like that."

"It is only the cooler mornings, Jimmy," Bridie called back over her shoulder.

As they approached the cottage, the pair settled their horses to a slow walk along the beach where the shingle disappeared beneath the softer sands.

"What's that ahead there, about one hundred yards?" Jimmy called, his finger directing Bridie's gaze to a bundle of something rocking with the rise and fall of the waves on the shoreline.

"Looks like debris, maybe a ship has gone down near here recently."

Both horses were guided towards the site to investigate this find. It was Bridie who first recognized what she was looking at. The sight of David's red hair floating in the shallows sent a scream tearing from her throat. She was off her horse before Welly had come to a stop. Bridie stumbled to her lover's body, where she fell to her knees. Water, mixed with sand and a thin stain of blood, washed up over her clothing as she rolled the body over and gathered the shattered head into her lap.

"David, David, speak to me," she begged, although commonsense told her that was not possible.

Jimmy's gasp at her side drew her back from the verge of collapse.

"God's truth, this be a bad business," he mumbled.

"Jimmy, go and tell Mr. Axel to bring a dray to carry David back to Clawhaven."

"But, Miss, I can no be leavin' you here alone."

"Go, Jimmy, go."

Bridie's tears began to fall and threatened never to stop. She knew she did not have the strength to drag David's body from the sea, so she held his head out of the water on her lap.

"David, David what has happened? I will never believe you fell from the cliff. Your feet were as steady as the rock upon which you always stood. Your poor beautiful face." One hand scooped up the seawater to dribble over the smashed bone of his forehead, nose and jaw. She stretched her own head down beside his. "David, please tell me this is only a bad dream and I will wake up soon?" She lifted her head and wailed at the sea. "Was it such a sin to love each other? What kind of merciful God of love are you that you allow this to happen?" She lay her head back beside his. "David, don't leave me like this. We have our baby to look after. Please do not go."

Bridie's body began to tremble, partly with shock and partly with the cold of the water and the breeze. When Jimmy returned, he found her almost comatose.

"Miss Bridie, wake up, Miss Bridie." He shook her shoulder with a light hand. "Miss Bridie, Mr Axel and Mr. Sanders are here with the dray."

The two men stood on the sand aghast at the sight of David Lewis's broken body.

Mr. Axel brought himself under control first. "Come away now, Miss Bridie. Mr. Sanders, Jimmy and I will need to carry Mr. Lewis to the dray. I cannot bring it down onto the soft sand, or we might get it bogged.

It was Jimmy who helped Bridie to stand. "I'll be fetchin' our horses as soon as we fix Mr. Lewis," he assured her.

Bridie went to thank the groom, but her teeth began to chatter. Jimmy patted her gently before moving over to carry the legs of the dead man while the two other men supported the upper body. Bridie followed close behind. With surprising gentleness, the men lay David in the dray covering him with an empty grain bag as they did so.

Mr. Axel and Mr. Sanders sat on the seat of the dray. The coachman flicked the reins along the backs of the two horses and called, "Walk On."

Jimmy wasted little time in collecting Flyer and Welly, who had met up and were eating the scant grasses on the edge of the forest.

"Can I be helpin' you mount, Miss Bridie?"

Bridie's vacant eyes peered at Jimmy. She lifted her head to gaze around her as if just waking up.

"No, Jimmy, I think I will walk for a bit if you do not mind."

Bridie and Jimmy walked, leading their horses behind. They walked right up to the stables at Clawhaven. Jimmy took the reins out of Bridie's hand and gave Welly a quick brush down. Bridie stood staring at nothing, while he did the same for Flyer. Grandpa Wellington found the pair heading towards the Manor.

"Oh, Bridie, my darling, I am so sorry." He drew her into a hug.

"I'm sorry, sir, but Miss Bridie's still in shock. She's quite dazed."

William looked over the top of his granddaughter's head. "Thanks, young Jimmy, I will take care of Bridie now. Can you give Mr. Axel and Mr. Sanders a hand at the back of the manor?"

"Yes, sir." Jimmy moved to go but then turned back for a moment as if to assure himself his Miss Bridie was adequately cared for.

Anna met William and Bridie on the steps of the manor. She took in Bridie's white face, open mouth, and the sag of her body. Anna's heart cried for this woman who was like a second daughter to her.

"Is she alright, William?" Anna did not wait for an answer. She had her answer in what her eyes told her. "Bring her up to her room and I will care for her there."

"Where is David?" Bridie whispered.

"Bridie, I have the men looking after him in the little room beside the back entrance. Now I want you to come upstairs with me, dear."

"Yes, Grandmama," Bridie offered listlessly.

Grey clouds in the cold sky seemed appropriate for the funeral of David Lewis, a popular church member and a wonderful organist. Bridie sat beside her grandparents in the front pew only an arm's reach from the polished timber coffin. It felt surreal to think of her David lying dead inside. She fought to chase away her final picture of him and recall their happier moments. Most of the service passed over her bent head. Tears ran unheeded down her cheeks. Bridie, with her grandparents, stood beside the Rector at the door to greet the parishioners offering their condolences, as they made their way slowly out of the church. Bridie's mind took in not a word of what was said to her. Only the Wellingtons and a few of those, who knew David best, gathered at the graveyard to witness his interment.

Bridie's gaze was fixated on the ground as the preacher spoke the last words of farewell to David.

Her ears heard not a word. Suspicion, blame and resentment filled her mind believing someone in her community had killed her lover, and was most likely in cohorts with her father.

Her gaze lifted to cast over each of the four pallbearers standing behind the minister. Gratitude and comfort at the presence of Mr. Axel and Jimmy Braydon brought tears to her eyes. The sight of Mr. Bacon who she knew had begged her grandfather to have the honour of this position, being an elder of the church nowadays, did not sit well with her peace of mind. She pondered this feeling inside herself. It had been her father who had chosen the fellow as her tutor. At the sight of Sanders, the man who had shown her how to ride her first horse and who was always present to drive the family carriage when any one of them travelled anywhere, she questioned her subconscious at lumping him in with her ex-tutor, Mr. Bacon. Was there a connection between him and her father too? This cannot be, Sanders always offered the family the greatest assistance and respect.

During the afternoon, Bridie took Welly and rode down to the cottage to rescue David's personal things she knew to be there. Mr Axel and Jimmy planned on coming later in the afternoon bringing a horse pulling the dogcart in which to carry David's things back to the Manor.

Bridie found the small leather case, sixteen by twelve by five inches deep with the well-worn metal clasps on each side of the leather handle. She caressed the leather, following David's long fingers over this music case that he handled more than anything else in the cottage. Inside it, he kept those musical scores he played frequently. The mountain of his other musical sheets she placed in several old fruit boxes along with the things from his writing table. Bridie discovered what she had hoped to find, the address for his mother in Wales, written on the letters the lady had sent to her son. Using the key found in his wallet on the kitchen shelf, she unlocked the wooden box under his bed. Along with some money and documents, Bridie found in a padded, velvet-lined metal container, two gold rings – one small enough to fit a female finger and the other suitable for a larger finger altogether. Bridie sobbed. She sobbed for the loss of her David. She sobbed for the life they were to have had together. She sobbed because the little time they expected to have together due to his ill health had been stolen by someone, for a reason she could not imagine. She sobbed for her little baby who was to grow up never knowing the wonderful man who was his or her father.

Back at the manor after dinner the same evening, in the flickering light of the lantern and with Anna to support her, Bridie wrote the letter to David's mother. A letter that was going to break another woman's heart. A letter which she had not planned on having to write for several years at least.

"Bridie, have you thought about David's piano at the cottage? It would be a logistical nightmare to send that back to Wales, I should think."

"Perhaps it can be donated to the school. How lovely if the children of Clawhaven Cliff Village learnt to play music on David's piano?" The thought set the tears streaming down Bridie's face again.

"Ask Mrs. Lewis if she would be agreeable to that. Perhaps she might like some of his sheet music back."

As Bridie completed the address on the front of the envelope, Anna hugged her granddaughter and escorted her to her room.

"Grandmama, I want to show you something." Bridie went to the cupboard by her bed and removed the container holding the two gold rings. "David had already purchased our rings for a wedding. He never breathed a word to me."

Both women sat in silence, each with their own thoughts. It was Anna who spoke first.

"If you want to have them made into a locket, I will paint you a miniature likeness of David to place inside it."

"Oh, Grandmama I will treasure it for life."

"Goodnight, my darling. Do you want me to stay with you until you fall asleep?"

Bridie hugged her back. "No thanks, Grandmama, I will be better on my own for a bit, I think."

"Night, dearest."

"Good night and thank you and Grandpa for being here for me."

Anna closed the door gently. Her soft footsteps padded down to her bedroom further along the hallway.

It was early in the morning two days after the funeral, when Bridie realised that she had lost her baby also. Gripping pains tore at her lower abdomen. Blood clots swam in her commode. Her hand clenched over her mouth to deaden the screech she felt pushing up her throat. She curled herself into a ball on the bed and pulled the pillow over her head.

It was Mary, Odette's nurse, who came to her rescue. She knocked softly on the door but entered anyway when she did not hear a reply.

"I'm so sorry, Miss Bridie. This will be from the shock, no doubt," she offered when discovering what had happened. "I'll clean this away and bring you another pan." She removed the pot and covered it with a cloth hanging on the side of the commode. "After that, I'll fix you an herbal mixture to help your body to recover." Mary stroked Bridie's forehead with the gentleness with which she soothed Odette when upset.

Bridie lifted a feeble head. "What about little Odette?"

"She'll sleep for an hour or two yet, Miss."

It was Mary who later brought a cup of hot tea and a small cup of warm herbal brew for Bridie to sip.

"Drink this, Miss Bridie. I'll just go and check on Odette." Mary reached out and patted Bridie's wrist. "Miss Bridie, you can rest assured not a word of this will pass my lips."

Anna and William went together to visit Bridie having been told by the nurse she was unwell. Bridie struggled to sit up and make polite conversation. She refused their offers of the services of the local apothecary.

"Thank you, Grandmama, but I just need time, to help me adjust to all that has happened."

Two days later a desultory Bridie made her way downstairs to join the family for breakfast. It was the child Odette, who brought a smile to her face, when the little arms wrapped around her legs and she spoke a word that sounded very much like, "Bridie."

Bridie settled for a plate of porridge and a cup of hot black tea.

"Bridie, it is good to see you up and about. I have had our friends asking after you. The most insistent has been young Jimmy. He said to tell you he will look after Welly for you until you want to go riding again." Anna informed her.

Bridie smiled – a watery smile. "I will take a walk to the stables later and say hello to him," Bridie paused as if speaking was all too much for her. She sighed before going on, "And to everyone else there." She sipped thoughtfully at her tea. "Grandpa, Grandmama, can we meet in the library after this, there is something I need to discuss with you?"

An anxious glance passed between her grandparents before her grandpa spoke.

"Yes, dear, of course."

Bridie pulled her knitted jacket tight around her as she and her grandparents made their way through the hall and into the library in the south-west corner of the ground floor. On entering the room, it was her grandpa who went and stoked the coals in the fireplace. Bridie stood to one side savouring the warmth.

"It feels like an early start to our winter this year," William said.

Anna sat in one of the three armchairs around the warmth, and when Bridie and William were settled in their chairs, she asked, "Bridie dear, what did you want to talk about?"

Bridie dragged her thoughts into some semblance of order and began to speak slowly at first, then her speech rushed forth as if the words could not wait to tumble out.

"Grandmama, Grandpa, I think David was pushed off the cliff." She lifted her eyes having expected, maybe even hoped for, their strong denials. "Oh, you have wondered about this too, then?"

William stroked the armrest of his chair, while his mind rearranged his thoughts.

"Bridie, we have been waiting for you to regain your strength, before telling you this." William glanced over at Anna as if seeking her opinion, before relaying his news. The greying head gave an almost faint nod. William went on, "We had Mr. Fields the coroner, Officer Graham the policeman, and the local Apothecary, Terrence Cairns, here to see David's body the day he was brought up from the sea. They could not make a definite decision on whether David had fallen by accident or had been attacked." William watched Bridie carefully to ensure she was coping with what he had to say. Once again, he pursued Anna's silent nod before he went on, "Apparently, they found wood slivers in David's facial wounds which would have been most unlikely to have come from the fall down the rocks. Mr. Axel took Officer Graham to the flat rock where David spent so much time. They discovered footprints of different shoe sizes to David's in the dirt behind the rock, and a wooden club with blood on the end discarded only a few yards away."

William stopped talking as if exhausted himself. It was Anna who delivered a summary of the professional's report.

"They suspect David was murdered by someone unknown." Anna leaned over to touch Bridie's hand. "When you are feeling able, the policeman will want to ask if you know of anyone who may have had a grudge against David."

Tears ran freely down Bridie's face. "I knew it," the words spewed from her mouth. "I just knew something was wrong. David would never have fallen from his 'lookout rock,' as he called the big flat rock at the top of the cliff. He was as surefooted as a mountain goat."

"The policeman will want to ask you if David had any enemies, or if you knew of anyone who might want to hurt you," William explained further.

"How could David have any enemies? He was as gentle as a lamb."

"Then who do you think might want to hurt you, through David?"

Without a second thought, "My father," fell out of Bridie's mouth into the room. "He said I should have higher prospects in my life than a musician – so he knew about my friendship with David."

"How did he know that do you think, dear?"

It was William who answered Anna's question.

"Douglas is not short of contacts in this area. It was he who sent Tutor Bacon to us and if I remember, I think Sanders, the horse-breaker, is a relative of his somehow."

"Sanders would never tell tales," Bridie defended the man who had taught her to ride ... yet the thoughts that had hounded her at the funeral popped into her head. *No, it cannot be*, Bridie shook her head to chase the unwelcome idea away. "The Tutor, well, that is another matter."

"But would he be so spiteful?"

"Yes," replied Bridie and William together. The three laughed despite the seriousness of the situation.

William nodded his head. "Your Grandmama and I had wondered about Douglas until we received a letter from George two days ago. He told of how Douglas had been completely bedridden since having a further turn just a few days after your last meeting there. I might add, that George in no way blames you for this. He is very much aware his father is his own worst enemy." William stretched his legs out in front of himself and pumped them back and forth a few times. "I guess there is the possibility he might have ordered the attack on David before his final stroke. I am sure he saw David as the one who caused his plans to fail. Douglas was never one to concede defeat."

"Strange you should say this, Grandpa. As soon as I saw David in the water that day, similar thoughts entered my head. The first candidate as the guilty party in my mind was the secretary of my Father, Alec Bacon-Dowd. He looks more like a dockworker or bully man than a secretary."

Both Bridie and William then looked over at Anna when she entered the conversation.

"We cannot disregard Tutor Bacon, remember. In recent months, I have been questioning my instinct about the man. I realized he and Bacon-Dowd may have a family connection."

"The policeman will be out here tomorrow and we will mention these ideas to him, but I doubt if there is any chance of us getting any proof." William brought the discussion to a close when he stood and suggested Bridie should retire to her room until lunchtime.

Anna smiled up at her granddaughter. "Will you be alright, dear? I hope young Odette is not too noisy for you."

"The child is an angel. I seldom hear her at all."

PART TWO

ODETTE MAYFORD

CHAPTER SIX

Odette at Clawhaven Manor

1879-1883

Mrs. Ogilvie's eyes lifted as she sat on the chair beating the eggs in the large china bowl. She watched the kitchen door open, then dropped her gaze to see only the top of a head of blond curls tied in a pink ribbon approach the large kitchen table.

"I wonder who those curls belong to?" She asked aloud.

Odette squealed softly as she jumped up and down. "It is me, Mrs. O'vie. It is me."

"Oh, yes, it is you too."

"I is four today."

"Oh, four what, four frogs? Is that why you are bouncing?"

"No, Mrs. O'vie. I four-year-old today. It is my birfday."

"Happy birthday, little birthday girl. Would you like to help me beat the butter and eggs for your cake?"

"Oh yes, please," Odette rushed over to stand by the cook, who handed her the large fork. After several whisks, Mrs. Ogilvie now began to add the other ingredients helping Odette stir the mixture with a large wooden spoon.

"Is this for my birfday cake?"

"Yes, Miss Birthday girl, it is. What colour icing would you like?"

"Pink, please?"

"With raspberries on top to match?"

"Yes, please. Aunt Bridie loves raspberries too. I have to be real quick to stop her eating them all."

When the cake mixture was beaten and poured into the greased pan, Mrs. Ogilvie made Odette stand well back while she placed it into the hot oven. She stirred the coals in the firebox of the stove.

"This afternoon I'll be making the wedding cake for Mary and Mr. Axel. If you come down, after you have your nap, you can help me with that too."

Odette's eyes grew large. She spun around and headed towards the doorway, at which point she spun back to thank the cook.

"I not sleep this afternoon, I come real early."

Odette almost knocked Bridie over as she entered the kitchen.

"Sorry, Aunt Bridie, I is going to cook Mary's wedding cake," she tossed back as she raced off to spread the news through the household, but most especially to her nurse, Mary.

"That child is like a whirlwind," Bridie laughed as she turned back to talk to the cook. "I hope she has not been any trouble for you here, Mrs. Ogilvie?"

"None whatsoever, Miss Bridie. I don't think she'll do me out of a job for a bit. She loves to help me with the mixing, but I can't trust her to wait for things to cook. We'd have burnt fare every meal if we depended on her to remember she has things baking in the oven," the cook laughed.

Bridie joined in as she took the mixing bowl from the cook's hand and began to scoop up the remnants of the mixture with her finger.

"Oh, that tastes beautiful."

"Don't you let your grandmother catch you doing that, my girl."

Bridie laughed again. "You have been telling me that since I was Odette's age."

Mrs. Ogilvie paused for a moment sorting something out in her memory.

"That will be going on eighteen or nineteen years ago now, Miss Bridie."

"Yes, you are right." Bridie smiled. "Now, I have come down with a message from Grandmama about the wedding cake. Mary has asked for a simple fruit cake with plain white icing."

"Yes, that will be no trouble, but I may make some icing roses on top. Just one or two, what do you think?"

"I think that will set it off beautifully."

Bridie made her way to the library, where she knew Grandmama and Mary were sorting out the wedding program before they left for town to attend Mary's dress fitting.

Grandpa sat in his most comfortable chair in the corner with Odette on his lap turning the pages of a storybook.

"I saw Sanders pulling the carriage up at the front," Bridie informed Anna and Mary. "Are you ready to go to the dressmaker?"

"Yes," Anna said as she made to rise from the chair. Mary jumped up to help her. Bridie noticed Odette look up from Grandpa's lap. Doubt filled the child's eyes. Compassion filled Bridie's smile. After almost two years of living at Clawhaven Manor, the child still liked to have Mary in her line of sight.

"Come, young Odette," Bridie held her hand out to her niece. "How about you and I go for a walk through the orchard and down to the beach? Do you think you are big enough to walk that far yet?"

"Oh, yes, I can walk the biggest way."

"Should we invite Grandpa too? The walk will do his bones the world of good."

"Yes, come on, Grandpa, up you get."

Bridie led the trio out through the back doorway.

Sanders hauled on the reins. Dust clouded around the feet of the horses pulling the carriage as they came to a halt outside the house of the dressmaker, Mrs. Turner. Mrs. Turner was the mother-in-law to Mary's matron-of-honour, Josephine, who was the wife of the local veterinarian. Donald Turner the veterinarian, was going to stand up beside Bernard Axel, the bridegroom.

Partially sewn frocks, suit coats, waistcoats and trousers hung from improvised racks, hooks and curtain rails in Mrs. Turner's spare room. A variety of materials tacked together covered one of the two work benches. A brown paper parcel sat on the corner of the other table, where a cloth covered a new hand-powered sewing machine.

"There is a small pair of pink soft shoes in there," Mrs Turner pointed to the brown parcel. "They may fit Odette if you want them, Mary. Josephine found them at a church stall some time ago." Mrs Turner lifted a small girl's white frock from a curtain rail. Mary and Anna sighed in unison.

"Oh, Mrs. Turner, the smocking is beautiful," Anna caressed the miniature pink flowers stitched within the intricate pleats of the fancywork on the bodice. A two-inch strip of similar smocking set off the bottom of the puffed sleeves. She turned to Mary, "What do you think, Mary?"

"Mrs. Wellington, I have never seen anything so beautiful." Tears welled in her eyes.

"Now, dear, let us see your dress."

Mrs. Turner brought forward from the curtain rail, a high-waisted, simply cut, long, grey frock with puffed upper sleeves which then hugged the arms to the wrist. A hand-tatted, lace vest covered the bodice.

"I'll need you to try it on, Mary, before I can make the final touches," Mrs. Turner instructed. "Josephine was over last night to have her final fitting." Mrs. Turner then took down a similar grey frock to the bride's dress but without the adornment of the lace.

While the women settled down to the fitting of their dresses, Sanders the coachman checked his horses, before wandering over to the large barn at the edge of the garden. It was only moments before Donald Turner seized him to help with a reluctant dog awaiting castration.

"Geez, Don, you can't blame the poor mutt for complaining, you know. How do you think you'd feel if someone wanted to lighten your load?" Sanders laughed.

The vet joined in the laughter. "Not as bad as Bernie Axel would feel with his wedding only two weeks away. I think Mary might throw him back if someone chopped his bits off. Now just keep that bag over the dog's head – he's been known to bite. That's why he's ended up as my patient."

For some moments, the two women inside the carriage sat in silence letting their thoughts rumble along with the wheels over the country track.

Mary broke the silence. She stuttered at first, trying to find the words she wanted to say.

"Mrs. Wellington, I want to thank you from the bottom of my heart for all you and the Colonel have done for me. Before I arrived here, few people in this world would've given me the time of day. I'm sure you know I'm not a worthy person. I was taken from the home for unmarried mothers to be a wet nurse for Odette. The Matron took my baby away to give to parents who couldn't have children. Mrs. Beatrice was kind enough to take me in to help with Odette and now you, the Colonel and Miss Bridie have treated me as one of the family. I'll never forget your kindness. It's because of you I've met Mr. Axel. I've told Mr. Axel the truth and he's accepted me as I am.

He's a good and kind man. I'll now be respectably married and will have children of my very own. This is a chance denied to many others with my past." Mary's voice faded away as she finished her last sentence.

Anna reached across and held Mary's hand. "Many women are pregnant before they are married, Mary, and none are the wiser. As a rule, it does not make them worse or better than anyone else. Every woman has her own story to tell. Bridie told me of her own pregnancy and how you helped save her when the miscarriage followed David's death. I can never repay all that I owe you for that alone." Anna stared out of the window seeing again Bridie's sunken pale face. "Not only that, you kept our Odette alive when she was a baby and unwanted. I think we are forever in your debt, Mary."

The last two weeks before Mary's wedding passed rapidly. Bridie paid extra attention to young Odette, who appeared to be in two minds at the thought of Mary moving out of the manor to live with Mr. Axel in his cottage a mile away.

During this time, Anna's thoughts often drifted to Bridie knowing the pain her granddaughter must be feeling in her heart having been denied her own wedding, but any tears she shed, and Anna believed they were probably many, Bridie shed alone.

The spring sunshine warmed the morning and brightened the smiles as the locals gathered at the church. Most of them had been there when Bernie Axel had married his first wife. They would have been there at her funeral following an illness less than eight years later. Now they wished a good man a happy future with this quiet but capable woman.

Bridie felt her cheeks aching having held the smile for what seemed like hours. She wished they could all move inside the church and get it over and done with. As she struggled to drag her thoughts back from the wedding she had planned for David and herself, William's clear whisper to Anna drew Bridie back to the present.

"Good heavens, our Bernie Axel has scrubbed up well. Just shows what a marriage can do to a man." Bridie heard his grunt when Anna nudged him with a sharp elbow. A soft ripple of laughter spread amongst the others in the nearby groups of well-wishers.

Bernie, and his friend Donald Turner, grinned at the exchange before they turned to enter the church. The guests followed their lead.

Bridie sat with Anna in the front seat on the opposite side of the aisle to the groom. Her grandpa waited outside for the bride to arrive in the Clawhaven Manor carriage.

The organ music echoed through the rafters of the church. Tears swam in Bridie's eyes when, through her ears, it was David's music that filled her soul. She strived to concentrate on this wedding and not the one never to be. The memory of Mary's earlier thoughtfulness almost overwhelmed Bridie. The two had been sitting in the garden watching Odette play with the puppy Mr. Axel had given the child for her fourth birthday.

"Bridie, I have asked Josephine Turner to be my matron-of-honour. I thought you may not wish to be too closely involved in the wedding since it is only two and a half years since you were planning your own wedding. I hope you understand."

As she now stood here in the church, where she should have been married, Bridie again felt the knife slash into her heart at the thought of her loss. She swallowed the excess tears running down the back of her throat. She knew full well that she could not have had the strength to stand at the front of the church beside Mary today. Bridie squashed down hard on her thoughts when a picture of David, as he lay in her arms on the beach instead of lying beside her on their marriage bed, threatened to overwhelm her. She stomped on the rising feelings of jealousy and her resentment at the legal process which had never solved what she knew was his murder.

At that moment, the music changed and everyone stood to watch as Mary, on the arm of Colonel Wellington, began her slow walk into the church. Bridie sucked in a deep breath. She felt her grandmother's fingers clasp her hand tightly. Their eyes met.

Bridie smiled a watery smile at Odette who fired off a small wave and a big grin to her great-grandmama and her aunt Bridie, as she strode by in her little pink soft shoes. Odette stole everyone's heart when she quietly refused to step back with the matron-of-honour when the bride stood beside her husband-to-be. She clung to the back of Mary's dress. Mary passed her bouquet of white flowers to Josephine, and with a smile, she reached down to wrap the palm of her hand gently around Odette's cheek. Once the child was reassured Mary was not going anywhere soon, she wandered back to sit on Bridie's knee and promptly fell into a light doze.

The supper was provided in the village hall by friends and family. Ale flowed freely amongst the local chaps plus a few bottles of alcohol of dubious origin. The women mostly drank tea.

With drooping eyes, Odette sat on Bridie's lap enthralled to watch those dancing to the piano music as they swept past. Occasionally her gaze shifted to follow Mary and Bernie, as they walked around their guests offering their thanks for their attendance and receiving their well wishes for the future.

Before the party became too boisterous, the Colonel led Anna, Bridie and Odette outside to the Clawhaven Manor carriage.

"Wait, Colonel Wellington, sir." It was Mr. Axel with his new wife on his arm who chased after the group. "Mary and I wanted to say thank you again for your very generous wedding present." He held his hand outstretched.

The men shook hands. Anna and Bridie smiled. They were happy William had decided to have the manager's cottage drawn up on a separate deed in the names of Mr. Axel and Mary.

Back in her room, Bridie had little time for feeling sorry for herself. This was Odette's first night to sleep in her small bed now settled in the corner of Bridie's room. The child's eyelashes lay soft upon her cheeks before the story Bridie told of ballrooms and sweeping skirts of women and tall handsome men in smart uniforms reached an end.

Odette's final words, before her breathing softened, barely reached Bridie's ears.

"Will you teach me to dance, Aunt Bridie?"

It was after Bridie slipped beneath the cool sheets on her own bed, that the tears fell, dampening the pillow under her head. In the morning, she awoke to find a small body in the bed beside her.

"Good morning, Aunt Bridie, will you teach me to dance now?"

1883-1887

The family was gathered in Anna's music room. Mrs. Berrington, Anna's friend from the village, stood up beside Bridie and Odette. Anna sat on the piano stool waiting for instructions.

Mrs. Berrington stepped back, having shown her students in dancing the first few steps of a waltz. Bridie towered over her eight-year-old niece, whose face spoke of serious concentration.

"Anna, can we have the first few bars of the Chopin waltz, please?" The dance teacher requested. She swept across the floor by herself as light as a whisper on a mischievous breeze. "Now Bridie and Odette let me see you do that."

156

Bridie and Odette's gazes met in a cheeky grin. They stumbled off.

Gladys Berrington clapped her hands repeatedly. "No, no, ladies, I want you on the balls of your feet, pointing your toes and moving with grace. You must feel yourself floating. Not like two sacks full of potatoes." Bridie and Odette stood with bowed heads, but their glances sparkled when they met. The teacher turned back to the pianist. "Can we try that again, Anna?"

After one hour and all her clapping, the palms of Mrs. Berrington's hands glowed red, similar to the colour of her cheeks.

"I think, ladies, we will rest now, until next time. You are both showing some improvement. Anna, these ladies will need to practise frequently."

"Of course, Gladys. Now I think you deserve a cup of tea and scones. Do you remember our first dancing lesson?"

Gladys smiled. "How could I forget? Mr. Capini, wasn't it? A name very like that anyway."

"Oh, yes, and how he got all het up if we faltered."

Gladys began to laugh. " 'What am I teaching here today, cattle lining up to be milked?' he often reprimanded us."

"Yes, he did, but give him his due, when he finished with us, we were sailing around the floor without no more noise than the swish of the wind through the trees." Anna turned to her great-granddaughter, "And so you will, with a little more practice. But now, young Odette, it is time for tea before you will need to return to your school lessons with your Aunt Bridie."

The mailman rode up just as Anna waved goodbye to her friend. His snowy hair gleamed in the sunlight, as he jumped from the back of his dark horse with four white feet. Rough, arthritic fingers delved into the bulky-shaped bag on the nearside of the animal.

"Good morning, Mrs. Wellington, it looks like spring is on the way in at last."

"Yes, Mr. Featherstone, and it cannot come soon enough for me. The cold seeps into my bones these days."

"That's what my father used to say, every winter. God rest his soul."

"I see you are still riding your horse for your deliveries. I have been reading how many postmen are riding bicycles in the bigger towns these days. Will you be getting one, do you think?"

Mr. Featherstone lifted his head, "When they make a bicycle that will keep my legs warm, I might consider it." He smiled.

"Now that is something I never thought about." Anna laughed.

He finished his search and stood back with several envelopes of various sizes and shapes in his hand. "Do you want me to give this mail to you, or should I give it to Mrs. Coburn?"

"Thanks, I will take it, as I am just going inside myself anyway. Mrs. Coburn is busy this week with the spring cleaning."

"Thank you, Mrs. Wellington, I'll be on my way. I've got two here for Mr. Axel and his wife next. They be a lovely couple, them two."

Anna smiled her agreement and turned to enter the hall. She began to flip through the envelopes as she enjoyed an extra few minutes of sunshine while standing on the top step. A frown deepened in her forehead at the sight of the black band in the corner of one envelope. She recognized Mr. Bacon-Dowd's handwriting.

"Oh, dear, this cannot be good."

Once inside, she made her way to the library where she knew William was sure to be sitting listening to Bridie teaching young Odette her lessons. He looked up when he noticed Anna's signal. They moved into the office next door. Anna passed over the black-edged letter.

William eased his long frame into his seat and opened the envelope. His eyes ran across the short note.

Dear Colonel Wellington and Mrs. Wellington
I write this letter on behalf of Mr. George Mayford who has instructed me to advise you of the passing of Mr. Douglas Mayford on the fifth of this month. He was taken with a final stroke from which he never recovered. Due to the inclement weather and snow at the time, Mr. Douglas Mayford has been interred beside his beloved wife, with just the local family in attendance.
Mr. George plans a memorial service in the middle of spring – at a date to be advised.
Yours sincerely
Alec Bacon-Dowd

William looked up into the eyes of his wife. "It is as you guessed, Anna. Douglas passed away during the snow and has been interred beside our Athena. They are holding a memorial service in a few weeks. Do you think we should go?"

"It might look a bit odd if we did not go, William, but I think it best to leave Bridie and Odette here in Sussex. I cannot say I trust George or Beatrice fully, and would not like to see our girls manipulated into remaining in London against their wills."

"I will agree with you there. They both regard Clawhaven as their home and neither show any inclination to venture back to the family in London."

"I do worry about Bridie though. She shows no proclivity to meet other people."

"You mean suitable as a marriage partner?"

"Yes, that is exactly what I mean. It has been six years since David's death. It is not good for her to mourn so long."

"That is a problem for another day, my love. You were saying you might like a trip to London on the railway this time. Is that the plan?" William moved the conversation along.

"It has been in my mind. We could travel by horse and carriage to the nearest station on the London to Portsmouth or Southampton line. On the other hand, I do worry a lot about all the crime we read about on the train carriages, though."

"Anna, dear, they have government inspectors on the trains now and the crime is not near what it was. I understand it is quite comfortable travel and so much quicker than on the roads. How often do we see travellers held up with a broken axle or such, due to unmaintained roadways."

Eventually, Anna decided to travel how she usually travelled.

"I prefer the privacy we have during the long hours, William. Sanders is such a good driver and looks after us so well. Would it bother you too much if we went in our carriage? I know it is slower." Anna's eyes twinkled, "It has not escaped my notice this desire you have to take a ride on the train. You have been like a small boy with a toy reading through all your papers and journals on the subject. Perhaps you could take Sanders with you on an exploration journey on the trains after we see Douglas suitably remembered."

"You know I think he might like that, but for now, I had best take a walk and let him know to prepare the carriage and horses for a trip to London in the near future."

Sanders looked up from shoeing the feet of one of the Clydesdale horses. He rested the hoof back to earth.

"Good morning, Colonel, what can I do for you?"

"Mrs. Wellington and I will need to travel to London in a few weeks. Our son-in-law has died and we will attend his memorial. Will you be so kind as to make sure the horses and carriage will be in a fit state for the trip?"

"Of course, sir." If William noticed the flash of glee in the eyes of the coachman at the news received, he did not mention it.

Sanders did not make his following comment until he was sure the colonel was out of earshot.

"Good riddance to bad rubbish, I say," he mumbled.

The two horses and the piebald pony, with their riders, plodded over the grassy track towards one of Odette's favourite sites on the estate. The child's excited prattle startled the birds in the trees and sent other fauna scuttling for cover in the hedgerows. Jimmy Braydon, in control of the lead attached to Pie, Odette's pony, rode ahead on the aging Flyer. Bringing up the rear on Welly, Bridie's smile never faltered as she watched the child's pleasure.

Odette gripped a handful of mane as she also clung to her reins. She squealed with delight when they arrived at what Jimmy Braydon called the brook-of-magic. Over the warmer months, this had turned into a regular jaunt on a Saturday morning – a picnic in the dappled shade of the oak and ash trees that lined either side of the stream. Their branches stretched across to make a green tunnel over the brook. A purple carpet of violets lined the banks. After letting their horses drink the cool water, Odette wasted little time in removing her shoes and socks and leaving them in Bridie's care. Under Jimmy's watchful eye, Odette explored the stream where the shallower waters chuckled over the larger stones. Bridie spread their repast along a wide fallen tree trunk, before stretching out on the grass with her back leaning against the timber. She inhaled the aromas of the wildflowers and the moist air above the running waters through the leafy tunnel.

"Look, Odette," called Jimmy as he pointed to the water turbulence made by the fish in the deeper stream, "the trout are here again today."

161

Odette ran back to draw Bridie's attention to their find. "Aunt Bridie, can we bring a fishing line and catch some trout for Mrs. Ogilvie to cook?"

"We can ask Mr. Axel if he has some fishing tackle hidden in his shed," Bridie suggested.

"Mary will help us to search," Odette never doubted her former nurse's support. Odette turned and stepped again into the stream with care not to roll her ankle on the occasional stones found in the sand and gravel stream bed.

Bridie closed her eyes. It was easy for her to imagine David Lewis alive and well, sitting by her side. Odette's young voice and laughter might easily have been that of her own offspring. It was Jimmy who caught her out.

"Miss Bridie, todays will lead into tomorrows and who knows what tomorrows will bring. Look forward never backward."

Bridie's eyes snapped open. A frown of annoyance flashed, but only briefly, as she looked up at her young friend.

"Clever clogs aren't you, Jimmy Braydon?"

"Will I set out the food and call young Odette in to eat?"

"Yes, Jimmy," Bridie watched her niece dancing in the waters and smiled. "A sweet thing like her will dissolve if she gets too wet."

"Besides that, your Mrs. Coburn will be wearing her not-happy face, if we be turnin' up with the child soakin' wet," Jimmy laughed.

Bridie joined him in laughter at her own memories of those times she incurred Mrs. Coburn's not-happy face when a child herself.

They sat upon the grass with plates of buttered toast and jam to be washed down with glasses of fresh milk when Odette asked, "When will Grandpa and Grandmama be back from Granddad's funeral?" She pronounced this new word slowly.

Bridie's eyes opened wide. Before she was able to ask why Odette thought that their grandparents had gone away to London for a funeral, the child asked another question.

"What is a funeral exactly?"

Bridie paused unsure how much to explain. Should she tell the child it was a memorial, not a funeral they were attending? Perhaps it was best to keep things simple. She realized Odette had been only two years of age when they buried David. The child would have no recollection of that horrendous day.

"Is it what happens when we die?"

Bridie felt as if she was sinking into a deep quagmire. It was Jimmy who rescued her.

"Odette, look over yonder near the stinking iris, is that a hedgehog?"

Odette jumped up and went to investigate.

"Don' you be touchin' that stinkin' plant next to the big boulder. You'll be walkin' home alone if you get smelly," Jimmy warned. "And if you find a hedgehog, remember its spikes will be settin' your skin on fire."

Bridie smiled at the interchange. "Jimmy you are so good with her."

"With three younguns to help Ma look after, I learnt pretty quick to send them off on other tracks."

"You'll be a good father one day, Jimmy Braydon. Have you not found a pretty maiden in Clawhaven Cliff Village to catch your eye yet?" Bridie grinned as a blush lit up her groom's face.

Jimmy stuttered for a moment, then laughed back, "They are lined up all the way from London town wantin' a glimpse of this handsome face."

Odette ran back to learn what it was had Bridie and Jimmy so amused.

"Jimmy has so many women falling at his feet he cannot decide who to marry," Bridie explained.

"I am going to marry Jimmy when I grow up," Odette affirmed.

"Whoa there, lassie, hold your horses. I'll be an old man by the time you grow up. You won' want to be lookin' after an old man now, would you?"

"Old, like Grandpa?"

"Much older I be thinkin'."

Odette turned to Bridie. "Will this be true, Aunt Bridie?"

Bridie's smile softened. "Odette if you look closely, you will see the grey hairs popping up on Jimmy's head already."

Odette walked around to where Jimmy sat. "Lift your cap, Jimmy, and let me look, please."

"Miss Odette, that will be too embarrassin'. You would'na' be makin' me do that?"

A frown settled on the girl's forehead. She walked back to Bridie and rested her hand on her aunt's shoulder.

"What does embarrassing mean?"

"It will hurt his feelings and we would never want to hurt Jimmy's feelings now, would we?"

"Sorry, Jimmy," Odette offered, but her expression changed to suspicion, as she looked at the dead-pan expressions on the faces of her audience.

"Now can I move on to a safer subject?" Jimmy laughed. "Mr. Axel's be sayin' the Colonel's plannin' me to work as assistant gard'ner as well as bein' the slave to you two young ladies."

Odette walked over and stood at Jimmy's shoulder. "You will still come with us on our morning rides, won't you Jimmy?"

"Yes, Miss Odette, of course. I be still your groom. I need you to finish teachin' me to speak proper, don' I?" Odette walked back to stand near Bridie.

"And you, Jimmy, what do you think of this?" As she spoke Bridie's arm slid around Odette's waist.

"Miss Bridie, I could not be more pleased. Mum and Aunt Eleanor have my two younger brothers helping them on the farm. I can work here full-time now. Mr. Axel explained if I work hard, I will become the full-time gard'ner/handyman in a few years. Mr. Baines be ailin' lately and needs the help, I un'erstand."

Bridie spoke more to herself than to the others. "I guess Grandpa is preparing for the retirement of Mr. Baines. The gardener is getting on in years and has not been too well lately."

On their return to the manor stables, Odette nearly fell from the horse in her excitement at the sight of Sanders releasing the carriage horses from the traces.

"Are Grandmama and Grandpa home, Mr. Sanders? Are they home from London?" She called as she twisted around to see the man better.

"Now hush, Odette, you know better than to be making all that noise around the animals," Bridie admonished.

Leaving Jimmy to care for the horses, Bridie did her best to restrain Odette to a walk.

"Grace and decorum, Odette. How often does Grandmama tell you, 'Grace and decorum'?"

Four months later, on a trip to Clawhaven Cliff Village with Odette and Mary, Bridie detoured to the Post Office to collect any mail. Her eyebrows lifted at the sight of a letter addressed to herself in an envelope that bespoke of someone private and not the occasional business mail she might receive. She slipped it, along with three other letters for her grandparents, into her reticule for perusal later in the privacy of her room.

After a light luncheon, the three climbed back into the carriage and knocked on the roof to let Sanders know they were ready to move on. The horses stopped at the front gate of the Axel's cottage to allow Odette and Mary out.

"I'll walk Odette home in the cool of the afternoon," Mary assured Bridie.

Bridie grinned, "Thank you, Mary, and best wishes with the little one."

Mary's eyebrows lifted, "You know?"

"I guessed."

"Thank you." Mary smiled – a glowing smile.

"What did Aunt Bridie mean, Mary?"

Bridie gave the roof a tap as Mary led Odette off to her house.

"I have no idea, Miss Odette." Mary was heard to say above the creak of timber and leather as the carriage wheels slowly turned.

It was mid-afternoon before Bridie had the time to retrieve her letter and read its content.

Dear Miss Bridie Mayford

This is a belated message of condolences. During my meeting with your grandparents at the memorial of Douglas Mayford, I learnt of the loss of your fiancé.

My thoughts reach out to you knowing just how much David meant to you.

I took your advice and listened to George. Now I am in the process of being included as a partner in the company. I have been fortunate in finding a delightful young woman Edith Murray who has agreed to be my wife. We will be married in three weeks and our honeymoon will be a trip to the Australian colonies where we plan on settling for some time and hopefully developing new shipping routes in the area.

Now do not go giving me that frown of yours and flashing those amazing blue eyes which have already burnt a strip off me. Miss Murray is fully in favour of this trip and almost as enthusiastic as myself.

Eventually, your pain will subside, Miss Bridie, and I wish you every happiness in your future.

Kindest regards

Stewart Cruickshank

For a moment, the broad-shouldered, narrow-hipped, brown-eyed gentleman of her father's dreams to lure her into the Blue Seas Shipping Company's future, brought a smile to Bridie's eyes. This was quickly replaced with the memory of her David lying in her arms on the seashore. She stood up sharply and walked to the window where she stared out at nothing until the bell rang for the evening meal.

1888-1891

Bridie sat in the library engrossed in reading the latest news from South Africa. She snorted in disgust.

William looked up from the report he was reading on the northern coal fields to see what had Bridie so involved.

"We'll be fighting another Boer War, if we are not careful," he offered his comment. "I suppose Odette is working on her art with your grandmother," he looked up from his reading, "and her music."

"Yes, and her music. She has outclassed me long ago. Perhaps I should give her David's musical scores, but ...."

William waited for some moments for Bridie to go on. "But what, Bridie?"

"I ... I cannot, Grandpa. I cannot bear to listen to her learning them."

"Is that why you hare off outside on one of your long walks, when either she or Anna play something that he played?"

"I am sorry, but yes. I do not know why after all this time, but it brings him right back into the room with me, and I cannot bear not to have him here in the flesh."

"You are right, it is a long time – eighteen seventy-seven or eight, wasn't it?"

Bridie smoothed the pages with trembling hands. "Yes, ten years, Grandpa."

"I am sorry, lass." He reached over and placed his bony hands on her arm. "You are not the only one who has trouble forgetting. I have known many wives who have never forgotten their husbands killed in the war. One I know of, still waits for Mr. Featherstone to bring a letter from her husband to this very day, and the Crimean War finished over thirty years ago. Love can be a powerful thing, my dear."

Odette was thirteen-years-old when she learnt the answer to the mystery of her great-grandmother's occasional faraway look, which was always filled with sadness and longing. At these times, she felt Great-Grandmama's attention absent from the room. Even the curious Odette hesitated to ask questions. For some reason, today was one of those days.

Odette sat in front of the low cupboard in the morning room searching for a particular painting brush misplaced by Anna. A not small number of sketch pages stacked in a tidy heap caught Odette's eye. She glanced up to see her great-grandmother dozing in the chair; something she tended to do these days.

When asked, Anna always replied, "What nonsense, I was not asleep. My mind has much to contemplate."

Odette's gaze dropped back to admire each sketch, most completed with her great-grandmother's tidy signature in the bottom right-hand corner. Wrapped in a soft, white, silk cloth she found two layers of glass with smoothed edges secured by small gold clasps. This glass protected a charcoal sketched portrait of two men each wearing the uniform of the British Cavalry.

Odette looked up to see Anna's faded blue gaze watching her.

"They were my two sons, Odette, Anthony and Abel. They were the brothers of your Aunt Bridie's mother. They were killed in the Crimean War." Anna sucked in her breath. "It was a long time ago," she whispered.

"Where are the girls, William?" Anna rubbed at the ache in her knee.

"Is your arthritis playing up again, Anna?"

"Just a little thanks for asking, William. It will be dusk shortly. I worry when they are not in the house before dark."

"Bridie has taken Odette out for a lesson in French."

"How do you teach French outside?"

William laughed. "They have gone for a walk along the beachfront and Bridie has demanded they both talk French the whole time."

Anna's soft chuckle wobbled a little – something developed along with her old age.

"Odette could well do with extra lessons in her French, I'll grant you that."

"Did I hear a big kerfuffle in the kitchen earlier?"

"Yes, William, I did warn you this morning. Mrs. Ogilvie and Mrs. Coburn will be leaving tomorrow. They are retiring to a small house on the beach near Portsmouth. It was Mrs. Coburn's parents' house. The new cook and the housekeeper will arrive today. They are mother and daughter. They have been working in Southampton until recently. According to Gladys Berrington, we were lucky to get them so quickly. Arriving today will give them a chance to see how things are done around here."

"Oh, dear, the older I become, I do find change irritating."

Anna chuckled again. "William you always found change irritating."

In the morning, William could find little to complain about. His porridge was hot and without lumps. The bacon and eggs were not overcooked and the toast was almost black – just perfect.

Anna winked at Bridie and Odette who found it hard to keep straight faces.

When the empty plates sat in front of them, Anna rang the small bell at her hand to summon Mrs. Coburn. The prompt arrival of the housekeeper suggested the woman may have been awaiting the summon.

"Will you bring in the new staff members, Mrs. Coburn?"

"Yes, Mrs. Wellington, right away."

The prompt arrival of those summoned further suggested they also may have been waiting outside the doorway.

Mrs. Coburn introduced the new staff members.

The new housekeeper, Mrs. Dempsey and her daughter, Rosa Dempsey, the new cook, curtsied.

William's eyebrows almost disappeared within his thinning grey hair. He whispered aside to Anna, while Bridie and Odette made conversation with the new staff members.

"Anna, the cook looks like she has barely climbed out of the cradle. She cannot be anything over twelve years of age."

"Enough, William, Rosa is twenty-three years of age and you did comment on the perfect breakfast she provided earlier." She turned to her old hands. "Now, Mrs. Coburn, Sanders will be ready to drive you and Mrs. Ogilvie to the nearest railway station at nine o'clock this morning. It is the least we can do for many years of loyal service."

"Thank you, Ma'am and Colonel Wellington." Each woman bobbed a curtsy.

William turned to Mrs. Dempsey and Rosa. He thanked them for coming to work at Clawhaven at such short notice. The Mayford family then exited the room.

Contrary to William's dreary forecast, the running of Clawhaven Manor showed little change, if not maybe an improvement. Odette spent her mornings in the library studying with either her great-grandfather or with Bridie, and the afternoons with Bridie in the music room, or with her great-grandmother in the morning room sketching, or engrossed in needlecraft. With Mrs. Berrington away in London for several months, their dancing lessons were curtailed. Today Anna and Odette admired the cream-coloured layette just completed for Mary's second baby due in four months.

"How is Mary, Odette, I have not seen her for a few weeks? She will have her hands full when the new one arrives. Young Donald has not long started to walk."

"I visited her yesterday. Mary admits to feeling tired and her feet are swollen by the end of each day."

"I will have Rosa cook something extra today and Jimmy can deliver it for us." Anna smoothed the new layette with her arthritic fingers. "Odette, you will find brown paper in the drawer. You can wrap this up to take with you next time you visit Mary."

≈

Jimmy Braydon's latest task as assistant gardener was to top up the shingle on the circular driveway at the front of the manor. A large Clydesdale horse, between the shafts of the loaded dray, stepped forward slowly with little more encouragement than intermittent grunts from Jimmy, while he shovelled the fresh shingles hauled up from the beach, out of the dray. After their third trip to the beach, perspiration poured down Jimmy's body, dripped from his chin and saturated his shirt.

He looked up at the sound of footsteps crunching across the new shingle. The new cook, carrying a large jug of rainwater and a tumbler, approached. The expression on his face may have been appreciation for the liquid, after all his tongue was as dry as a preacher's wit, or it may have been for the sight of this new staff member whom he had not had the chance to meet yet.

"Hello, I'm Rosa, the new cook. I hear you're called Jimmy. I was busy in the vegetable room when you came in for your meal last night."

"Er ... yeah, I be called Jimmy." Surely it was only his dry throat that had him struggling to find words to say. His gaze took in the well-rounded woman with sparkling black eyes and short dark curls, many of which had escaped from under the cap on her head. Jimmy estimated she was maybe a few years younger than himself. Slowly his grin recovered. "Pleased to meet you, Rosa." He lifted the tumbler. "I really needed a drink, thank you."

The dairy hands were hard at work in the milking shed when Bridie and Odette mounted their horses as the sun broke above the skyline. Jimmy Braydon double-checked the saddlery before the three riders set off on their morning outing. It was Bridie who led them towards the cottage on Clawhaven Cliff. She planned a foray into the long-empty cottage. Jimmy questioned her with a glance and raised eyebrows.

"It is alright, Jimmy, I need to do this, and it is better I do it with you and Odette beside me." Last evening, before retiring, she finally opened the large brown envelope in which, ten years ago, the solicitor had assured her were the land deeds for the cottage willed to her by her lover David Lewis.

As the track narrowed, Jimmy angled his horse to slip in behind Bridie. He smiled a nod to Odette. Confusion and interest filled the face of the younger woman, but she held back a little, as they wound up the path to where the stone cottage sat in the shelter of boulders at the top of the cliff. Odette knew very little about Bridie's fiancé, only small snippets told to her by her old nurse Mary Axel. She did know he was an accomplished musician, he had lived in this cottage, and he was killed when falling from Clawhaven Cliff.

Bridie stood back near where they tied the horses. She searched the ground in front of her. Not seeing any fresh footprints, she led Jimmy and Odette to the door facing the sea. They watched the waves crash in regular rhythm onto the rocks below.

Bridie took a deep breath and turned towards the door. She lifted the bolt. It took a good shoulder shove by Jimmy to shift the swollen timbers and open the doorway. He stood aside to allow Bridie to pass through. She stepped into the entrance. Her gaze roamed past the doorway and into the kitchen, where it settled on the table. The table on which they had first made love. She again felt David's hands on her body. She felt his breath upon her neck and his whisper in her ear.

Bridie spun about. "I cannot do this, Jimmy. I should not have come here. I must get out."

Bridie pushed past her two friends and ran outside. Jimmy ushered the mystified Odette out to the horses. The pair followed at a sedate pace, while Bridie raced her horse down onto the beach path, where the dust blew up in a cloud behind horse and rider.

CHAPTER SEVEN

New Veterinarian

1892 – 1895

On the first day of April 1892, Bridie woke to the sound of fine gravel stones hitting her window. She dragged herself from her bed and opened it. Jimmy waved his arms back and forth.

"Come quick, Miss Bridie, and bring Miss Odette. Her birthday present is about to be born."

Odette and Bridie ran towards the stable, their skirts held high above their ankles.

"What about grace and decorum, Aunt Bridie? You are always telling me to remember, decorum and grace."

"Today we are excused," she said between panting and laughing at the same time.

"What is the rush?"

"Have you forgotten? Today is your seventeenth birthday. Grandpa, Mr. Axel and Mr. Sanders are just about to present you with your present from all of us at Clawhaven."

The pair pulled up to catch their breath when they turned the corner to the brood mare's loose box. They brushed down their skirts. Odette wondered at Bridie's excitement until she noticed the mare, Sunshine, lying on a thick layer of straw.

Grandpa drew her near. "Come closer, Odette."

In the loose box, Mr. Axel and Mr. Sanders stood back against the wall, while the mare in foal pulled herself to her feet and shuffled around the enclosure. The audience all turned when a tall, slim young man carrying a brown Gladstone bag entered the stable. He pulled the door shut with a clatter. At the sight of the two women present, he dragged a knitted cap from his head to reveal a mop of unbrushed, curly, brown hair.

"Good morning, Colonel Wellington, Mr. Axel, Sanders, I came as fast as I could. I've been over at the Braydon farm. The ladies had twin foals born last night."

The men shared greetings. It was left to William Wellington to introduce his granddaughters.

"Mr. Peter Treloar, veterinarian partner with Donald Turner, I'd like you to meet my granddaughter, Miss Bridie Mayford." Bridie smiled with a nod of her head. "And my great-granddaughter, Miss Odette Mayford." Odette's face flushed red as she curtseyed. Her gaze was captured by glittering grey eyes and a shy smile.

"Pleased to meet you both." He turned to Sanders. "Mr. Sanders, didn't you say this foal was for Miss Odette's birthday?"

It was William who answered. "Yes, it is, Mr. Treloar. And today is Odette's birthday." He smiled his gentle smile. "We are depending on you to make sure this is a successful day."

"Wow, my head is on the chopping block, then?" He smiled and turned to face his patient. Peter watched as the mare settled to the floor again. The audience now receded in his mind. The mare held his complete focus, as he observed and palpated while talking soft words to the animal.

When the front hooves of the newborn were sighted a sigh ran around the stable. The small muzzle appeared and within the next ten minutes, the foal lay exhausted in the straw.

"It's a filly," Peter Treloar advised everyone.

After a brief pause, the mare shook her head and began to rise. The small group left the stable and watched over the half-door as the mare

175

licked her newborn clean and welcomed it into the world. Each time the foal struggled to rise, the mother's attention ruined its efforts to make sense of its long legs. Eventually, the foal found its balance and tottered around its mother until her head guided the baby to the udder.

William hugged his great-granddaughter, "Odette, happy seventeenth birthday, my dear, from everyone at Clawhaven."

"Thank you, Grandpa, and thank you, everyone, especially Mr. Treloar for being here." Her face flushed red once again.

"You are welcome, Miss Odette, and a happy birthday."

Odette would have been happy to stay and listen to the warm voice of Peter Treloar for the remainder of the day, but Grandpa reminded her of her other duties.

"Come, Odette, your grandmama will be quite anxious. We had best get back to the manor and let her know it all went splendidly."

Later, as the evening drew in around the manor and the family folded the table napkins after eating, Odette smiled.

"Thank you, Aunt Bridie, for a wonderful birthday." The smile had not left Odette's face throughout the entire day.

Bridie grinned. "It was Grandpa who organized the foal for you. I hope you thanked him and Grandmama too."

"Hmmm. Oh yes, of course I did."

Bridie rested her arm on Odette's shoulder as they walked abreast up the staircase.

"No need to call me 'Aunt,' now you are seventeen, Odette. It makes me feel so old hearing 'Aunt' from a young woman of your age." Bridie tucked some errant locks behind Odette's ear. "Do I assume the best part of your day was meeting the new vet? What was his name again?"

"Peter," Odette drew out the name with a sigh. "Peter Treloar."

This time Bridie's grin turned to a chuckle. "Do I take it Mr. Peter Treloar has rather impressed you?"

Odette wiped the foolish grin from her face and looked as innocent as she could.

"Oh, I hardly noticed him."

"I am not sure whether I believe that or not. He is rather charming if you look behind the work clothes and the ungroomed appearance."

"I liked his grey eyes and his shy smile the best."

At Odette's door, Bridie kissed the top of her niece's head and said goodnight. "Sweet dreams," she added.

Laughter and boisterous voices burst across the village green as the men, some a little more than merry, drifted through the twilight on their way home to where their dinner waited. Squeals of young boys joined in as they re-enacted the better cricket shots they had witnessed during the afternoon game.

Sanders exhibited a pronounced limp in his right leg, as he and Officer Rogers walked together along the shortcut past Tutor Bacon's schoolhouse. Rogers headed towards the police house and home. Sanders made his way to the blacksmith's workshop. He planned to collect his horse and dray left there earlier. Blacky was to fit new horseshoes to the animal.

They passed close to the back door of the school master's small cottage where the feeble light of a lantern struggled out through a partially open doorway and over the yard.

"What's that?" the policeman asked.

"What's what?" Sanders looked around him to see what Rogers might be referring to.

"That, lying in the doorway," Officer Rogers changed direction.

Sanders followed suit. As the two men neared the house, they were able to distinguish a curious bundle holding the door ajar.

"Good grief, it's the schoolmaster." Rogers broke into a trot. Sanders limped along at his side.

Rogers dropped to his knees beside the bundle. "Can you fetch the lantern out here, Sanders? I can't see a darn thing." Blood dripped from a wound at the top of the man's head. "He's not breathing." When Rogers then felt the man's wrist he announced, "There's no pulse either."

"Roll him onto his side," Sanders suggested.

The pair had little trouble rolling the tutor's bony body onto its left side. Their gazes met in alarm as a soft sigh escaped from between the blue lips, when the last breath, caught in the man's throat, was expelled into the dusk.

Rogers again checked for pulse and respirations but found none. He shook his head.

"It's no point in asking you to run for the doctor," the policeman nodded towards Sanders' leg, that had been injured during their cricket match earlier. "You stay here and do not touch anything. I will fetch Doctor Rains."

"Not a thing, Officer," Sanders smiled, but his thoughts raced.

Years of suspicions towards the tutor following odd things he had witnessed himself, and the unconfirmed gossip that originated with the children at the school had often left Sanders curious about the man. The knowledge of his connection to the long-dead Douglas Mayford, his nemesis, and his long-held interest in Douglas's secretary named Bacon-Dowd, seemed to fill his head to bursting point.

Sanders watched Rogers' long legs loping across the field. It was hard to see clearly with the fading light. Rogers leapt over the one-rail wooden fence and jumped across the ditch at the side of the road before he could be seen in the light of the doctor's porch. Sanders moved out further to where the glow from the lantern light did not detract from his vision. Not a thing moved. He went back to lift the lantern and take it into the one-roomed residence. Everything was in disarray. Books and papers had been dragged from shelves and cupboards. The mattress had been upended and lay across the bed frame. The contents of the table drawers had been tossed over two upturned chairs nearby. His sharp eyes caught sight of what might be a tear in the edge of the mattress ticking. It was almost invisible and did not appear to have been disturbed by the earlier intruder.

Sanders slid his fingers inside the slit in the ticking. Within the horsehair packing, he touched what felt like the edge of a book. He eased it out to discover a hard-covered notebook filled with journal entries and pictures. He flicked through the pages listening intently for the sound of the returning police officer. Many pages were filled with sketches of children's faces – all girls. Below each face and separate from the face, budding naked bodies all similar in design filled the remaining page. Some pages were full of written words in erratic sloping text.

The ache in his leg convinced him to take one of the fallen chairs and lift it upright. He sat down and held his find closer to the lantern light on the floor.

Sanders recognized the face on the first page. This was Bridie Mayford, if he was not mistaken, at the age she was when he first met her. Looking closer he recognised many of the village children. In the pages of script, the repeated underline beneath the name David Lewis caught his eye. He scanned the pages. Sanders gasped. This was a confession. Next, it was the name of Bridie Mayford he found underlined. He discovered the man was infatuated with the then-young girl. Sanders was torn. He knew Miss Bridie wanted so much to know who had killed David Lewis, but what else might be in here she did not want to be known. Should he expose this or hide it again? The creak of the wagon timbers and the plod of horse's feet left him with no time to ponder further. He stuffed the book back where he found it.

He sat back on the chair with his head bowed as if resting. Before Rogers could admonish him for entering the room he spoke first.

"Sorry, I know you said not to come in here, but I needed to sit and rest the leg. This is just how I found it. I touched nothing except I stood this chair upright." Any qualms in telling such a blatant lie did not bother him too much. "Looks like someone was searching for something."

"Hopefully he has not found it. I'll have a look when we get this body sorted."

Sanders followed Rogers' gaze to where Doctor Rains knelt beside the body.

Rogers picked up the lantern from the floor near Sanders' chair and took it closer to the body in the doorway.

"He's not been dead too long. The body's quite warm and blood's still dripping from the wound. No sign at all of rigor mortis yet." Doctor Rains passed his professional opinion.

"Maybe we did interrupt whomever when we chanced by," the policeman spoke thoughtfully. "Maybe we will find whatever the culprit missed."

Water squelched underfoot as Jimmy and Sanders headed towards the stables. They watched Doctor Rains and Officer Rogers pull up their horses at the tying rail in front of the manor.

"Wonder what those two be doing here?"

Sanders turned to Jimmy. "Now if I knew that, they wouldn't have had to make the long trip out here. I could have delivered the message myself."

Jimmy's eyebrows lifted. Sometimes Sanders could be a prickly wart. 'Comes of being a loner,' as Mr. Axel would say, but Jimmy forgave him a lot appreciating that the man had taught him so much.

The two were just settling into the saddles on the two freshly broken grey horses, one light and one darker, that Sanders wanted exercised this afternoon. They heard Mrs. Dempsey usher the visitors inside.

"Please come in, Doctor Rains and Officer Rogers. I didn't realize you were coming to see Mrs. Wellington, Doctor."

"I'll pop in and see her before I go, but first we would like to talk to Miss Bridie Mayford."

Upstairs in her bed, Anna Wellington's chesty wheeze filled the room. The bed seemed way too large for her frail frame where she lay with her grey hair fanned out over the pillow behind her head. The nurse sat quietly in the background rolling cotton balls for future use in her nursing care. On Anna's right, William sat with his head bowed. At regular intervals, his restless fingers rubbed his scalp leaving the thinning strands of grey hair all askew. When not abusing his pate, William nestled Anna's hand in his own. He stroked her cold fingers.

On the other side of the bed, Bridie and Odette sat sentinel also. Bridie held Odette's hand. The three in the chairs looked up at the soft knock on the door before it opened slowly.

"Miss Bridie, will you be able to come downstairs? Doctor Rains and Officer Rogers wish to see you. I have them waiting in the parlour."

Bridie looked askance at the housekeeper.

"He didn't say what for, Miss Bridie, but the doctor did say he'll look in on Mrs. Wellington before he leaves."

Bridie disentangled herself from Odette's hold. "I will not be long, dear. Stay here and look after Grandpa and Grandmama."

Bridie's feet felt heavy as she descended the stairs to the hall and entered the parlour next to the front door.

The two gentlemen rose to their feet when Bridie arrived. She made her way to her favourite chair and invited the men to sit.

"What can I do for you, gentlemen?"

At that moment, Mrs. Dempsey entered with a tray of tea and biscuits.

"Thank you, Mrs. Dempsey. I will pour," Bridie offered a grateful smile to the housekeeper.

While Bridie poured the tea for the visitors and passed the drinks and biscuits to each, she asked again, "How can I help you?"

It was Officer Rogers who spoke first. "Miss Mayford, I have some news for you. While it may offer some satisfaction, it may also be rather disturbing."

Bridie sat straighter in her chair. She swallowed a large sip of tea.

"Well, best you tell me what you have to say."

"We have discovered who murdered your fiancé, David Lewis."

The cup made a soft clunk, as Bridie sat it on the table by her side.

"Good heavens, that was over fourteen years ago." She stared off into space. She felt her heart pound in her chest. She blinked the tears from her eyes. After clearing her throat she asked, "What new evidence have you turned up?"

"You may have heard, that the schoolmaster Bacon was murdered several weeks ago. We don't know who the guilty party was for that, but in the evidence from within his house we found a journal he kept, covering many years." Rogers paused. He felt in two minds about reporting the disgusting pictures they had discovered in the journal, and eventually decided there was no point upsetting Bridie any further. One day, if they find the tutor's killer, it may become public knowledge, but for now, he saw no reason to upset people without good cause. "The man killed the musician for what reason we cannot fathom." Again, the policeman thought it best not to explain how the man had an unhealthy attraction for the young Bridie, to the point of killing the man she planned to marry.

For a moment Bridie's mind froze, before thoughts raced about like a whirling dervish inside her head. *Had they been right in thinking the tutor worked for her father? Was that why he murdered David? What other reason could there be?*

If the policeman had any idea of Bridie's thoughts, he would have explained further, rather than have the lady continue to distrust her own father – but he had no idea.

The doctor spoke up. "I am sorry, Miss Bridie, but I felt you would prefer to be told. I realize how upset you have been for so long, not knowing."

Bridie struggled to stem the tears. She felt her limbs did not belong to her. It seemed that her brain shut down – unable to function after this shock. She nodded her head. Eventually, she was able to speak.

"Thank you, both. This has been a most distressing job for you today. I do appreciate you letting me know."

"You are welcome," the men replied in unison.

"You were right. I did want, no, needed, to know this." She stood up.

Both men followed. The doctor spoke first. "I'll come with you to see how Mrs. Wellington is now if that is suitable." He picked up his bag from near the chair.

"Er … yes, please … of course, Doctor, follow me." Bridie turned to the policeman. "Thank you, Officer Rogers. Will you find your way out?"

183

"Yes thanks, Miss Bridie, I'll duck over to the stables, if that is alright with you. I want to check on Sanders' report on this incident. He was with me when we found the tutor."

Bridie was at the point where she could only nod her head. She led the doctor to her grandmother's room.

When the doctor entered, the nurse rose and approached the bedside.

The doctor listened to Anna's chest and stepped back.

"I am sorry, Colonel, it seems your wife is nearing the end. There's nothing more we can do except make her comfortable.

Bridie stepped forward to take the weeping Odette into her arms. "Hush, child, hush."

That night as she lay in bed half asleep waiting for the inevitable call from the nurse, Bridie realized this was the first time since she witnessed David's burial in the village churchyard that she felt able to visit his gravesite again.

Daylight was still several hours away when Bridie felt the hand shake her shoulders. The nurse's soft voice brought her to wakefulness.

"Miss Bridie, your grandmother is close to passing."

Her eyes were still closed as her legs swung over the side of the bed. With her last arm still finding its way into the sleeve of her dressing gown, Bridie opened the door to her grandmother's room. Her gaze swung towards this woman who had been a mother to her since her birth. *When had Grandmama become this frail old lady? She was always a driving force in my life.* Tears threatened to spill, yet her sorrow ran so deep it seemed impossible to cry.

Bridie's gaze then turned to see Grandpa in his chair by the bed. He obviously had not moved since she bade him goodnight late last night. She walked over and leant down to wrap her arms around his shoulders. At that moment, Odette entered the room – her step tentative.

Bridie reached an arm out to this young woman, who was like a sister rather than a niece. Odette ran to join her great-grandpa and her aunt at the bedside. Her feelings also ran deep as she gazed, almost in disbelief, at the woman who had mothered her since she was two years of age.

It was Bridie who asked, "Grandpa, have you had any sleep? You did not go to bed like you said you were going to do, did you?"

"I could not leave her alone, my dear. We have never been apart since I returned from the army. I do not know how I will manage without her by my side. She opened her eyes and looked at me as she took her last breath. My sweet Anna knew I was here."

Bridie swallowed the lump in her throat. "Grandpa, will you let me take you to your bed now? Try to catch a little sleep. Once the news gets out to our people, and then the village, there will be little sleep to be had for some time, I should imagine."

William Wellington sighed a deep and lingering sigh.

"You are right, Bridie, my love, but it is hard to accept the golden chains that held us together are gone." He started to rise. Bridie helped to lift him from the chair. With Odette supporting one arm and Bridie the other, they escorted him to the bed in the next room.

"Sleep, Grandpa," they advised in whispers.

Colonel William Wellington sat with jaws clenched, his face pale, in the front pew of the village church. Bridie Mayford and Odette Mayford sat on either side of him, their black silk weeping veils hiding the errant tears streaming down their faces. At intervals, white handkerchiefs were surreptitiously raised to mop their cheeks. Behind the family sat the staff of the manor, while against the wall stood the four pallbearers; Mr. Axel, Sanders, Jimmy Braydon, and Peter Treloar standing in for Donald Turner the veterinarian.

The church pews were filled and many mourners stood in three layers against the walls. Other folk who could not fit inside the church crowded on the narrow verandah outside to peer through the windows.

Bridie felt her sorrow for the loss of her grandmother blend with the loss she felt for her lover David Lewis, even though so many years separated the two. Knowing now there was no doubt he did not fall, but had been pushed from the cliff, allowed her to finally say goodbye to her lover. The service passed as if in a dream. Several times she clutched her grandfather's upper arm when he sucked in a rasping breath.

When the last organ chord to the final hymn vibrated throughout the church, the four pallbearers moved over to lift the coffin from the table at the front of the congregation. Feet shuffled as the people rose from their seats. William Wellington, with Bridie and Odette on either side, led the slow procession down the aisle and outside to where the coffin, with the efforts of the pallbearers, slid up onto the floor of a wooden dray. With Mr. Axel at the reins, the four dark horses pulling the dray which carried Anna Wellington's coffin and the bearers, led off in the direction of Clawhaven Manor, to wait for the colonel and his granddaughters at the family vault.

William Wellington felt as if he floated several feet above his body watching himself thanking everyone and making polite conversation with the minister and villagers who had gathered to farewell his wife.

He appreciated Bridie and Odette's company, one at each side. He reached over to his girls and patted their arms to remind them, they were not alone either. Their wan smiles strengthened his own resolve.

Eventually, the three climbed into their carriage to follow Anna to her final resting place.

On the ninth day of April 1892, the casket holding Anna Margaret Wellington became a new addition to the family vault with only the immediate family, pallbearers and other of the servants from the house, who had been unable to attend the church service due to duties in the preparation of the wake, present.

Spring 1893

Since they buried their grandmama last year, Bridie and Odette were determined to ensure one or the other was always within calling distance of their grandfather. Both women felt concerned at his deepening despondency since her passing. Today, it was Bridie's turn to leave the house and go riding with the groom Jimmy Braydon.

"Jimmy, you are as good a company as a burr in the saddle. What is bothering you?" Bridie paused when she realized his droopy lip might have something to do with the sparkling eyes of their cook, Rosa. She had seen the pair, on more than one occasion, canoodling in the orchard of an evening. "Has the beautiful Rosa upset you? Should I send her packing?"

Jimmy's head swung around. "Oh, no, please don't do that, Miss Bridie."

"Well, give me a smile then."

Jimmy's infectious grin sent them both into fits of laughter.

"So, Jimmy, what has you in such a gloomy mood? Will she not marry you?"

"Oh yes, she'll do that alright, but they be wantin' a joint weddin'."

"Now you have lost me, Jimmy. Who wants a joint wedding?"

"It's Mrs. Dempsey see, Rosa's mum. She doesn' have a lot of money being a widow and all. She canny afford a weddin' for Rosa and herself separately."

"Herself, what are you saying, is she planning on marrying too?"

"Oh my, you are far behind, Miss. I canny blame you – with all you have on your mind lately. Her and Sanders be a couple, these days." Jimmy paused as if choosing his words. "Sanders is not the sullen, prickly bloke I thought him to be. He just be a man of few words, who happens to have a straight face. I'd hate to play cards with him, I know that. A bit of a loner is all."

"I cannot turn my back on you lot for five minutes and see what happens. Well, what is all the pother? Why not a joint wedding to save money? After which, you and your sweet Rosa can live in the gardener's cottage now that Mr. Baines has retired. It is big enough, is it not?"

"Yes, yes, Miss Bridie, I was told to ask you if that was allowed. And Sanders has bought a small cottage opposite Mr. Axel's house. It be the stone cottage with the crooked chimney on that odd-shaped corner this side of the stream on my mother's farm. He be out fixin' it every spare moment he has."

"Jimmy, that is lovely. Mary will be so happy to have a neighbour so close, for company. So, why all the misery?" Bridie paused thinking about this new organization of the staff at Clawhaven. "I will discuss it with Grandpa this evening. Maybe we can pay for the cost of a wedding feast at the village hall as our gift to both couples. If we have the cricket wives cater, we will pay for the food, and they will earn money for the cricket club. I understand they need a new scoreboard at the hut. I will ask him about that also."

"Thank you, Miss Bridie." For once Jimmy found himself at a loss for words.

Bridie kicked up her horse and called back over her shoulder, "Well, come on then, slow coach, I was hoping to get back home before dark."

When the subject was broached with William Wellington three days later, he agreed with a proviso.

"It will need to be a subdued affair so soon after your grandmother's funeral, Bridie. I most certainly cannot attend. Even you and Odette will need to keep a low profile because you are still in mourning."

"Yes, Grandpa, I understand." She felt as if a knife buried itself into her heart. Bridie bit down on the urge to remind her grandfather twelve months had now passed since Grandmama died, but how could she steal another level of his confidence?

Later as Bridie sat in the morning room planning everything, Odette arrived in the doorway securing the last pins into her hair.

"Good morning, Odette, did you have a nice ride this morning? It is rather late."

"Oh yes, Peter, er … Mr. Treloar, is checking over the new foal in the stables. Jimmy is well. He told me a hundred times to say thank you for the wedding feast. Even Sanders grinned a thank-you. The shock of his grin almost set me into a fit of the vapours." Odette gave a cheeky grin of her own.

"So, Mr. Peter Treloar visited, not Mr. Turner. Your Peter seems to have a lot of calls to make here lately."

Odette bowed – her face red. Bridie hid a smile.

One evening a week later, William stormed into the library where Bridie sat reading the latest papers.

"This place is a mad house. I went to the kitchen to order a warm milk drink. I found the women all fussing about at the table with sewing needles and yards of material spread all over the chairs."

"It is for the joint wedding next week, Grandpa. Remember I told you?"

William's face went blank for a moment before he looked up. "Yes, yes of course I remember. I just hope we are going to get fed somewhere between now and then."

Bridie smiled. "I will go and fix you a hot toddy. Now, you make your way up to bed and I will bring it up myself."

Spring blossoms weighed down the branches. Petals carpeted the churchyard. The two couples, Rosa and Jimmy on the left and Sally Dempsey and Sanders on the right faced the Rector, following his prompts as the ceremony progressed.

Bridie and Odette, dressed in subdued clothing with their heads covered in dark crepe, sat in a front pew. On Bridie's left, a gentleman separated two women, neither of which were much older than Odette. They were the married daughters of Sally Dempsey and the sisters of Rosa. After having been introduced to the group earlier, Bridie invited them to join her and Odette. Meg, and her husband Bill McLeish, a groundsman, lived in Southampton. The other sister was Patsy Chambers from Portsmouth. Her husband, a farmhand, was unable to attend. The remainder of the church was taken up with the staff of Clawhaven Manor and Estate, the members of the cricket club, and several of the local rural community.

Bridie's face slipped into a grin at the sight of Jimmy all spruced up. Her thoughts ran back to when she first met him. *When did Jimmy turn into this tall, muscled man? It does not seem that long since his skinny limbs scrambled up the side of his horse, Flyer.* Her sharp eyes did not miss the few grey hairs now resident at his temple. *He is only thirty-three years of age. He is five years younger than me.* She struggled to concentrate on the ceremony and not think about the urge she had to search for any hidden grey hairs on her own head.

Across the aisle, Jimmy's mother Teresa Braydon, and his aunt Eleanor, stood proud, while his sister and two brothers nudged and grinned at each other.

Jimmy shuffled his restless feet pulling at his collar and generally fidgeting like a dog with fleas. Rosa, wearing a slim pale blue frock sweeping wide at the ankles, nudged him in the ribs at regular intervals. Her mother, Sally Dempsey dressed in a soft grey, but similar styled frock to her daughter's, kept her head lowered as she clasped Sanders' elbow with a grip that threatened to break his arm.

When the preacher spoke Sanders' full name, Bridie and Odette exchanged surprised glances. Later, as they climbed into the carriage taking them home, with Peter Treloar at the reins, Odette whispered to Bridie, "Did you know that?"

"What," Bridie covered a grin, "Sanders' real name?"

Odette nodded her head, her eyes twinkling, "What a mouthful, Alexander Mayford Douglas Wales, no wonder he just tells people to call him Sanders." Her smile turned to confusion, "but how come he has Mayford for a Christian name too – and Douglas?"

Bridie sat silent for a moment, deep in thought. *I remember Grandmama mentioning he and my father had some connection, but I have no idea how or where.* Her thoughts took her back to that dreadful day when they brought David's body back to the manor. She recalled the later conversation after the funeral when they discussed the possibility of her father having something to do with his death. She bit her lip. They had been wrong. The policeman discovered indisputable evidence from the murderer himself. Tutor Bacon as much as confessed. She shook her head slightly as if to shake away any other thoughts on the subject.

When Peter helped them step down from the carriage, Bridie asked him if he would like to join them in a cup of tea or perhaps something stronger.

"Grandpa would benefit from a little company, if you have the time, Mr. Treloar."

Peter grinned; a soft flush swept over Odette's bowed face. When she glanced up her eyes glowed with pleasure.

"Thank you, Miss Bridie, I would like that very much. I'll just unharness the horses first."

Bridie led Odette inside, where everything was unusually silent. The staff were away for the celebrations of the weddings.

"Aunt Bridie, Bridie," Odette remembered her aunt's request about dropping the 'aunt,' "Thank you for inviting Peter in for a drink. As you hardly know the difference between a wood stove and an ice box in the kitchen, I will go and sort the drinks, while you see if Grandpa will join us."

"Just be grateful Rosa and Mrs. Dempsey …," Bridie stopped speaking. "Oh dear, we will need to remember she is now Mrs. Sanders." Bridie made a mental note not to make such a mistake in front of her housekeeper. "What I was going to say is, we can be grateful neither of the brides are planning on being away for more than three days, and we have Mrs. Padgett from the village filling in during that time. At least you will not be commandeered into the kitchen full-time."

Odette smiled. "I don't know, I rather enjoy helping Rosa in the kitchen. I remember when I was very little how Mrs. Ogilvie taught me how to cook a few things."

Winter - February 1894

At the sound of the knock on the library door, Bridie looked up from the book of maps she had been studying.

"Yes, Mrs. Sanders, come in."

"We have visitors, Miss Bridie. I think it is Mr. Mayford's carriage."

At that moment, the front doorbell clanged throughout the manor.

"Send whoever it is into the parlour, I will be out in a moment." When Mrs. Sanders left, closing the door softly behind her, Bridie mumbled, "Why can't my brother have the good manners to send us some warning of his arrival." Bridie stood up and walked to the far end of the table to where her grandpa sat snoozing in his favourite chair. The date above the headline on the newspaper on his lap caught her eye. She felt surprised; it was already the first day of February of 1894. She touched his arm gently. "Grandpa, are you awake?"

"I am now, Bridie, what is it?"

"It seems we may have brother George at the door. He must be in a hurry to be out travelling when the snows are only just easing off."

Mrs. Sanders returned to advise Bridie that Mr. George and Mr. Edward Mayford had arrived. They were now ensconced in the parlour and she was on her way to order morning tea for their guests.

"Did you want to see them, Grandpa?"

"I am not so old I cannot meet our visitors, Bridie. Do not fuss now." William forced a wry smile.

Bridie smiled in return as she helped William to rise from his deep chair. The weight of him on her arm surprised Bridie. She straightened up and leaned in closer. They made slow progress across the foyer and into the parlour. They stood aside to allow Mrs. Sanders to place the tea tray on the low table.

George and Edward rose to their feet as Bridie entered the room. Bridie did not miss the raised eyebrows of her brother and her nephew at the sight of her grandpa's tentative step.

"How do you do, gentlemen? This is a surprise." Suspicion lurked in Bridie's gaze.

She helped William into a chair and began to pour the tea.

193

"Please be seated, George...," She then nodded to Odette's elder brother, "... Edward. Now, how do you take your tea?"

Once everyone was settled with their refreshments, it was George who offered condolences and apologies to his grandfather.

"Sorry to hear of Grandmama's passing last year, Grandpa. We were unable to make it to the funeral in time."

William grunted and sipped at his teacup.

George turned to his sister. "How are you coping, Bridie? I guess much of Grandmama's work has fallen onto your shoulders."

Bridie cast a wary glance at her brother. She had learnt a long time ago never to trust her father and now she intended never to place any faith in her brother's motives. Bridie cast her glance towards Edward.

"Edward, I do not think we have had the pleasure of your company at Clawhaven."

"This is my first visit, Aunt Bridie. I am running the shipping company now. Father has stepped aside."

"Goodness me, how old are you? Oh yes, you must be twenty-two or is it three?"

"Twenty-two, Grandfather Mayford took me under his wing before I was thirteen."

George sat up higher in his chair and addressed his sister, "Remember our father was only twenty-one when he had to take up the reins of the company. Edward is doing a sterling job, Bridie."

Bridie did not miss the pride that shone in George's eye for all to see as he looked at his son, but the sight of a shadow of something she could not fathom skulked in the depths, and sent a jolt through her stomach.

"I am pleased to hear you have the company running smoothly, Edward." Bridie glanced over to see her grandfather's eyelids drooping. A worried frown was quickly dispersed. "How is your mother managing these days?"

Edward at least had the decency to squirm in his seat a little before he answered.

"I have no idea. She remains locked up in her own quarters and I have never been invited."

"Oh," Bridie was left short of words.

George took up the conversation. "Where is young Odette? I hear she goes riding each morning."

Bridie struggled not to flinch. She hoped today was not a day when Odette was out riding with Peter Treloar.

"Yes, we take it in turns to get out of the house for a little each day."

"Perhaps she might like to return to Blue Seas and run the house in London now she is older."

Bridie's suspicions hung thick in the room like the smoke from a hearth with a blocked flue.

"George, Odette still has nightmares about her first two years at Blue Seas House. She spends her time doing her best not to think about her London home."

Edward butted in, "She is a Mayford and must do what is right by her family."

Bridie saw William stir in his chair. She bit hard on her lip before she replied.

"Edward, there is a good lesson your great-grandfather taught me, which you may find useful. 'It is the wise man who knows he will get more from his beast of burden with a carrot than he will with a stick.'" Bridie drew a deep breath and swallowed the sour taste in her mouth before going on. "Some things can only be learnt from experience, but I am sure you have already discovered this being astute as you are."

"What would you know, Aunt Bridie? You are only a woman. I do not need you to tell me how to run our business. Nor do I need those women's rights people sprouting their rubbish in the streets and newspapers every day."

Bridie's disgust cleared the room of suspicion. She now knew exactly how the land lay. For all that, it was George who spoke first.

"You are right, Bridie. Edward still has a lot to learn and patience may be the thing most sadly lacking. I am sorry we have missed Odette," he turned to William who sat with eyes closed, "I see Grandpa is not too well today. We will depart. There are a few friends I wanted to see in town before we begin the journey home."

Edward went to interrupt, but George silenced him with a glare.

Odette was in fact, not too far away. She and Peter pulled their mounts to a stop in the orchard. They dismounted and moved to kiss each other goodbye when Rosa came flying out through the back door.

"Miss Odette," she whispered loudly, "your father and brother are inside. They appear to be just rising to leave."

Odette caught Peter's hand and led him and the horses behind the shelter of the hawthorn hedge dividing the laundry shed and the orchard.

"What is going on?" Confusion filled Peter's eyes. "This might be a good time to talk to your father."

"Hush, my dear, I suspect there is no such thing as a good time to talk to my father or my brother."

"B-b-but …," Odette covered Peter's lips with her own.

Ten minutes later, Rosa appeared at the back doorway with a grin on her face.

"All clear, they've gone," she called softly.

Bridie watched the coach disappear down the track in a cloud of dust. She turned on her heel and made her way to the parlour, where Grandpa was in the process of struggling to his feet.

"I find that young pup of George's objectionable," he complained, as he straightened up with his hand resting on the sideboard.

"I will not argue with you there, Grandpa."

"I wonder who these people are George calls 'friends' that he wants to see around this district."

"He seems to know a lot about what we are up to, I think."

"Whatever it is, I think we might be advised to keep an eye on Odette and Peter. I do not want a repetition of what happened to David."

"Grandpa, he would not, would he? I find that hard to believe of George."

"George may have some scruples, but I would put nothing past that whelp of his."

Bridie spent much of the remainder of the day pondering over the early visitors and the conversation of the morning. The pain at the loss of David Lewis flowed back to fill her heart and soul. Had she accepted the evidence, as mentioned by Officer Rogers, of Tutor Bacon's journal, too easily? Had her father and his friends been involved somehow? Were her father's friends, the friends George spoke of this morning? She tried to remember those names her grandmother had mentioned as people of interest. Had the tutor been one of her father's spies? Had there been more people here at Clawhaven Estate, or even in the village, who reported back to her father and now to George and/or her nephew Edward? One of Sanders' Christian names was Mayford. How did he fit in? Bridie shrugged, unwilling to believe he could be involved in any way.

"Oh, this is all too much." Bridie tied the scarf holding her hat tight on her head and slipped into her outdoor shoes. She walked out through the back doorway and strode off through the orchard towards the beachfront.

Bridie's footsteps climbed the path to the cliff allowing the sea breezes, whipping up the wavelets, to sweep the swirling questions from her mind. She felt a peace descend upon her as she sat on the rock where she and David had spent so many wonderful hours making plans for their future. How young and innocent she was then.

The weeks passed. The spring draped the countryside in its beauty. It came and went, but always the question of the Mayford men and their ambitions hovered at the back of Bridie's mind. One Saturday afternoon, while watching Odette and Grandpa engrossed in a game of chess, it broke her heart to see her once alert and intelligent grandfather now becoming more and more forgetful and slower to dredge up any memory. On several occasions, she became aware of his reading a newspaper repeatedly, as if not realizing it had already been read once.

Bridie slipped away from the chess players in the library and made her way to the back door. She changed her shoes and threw a light jacket around her shoulders against the summer showers. She secured her bonnet to her head. As she stepped out into the sunshine muted by swift-moving clouds above, she drew in a deep breath of fresh air and began to walk.

Bridie noticed Sanders on the track with his back against the beech hedge protecting the stables. He stared out across the pastures where the black Angus cattle grazed peacefully. There was something in his stature that brought her father to mind. All her questions about her father exploded in her head. This was a perfect opportunity to seek answers.

"Penny for your thoughts, Sanders."

He drew himself to attention and tossed the reins, hanging loose in his hand, over his shoulder.

"Good afternoon, Miss Bridie, a lovely day for a brisk walk."

"It is that, Sanders. Nothing like a chill air to clear one's tangled thoughts."

"Now, what thoughts would you be having that require untangling?"

"You know, Sanders, you may be able to solve something that has bothered me for years."

"Me, solve your tangled thoughts, how can I do that?"

Bridie paused, trying to word her question in a way so as not to upset the man whom she had always admired.

"Sanders, you knew my father, didn't you?"

"Yes, Miss, I did."

"Was he an honourable man?"

Sanders' eyebrows rose high on his forehead. "Miss Bridie, I am sure he must have been."

"I asked, was he?"

Sanders scratched his head. "Where is this going, Miss Bridie?"

"I am asking, do you think my father was capable of doing something underhanded, illegal, maybe even order a murder?"

Sanders sucked in a deep breath, which set up a coughing attack.

"Oh, Miss, I can't say I knew him that well. Whose murder are we talking about?"

"That of David Lewis for a start." A frown brought Bridie's eyebrows almost together. "And do you think he might have ordered the murder of Tutor Bacon?"

"As far as I am aware the police have never worked out who killed the tutor, but I do know he attracted enemies like salted meat when cooking will attract flies." Sanders tugged at his ear. He swallowed his own suspicions on what parent or parents in the village may have had every reason to kill the fellow.

Sanders would have given anything to have his pipe in his hand right at this moment, but it had been left at home out of his sight, thanks to the encouragement of his wife.

"Officer Rogers told you of the confession found in Tutor Bacon's journal, didn't he?"

"Yes, he did, but why would the man want to kill David, if it wasn't at someone else's bidding?"

Sanders' coughing attack returned. He cursed silently. *Didn't the copper tell her of the unhealthy attraction Bacon had for her and his jealousy of David? What on earth am I going to say now?*

Before Sanders was able to think of an answer to this question, Bridie posed another.

"I noticed one of your names is Mayford. Did you know my father, Sanders?"

"Now wait a minute, Miss Bridie. I had nothing to do with David's death."

"I believe you, Sanders, but did you know my father?"

Sanders gasped and shuffled his feet in the dirt. He cleared his throat a few times before the words fell out uncensored.

"Your father was my father, Miss Bridie. He had an illicit love affair with my mother, and I was the result. He ensured I had an education to university level and paid for my commission into the army. The only thing was I did something foolish and would have been drummed out with a dishonourable discharge, but Douglas Mayford did a deal with the Colonel, and I retired with my reputation intact."

"What dishonourable deed?"

"I… er… the er… lieutenant found me in bed with his wife."

"Hmmm, the apple did not fall far from the tree."

Sanders looked up with almost a smile on his face. "That is what Douglas Mayford said when he was told." He quickly removed the smile and went on, "Miss Bridie, there are few men who can say they have always been honourable men, and I would think in the shipping industry that might apply more so. It is a hard industry filled with hard men. A man had to be hard to survive."

"But murder? Would my father be capable of murder?" Bridie stopped for a moment, then, "either directly or indirectly?"

Sanders stood watching the cattle as if he had not heard. Bridie was almost ready to repeat the question, when Sanders spoke.

"I think Douglas Mayford was capable of many things. I know he blackmailed me to have me settle in up here." Sanders saw Bridie open her mouth ready to jump in again with more questions, but he went on, "I think he loved you in his own way. He planted me here to make sure you were safe. I was instructed to report on visitors who came and went. If at any time I thought you were in danger, I was to do whatever was necessary to keep you safe. If I refused, he threatened to have the honourable discharge turn into a dishonourable one." Sanders paused, thinking back on those early days at Clawhaven. "I wasn't too happy at first, looking after a pint-sized precocious midget. I craved the streets of London." Before Bridie interrupted, he went on again. "I soon realized I rather liked it here and I quickly learnt Douglas was happy just for me to be here. I only ever saw him a handful of times as you grew up. Mind you, there was never anything untoward to report anyway. Your grandparents were wonderful people to you and the staff."

This time Bridie threw her question into the ring before Sanders could go on.

"What about Alec Bacon-Dowd, did you know him, Sanders?"

Sanders' eyes narrowed. "You mean Douglas's secretary? Yes, I did. He was a man who would as soon cut your throat as shake your hand. He was killed in a dockyard brawl a few weeks after Douglas died, I understand."

"Why did you not leave when Father died?"

"Why would I want to? I had a job I enjoyed and the lights of London had faded in my mind by that time." Sanders considered how much he should say about Tutor Bacon's death, but decided to take the policeman's easy path. "Miss Bridie, I had little love for my father, but I believe strongly that he had nothing to do with the death of David Lewis. Maybe Tutor Bacon was jealous of your happiness, or maybe he never forgave your grandfather for his ignoble dismissal."

"Do you not feel resentful of my father because he never included you in his business? You were his son after all."

"An illegitimate son, Miss Bridie, and therefore with no entitlements." Sanders gave a sharp chuckle. "Anyway, I'm a horseman first and foremost. What do I know or care about ships and the sea? Besides, he loved your mother beyond all else, and I would never want the world to know of my own mother's indiscretion."

Winter - January 1895

"I thought you must have gone for a walk, Grandpa. I looked everywhere for you," Bridie opened the music room door further and entered. Her gaze cast about the room taking in the hot coals at the fireplace, the view of a light snow falling seen through the gap in the window curtains, and the undisturbed dust cover over Grandmama Wellington's piano.

William turned and smiled a rueful smile. "Not everywhere then, lass. I think my walks on the beach may have come to an end, my dear, don't you?" A trembling hand slapped at his chest when the wheeze stole his speech for a moment.

"What are you looking at, Grandpa?"

"I cannot remember the snow being so deep on the front drive before. Not since your grandmother and I first settled here when my father was failing."

Bridie moved over to wrap her arm around his shoulders. "Would you like to sit down and I'll play some of Grandmama's favourite pieces?"

"I would love to hear the piano in use again, Bridie."

Bridie assisted her grandfather into his comfortable chair, the one in which he used to sit for hours listening to Anna playing. Bridie removed the dust cover from the piano, opened the keyboard and ran her fingers lightly up and down the ivories. In silence, she admonished herself for not realizing how Grandpa must have missed his wife's music throughout the house. She promised herself not to be so thoughtless in the future. The idle scales evolved into a selection of the musical scores learnt at her grandmother's knee. She glanced up when Odette entered the room and sat in the chair beside Grandpa.

It seemed only minutes had passed when Mrs Sanders arrived at the door to inform the family lunch was served. Bridie looked up in surprise. She slid her bottom around on the piano seat.

"Grandpa, will you have some lunch with us today? You have been eating like a sparrow lately."

Grandpa's head drooped onto his chest.

"I did not think I had been playing any lullabies, Grandpa." Bridie smiled.

It was the expression on Odette's face when she turned towards her grandfather that alerted Bridie to the fact something was not right. Odette's mouth hung agape, her eyes stretched wide and her hesitant hand reached up to touch his shoulder.

"Grandpa, are you awake?" Odette gave a gentle shake. Grandpa's hand dropped onto his lap from where the bony fingers had been tangled in his shirt.

"Noooo," Odette covered her mouth to suffocate the scream threatening to escape.

Bridie rushed to her side and held her tight. Both ladies stared down at their grandfather's lifeless body. Mrs. Sanders found them there fifteen minutes later, when she came looking to remind them lunch was served.

"I'll have Mr. Axel send the stable boy for the doctor, that is if the road is at all passable. I think we should have Sanders and Jimmy set up a temporary bed in the next room to lay the master on."

Bridie shook herself. "Thank you, Mrs. Sanders, that will be a very good idea." She felt as if her world had ceased. Bridie's mind found it hard to accept her grandfather was dead. The confusion settled into the weight of a boulder in her chest. It seemed only yesterday that they buried her grandmother. Her gaze turned to her niece. "Are you alright, Odette? We must help prepare the bed for Grandpa. It will make things so much easier for everyone." With unwilling legs, she forced herself into action.

It was the 31st of January 1895 when they installed William Wellington's coffin beside that of his wife in the vault on Clawhaven Estate. To Bridie and Odette, the days passed in a haze of disbelief. It seemed hard to comprehend that it had been nearly three years since they said their final farewells to Grandmama. With Peter Treloar, they walked back up to the manor hand in hand. The ache in their hearts deadened the chill of the snow on their feet through the thick socks and boots they wore.

It was Bridie who spoke first. "It is sad for us to say goodbye to Grandpa, but I think he welcomed the chance to be with his beloved Anna again." Her throat in spasm threatened to strangle the words. Tears almost froze on her cheeks.

Odette's eyes blinked furiously as she nodded her head. Peter clenched her hand tighter.

Mrs. Sanders and Rosa, with the help of the two housemaids, prepared nourishment set out in the parlour. After holding off all morning, as if out of respect for a good and honourable man, a light sprinkle of snow began to fall just when the numerous guests set off on their journey to their homes.

Mr. Birmingham and his secretary Mr. Burke, sat in the chairs opposite to where Bridie and Odette sat at the Colonel's large desk. Mr. Burke, a small vibrant man sat behind a mountain of papers with only his eyes peering over the top. Mr. Birmingham's slim fingers stroked the thick file headlined with the words The Last Will and Testament of William Anthony James Wellington.

"Miss Mayford," he spoke to Bridie, "other than gifts of appreciation to the long-time staff here at Clawhaven, the essence of this Will declares you as the sole beneficiary of William's fortune. He updated this Will several weeks after the passing of his wife. It contains the proviso that you continue to support and assist your niece Miss Odette Mayford until she reaches her maturity, after which she will receive a half partnership in everything during both your lifetimes. My cousin is a barrister in London specializing in the law around Women's Rights. He has perused this Will, at your grandfather's request, to ensure it has guaranteed only you two women will benefit in any way, which is possible following the Women's Property Rights twenty years ago."

At that moment, a knock on the door lifted the four heads. "Come in, Mrs, Sanders," Bridie called. She turned to the two visitors. "You will take refreshment, gentlemen?"

The housekeeper rested the tray on the side table. "Will I serve, Miss Bridie?"

"No, Mrs. Sanders, I will manage," Bridie smiled. "Thank you very much and thank Rosa too, please."

Once everyone sat with a cup of hot tea and buttered scones in front of them, Bridie discussed the specifics of Odette's upcoming twenty-first birthday and the threat of her brother's dominance over her rights and property. It was explained to them that unless Bridie had been made Odette's guardian officially, Odette would need her father's permission to marry, if she did so before turning twenty-one years of age.

When all the questions had been addressed, the men rose to leave.

"Please do not hesitate to let me know if there is anything else you wish clarified, ladies."

As Bridie and Odette escorted their guests to their carriage, Bridie's mind swirled with plans for them leading up to Odette's next birthday in just over twelve months.

Autumn 1895

Autumn leaves blew across the front driveway. On her return from the stables, Bridie, with her hand on the front door of the manor, turned at the sound of the horse's hooves. The mail deliverer Mr. Featherstone, dismounted from his white-footed gelding. Bridie stepped down from the patio to greet the postman and receive the mail. As Mr. Featherstone guided the horse back up the driveway,

Bridie flicked through the letters in her hand. The two with the postmark from Blue Seas House caught her eye. After examining the script, Bridie felt sure the one addressed to her was from her brother George, and the other one, addressed to Odette, she assumed to be from Edward or his secretary.

Odette stood at the now open doorway with a tray in one hand. "How is our mailman today?"

Bridie smiled, "He is in fine fettle, as usual. Where have you been this morning? I was about to come looking for you."

The two women entered the hall together. "I have been in the library reading Grandpa's diaries. He was no fool, was he Bridie?"

"No, Odette, nobody could call Grandpa a fool. Other than his time in the army, he spent most of his life here in the country, but his readings embraced the whole world and those people who inhabit it. Why do you say that?" Bridie shut the door behind them.

"Have you read them?"

"Some, but not all. I often told Grandpa he should write a book on his life, but he pretended not to hear." Bridie waved the two envelopes from Blue Seas House in front of Odette. "Come, let us go to the office and see what these are all about."

While Odette returned the tray to the kitchen, Bridie sat with the two envelopes in front of her as if reluctant to learn their content. When Odette entered to see Bridie procrastinating, she reminded her aunt of their grandfather's advice when faced with vegetables on their plate which they did not like to eat.

"Like Grandpa always said, Bridie, 'Eat the worst vegetables first, then you can really enjoy those that you favour.'"

"Did he ever mention what we should do if there was nothing on the plate that we really wanted to eat?" A wry grin accompanied her words.

"We will never know, while we sit here wondering."

Bridie's wry grin turned into a chuckle. "While ever you are alive, Odette, our Grandmama will never die." She took up the paper knife and passed it and the envelope addressed to Odette across to her. "You open your letter first. I suspect it is from your brother.

To Miss Odette Mayford

Dear Sister

Please accept the condolences to you and Aunt Bridie from everyone here at Blue Seas House on the loss of our great-grandfather.

You are nearing your twenty-first birthday and maturity next spring. I am sure you realize your duty now lies with the family company and will endeavour to support it in any way you can. With our father now semi-retired and I having taken responsibility for the running of the family company, I, on his behalf will therefore be responsible for the decisions in your life.

In that vein, I have taken the opportunity to seek a marriage which will appeal to you and improve the finances of the company.

One such candidate is an old school friend of mine who is amply provided with family funds and having met you briefly at church in Sussex recently has shown interest in asking for your hand in marriage. When the nuptials are completed, he will invest heavily in our company and become a full partner at the same time. You will remember Roger Armstrong as a pleasant fellow to look upon and a man with an agreeable personality to match.

I think it might be advisable to arrange this at your earliest opportunity – preferably before your birthday on the 30th of April next year. I would not like to see you experience the heartache our Aunt Bridie suffered years ago.

At this point, Odette sucked in a deep and noisy breath.

"I cannot believe the audacity of my brother." She glanced over the solicitations at the bottom of the page. "And will you look at that, he does not even know the date of my birthday – a fine brother."

"What audacity is that, Odette?" Bridie looked up – eyebrows raised. She reached over to take the letter her niece passed across the desk. Her gaze skimmed the written words.

"The foolish pup – he has hardly made any attempt to cover what can only be called an outright threat. Do you remember meeting this Roger Armstrong he mentions?"

A furrow deepened between Odette's eyebrows. "There were a few newcomers at church about six months ago. They seemed amiable, but I have no real recollection of them." She searched Bridie's face for answers. "What am I going to do, Bridie?"

"Firstly, let me assure you, I am sure Edward is overstating his responsibilities. Let us read what your father has to say in his letter, and if we do not have any joy with it, we will plan how to use Edward's ignorance of your birth date to outwit him."

"I assumed that might be a written error."

"Unlikely," Bridie offered, as she slit the second envelope.

Dear Bridie

I am hoping you will receive this epistle before the one Edward has been threatening to write for the past week, arrives at your doorstep. I am sure you will note an error in the day of Odette's birthday. I deliberately told him the 30th of April in the hope you may use the extra four weeks gained between the 1st and the 30th in outwitting his schemes for Odette's future.

I know you thought our father was an arrogant, hard-hearted and unkind man with few kind words for anyone. I am afraid to say my son is one hundred times worse. I wonder how I begat such a cruel and thoughtless man.

One other thing you may wish to discuss with your solicitor. I gave William sole guardianship of Odette when first she moved to Clawhaven as a baby. If that automatically returns to me, I now declare that guardianship is transferred to you, Bridie. Will you see this legally transferred at your earliest opportunity? I am afraid it is best not to send communication relating to this through usual channels – I know Edward examines all my incoming and outgoing correspondence. My personal attendant Graham Turnbull will ensure the safe delivery of correspondence to me. See his address below.

I owe Odette a deep apology for not having done more for her as a child, but I had full confidence in William and Anna Wellington, especially after the superb way they cared for you.

Your repentant brother who loves you both.

George.

Bridie noticed the address for Graham Turnbull at the bottom of the page. She handed the letter across to Odette.

"You will find this interesting."

Bride sat in deep thought while Odette absorbed her father's correspondence. She waited until Odette placed the epistle on the desk.

"I think a visit to Mr. Birmingham is called for. I will write a letter immediately and send Sanders to the village post office today before the mailbag goes."

CHAPTER EIGHT

Endings and Beginnings

1896

"Bridie, I love Peter very much and admire his work with the animals, but I wish he might arrive for dinner at the correct time. It is such bad manners to be tardy like this." With a snap, Odette flicked her table napkin open on her lap and smoothed it with a stroke of her hand. The candle lights flickered above the two candelabra, one on each end of the table.

"Peter's time is not his own, you know. Animals do not calve or foal to suit your mealtimes. They do not think to time their illnesses to suit your schedule. In fact, I think I can guarantee their problems will occur at the most inconvenient times."

Odette sighed. She took up her soup spoon and dipped it in the bowl of steaming soup in front of her.

"It seems an age since he was here. Mr. Turner was supposed to be back from London this week to take over the on-call work, but he has been delayed for some reason, and Peter is still working all the hours that God gives."

"I guess that is something one has to learn to live with if one chooses to love a veterinarian."

"When we are married, Peter will not have to work anymore. Mr. Turner will have to find another man to be his business partner."

Bridie's eyebrows lifted. A tolerant smile flittered over her lips.

"Have you discussed this with Peter?"

Odette had the grace to drop her gaze. "Well, no, not exactly. But I am sure he will agree when I tell him I will need him to be with me most of the time."

It was Bridie's turn to sigh. "Have you asked him why he became a veterinarian? It is how he earns an income. Maybe he loves his work. Maybe that is why he spent so many hours at the university to become a veterinary surgeon. Not all men …," At this point, Bridie paused in thought before continuing, "and women, go to university just to keep up appearances, or because their father pushes them into a career. Many people do so because they have a desire for knowledge of their chosen subject."

"I cannot remember." Odette swirled the soup in her plate with her spoon.

"As far as I can see, Peter loves his work. His facial expression reveals his satisfaction each time an animal that he has rescued returns to full health. You only need to see the devastation revealed when he is unable to save some other animal no matter how hard he tries."

Odette sipped her soup with little appreciation as she considered her aunt's advice.

"Am I being selfish?"

"I think you are being inexperienced. Perhaps you need to take more notice of the people around you, and what they do all day every day. I think you and Peter need to sit down and discuss what you both expect out of married life. Perhaps even discuss how you might make things easier for him."

Only the soft scrape of the metal cutlery on the china plates broke the silence for some time as Odette absorbed these words.

"How did you become so wise, Bridie?" Odette eventually spoke.

Bridie pressed the white, ironed table napkin to her lips.

"Observation," she tidied her napkin on her lap again, "and I like to read a lot." She smiled a gentle smile. "Most of any wisdom I may have has been thanks to Grandpa and Grandmama. Together their wisdom was never-ending."

Odette reached over to touch Bridie's hand. "Tonight, Peter was going to ask if you would approve of us being married."

Bridie clasped Odette's hand. "My dear, that is wonderful news. So, is the extra pink in your cheeks just excitement and not extra colouring?"

Pink turned to red as the blush rose on Odette's face.

A shudder ran through Bridie's limbs. A flash in her mind of a man's broken body lying in her aching arms – her man, David – filled her vision. A thin stream of diluted blood ran with the salt water from the shattered face. She felt again the cold water of the sea lapping about her legs as she sat in the shallows holding him tight – the last time she was able to hold him tight.

"Bridie, are you alright?" Odette spoke for the second time – her voice rang with an urgency.

Bridie shuddered again and looked up. "Sorry, dear." She sucked in a deep breath and sat higher in her chair. "Sorry, Odette, I am fine. 'The fairies must be walking in the graveyard tonight,' as Grandmama would say."

"You gave me quite a start. Your face turned red and then it went white, but now it is back to normal. Are you sure you are alright?"

"Yes, dear, I am fine."

At that moment, Mrs. Sanders entered the room with a plate of hot food in her hands and Peter Treloar at her side.

"I found this gentleman at the back door."

Odette's head snapped up – her eyes wide – her smile wider.

"Oh, Peter, you poor thing, you look tired." Odette turned to the housekeeper, "Thank you, Mrs. Sanders, Mr. Treloar will sit here next to me."

Peter took Odette's hand and kissed the palm. He turned to Bridie, "I apologize for being late. We had a cow and calf in trouble, but all is well now."

Bridie sighed. It surprised her to realize just how apprehensive she had become about his safety.

"Well done, Peter, now sit and eat, you must be ravenous."

"I am that, yes."

Odette chattered while Peter ate, only nodding his head when required.

Bridie's smile remained fixed on her face, but inside her, the anxiety swirled. Her heart thumped in her chest; her breath panted through her nostrils in an irregular rhythm. She placed her hands on her lap to hide the tremor and to prevent her knees from trembling. She struggled to squash the vision as it threatened to return.

"We really must do something to protect Peter." Her voice rushed out like water through a hole in a dam wall interrupting the conversation between the lovers. Their heads turned.

"Whatever do you mean?" Odette asked.

"Er … sorry … did I say that out aloud? I am sure I am only fussing."

Odette and Peter's confused gazes met.

"Odette, Peter, will you please excuse me? I really must do something. Will you join me in the library when you are finished here?"

Only five minutes behind, Peter followed Bridie into the library.

"Odette won't be too long; she has gone to organize drinks."

Bridie smiled as she indicated the chair on the opposite side of the table.

214

"Then you'd best make haste to say what you have to say."

Peter flushed. "It sounds like you may already know what it is I wish to ask."

"Well, you must admit Odette has been rather excited tonight. I see the way the pair of you look at each other."

Peter scratched his head.

"Sit down, Peter, you are giving me a crick in my neck having to look up at you."

The chair scraped on the polished wooden floorboards and Peter sat with his hands clasped in a strangle hold on the library table in front of him.

"Miss Mayford, as Odette's guardian until she turns twenty-one, will you give me permission to propose marriage to Miss Odette Mayford?"

"I should deny you permission just for being so formal and calling me Miss Mayford. Miss Bridie would have done just nicely, but then if you are to be my nephew-in-law, I guess you should just be calling me Bridie and be done with it."

Peter's face questioned her remark and his lips flashed a soft smile as he struggled to fathom the answer.

"Is that a yes, Bridie?"

"Odette would never forgive me if I refused you. Yes, Peter, that is a yes." The girl herself flew into the room her eyes sparkling. Bridie's eyebrows lifted. "Am I to assume you were eavesdropping on our conversation?" Her eyes rolled when her question went unanswered.

Odette wrapped Peter in her arms almost strangling him in the process.

"I told you, Peter. I told you Bridie would say 'yes,' didn't I? Can I see the ring now?"

Peter disentangled himself and stood. He delved into his right hip pocket and then bent to one knee.

"Odette Margaret Mayford, will you marry me?"

"Yes, yes, you silly." Odette almost had them both on the floor as she threw herself into Peter's arms. He dragged them upright. Odette stretched out her left hand and the tears flowed as Peter slipped the ring onto her finger. She held her hand up to stare in disbelief at the gold ring with a modest diamond surrounded by small amethysts. She slipped it off and held it across for Bridie to see the fine inscription inside. *Detta - Peter.* Bridie only glimpsed the words before Odette returned the ring to her finger. "I will never take this off," she vowed.

"I do hope you have drinks coming, Odette?" Bridie interrupted, "I think we need to seal this moment in time."

With drinks poured and toasts made they sat in silence around the library table.

"I do wish Grandmama and Grandpa were here to see this, Bridie."

"I am sure they are both right here in this room with us tonight, dear." Bridie padded at the tears leaking from her eyes. She could not have honestly said whether they were for Odette's happiness, or for her own regret at what she and David had missed, or for her sorrow at the loss of the two people who shaped her life.

"Odette, if you will put Peter down for a moment, I wish to talk to him."

With peace returned, Bridie's thoughts raced one way and then another, before she settled down and spoke.

"Peter, I know you will have the approval of my brother George, Odette's father, but her brother Edward, who runs the family company now, will be furious. Edward had his own plans to use Odette to lure an unsuspecting investor into the company. I was in a similar situation years ago. You may have heard of what happened to my fiancé at that time. I cannot blame Edward for that, he was much too young and we have had a man confess to the murder since, but I was never convinced that my father was not involved in some way. Young Edward reminds me so much of his grandfather who never liked to be beaten."

"Surely, in this day and age, such a thing is unthinkable, Bridie. We are almost into the twentieth century," Peter spoke with the assurance of the young.

"Odette will be twenty-one years of age on the first of April. Until then I will give my permission as her guardian. I believe the most dangerous time will be between Edward learning of your betrothal and her turning twenty-one. Please do not think for one minute that because he lives in London, he has no idea of what goes on in this district. We know the Mayford family has friends here in the village. I want you to always be on the alert and avoid strangers. I have been thinking about this for a long time and have considered moving us all to another country."

"Bridie, you cannot think Peter is in danger?"

"Never did I think David was at risk either, until it was too late. We cannot be too complacent. Grandpa and Grandmama often discussed who might be the spy here at Clawhaven passing information back to London." Bridie stopped to sip her wine, while she watched the glances passing between the betrothed couple. "Once the staff has retired, I will show you something, Peter. Who knows, it might come in handy one day."

At the sound of Rosa's voice calling goodnight to her mother and the rumble of the horse and dog cart driven by Sanders leaving with his wife, Bridie turned to Odette.

"Will you bring our coats from the back door and collect Peter's coat also, dear? We will be in the office."

Curiosity hastened Odette's feet.

217

Picking up the lamp, Bridie led Peter to the office next door. She placed the lamp on the table and thought to check the oil level in the bowl. When Odette arrived with the coats, Bridie slipped into hers and waited while Odette and Peter donned their jackets.

"At this time of night, it will be cold where we are going."

Peter and Odette shared questioning glances, but neither knew what Bridie was up to.

"Slip your hand in behind this book, Peter," she directed him to feel behind the solid tome on *Good Manners in the Nineteenth Century*, "can you feel that lever behind the thin block of wood that holds the book in its place?"

At first, Peter looked blank, and then his grey eyes lit up in the lamplight. "Here, Sweetheart, feel there." He moved aside for Odette to find the secret lever.

It was Bridie who instructed her niece, "Push it gently upwards, Odette. It does not need too much pressure."

Peter gasped and Odette gave a sharp cry when the panel between the bookcase and the corner swung open. With her lamp in her hand, Bridie led the way into the space in the wall behind the office. Odette and Peter followed.

"Sorry, this is a tight squeeze with the three of us. There always seemed ample room before."

Bridie showed them both the ledge with the emergency candles and flint before leading them down the stone stairs and into the tunnel true.

"Good grief, what is this place?" Peter asked.

"How long have you known this tunnel was here, Bridie?" Odette questioned.

"I discovered it when I was seven years of age. I found it by accident. Grandpa knew all about it and showed me how he maintained the swinging panels."

As the trio moved deeper into the tunnel, the cool air caused Odette to shiver.

"I do not think I would like to be here without a coat. It is so cold."

When they came to the T-piece, Peter wanted to know where the second tunnel went.

"It leads to the old dairy. In generations gone by, I guess it gave the family two options for escape if the need arose."

The lamp light flickered shadows against the rough stone walls as they moved through the narrow space. After ten minutes passed, with only the sound of their shoes on the stone floor and the heavy breathing, it was Odette who asked, "Is this ever going to end, it feels like we have been down here for ages."

Peter moved closer to her and held her hand. "Don't be afraid, Detta dear, I'm sure Bridie knows what she is doing."

It was only a short time later they reached the bottom of the stairs leading up to the hidden chamber behind the angel in the coffin room. Once again Bridie made both Peter and Odette find and touch the release lever to open the panel. She led them through the gap. Odette gave a soft squeal as the panel closed softly.

"This is the family vault." Bridie glanced over to send a silent nod of respect to the coffins of her grandparents. "We cannot delay because I do not want anyone who may be wandering around in the forest outside to report strange lights coming from the vault." Bridie led them to the door that opened out onto the edge of the forest and explained how to open it from the inside. She then showed them how to twist the angel statue's arm to open the panel again. She pointed out the candles and flint available on the ledge in this chamber also.

"Oh, can we go back now, Bridie? I am scared in this place."

"Yes, dear, we will go back now. I just wanted Peter to know this is here, in case one day the need arises."

"Are you trying to warn my fiancé off, Bridie?"

"No, dear, but I am trying to impress upon both of you to be prepared for anything and everything."

Once again only the shuffle of their feet on the floor was heard above their breathing as they walked the approximate five hundred yards back to the house.

March 1896

The early buds dotted the foliage in front of the dairy as Sanders called goodbye to Mr. Axel. He rode tall in the saddle on Copper, the large horse he used to steady his geldings-in-training. Following on the lead in single file were the two latest thoroughbreds – their coats freshly brushed to the sheen of polished bronze. Birds in full chorus darted through the branches of the trees, as they threw off the winter chill and announced the beginning of springtime.

When the small procession turned the corner between his own house and that of the estate manager, Sanders waved to Mary Axel who supervised her two sons as they collected firewood for the stove.

"Good morning, Mister Sanders," the lads called.

"Morning." If Sanders was going to speak any further, he changed his mind at the sight of the two strangers approaching in the distance. The pair moved apart to ride one on either side of the road which would force Sanders to ride between them. Sanders' eyes narrowed. He slowed his animals, speaking softly to them as the newly broken pair threatened to take offence at these newcomers. Sanders took in the approaching two men. The one riding the bay horse and wearing a sharp hat like those worn by the men in the city would pass on his right. Despite his face being in shadow, he knew him to be young, and vaguely familiar. The nose of the large, broad, hatless man on the grey horse lay twisted between eyebrows distorted by multiple scars. He wore a sour expression; the kind Sanders had seen on many men within the British army in his younger days – bullies every one of them. As the distance between those facing the east and himself facing the west lessened, his gaze flicked back to the city man and recognized him to be the type of man he would never gamble with. This was a man most likely to carry a knife or even a Derringer up his sleeve to be used if things were not going his way. Sanders felt annoyed at not recalling the fellow's name or where he had met him previously. He knew he should. His nerve endings tingled.

Sanders' face remained expressionless when the pair pulled their horses to a stop. He sat loose in the saddle with his right hand lightly on the reins of his mount and his left hand holding the lead rein on his left thigh.

It was the city man who spoke first.

"Sanders is it not? My name is Edward Mayford of the Mayford Shipping Company."

As soon as the name Mayford was mentioned, Sanders realized who addressed him, but his expression never gave anything away despite the thoughts running through his head. *So, this is George's whelp, all grown up and every bit as bad as, if not worse than, his grandfather, I'd be judging.*

He let himself go limp and sagged in the saddle. His voice changed to his scrambled version of the countryman's dialect.

"Oh, yes, you be related to Miss Bridie of the Clawhaven Estate." He paused and nearly choked in saying the next word, "Sir." It was Colonel Wellington's advice to him many years ago when he was wont to go off half-cocked, that caused him to hold his tongue. *Something I learned a long time ago in the army, Sanders, there is more than one way to kill the cat. You can just as easily choke it with cream.*

The ears of the grey horse flicked at the sound of the loud snap when its rider, a brute of a man, cracked his knuckles. The newly broken horses shuffled their feet. The brown Clydesdale remained unmoved beneath Sanders.

"I now run the company and have discovered my grandfather's journal."

If he hoped for a response from Sanders, Edward was sorely disappointed despite the thoughts running amok in the horseman's brain.

That could very well be a minefield, but if Douglas had meant Edward to see his secret notes, then he would have shown them to his grandson – not left them around on the off chance of them being discovered by anyone. Douglas would have destroyed them if not going to show them to Edward or at least, buried them very deep. He stamped down on the grin that threatened to erupt.

"That be good, be it not?" Sanders asked without displaying any guile.

Annoyance distorted the rather handsome face. "My grandfather gave you this job here at Clawhaven, I believe."

Sanders remained schtum.

Dark clouds filled Edward's expression. "Well don't sit there like a numbskull. Answer me when I ask you something, or should I have my friend Hammers help your memory?"

"Sorry, sir, I did not know that be a question. I thought you be tellin' me something." Despite Sanders' effort to restrain his voice and his assumed accent, sarcasm dripped from his words.

"Do not get uppity with me. I will have you sent on your way quick smart. Now, answer my question."

"Yes, sir, er ... what be the question again?" Sanders knew he was being foolish, but this upstart irritated him beyond measure. He ensured the bully boy remained on the edge of his vision.

"Did my father give you this job at Clawhaven?"

"No, sir, he did not. Colonel Wellington took me on and now Miss Bridie Mayford uses my services also."

Edward Mayford sat scowling. He was sure his grandfather had something to do with this man coming here to Sussex, but search as he might he could not find the black journal which he remembered usually lived in the locked drawer in his grandfather's desk.

"Well, would you like to earn an extra handout by keeping me informed on the goings on out here at Clawhaven Estate?"

Sanders lifted his soft cap and scratched the thick brown locks on his head. Even his wife would be at a loss to recognize the look of vacancy on her husband's face.

"Sir, I knowin' aught of goings-on round these parts unless it be the horses. I be knowin' all the horses hereabouts. I knowin' aught how of writtin' words. I never be learnin' me letters, yer see." If the interlopers suspected Sanders' distorted dialect, they never mentioned it.

"Sir, do you want me to teach this oaf a lesson?"

Edward sat for several moments staring at the wide innocent eyes of the horseman.

"Nah, Hammers, it looks like we have been on a false trail. It seems to me there is only horse dung between those ears."

"Will you be going up to the manor this trip, sir?" Hammers asked

"No, I need to call in on the preacher fellow and have a chat. After that, I want to travel on to Portsmouth. I must speak to the harbourmaster tomorrow morning about a ship he has for sale in his dock. From there we will catch the train back to London." His gaze fell once more upon Sanders' face. "Take a word of advice, Sanders, not a word of this meeting to Miss Bridie Mayford, if you know what is good for you."

"If you be sayin' so, sir."

Sanders watched the departure of the unpleasant men until they were out of sight.

"You can come out now, Mary," he called. Sanders watched Mary push aside the branches of the shrubs and bushes within the grove of trees beside the road. She climbed out onto the roadway. "If they were hell-bent on serious trouble, you might have been hurt if they discovered you there."

"An unsavoury pair if ever there was. I wanted to make sure you were alright." Mary screwed up her face in distaste. "Sanders, I think that must have been young Edward, Odette's brother. What does he think he is up to? I have never seen the other fellow that I can recall."

"Yes, Mary, I agree. Together they make a despicable pair. Now, you best be getting home to the boys."

It was several hours later when the young horses were returned from their exercise, that Sanders stood in front of Bridie's desk in the office. Bridie finished the column of figures she was adding up and wrote her tally in a neat hand. She placed the pen in its holder and blotted her work.

"Sorry, Sanders, please sit down. What brings you up here to the manor?"

Sanders sat, but not with the grace with which he sat a saddle. While Bridie listened, her frown deepened. Sanders related the tale of his morning's encounter with Mr. Edward Mayford and the bodyguard.

Bridie rested her head on the bridge of her hands under her chin, while her thoughts reflected on the report from her trusted employee.

"What did you make of it, Sanders?"

"I would not trust that man if my life depended on it, Miss Bridie. I think he would be more likely to hand a man a poisonous viper before a rope if I were falling."

"Hmm, it sounds like it. And what is he doing snooping around Clawhaven wanting information? When I think of it, these are similar questions to those my grandparents posed after David was killed." Bridie stood and strode back and forth behind the desk. "If it was all innocent, why did they not turn up here at the manor, while they were in the area? I think you are right to be suspicious."

"And, Miss Bridie, you need to ask yourself, what does he need to have a chat with the preacher about? I cannot see him being interested in joining the congregation, can you?"

"Most unlikely."

≈

Odette was pleased to have Mary and the two boys with her at the church service today. With Bridie at home in bed nursing a head cold and Peter sending a message via Donald Turner that he expected to be late due to an animal call-out, she would have felt very exposed sitting in the front pew on her own. The eldest boy sat on her left between her and Mary. Arthur, the youngest son sat on Odette's right where Bridie usually sat.

The organ music dampened the murmur of soft voices and the rustle of clothing. The door behind the pulpit opened just enough for Odette to see the face of Roger Armstrong, whom she had met at this church some months ago. The determination on his face and the articulation of the quiet words spoken indicated he was laying the law down about something to someone whom she could not see – someone she suspected could be the minister. Roger moved out into the church. With a frown on his face and a measured step, he strode towards the rear seats of the congregation. It was some minutes later before the preacher also entered the church proper, shutting the door quietly behind him.

Odette thought the scene she had witnessed rather odd but soon forgot it once the service began.

It was during the sermon that Arthur began to wiggle in his seat as he emptied his pockets. Odette's attention fell to the shiny amber-coloured stone, which the boy stroked with his thumb before he gave it a good strong polish on his trousers. This was placed on the wooden seat beside him with great care before he examined a white bird feather. He ran it up and down his face several times enjoying the feel of it on his skin. The next item to be retrieved was an old bent and none-too-clean horseshoe nail. It left a dirt stain on his clean grey shirt. When Arthur attempted to remove the evidence, the stain only expanded further. With a final brush of his hand, he moved on to bring out a small coloured glass ball. Odette watched entranced as the pattern of black and white within the glass twirled with each roll of the ball in the boy's hand. Neither she nor the child considered the disruption to the minister's dreary sermon if the ball should fall to the floor.

A small squeak escaped Odette's lips, when next she looked down to see a small dark, cream-striped frog on Arthur's lap. She held her lace-edged handkerchief to her nose as if to cover a sneeze. The cream colour, on the top lip of the frog, bobbed each time the small finger patted the frog's head. The people of the congregation were not the only ones losing interest in the dry sermon, even the frog decided to move on. It leapt off Arthur's lap, bounced off his right foot and landed in the middle of the aisle.

"Oh, Fropper, come back," Arthur called. The boy would have set off on a rescue mission, but his mother's fierce whisper held him in check.

"Don't you move, Arthur."

With a broken expression guaranteed to soften all but a strict mother's heart, he whispered back.

"But it's Fropper my frog, he's gone."

"Serve you right for playing with it in church. Now sit still."

Odette stuck her hand out to pat that of little Arthur. The lad's sniffly tears broke her heart.

When eventually the congregation was released and they followed the minister outside, it was Roger Armstrong who brought a wide smile to the boy's face.

"This is yours, I think." He held out the palm of his hand on which sat a small cream and brown striped frog looking none the worse for its adventures.

"Thank you, mister, thank you." Arthur had the sense to take the frog and disappear outside post-haste before his mother could intercept.

Roger Armstrong greeted Odette, "Good morning, Miss Mayford." They continued towards the exit not wishing to cause a backup of people.

Odette's mind was more on the conundrum of why this man and the Rector might be having words earlier, than on his greeting.

"Good morning, Mr. Armstrong, isn't it?"

"Yes, Roger, please. I was hoping we might meet again."

Odette stood stunned for a moment until Peter Treloar arrived at her side and rescued her. He slipped his hand into hers.

"Sorry, dear, things took longer than I expected."

Odette clasped his hand tightly. Peter's gaze looked askance.

"Oh, Peter, you're here," Odette began the introductions. "Peter, have you met the recent member of our church, Roger Armstrong? Roger is a friend of my brother Edward, in London." She turned, "Mr. Armstrong, I would like to introduce my fiancé Peter Treloar, one of our local veterinarians."

A frown accompanied by a shadow within the dark eyes flashed across the man's face.

"Oh, your fiancé, I am sorry, I did not realize."

As she watched Roger Armstrong move off to join another group of people, Odette felt a chill run down her spine.

≈

"Bridie, are you sure you do not want me to come with you?" Odette held Bridie's hand through the carriage window, while Jimmy loaded the suitcase onto the roof.

"No, dear, I need you here to keep the appearance of everything as usual for the few nights I will be away at Portsmouth speaking with Mr. Birmingham."

"I will miss you."

"I will miss you too, but we will be back before Friday. You will not forget to take care of the Easter arrangements will you, dear?"

"Bridie, am I likely to forget Easter?"

"Of course not, sorry, I am fussing. Now remember to take Sanders with you when you go riding, and keep yourself alert. He and Mrs. Sanders are going to sleep in the manor until Jimmy and I return."

Odette stepped back as Jimmy settled himself onto the driving seat. Bridie called to her, "Tell Peter to take care."

Odette touched the lace handkerchief to her eyes. "Of course, and you keep safe too."

"I'll take good care of her, Miss Odette." Jimmy flicked the reins over the horses' backs.

Later in the evening, when the knock sounded on the door, Odette's feet threatened to break into a run as she descended the staircase. Her great-grandmother's voice sounded inside her head - *Ladies do not rush about, Odette. It is unbecoming. Grace is essential in a lady at all times. I sometimes think you and Bridie must have wings on your feet.*

Mrs. Sanders reached the front door moments before her. "Good evening, Mr. Treloar, please come in."

Odette could not contain herself a moment longer. As the housekeeper shut the front door behind him, Peter grunted when his fiancée hurled herself into his arms, twirling them both around in a spin.

"One day you will have us both in a heap on the floor, my love," he laughed.

"Dinner will be served in fifteen minutes," Mrs. Sanders informed them.

"Thank you, Mrs. Sanders."

"Play for me, Odette, please, I need some soothing music."

Odette led Peter into the music room. "You have had a hard day, my love?"

"A long one, that's for sure, but now I can relax with my sweetheart."

When the dinner gong sounded, Peter jumped in his seat. He rubbed at his eyes then reached up and took the hand Odette stretched out to him.

"Come, my love, let us feed you."

His arm snaked around her waist. "I'd rather we made love, my sweet," he whispered.

"Hush, my darling, Mr. and Mrs. Sanders will be sleeping in the house tonight," her eyes sparkled in the lamplight. "They are sleeping downstairs. My room is upstairs."

Hope reflected in Peter's eyes. "Is that an invitation?"

"It would be improper for me to make such an invitation. I just thought you might like to know."

He planted a gentle kiss upon her forehead. "Come, we do not want to upset your housekeeper."

After dinner, Odette sat on the floor near the cupboard that held Grandmama's paintings – those that had not made it to the walls of the manor.

"Your grandmother was certainly a talented artist." From where he lay stretched out upon the large sofa, Peter examined a sketch of the cottage on Clawhaven Cliff. He recognized it immediately, having had the story reported to him by Odette on their many walks along the beach.

"Grandmama kept this one hidden out of respect for Bridie's feelings. I do not think she ever did show it to her."

When Peter viewed the portraits of Bridie and Odette as ten-year-olds, he was surprised at how alike the pair were, other than in their hair colour. He laughed at his companion. "I like you with your plaits. Why do you not wear your hair in plaits for me?"

Both looked up when Mrs. Sanders spoke from the doorway. "Sanders is inside. He has locked the doors. Miss Odette, will you re-lock the front door when Mr. Treloar leaves? I'm off to my bed."

"Yes, of course, thanks, Mrs. Sanders."

"I won't be too late. I've another long day tomorrow. Good night, Mrs. Sanders."

"Goodnight, Mr. Treloar. Now don't keep Miss Odette up. Ladies need their beauty sleep."

As Mrs. Sanders' lantern light disappeared along the hall, Peter chuckled. "Beauty sleep, I think Mrs. Sanders is going blind. You are a most beautiful creature just as you are."

Odette lay down her great-grandmother's sketchbooks and shuffled along on her knees to settle on the floor with her head on the sofa beside Peter's face.

"Peter, when we are married, will you continue with your veterinarian work? I will understand if you want to do so, of course, but you will not have to if you do not wish to. Did I tell you Bridie is talking of closing the manor and emigrating to Australia? You will come with us if we do that, won't you? I mean we will be getting married before we leave here, you see." Odette stretched her legs out and pressed her back against the couch with her blond hair intermingled with Peter's brown locks.

Peter allowed her soft voice to flow over him like liquid honey, even though the words she spoke never registered. His breathing deepened. A soft snuffling snore spluttered forth with each inhalation.

When Odette realized her audience was reduced by one, her words slowed in disbelief until they ceased altogether. She swivelled around until she faced her sleeping guest. The sight of the innocence before her melted her heart. She watched for long moments until, like her voice, her hopes came to a full stop. With a gentle smile, she stood and retrieved a thick blanket from the hall cupboard and spread it lightly over the sleeping form. She turned down the lamp and guided by the slivers of the moonlight through the drapes, made her way up to her bed.

It was some hours later when a rough hand on Peter's shoulder dragged him from his slumbers.

"Wake up, Peter, that damn horse of yours is keeping me awake chomping on the grass outside my room. You'll have to take him over to the stables."

With a grunt, Peter threw his legs out onto the floor and stood.

"Sorry, Sanders," he mumbled. "I'll get on home. I have an early start in the morning, anyhow."

"Do you want a lantern to find your way?"

"No, there's a full moon out there. That's all I will need."

≈

"Miss Mayford, welcome. I trust you had a good trip."

"Thank you, Mr. Birmingham, yes, at least the weather was kind and the country looks splendid with the new spring foliage. I cannot say the roads were at their best after the recent rain. I see the docks out there have expanded even further."

"Oh, yes, the shipping traffic through this port increases every day. Please sit." He pointed towards the windows where two chairs sat at a small round table draped in a colourful cloth. A dull light streamed in through the open drapes. "Will you join me in morning tea?"

"Thank you, I would like that."

At that moment, a discreet knock sounded on the heavy oak door.

"Enter," Mr. Birmingham called.

It was the secretary Mr. Burke, who entered the room carrying a large silver tray holding a matching teapot, milk jug, sugar bowl and fine china cups and saucers. He set the tray down on the table and with a small bow, exited the room on silent feet. Mr. Birmingham held Bridie's chair while she sat. He then settled in his chair on the opposite side of the table.

The two made polite discussion on current affairs and local political issues, subjects which Mr. Birmingham still found hard to become accustomed to when conversing with a woman, but he had learnt twenty years previously, when he first met Bridie with her grandfather, she was no ordinary woman and always proved informed and interesting.

When the tea cups sat empty on the tray, Mr. Birmingham rested back in his chair.

"Now, Miss Mayford, I understand from your recent correspondence, that you have many legal questions to be answered. You did not explain what has prompted this inquiry." Mr. Birmingham's astute mind had seen and heard most things, but from the little he understood, he was about to learn much more than he expected. He sighed and thought. *Families at all levels of society are never short of dramas of all kinds.* After years of discussions with Colonel Wellington, he knew this family had more than their share of such things, particularly Miss Bridie when she was about Miss Odette's age.

Bridie took a deep breath. Her words began slowly, but as she gathered everything together in her head, the story flowed forth. She spoke briefly on her experience with the expectations of the Mayford men's beliefs of a woman's role in the family company. She confessed to the lingering doubts she retained about the role the male counterparts in her family may have played in her fiancé's death. She told Mr. Birmingham of her fear it was all happening again for Odette. She held up her fingers as she counted off the evidence they witnessed of veiled threats and the not-so-veiled threats presented to her and Odette and recently to Sanders.

Bridie drew a breath. "I am sure you are wondering why you need to hear all this, no doubt. I am seriously considering emigrating to Australia along with Odette and Peter Treloar her fiancé – soon-to-be husband – preferably the sooner the better."

"Good heavens, Miss Mayford, your grandfather had mentioned some of the concerns he held regarding David Lewis's demise, but would anyone consider such measures to get their own way in this day and age?"

"One would like to believe not, but we cannot ignore the threats. I think Peter's life could very well be in danger."

A silence settled over the pair sitting at the small round table. Mr. Birmingham gave his initial thoughts of an overwrought female, short rein. He knew the woman beside him had proved herself to be intelligent and rational in many difficult circumstances.

Bridie stared out at the glimpses she had of the very busy harbour waters of Portsmouth with the dull reflection of the clouds from the sky above. The bang and crash of heavy machinery and raucous orders became muted as they echoed up the winding street from the quay.

Eventually, Mr. Birmingham spoke, "Emigrate, you say – is that not a bit dramatic? Maybe you should take a holiday over there first and test the waters, so to speak."

"Yes, I had considered that. The three of us could travel there on speculation, and if we decided to stay, I would invest in a residence and leave Odette and Peter there, while I returned to settle things here." Bridie sat in contemplation for some time. "If we decide to live there, I am hoping I can talk Jimmy Braydon and Rosa into joining us."

"Yes, I can see it is a big decision."

"Hmmm, but I believe it is easier just to make the complete move right up front. I would leave Clawhaven as a going concern with the workers we have, so if we needed to return, we could retain Clawhaven Manor. Mr. Axel will remain as manager and his eldest son will follow in his footsteps; I think. The thing is, Mr. Axel's education includes only the farming component of running the place, so I would ask Sanders, who has had a more extensive education, to be the caretaker and business manager, reporting to Mr. Langford our usual accountant's firm here in Portsmouth. The dairy hands and farm labourers will be hired from the local community as usual. Sanders' wife is our housekeeper and she will be asked to supervise the upkeep of the manor." Again, Bridie's voice trailed off and she sat gazing down at the busy harbour and the bustle on the streets.

"Do I take it you want me to set something up legally to see all this unfolds as you envisage?"

"Yes, Mr. Birmingham, that is what I am asking."

"When are you planning to do all this?"

"Odette will turn twenty-one on the 1st of April, that is in the week pre-Easter. I was thinking of having Reverend Andrews out to the manor for an evening meal, immediately after Easter, to have him perform the marriage – just between ourselves." Bridie paused and then with a wry grin, "I may even hijack him into doing so if necessary." Bridie rolled her eyes and the grin widened. "That will depend on Odette's wishes, of course."

"Why do you think such an extreme measure is necessary, Miss Mayford?" Mr. Birmingham tried to keep the surprise from his face. He sat in silence running his forefinger up and down the side of his teacup. His gaze lifted to analyse the expression on the face of his guest. "Will your minister be given any warning of the cost to him of a free meal?"

Again, a silence, other than the muted noises drifting up the hill outside, filled the room for some moments. On her lap, Bridie's thumbs rubbed together slowly in her clasped hands.

"Recently, I have become concerned as to the minister's friendship with Edward and some of Edward's cohorts." The reports from Sanders after his encounter with Edward and the unknown man called Hammers filtered through her mind. "Maybe we have become paranoid over time," she glanced up wearing a wry smile. "I would prefer to stay extra vigilant, especially when a friend of Edward's, whom we had never met until recently, is a close friend of our local preacher. He turned up again at the village church service recently. Roger Armstrong may be a messenger boy of Edward's or he may just be infatuated with Odette." Silence fell in the room again, until Bridie continued, "I learnt a hard lesson a long time ago when I underestimated the evilness of power and greed."

April 1896

It was the Thursday after Easter when the Rector, Reverend Andrews, arrived at the manor in his spring cart drawn by his aging brown horse. The clock inside the hall chimed seven o'clock in the evening just as Mrs. Sanders opened the front door to the preacher's knock. She welcomed the man and directed him to the parlour room where Bridie, Odette and Peter standing by the window, cut off their conversation mid-flow.

After their greetings, the women sat while Peter stood and poured a glass of sherry for their guest.

"Please sit, Reverend," Bridie pointed to a chair near the door. "I trust it was a pleasant drive on a mild evening such as this."

"Thank you, Miss Mayford, a pleasant and balmy evening indeed." He thanked Peter as he accepted the drink.

Bridie felt a twinge of guilt when she noticed the man seemed ill at ease. She bit her lip but did not interrupt when the uncharitable voice inside her head whispered, *Serve him right*. It was her grandfather's voice next which reminded her of his favourite saying, *There is more than one way to kill the cat. You can just as easily choke it with cream.* She bit her tongue this time and pulled her thoughts together. *Tonight is all about Odette and Peter taking their vows. I will walk over hot coals if necessary to make this happen.*

"Bridie, are you alright?" Peter asked from where he sat on the sofa holding Odette's hand.

"Yes, sorry," Bridie realized it was up to her to carry this night to its climax. Odette appeared quite pale. "Now, Reverend Andrews, you spoke last week of your plan to hold a little Sunday School during the church hour on our days of worship. That sounds like a wonderful plan. I am sure the adults will appreciate the peace of contemplation this will bring them in their prayers. No doubt the small ones will appreciate the chance to relax. Their power of concentration is far from endless."

Bridie began to wish she had not mentioned the Rector's favourite topic of the moment as he then went on for such a long time. She looked up with a grateful smile when Mrs. Sanders rang the gong for the evening meal.

With their guest settled at the dining table, Mrs. Sanders, at Miss Bridie's special request, dismissed the parlour maid and filled the plates herself from the serving dishes on the sideboard. She delivered the food to the Rector first and then to the family. Once again, the little imp inside Bridie's head spoke to her. *I do hope the Rector does not go on for hours with his grace, I do not want my meal to be stone cold.* She was very pleased to find the man must have been hungry because his words of thanks were brief.

Roast beef, gravy, horseradish sauce and seasonal vegetables kept the conversation to a minimum as everyone enjoyed Rosa's culinary skills. Bridie spoke very little as she struggled with her conscience knowing she must refer again to Reverend Andrews' favourite topic. Not that she wanted to, but it was her means of bribery to have the night end as she and Odette wished. She sighed silently and soothed her conscience again. *God forgive me the hypocrisy.*

It was during the dessert of Yorkshire pudding that Bridie raised the subject again.

"Reverend, this Sunday school idea of yours, where exactly are you hoping to hold this class?"

Like an athlete at the starting pistol, his voice took off. "I am hoping we might have a separate small building built on the church grounds – close but not too close to the church." He continued his spiel. While he spoke, Bridie's glance fell on Odette and Peter. Discreetly, she rolled her eyes. Eventually, she hauled their guest in.

"Well, sir, I think we may be able to help with that. It does sound like a wonderful idea and worthy of our support. We have something we wish you to do for us this evening, and in return, I will see a church hall built in which the children can receive their Sunday lessons, and which the congregation may use for innumerable other purposes."

The man's mouth hung open. The spoon in his hands settled in the last of his custard.

"Anything, Miss Mayford, anything at all. That is very generous of you."

Bridie, Odette and Peter were each filled with their own thoughts for the remainder of the meal, while the Rector did indeed expand on his hopes and dreams.

Mrs. Sanders' presence at the doorway was the excuse Bridie needed.

"Rector, we really must allow the staff to clear up. Please join us in the library."

"Goodness me," the preacher exclaimed when he entered the room, "this is indeed a magnificent library." His gaze took in the length of the polished oak table and matching lines of shelving around every wall. All the chairs were tucked in under the table. "I have never been into this room. What a wealth of information you have in such a book collection, Miss Mayford."

"Yes, I have been very privileged." Bridie guided her guest to the far end of the table, where several papers were lined up in army-like precision on the tabletop. The light from the candles in the candelabra provided ample illumination.

Peter led Odette to the far side of the table and stood still as Bridie explained, in a gentle manner to their visitor, what he had to do to get his church hall.

"Er …er… you want me to marry Miss Odette and Mr. Treloar right now, here in this room?" The Rector's voice erupted in a soft screech. "That is impossible. Er … er… it cannot be done." He swung an arm around taking in the whole room.

Bridie gently took his arm and pointed to the papers provided by her friend and solicitor Mr. Birmingham.

"I think you will find everything here that you will need."

"B-b-but is Odette of legal age yet? I understood her birthday was not until the end of the month and her brother was her guardian."

Both Odette and Bridie's glances met across the room – their eyebrows raised. Why would this man say these things, when the two of them were the only ones who knew about the trickery with the birth dates and the misconception of Edward's beliefs in his position?

At this moment, Mrs. Sanders, Jimmy Braydon and his wife Rosa joined them bringing champagne and glasses.

"Come in, everyone, please," Bridie invited the staff before she reached across the table to where a single sheet of paper sat folded. She looked back at the Anglican priest. "Mr. Birmingham has written his name and address upon this page to remind you where to send the quotes and then the accounts for the church hall, Reverend Andrews." Bridie picked it up and held it close to her chest.

"T-T-The banns."

"Is there anyone in this area who might argue Odette has not lived here all but two years of her life? If you check with Donald Turner, you will discover Peter has been in his employ for more than the required time for any banns." Bridie pointed to the chair, "Please make yourself comfortable. Have you enough light to see there?

These people and myself will be the required witnesses." Bridie's sweep of her hand took in the latest arrivals.

After reading the legal documents on the table in front of him and unable to think of further excuses, the church minister rose and prepared to begin the private ceremony with the lure of his church hall at the back of his mind.

Peter withdrew the single band of gold he had been twiddling in his pocket. After the vows were recited, he slipped it over Odette's ring finger to rest alongside her engagement ring. Lamplight reflected in his bride's tears and sparkled within the violet of her eyes. Peter slipped his arms around her pulling her close to him.

"Hello, my darling wife."

"Oh, Peter," she pulled his head down to hers. Their kiss lasted a long time.

Jimmy began to laugh. "Put that lass down, Pete, she may be someone's wife."

Peter lifted his head. "She is that, Jimmy lad, she is my wife." Peter stared into Odette's eyes as if disbelieving his dreams had reached fruition. They held each other close.

When all the papers were signed, Rosa poured the champagne for everyone.

The group, including the bride and groom, went out to see their guest safely on his way. Bridie stepped forward to lean into the spring cart and speak quietly to the parish priest.

"The new hall will hold a large bronze plate inscribed: *In memory of David Lewis a gifted organist*." Bridie's eyes so like her father's, when he wished to make a point, burned into the preacher's soul.

Back inside, Odette led her husband upstairs to the refurbished room previously used by William and Anna Wellington.

≈

Odette and Peter spent three glorious days sleeping late, walking in the countryside, and eating the best food served up by Rosa's hand. Bridie and Jimmy took another trip to Portsmouth to deliver the precious papers into Mr. Birmingham's care. Bridie spent several days within the town library, while Jimmy revelled in his hours exploring either the railway depot or the harbour. He discovered a passion for trains and ships.

Odette partially opened the bedroom door. A thin stream of sunlight through the gap between the curtains revealed the body of Peter lying sprawled across their bed. She smiled at the sight of his ruffled hair. Odette longed to push the locks away from his closed eyelids. She watched his even breathing. Inside her chest, her heart beat faster at the memory of the pleasurable response his muscled body stirred within her. The clock downstairs chimed ten o'clock. How she missed his presence in her bed last night when he had not returned from work until well after the stroke of midnight.

"I know you are watching me, Detta," his voice mumbled through dry lips.

Odette's soft laugh filled the room as she ran over and threw herself down beside her husband of only two weeks. He grinned and rolled over to wrap his wife in his arms.

"What time is it?"

"Time you and I had time to ourselves."

Peter squeezed Odette and kissed the top of her head. "Don't tempt me, my love, I have a new foal to check over on the Braydon farm. It had a difficult birth and when I left, I wasn't too sure if it would survive the night. I'm hoping the mare will fare better."

Peter kissed her warmly and lay her gently aside. "I really have to go, Detta, my dear."

Outside the back door, he banged the mud from his work boots on the stump. He looked up when Mrs. Sanders spoke to him on her way to the kitchen.

"There is a letter in the hall addressed to you, Mr. Treloar. It came in this morning's mail."

"Thank you, Mrs. Sanders, I'll pick it up when I get back."

In the stables, he gave the girth strap one last pull and straightened the stirrups, when a voice spoke from the doorway.

"Peter, are you off to my mother's place to check on Black Daisy and her foal?"

"Good morning, Jimmy, yes, I am on my way there before I start my rounds."

"If you be waitin' a bit, I'll keep you company. I need to be talkin' to Aunt Eleanor and my mother."

In the timber shelter at the Braydon Riding School, Peter was glad to find the new foal alive and sucking strongly on Black Daisy's udder. None-too-gentle head butts demanded more milk.

Eleanor, Jimmy and Teresa, Jimmy's mother, stood watching with smiles on their faces.

"You've done a fine job, Peter, with a very difficult birth. Thank you," Eleanor said.

"It was Black Daisy who did all the hard work. It is a beautiful sight, I must admit." Peter took one more look at his two patients before moving off on his rounds.

Bridie sat in the office reading the morning mail delivered by Mrs. Sanders – along with a tray of tea and biscuits. Odette arrived just in time to pour the tea.

"This is from your father, Odette." Bridie continued to read. "Oh, dear, this is a warning to us. He fears Edward is planning a surprise visit here in the next week or so. George has not been well and cannot join him to intercede on our behalf. Not that he could do anything much these days even if he were here."

"It must be his man Turnbull, who posted the letter for him."

"I am sure you are right. Remember, Edward thinks your birthday is on the 30th. He does not realize he is too late, and that you are already twenty-one years of age and married as well." Bridie re-read the short letter again, before pushing her chair back. "I must go and warn the staff of possible visitors in the near future. I will assure them I am not going to invite these visitors to stay."

Odette gathered the tea tray items together.

"Bridie, will you deliver these to the kitchen, as you are going that way? I shall go for a walk to the sheds and let Mr. Axel, Sanders and Jimmy know to keep their eyes peeled."

"Good, thanks, Odette."

Peter arrived back at Clawhaven Manor in the evening just as the hall clock chimed five. After a scrub in the outside bathhouse near the laundry shed, he dried himself and pulled on clean clothes left out for him by Odette. He smiled at the rustle of a note found in the shirt pocket. This had become a regular habit of hers. He pulled it out and spread it open to read.

My darling, my heart will not start beating again until I see your smile.

He chuckled in anticipation of a pleasant evening.

"Don't forget your letter, Mr. Treloar," Mrs. Sanders called as he stomped his feet at the back door.

Peter collected the letter from the hall mantlepiece and noticed the handwriting on the outside as that of his elder brother Mark. He made his way upstairs to his and Odette's room. He smiled at his selfish wave of disappointment when he found no Detta waiting for him. The chair by the window moaned as he sat and began to tear the envelope open.

Dear brother,

I am sorry this letter is not one of good news. Our mother took a turn the other day, and even though she is sitting out of bed today, the doctor has warned us her heart is not strong and she may not have too long in this world. We feel she has given in and cannot wait to, as she puts it, 'Meet my maker and my loving husband.'

Maybe you can come and talk some sense into her if you are able. You were always the only one she ever listened to.

Everyone else doing fine here and the farm has had a good year.

From your siblings, Mark, Johnny, Maggie and Sarah.

Odette found her husband staring out towards the orchard, as he sat still holding a letter in his hand. She paused at the doorway and slowed her step as she approached.

"Peter, is everything alright? Is that letter a message of bad news, my dear."

Peter looked up and smiled. "It is news to be expected, Detta. My brother has written to tell me my mother has not been well. I'm thinking I may take a quick trip to the border to spend a day or two with her. If we do decide to travel to Australia, this may be the last chance I get to see her and the family."

Odette rushed forward and wrapped her arms around his shoulders.

"Oh, Peter, I am so sorry. I would love to meet your mother, may I come with you?"

Peter stood up holding Odette close. "My dearest, as much as I would love your company, a hasty trip in conditions short of comforts might be asking too much of you. I am sure Bridie would never agree to you taking such a risk with the threat that she perceives we face. If there is anything in her concerns, it will be easier for me to avoid trouble if alone, rather than if I must protect you too, my treasure."

Tears trembled upon Odette's eyelids. She clung to Peter's arms.

"When do you plan on leaving?" Odette's voice quavered.

Peter stroked her cheek as he gazed outside the window, while his thoughts tossed and turned over this decision.

"I'll talk to Donald in the morning and see what will suit him best. Hopefully by the end of this week."

"Bridie received a letter from my father this morning. He warned us that Edward plans on a surprise visit here within days. I do hope you get away before he arrives, then I know you will be safe if you are not here."

"What?" Peter's voice lifted. "I cannot leave here if that brother of yours is expected. That would not be right."

"Now, Peter, do not fuss. He will not hurt me. Anyway, I am twenty-one now, which he does not realize yet, and he can only hurt me through you and your safety. Besides, if I know Bridie, she will have Jimmy, Sanders and Mr. Axel sleeping within arms' reach until we know Edward is long gone." Odette pulled out of his embrace and looked up into Peter's face. "Perhaps we should send one of them with you to the Cumberlands to ensure you are safe."

"I don't need a keeper, my love."

Two days later, Peter arrived home from work in the twilight to see two strange horses tied up at the hitching post in front of the manor. He had barely led his horse into the stables when Rosa arrived like a whirling dervish. She held a note out to him.

"It's from Miss Bridie, Mr. Treloar." Rosa shoved the note into his hand before she spun on her heel and ran back towards the kitchen.

Peter unfolded the sheet of paper and held it up to the last of the fading light.

Ed here. Use tunnel. DO NOT come into the office. Stay hidden. Jimmy & Sanders inside. Bridie

Peter felt torn. He did not want to go hiding behind the women's skirts, but then they knew this fellow much better than he did. Bridie did say she had Jimmy and Sanders on hand, which gave him confidence. Both men, particularly Jimmy, would die before anyone hurt a hair on Bridie's head. His feet turned towards the manor, but he knew he might upset their pre-arranged plans, which he was loath to do. He swung about and made his way towards the copse of trees near the family vault. He paused at the edge of the trees, before approaching the entrance.

It took him a moment to figure out how to shut the heavy door from the inside. In the poor light, he stifled a groan when he hit his knee on the coffin near the angel with the hand to twist. His own hands felt large and useless, as he tried twice to entice the twist to operate as it should. A sigh of relief filled the room as the panel opened with a swish. He slipped through and into the small space where the candles were kept on the ledge. Peter turned and watched, as the angel disappeared back into the vault room. He felt his heart skip a beat. He took a deep breath. His lungs filled with dust which had drifted in through the grid pattern in the top of the wall. The dust was tainted with the stale air from within the tunnel itself. He coughed.

It did not take him too long, using the tinder box, to light a candle before he started off on the underground journey across to the manor. It seemed to be so much further without the company of the others. When he felt the steps rising towards the office, he blew out the candle and shuffled along on silent feet towards the fine stream of light shining through the small hole in the office wall. His ears picked up the sound of muffled voices.

Peter placed his eye to the peephole. His heart thudded inside his chest at the sight of the partial backs of Bridie and Odette sitting at the near side of the office desk. He assumed the better-dressed man – the fellow with the dark curly hair – standing on the opposite side of the desk was Odette's brother Edward. Thin lips and a narrow nose accentuated the deep frown on his face. Another man stood to the left of Peter's brother-in-law – a larger and well-muscled fellow. Peter twisted his head a little to improve his view. He gulped at the sight of the cruel face which appeared to be looking right back at him. He drew back his head until he quickly realized the man had no way of seeing through the peephole. He looked again into the manor office. The partial door seen behind the big fellow had been left ajar. Bridie's voice was heard interrupting her nephew.

"Edward, may I ask what right you think you have to come barging into our home?"

Peter felt his anxiety lift at the lack of fear in Bridie's voice. Edward did not look like a man to be trifled with and the fellow with him looked little more than a thug. Peter was in a dilemma. He felt it was his duty to face these men and send them packing. His years of boxing at university had taught him to defend himself. Yet, Bridie had been specific. She did not want him to come into the office. He tried to concentrate on the conversation.

"… I am Odette's older brother and as her guardian, I have come to take her back to London where she will take her place doing her duties for the family company. She will not be allowed to become the traitor that you were, Aunt Bridie." Peter almost missed the answer.

Bridie ignored the slur. "And what might those duties be, Edward?"

"She will marry Roger Armstrong, who in turn will fill the company coffers." His sneer took in his sister, "You should be grateful, you sprat. Roger is a pleasant fellow with deep pockets."

Peter nearly fell over when he heard Odette answer the man. Her usually gentle voice came out loud and strong. "I have met your friend, brother Edward, and I concur he is an agreeable fellow, no doubt, but you see it would be bigamy if I were to marry him. Edward, I am already a married woman."

Peter jumped when the man slammed his fists on the desk in front of Bridie and Odette. Unseen by him the women did little more than blink.

"This cannot be. I will soon have annulled any marriage you may think you have engaged in. I have not given my consent and you are not yet of age to make the decision yourself." Spittle flew across the desk to be absorbed on the sheet of blotting paper edged by Bridie's forearms.

Bridie took a handkerchief from inside her sleeve and wiped the moisture away before dropping the laced material into the bin beside her desk. Peter saw briefly the look of disdain on her face.

Peter pressed his eye harder against the spyhole when Bridie stood slowly pushing the chair back with her knees. The top half of her body rose out of his vision. Peter did not see the contempt in her eyes as she threw her head back and stared at her nephew.

"Edward, you seem to forget your sister's birthday was several weeks ago. She is of age, as you put it. She is already a married woman in the eyes of the law and in the eyes of the church – although,

I guess that would not bother you being such an unchristian chap yourself who delights in bullying women."

Peter's heart rolled over. Bridie's steady figure prevented him from seeing properly all that was happening in the room. *What did Bridie think she was doing aggravating the fellow like this?* He only partly saw Edward's signal, as he stepped back indicating to his henchman to do as he wished with these two upstarts. He did see a flurry near the doorway. The arms of Edward's bully friend were clamped firmly on either side of his body, by the working hands of an unseen man whom he believed beyond doubt to be Sanders. The addition of Odette standing firmly at Bridie's side almost reduced his vision to nil of what was happening in the room.

A punch, so swift from Jimmy Braydon that Peter did not see it, felled Edward.

"Pick up your rubbish and get out of our house," Bridie demanded of the man of muscle. In a kinder voice, she spoke to her friends, "Thank you, Jimmy, thank you, Sanders. I take it this is the fellow you met with Edward hanging around the farm recently?"

"Yes, Miss Bridie, Hammers, Mr. Mayford called him."

"Well, can you release Hammers and escort him and the unconscious man out of the house."

Bridie followed the procession towards the front door. Odette moved to the corner of the room and whispered at the wall.

"Are you there, Peter?" After a few moments taken to find the lever, the secret panel swung back and Peter stumbled out on all fours to be dragged up into his wife's arms.

Bridie, Peter and Odette sat at the breakfast table all looking a little subdued. Bridie turned to Peter and asked, "Peter, when were you thinking of visiting your mother?"

Peter swallowed his spoonful of hot porridge almost burning his mouth in the process.

"I think perhaps I will forgo the visit, Bridie. I cannot leave you and Odette alone here with Edward and his thug on the loose. I feel bad enough about hiding in the tunnel while you two women faced up to him last evening."

Bridie reached across the table and lay her fingers gently on his arm.

"Peter, I am sorry if my plan made you feel left out. I did not want the tunnel revealed to anyone but us three. Odette and I were safe enough with Sanders and Jimmy in the hallway. I cannot be responsible for anything bad happening to you. Odette is like a daughter to me, and I will do everything in my power to ensure she is not left bereft, as I was for my David." With a sharp tap on Peter's wrist, Bridie sat up straight. "Now, we must get you away north to visit your ailing mother."

Peter opened his mouth to argue the point but closed it again when Odette's hand hidden by the tablecloth clamped his thigh. Her violet eyes laughed up into his own grey eyes.

"Peter, my dearest, you must visit your mother. Neither Bridie nor I knew our mothers, but we do understand a mother is someone to treasure. We will remain here at the manor until you return. With Mr. Axel and the men on the farm, we are safe."

Peter made to reply, but Bridie spoke first. "I would like Sanders to travel with you, if for no better reason than to reassure Odette."

"That is totally unnecessary, Bridie. I can handle myself."

"I am sure you can, but you cannot stay awake twenty-four hours a day."

"Bridie, enough. I cannot have Sanders protecting me when I prefer that he remain here to watch over you and Odette." He turned to look into Odette's beseeching eyes. "Detta, darling, how could those pair know of my plans to go north? I will travel on the train, so what chances will they have of hurting me, even if they were aware of my travel plans, of which at this point I am not sure myself?"

Three days later, before the sun fully breached the horizon, the hoof beats of two horses sounded through the morning mist. Long after the echo of the hoof beats faded, Bridie and Odette stood in front of the manor staring out at the empty road.

Peter rode his bay horse in silence, with Sanders on the back of a grey horse at his left, whistling a soft country folksong.

"I am sorry to have dragged you from your work, Sanders. I am sure this is only a storm in a teacup."

Sanders grinned. "My work is what Miss Bridie tells me to do, and right now I am to be your guardian on the train as far as London, at least. She did instruct me to try to convince you I should remain at your side all the way to the border, but I know when I am beat."

"Are you sure they will be safe enough there at Clawhaven? Perhaps I should give this trip a miss. Odette is my wife and it is my responsibility to protect her."

"Be assured, man, Clawhaven is a closed community. All our people adore those two women and will close ranks about them even at risk to their own lives. Now, it is becoming too hot to argue, can we cease this pointless discussion and hasten to the railway junction to meet today's London train from Portsmouth? I don't like the thought of camping out there waiting for the next one."

With their horses settled in the railway paddock until Sanders' return, the pair jumped aboard the train just as the squeal of steel on steel echoed across the valley when the wheels began to gain traction.

They laughed as they landed on the small platform at the back of the second carriage behind the engine. While Sanders opened the door into the carriage, Peter dropped the latch over the little gate of the platform. He followed Sanders inside and along the small corridor on the right-hand side of the moving carriage. When Sanders stopped dead in his tracks, Peter slammed into his back. Sanders turned and pushed Peter backward. He held his fingers to his lips.

"What's the matter?"

Sanders did not speak until they were once more outside the carriage door on the little platform. The wind whistled past their ears. Sanders had to place his mouth close to the side of Peter's head to make him hear.

"Of all the damnable bad luck. Edward Mayford and Hammers are sitting in the second compartment inside that carriage."

"That is impossible. Are you sure it's them? How did they get there?"

"It's them. I have met them twice. I am not going to forget them in a hurry." Sanders stood hanging onto the bouncing platform staring into space wearing a thoughtful expression.

"They must have gone on to Portsmouth the other day after visiting Clawhaven and are now returning to London. I know he has business at the port."

"Well, we can't hang on outside here all the way to London. All my teeth will have rattled clear out of my head before we arrive. We'll have to move back a few carriages to find a seat." Peter went to change direction when he held up his hand. "I need to see them both properly so I will recognize them in the future," Peter remembered he had not met the two before, and his limited vision of them from the secret tunnel was not reliable.

"We'll watch everyone who leaves the train between here and London and when they exit, I'll point them out to you."

Where the two carriages met, the steel plates slid back and forth against each other which made it a dangerous exercise to walk from one carriage to the next. The two men jumped across the narrow lane of sliding steel onto the small platform of the third carriage. They found seats in the first compartment of carriage number three and settled down to wait.

Night had fallen when the train hissed and puffed its way into the London railway station. Both Peter and Sanders sat with pages from a discarded newspaper covering their lower faces while they stared through the window. When Edward, followed by Hammers, stepped down from the train, Peter had only a moment to identify them before they quickly disappeared into the dark shadows of the railway platform.

Peter and Sanders' gazes followed Edward and the man named Hammers as far as their vision allowed. So engrossed in watching the two men they expected to see, they did not therefore notice Roger Armstrong, hidden in the shadows watching the back of his friend Edward and that of the man Hammers. Even in the poor lighting, Roger Armstrong recognized Peter the instant he stepped off the carriage and onto the platform. Edward's friend stepped back out of sight. Jealousy twisted Roger's face as he watched his rival and the chap he knew as Sanders make their way towards where the hansom cabs waited to deliver travellers to other London railway stations. Surreptitiously he followed the pair and heard the instructions given to the driver of the cab.

Edward Mayford's foot almost slipped on the small step as Roger Armstrong came swinging around the back of his carriage in the darkness.

"What on earth are you doing, Roger, you nearly had me on my knees. Where have you been? I was looking for you in there. What is all the fuss?"

Roger knew full well that Edward was a moody beggar. Dismissing all but the most important question, Roger directed his attention to it.

"Did you realize that vet chap from Clawhaven Cliff got off the same train as you – along with the fellow called Sanders?"

"They didn't."

"Yes, they did."

"Where are they now?"

Roger repeated the instructions given by Peter to the hansom cab driver.

"He is catching the northern train to the Scottish border."

"Jump in," Edward indicated to Roger and turned to deliver instructions to Hammers. "Hurry up, Hammers, jump up top with the driver. I want you and Roger to follow the vet to the Scottish border if necessary. I do not want him to return. You can remove the other fellow if he gets in the way also."

Roger's enthusiasm took a nosedive. "I was hoping for a hot feed, not a train journey anywhere, Ed."

"Stop grumbling, I'll make it worth your while."

$$\approx$$

Using the twilight in the woodlands outside Preston, the tall poacher, with long unbrushed hair tied back with a piece of string, bent to bait and reset the trap. A lad of twelve years or thereabouts watched his every move.

"Come on, lad, they'll be needing our catch in the pot back at the camp, if anyone hopes to eat tonight." Picking up the two limp furry bodies from the grass, the man rose to his feet.

The pair turned to go when the whistle of a night train spread across the countryside. They stood on the bank of the small brook watching the lights inside the carriages flashing by.

"Look, Da, them fella's be pushing the man off the train."

"'Tis none of our business, lad," but the poacher's gaze was held by the fight in progress on the platform of a carriage.

The boy gasped when one of these men flew from the train, bounced off the edge of the railway line and into the brook below.

"None of our business," the poacher reiterated.

CHAPTER NINE

Mystery

1896

"After Edward and the man he called Hammers, disappeared on their way towards the exit, Peter and I made our way to the northern train platform. I saw Peter onto the train travelling the west coast route." Sanders finished his report to Bridie.

"Thank you, Sanders." Bridie fiddled with the ruler in her hand. "I suppose there was no chance he was going to let you join him as far as the Scottish border?"

"No, Miss, and I cannot say as I blame him. We had no reason to think he was in any danger from his brother-in-law, at that point."

"Thank you, again. I will tell Mrs. Odette."

"It has been five days since Peter left, Bridie. He promised to write a letter to let me know when he arrived safely. There has not been a word."

"Maybe in all the excitement of meeting his family again, he has been delayed in getting the letter away. You did say he lived on a remote farm, Odette. Maybe we should allow another day or two for the mail deliveries."

"But Peter said he was only going to visit his family for a couple of days. Surely by now, he will be thinking of returning."

"Maybe his mother's condition has worsened. Maybe his brothers need his help with something. I do not think we need to be fretting just yet."

"And what if he is lying wounded somewhere? What if he never made it to his family."

"Odette, my dear, we do not have any reason to be thinking such morbid thoughts. Sanders said they saw no-one of interest board the northern train in London."

"Well, I cannot help it. I have this dreadful premonition inside me."

Bridie felt a shiver run down her spine at Odette's words. She had to admit things did not feel right. She believed Peter to be very reliable, and if he said he was going to write to Odette, he would do just that.

"If a letter does not arrive in the mail today, we will take a trip into the village and talk to Officer Rogers at the police station."

"Oh, Bridie, thank you." Odette rushed over and wrapped her arms around her aunt.

"I am sure there is nothing to worry about. Now I hope those tears of yours are not going to saturate my clothes," Bridie attempted to chuckle. She stamped down upon the swirl of her stomach and the clamp around her throat. *How have I let history repeat itself?* She berated herself. Odette's weepy smile joined her own.

Odette turned to go but swung back to face her aunt. "I think you will find Officer Rogers has been replaced with another fellow. I heard Mary and Donald Turner's wife talking at church last week." A small frown creased her forehead as she struggled to remember. Her eyes lit up. "Officer Stone, yes, Officer Stone is the name of the new policeman."

After lunch, when Odette stood on the front porch to watch Mrs. Sanders collect the mail from Mr. Featherstone, she barely noticed the man now had a new piebald horse hitched up to the dog-cart he had taken to using in recent years. He handed several letters to the housekeeper. Odette's heart rolled over in her chest. She struggled to draw air into her lungs. It seemed to take forever for the man to climb back into his seat and depart. How she wished she could go and snatch the mail from Mrs. Sanders' hands. Inside her head, she realized this would have been impossible. Her legs felt like solid lead. She doubted they would move even if instructed to do so. It was the deep sorrow in the face of Mrs. Sanders, that triggered the well of tears trembling on Odette's eyelashes.

"Come away in, lass," Mrs. Sanders put an arm around Odette's shoulders and led her into the library, where Bridie had settled at the end of the table. Bridie looked up and at the warning glance from Mrs. Sanders, she realised the mail delivered held no news for Odette. Bridie jumped up and helped Odette into a chair.

"Thank you, Mrs. Sanders. I will see to Odette now." Bridie's voice wobbled. "Will you call Jimmy, please? I will send him to ask the village policeman to call this afternoon."

Odette found it hard to settle as the hall clock chimed out the hours during the afternoon. Her footsteps paced from the front windows of the parlour room back to the chair that held her novel. After only several moments of sitting and reading, but not seeing or understanding, she stood again to pace once more.

Bridie sat in the chair opposite feeling helpless. The memory of her heartbreak at the loss of her fiancé flowed strongly inside her. When Odette spoke, Bridie took a moment to return her thoughts to the present.

"The policeman is here," Odette whispered loudly as she scuttled back to her chair.

When the young lad – and that is just how Bridie saw him, a lad barely out of short pants – was escorted into the room by Mrs. Sanders, Bridie and Odette looked up to greet him. Short, cropped hair and the darkest eyes she had ever seen were all Bridie remembered after Mrs. Sanders introduced him as "Officer Stone" and pointed him to a chair.

"Will you send in some tea and biscuits, thanks Mrs. Sanders," Bridie informed her housekeeper.

The lad's eyes widened as his gaze travelled around the room taking in the furnishings and large paintings hanging from the walls. When he turned back to Bridie and Odette sitting in the two chairs opposite his own, he stuttered, "Y-y-you wished to see me, Miss Mayford?"

"Yes, Officer, I am hoping you might send a message to the Inspector of Detectives at the new Criminal Investigation Department in London."

"The C.I.D., Ma'am?"

"Yes, Officer, is that too much trouble?"

"No, no, not at all, Ma'am. Er, may I ask concerning what?" The young man took a folded piece of paper from his top pocket and a stubby pencil. "He, er, the Inspector will want me to report on what it is you wish to speak to him about, please, Ma'am."

Bridie and Odette's glances met. Both knew the other was thinking that it might have been quicker to have travelled directly to London themselves. Bridie struggled not to let her eyes roll. She nodded instead to Odette to let her tell their story.

"My husband has disappeared on his way to the Scottish border. We suspect he may have been murdered. He was travelling by rail."

The policeman's wide, dark eyes expanded. "Murdered, you say?"

"Yes, Officer, murdered. His life has been threatened on more than one occasion."

"What is the name of your husband, Miss – er – Mrs Treloar isn't it?"

"Peter Treloar, Officer, my husband of only a few weeks."

"The vet fellow, in the village then? He has gone missing?"

This time Bridie did roll her eyes and turned to her niece. "Perhaps you had better start at the beginning and explain, Odette."

As Odette spoke, the policeman made notes on his paper, licking the end of his pencil at times to darken the writing.

When Odette finished her story, only the sound of Bridie pouring the tea was heard within the room. She drew in a sharp and loud breath when Officer Stone asked his next question.

"Mrs. Treloar, surely no one would want to kill your husband. I am sure he is quite safe with his family," – he flicked through his notes – in the Cumberlands, and has forgotten to send you a letter. What evidence do you have that he might be murdered?"

"Because we, and members of our staff, were witness to the threats made by my brother Edward Mayford, to Peter. Now do you want to take this seriously, or do we have to go to London and talk to the Inspector ourselves?"

Bridie was surprised that Odette's outburst did not seem to affect the young man. In fact, he looked up and asked Bridie the next question.

"Pardon me, Ma'am, but it was your fiancé that was murdered here twenty years ago, was it not? Do you not think you are both over-reacting in this case, when a full-grown man has taken the train north to visit his family? Perhaps you see a mystery where there is no mystery."

Bridie sat the teapot down gently on the table and made no effort to pass anything to their guest. It was Odette who spoke up, her voice harsh.

"No, Officer, we have explained the threats and NO, we do not think we are over-reacting,"

The policeman rubbed a chin that looked as if it had never seen a razor yet. He turned to Bridie.

"Miss Mayford, the death of David Lewis was resolved with the discovery of the murdered Tutor Bacon was it not?"

"Maybe in the minds of the police, but knowing David Lewis had threats made against him by my father, I was never satisfied Tutor Bacon did what he did out of vindictiveness. I have always suspected someone ordered, and maybe paid, the teacher to do what he did."

"The man was a pervert, Ma'am. Surely, they told you of the evidence found?"

Bridie sucked in a breath. Her head reeled. "No one told me that. And what do you know of it anyway? Have the police made a gossip party of my tragedy?" She drew in another noisy breath. "I cannot imagine Officer Rogers betraying our trust like that. I will get to the bottom of this, I can assure you, and you will not be turning Odette's heartache into the policemen's entertainment." Her mouth opened and shut, but no further words fell out. It was Odette who stood and spoke in her place.

"I think it best if you leave now. We will go to London tomorrow and see the inspector ourselves and mention your non-help here this afternoon."

"Please, Missus, I am sorry to have upset you both. I had no intention of upsetting anyone, but I must look at all aspects of the situation, and the possible repercussions from the events. I am also dreadfully sorry if you think your tragic loss was ever used as entertainment for anyone. I knew Officer Rogers and I know full well he would never do such a thing. It seems obvious he omitted to tell you of those details to protect you as a young woman. I only found out because, when you asked me to call, it was routine for me to examine any files we had of calls to these premises. I am truly sorry. I apologize if I have caused you any unnecessary distress."

Bridie almost dropped to her seat. She pointed to the tea and spoke to Odette.

"Odette, I think we all need a cup of tea, will you serve?" Odette moved over in front of the tray.

The peeler continued, "The Inspector should pass through the village after lunch tomorrow, on his way back from Southampton and Portsmouth. I will endeavour to have him call out here to see you, or did you want to come to the police station in the village?" He posed the question for Bridie.

"If it is not too inconvenient for the inspector, we would like to welcome him here."

As she placed the cup in front of her aunt, Odette's hand trembled, spilling a little tea into the saucer. Her aunt was not wont to throw out invitations to guests, willy nilly.

When Sanders arrived in the early evening to collect Mrs. Sanders at the end of her duty, Bridie went out and spoke to him where he waited at the horse and dog cart.

"Good evening, Sanders."

"Good evening, Miss Bridie, it's a beautiful night."

"It is Sanders. I would like to ask you a question about the events around finding the body of Tutor Bacon all those years ago?"

"Of course, but that was a long time ago, I'm not sure I can remember it all that well."

"That young policeman, who was here this afternoon, said the tutor was a pervert." Bridie struggled to force the word out between her lips. "Officer Rogers never said anything about that to me."

Sanders pulled at his right ear, something Bridie had noticed over the years Sanders often did when put on the spot.

"As I said, Miss Bridie, it was a long time ago. I'm sure if you were not told everything, it was out of the kindness of Officer Roger's heart. No doubt he told the Colonel everything and maybe he preferred you heard the diluted version. I wasn't privy to all that transpired that night."

Bridie watched Sanders' eyes, but she saw no falsehood there. "Thank you, Sanders, you are most likely correct."

Sanders let out a soft, long breath when at that moment, Mrs. Sanders arrived with her basket.

"Is everything alright, Miss Bridie?"

"Yes, thanks, Mrs. Sanders, I just had to ask your husband something."

It was early afternoon, when the Inspector of the London Criminal Investigation Division arrived alone at the front door of Clawhaven Manor, having left the young officer back at the village station.

Bridie and Odette sat in the library going through all their notes on what they wished to speak to their expected guest about. Mrs. Sanders ushered Inspector Davies, a tall slim man with grey hair and a thick moustache, into the room. Close on his heels, the maid arrived with the afternoon tea tray.

"I am very pleased to meet you, Miss Mayford, and Mrs. Treloar. I knew of the Colonel's admirable reputation as a soldier and a gentleman. It is my privilege to meet his granddaughter and great-granddaughter."

When the Inspector was seated, Bridie poured the tea and offered the seed cake sliced on a plate.

"How did you know of our grandfather, Inspector?"

"My grandfather was in the Colonel's Division and only had good to say of the man." He cast his glance around the library. "What we would not give to have a resource room like this at the C.I.D." He smiled, "But then, I should not complain – we are making progress, slow though it might be. We are teaching the men to retrieve fingerprints and take photographs when examining a crime scene these days. This is progress. The telegraph has been a wonderful step ahead too."

With the niceties over and the tea tray pushed aside, the Inspector asked Odette to tell of her concerns for the safety of her husband.

Inspector Davies listened, took notes, and only interrupted when he wanted something clarified. After Odette finished speaking, he looked over at Bridie.

"I take it you will concur with everything Mrs. Treloar has told me?"

"Yes, Inspector, and I must add I have known Peter for over two years now, and I believe if he said he was going to write to ease Odette's fears he would do so, no matter what." Bridie reached over and squeezed Odette's hand when she noticed the tears trickling down her face. "What also worried us was not only the fact that we heard the threats made by my nephew, but two of my staff were witnesses also. In fact, one, Sanders, had been accosted with similar threats when out on the roads working his horses."

"Thank you. Will there be any chance of having a word with these witnesses too?"

"Yes, of course, Inspector. I have Jimmy and Sanders working close at hand, for your convenience."

"That's very thoughtful, Miss Mayford."

The sky hung heavy with dark grey clouds when the Inspector offered his farewells. Perspiration stood out on his forehead.

"Miss Mayford, Mrs. Treloar, thank you very much for your hospitality. I am sorry to hear of your concerns and I will have a team follow up on the mysterious disappearance of Peter Treloar as soon as I return to my office in London." He bowed a short nod and swung up into the saddle on his dark horse with its gleaming coat. His hand reached down and patted the animal's neck. "You can be assured I will keep you abreast of any discoveries, ladies."

"Thank you, Inspector, if we have any news from here, we will notify you immediately. Safe travelling." Bridie called as he turned to canter down the driveway.

Odette and Bridie stood on the porch for some time after the inspector had disappeared, each deep in thought.

"I feel better having talked with Inspector Davies, Bridie, but I still feel this weight within my chest. I think we are too late. If Peter was still alive, he would have sent word to us already."

Bridie reached over and wrapped her arm around her niece's shoulders. She did not speak aloud, but her thoughts ran parallel to Odette's.

"Perhaps we should not lose hope until the Inspector has had his team investigate the train journey on the night in question."

"Yes, of course, but if there is no hope left, I am all for moving to Australia as you suggested weeks, or was it months ago."

"For the moment, we will wait until we hear from the inspector."

Four anxious weeks later, two letters addressed to Odette were passed over to Mrs. Sanders from Mr. Featherstone's new assistant Billy Featherstone, his son.

When Bridie received them in her office, she noted the thick one was from the office of the Criminal Investigation Department in London, and the other was written in a shaky scrawl and sent from the Cumberland district in the northwest of England. The sight of the postmark sent her spirits flying until almost immediately her hopes faded when she realized this was not from Peter. She remembered Peter's neat script. Both envelopes were placed on the corner of the desk.

"Where is Odette, Mrs. Sanders? I have not seen her since breakfast time."

Mrs. Sanders' hesitancy in answering drew Bridie's attention.

"Well, … I … er, I think Miss Bridie, Mrs. Odette is a little indisposed."

"In what way indisposed? Is she alright?"

"She has been nauseous every morning this week." Mrs. Sanders' eyes sparkled in the usually expressionless face.

"You mean …," Bridie switched her attention from the letters to her niece, "you mean to say … do you think …."

"I am as sure as one can be. Yes, it would seem Mrs. Odette may be pregnant."

"Oh."

Bridie found it impossible to concentrate on the accounts, while her thoughts swirled with the possibility of Odette's pregnancy. Her gaze returned to the mail. How were the contents going to affect Odette? Within herself, a wave of hope rose up and up only to crash down onto the sands of rational thought and drain away into sorrow and compassion for her niece. Bridie's spirits lifted. *Maybe a pregnancy will offer Odette hope.* She turned back to the columns of figures.

Bridie raised her head at the sound of Odette's voice talking to Mrs. Sanders in the hall. Odette rushed into the room her eyes alight and colour brightened her face – a change from the pallor of her features of late.

"Mrs. Sanders said there is a letter here from the Cumberlands."

Bridie handed over the letters with a wary heart. It was all she could do not to tap her feet with impatience as Odette stared at the two envelopes.

"I do not know which one I should open first." Odette sat on the nearest chair and shuffled the letters on her lap.

"We both hold out little hope for a positive result from the inspector. Maybe the one from Cumberland may hold more promise." Bridie felt she wanted to scream. *Just open one or the other.*

Odette took up Grandpa Wellington's paper knife and slit open the envelope. She took a deep breath and smoothed the letter open on the desktop. Bridie clenched her hands out of sight on her lap. She did not wish to betray her nervousness. When she first noticed the tears leaking down Odette's cheeks, she was not sure whether they might be tears of joy or sorrow. Her last ray of hope shattered at the sight of Odette's stricken face, when she looked up.

"Bridie, they have seen no sign of Peter. He has not arrived at the family farm."

Bridie stood up and walked around the desk. She pushed the door shut with her foot before wrapping her arms around Odette's shoulders. Her niece sobbed, deep convulsive sobs. Gradually these subsided to soft gasps. Odette clung tightly to her aunt.

When Odette quietened, Bridie asked, "May I read the letter?" Odette nodded and passed the paper across the desk.

Dear Odette,
Not long after we received my brother's letter to inform us of his marriage, we had a local policeman here at the farm making inquiries about whether Peter had arrived. We had not realized he

intended to return home to visit our ailing mother. We did not know until then of his disappearance under mysterious circumstances.

Odette, I am so sorry but we have no answer for you as to what has happened to our brother. If he has been delayed for whatever reason, we will ensure he sends word to you immediately when he does arrive. May we offer a belated welcome into our family and I am sure Peter will turn up safe and well shortly. He did have a way of getting caught up in helping someone in need. It is not unlikely he may be doing someone a favour and will turn up on our doorstep any day soon.

May this note go with God's Blessing

May He keep our brother safe.

From Mark, Johnny, Maggie, Sarah.

Peter's siblings, and from our mother

"Mark said there that Peter is often getting caught up helping people, and I very much believe it, knowing him as I do."

Feeling that the essence of the letter was more like a family grasping at straws, Bridie kept her own counsel.

"Anything is possible, dear," she muttered before tapping the table with her fingers. "Perhaps you should open the inspector's letter and see if he has something worthwhile to contribute."

Bridie watched Odette chew her bottom lip as she waded through the several sheets of paper. When her niece's glance lifted, Bridie only read black despair therein. Without a word, Odette passed the pages across the desk.

Bridie lay the pages on the sheet of blotting paper and took up the one from the inspector.

Dear Mrs. Treloar and Miss Mayford

Firstly, I would like to thank you both again for the warm hospitality offered to me during my visit to Clawhaven Manor.

I have had my officers examine every section of the railway line all the way from London through to the Scottish border. They have been out on foot searching on both sides of the railway tracks for any evidence of foul play. Officers were charged with speaking to all staff on duty on the train that night and those at the stations en route.

I have had my secretary make a copy of the summary of these reports and have included them here. I visited Mr. Edward Mayford whom I found lived up to your report on his reliability. The man denied all knowledge of Peter Treloar, which you will be aware is contrary to what your reliable witnesses told me. I will keep that discrepancy in mind in case it ever becomes necessary to call him to attention in the future.

I am sorry my news is not of a more pleasant nature.
Yours sincerely

A sweeping signature filled the lower section of the writing paper. Bridie felt Odette's pain as, with a reluctant hand, she took up the individual summaries of the investigations and began to read them one by one.

The sound of shuffling papers ceased. The sheets of paper sat stacked in a tidy heap. Odette's soft weeping tore at Bridie's heart. She pushed her chair back and stood up.

"Come, Odette, let us take a walk along the seafront. I, for one, need the salt air to clear my head and I am sure it will do you no harm either."

The two women walked along the bridle path each deep in their own thoughts, while the breeze played havoc with their hair and ruffled their heavy petticoats. When Bridie looked up and realized she stood at the base of the rise to the cottage on the cliff, she swung about and led Odette back the way they had come.

Odette opened her mouth to speak, but her words were whipped aside by the strong breeze. She closed her mouth and with her head down placed one foot in front of the other by rote. It was not until they passed under the trees deep in the orchard that she spoke again.

"Bridie, do you think we can really just pack up and emigrate to Australia?"

Bridie stopped walking. She reached over and placed her hands upon Odette's shoulders.

"Is that what you want to do, Odette? If I am to believe the evidence, you may be carrying Peter's child."

"I am sure that is so, and I fear for the baby's safety and for my safety too. Edward is a vindictive man. I am sure he is not of sound mind."

Bridie wrapped her arms further around her niece. "Dearest Odette, I would like to say such a thing is impossible, but I agree with you, Edward is not of sound mind." She unwrapped her arms and now, with both hands resting on Odette's shoulders, Bridie held her niece away to look into the violet eyes. "I think we should consider Mr. Birmingham's advice. Do we take an extended trip to Australia first, and then, depending on how we feel in several months, maybe even a year, we may or may not take the more permanent step."

The pair moved on and by mutual unspoken agreement, they sat at the table on the edge of the fruit trees near the back door of the manor.

"What will we do with the manor ... and the estate?" Odette's words were more a thought than a question.

"The staff will remain of course. I have full confidence in Mr. Axel and Sanders to manage the place satisfactorily – that is what they are doing now anyway. They will have access to our accountant at Langford's accountancy firm and to Mr. Birmingham our solicitor. Mrs. Sanders loves the manor and will take good care of it. I would like to ask Jimmy and Rosa to come with us, they are very resourceful people, who may be relied on to take care of us. We know Mrs. Sanders' other two daughters who live in the Portsmouth, and Southampton areas are married – one to a farmhand and the other to a gardener with the council. We might entice them and their families to move here. Mrs. Sanders would appreciate that, I am sure. She is often fretting about them."

"You have given this quite a bit of thought, Bridie."

"It has been on my mind as an option. I did not know how you would feel."

"To be honest I am torn between going and waiting in the hope Peter turns up," Odette choked on a sob.

When no further evidence came to light on Peter's absence, Bridie called Jimmy and Rosa into the library, where she discussed with them the plans for herself and Odette to travel to, and maybe live in Australia. She explained her desire to have them join her for their help and service.

"Your fares will be paid for, and you will receive the same wages as you currently receive." Bridie stood watching the waves of expressions wafting back and forth across their faces. "I know this is a big decision for you, and I will let you think about it for some weeks. I am sorry, but I do not want you to discuss this with the others until I make a formal announcement in a fortnight, when I have all the information I need from the solicitor and the accountant. Mr. Birmingham has a nephew living and working in Australia in a place called Townsville. It is a developing port on the north-east coast. The country produces crops to the north and south and cattle to the west. He says it is a large town and growing all the time. It sounds interesting and I think that will be our destination. Mr. Birmingham visited Townsville the year before last, and he plans to book us on the same ship on which he and his wife sailed. He said it took them a little while to get used to the limited living space on the ship, but it was all very lush and comfortable. He has advised me to book a suite for Mrs. Odette and myself and the adjacent first-class cabin for you both. This way you can be close by. The ship on which they travelled had one suite set up at the end of a corridor of first-class cabins. At the other end of the corridor was a spacious saloon in which everyone in first-class ate and spent much of their time when not out on the deck playing games, or in Mr. Birmingham's case, watching games and attending other entertainment events." Bridie sipped at her tea before going on. "If you choose to come with us, I will make replacements for the staff here as required."

Jimmy and Rosa exchanged prolonged glances. It was Rosa who posed the question, "May we offer a tentative acceptance at this stage? We will make a firm answer after you have spoken to the others and we can discuss things with my mother."

Bridie reached over and laid her hand on Rosa's. "Thank you, Rosa," she looked up at Jimmy, "and to you, Jimmy. I cannot expect more at this time." Bridie gathered up the papers on the table and made to call the meeting to an end.

During the next two weeks, which passed without any positive news regarding Peter Treloar, Bridie and Odette perused all the legal and monetary advice produced by both Mr. Birmingham, the solicitor, and Mr. Langford, the accountant. Bridie called a meeting at the manor for the senior staff at Clawhaven Estate and those of the manor.

"In the dining room, thanks Rosa, and open the windows. It is the coolest room in the summer."

Mr. Axel, Sanders and Jimmy, the staff from outside, sat on one side of the table. Mrs. Sanders and Rosa faced them from the opposite side. Bridie and Odette sat at either end of the table.

When everyone was settled, Bridie spoke.

"I will need the assurance from everyone here that what we are about to discuss this morning will go no further than this room."

The murmurs of assent flowed around the table.

"Everyone present here is fully abreast of the recent tragedy involving our family, similar in nature to one nearly eighteen years ago. Odette and myself are very much in need of an escape and have chosen to take a trip to Australia. I have full trust in all of you here to maintain the running of the estate," Bridie nodded to the men, "And the upkeep of the manor itself." She smiled at Mrs. Sanders. "Most likely we may need more staff, and I will discuss this with you, Mr. Axel, and with you, Mrs. Sanders, shortly."

Bridie went into more depth on her arrangements made for the supervision by the accountant and the solicitor in her and Odette's absence.

"We have asked Jimmy and Rosa to come with us on this venture and they are currently considering this request. If they do come with us, you would need another farm hand, Mr. Axel, plus a gardener to ensure the grounds at the manor are maintained." Bridie turned towards Mrs. Sanders, "Do you think your two daughters, Meg and Patsy with their husbands might be interested? If I recall, Meg's husband Bill McLeish is a groundsman with the city in Southampton, and Patsy's husband is a farmhand outside Portsmouth – I never got to meet him at the weddings."

"No, that is right, he was unable to get away. His name is Doug Chambers," excitement almost stole Mrs. Sanders' words.

"If we were to provide accommodation for them here on the estate, do you think they might consider moving to this area?"

Mrs. Sanders' eyes lit up. She looked over at her husband who grinned back at her. Bridie thought for a moment the always-composed Mrs. Sanders might even cry – something never heard of before.

Sanders spoke to Bridie, "The Missus has been fretting for years about the girls being so far away. She won't put up any sort of argument, Miss Bridie."

Ten days later, when acceptance had been received from the new farmhand and the replacement gardener, Bridie summoned Mrs. Sanders to her grandfather's office. Bridie looked up from the papers on the desk when the housekeeper arrived.

"Mrs. Sanders, I have a proposition to put to you and Sanders. If we converted the dining room and the smoking room into a bedroom and living area for you, the parlour room can become a storage for the furniture from those two rooms. That side of the downstairs area will be shut off from the main manor. I would feel much happier knowing you and Mr. Sanders lived inside the manor itself, and it was not left empty. You may like it if your daughter, married to the gardener, lived in your home, and the farmhand, married to your other daughter, lived in cottage number three, up from the dairy."

Relief washed over Bridie when she noticed the excitement flash across her housekeeper's face, only visible for seconds.

"Miss Bridie, I could not be happier. I agree, it will be much easier to keep an eye on things here if we are living inside." Mrs. Sanders drew a sharp breath, "You do realize we have only about three months before you leave. I wonder if we will have time to do everything."

"I have full confidence in your skills at making things happen, Mrs. Sanders."

Bridie tripped lightly up the staircase with the agility of someone much younger. She found Odette with a thick ledger book in her hands taking note of the furnishings, paintings and other treasures within each room.

"How is your inventory going?"

"This is the last room, thank goodness. It is such a tiresome job. It was hard at times not to stop and investigate things much more closely, but if I did that, I would still be in the first room."

"It is amazing some of the things gathered over the generations." Bridie cast her gaze slowly around the room. "It will be very sad to leave all this."

"Are you having second thoughts, Bridie?"

"No, my dear, I just remind myself that all these beautiful things have not brought a lot of happiness to you or me."

With only ten days until their departure, Odette entered the kitchen to find Rosa, under Mrs. Sanders' supervision, showing her two sisters around the kitchen.

"I am glad I have you all together. Miss Bridie and I have sorted our clothing and we have several large boxes to be sent off to the church to raise funds for the Rector's latest project. You ladies are more than welcome to sort through them and take any you think you might like. They are in the music room."

Mrs. Sanders spoke up first. "That is kind of you, Mrs. Odette, our Rosa was only saying this morning she might need a better dress if she is going to be in the first-class area on the ship."

"Rosa, please feel free to browse. If you could let Mary Axel know that she is welcome to do the same, I would be most grateful."

On the evening before they departed from Clawhaven Manor, a thick tarpaulin covered the bulky contents on the large dray standing in the front driveway. Sanders planned on hitching the four Clydesdale horses up first thing in the morning. In the stable, young Ben Hodges was beside himself with excitement. Tomorrow he would drive the dray to Portsmouth under Mr. Sanders' supervision. On their homeward journey, while Mr. Sanders returned the coach to Clawhaven, he was to drive the dray and horses by himself. Last minute luggage waiting for loading onto the coach at daylight, stood in the corner of the manor hall.

"Are we doing the right thing?" Bridie spoke more to herself than Odette standing at her side. "I have to admit some concern with you being in your delicate condition."

"I think it is the right thing for us at this moment, and we have left things open to return if we wish to do so." Odette reached over and held Bridie's hand as a reassurance to herself as well as a comfort to her aunt. "I am sure lots of women in Australia have babies too. We may just need to delay our return if that is what we want until the child is a little older perhaps."

"You are right. If nothing else, we will have a very interesting holiday." Bridie ran her gaze over the new dress Odette wore today. The soft muslin material gathered under her breasts by a small satin bow flared out to conceal her expanding abdomen below. "That dress looks so comfortable, dear."

"It is. Mrs. Turner wanted to make me a larger corset to pull my tummy in, but I did not think the baby would appreciate it."

"Sounds most uncomfortable for both of you. Did she mind – Mrs. Turner?"

"No, but she was surprised, I think. She did not mind when I ordered three more dresses like this." Odette ran her hands along the flowing material. A soft smile curled her lips. She looked back up to her aunt. "Bridie, will you come with me to the office? I am going to leave a note for Peter in the secret tunnel. If he does return and we are not here, I am sure he will expect me to leave a note somewhere, and where could be safer?"

"Of course, Odette. We can always hope. Stranger things have happened before." Bridie's glance of compassion held little sign of belief. A shiver ran through her body, which had nothing to do with the cooling evening. "How are you coping with the morning sickness?" Bridie asked as they put aside their lists of all they had to complete before retiring after dinner. The pair walked down the staircase hand in hand.

"Lately, it has been little more than a vague thought. Rosa's potions have done wonders. She promised to bring some with her on the ship to relieve any sea sickness we might experience."

"I did not realize she had such a knowledge of herbs."

"According to her mother, Rosa learnt at her grandmother's knee. She was a renowned healer in the Midlands somewhere." Odette opened the door to the office and sat at the desk. She took up a clean sheet of paper, checked the nib in the pen and lifted the lid on the ink pot.

While Odette wrote her note accompanied by the soft scratch of the pen nib on the paper, Bridie walked around the almost bare shelves and checked that all the cupboards containing current files were locked. Older files were in storage upstairs. She turned back to the desk when she heard the flutter of the notepaper as Odette dried the ink.

"There are envelopes in the top drawer, alongside the list of instructions we left for Mr. Axel and Sanders."

Bridie watched as the secret panel opened and Odette entered the chamber at the manor end of the tunnel. When her niece emerged, she was seen to wipe tears from her eyes. The well-maintained panel closed silently. They walked hand in hand to their bedrooms.

PART THREE

AUSTRALIA

CHAPTER TEN

Departures

1896

As the flotilla of smaller vessels turned back towards the harbour, their sails sagged and flapped until the breeze caught up with them. Smoke from the ship's engine billowed up from the funnel to be dispersed at the whim of the wind. The gusts whipped at the canvas of the triangular try-sail – the only sail on the three otherwise bare masts of the passenger ship – making it crack like rifle shots that echoed across the water. The afternoon sun appeared moodily between the gathering grey clouds.

"Try-sail help captain with steering, Missus," the bare-footed, dark-skinned lascar crew member wearing a neat beret and a grey cotton shirt that hung loosely over a pair of whiter-than-white cotton trousers, pointed with his long slim fingers, as he answered Bridie's question from where she stood at the ship's rail watching the shore disappearing in the distance. Bridie smiled her thanks for the information.

A cold breeze cut across the bow of the ship reminding everyone they were leaving behind an approaching winter en route to what was likely to be a summer of unknown depths. Rolling waves set the ship angling down the troughs to then rise upon the looming crests, as they ploughed ahead in a south-westerly direction.

Bridie was happy to see colour returning to Odette's cheeks after months of such pallor. The two women stood with their elbows linked. The wind ruffled their skirts and threatened the security of the extra hat pins applied. Their glances met. Their smiles widened.

A little astern of them, Rosa clutched Jimmy's arm with one hand while her other held the bonnet on her head.

"Let me arm go, me dearest, or it's likely to fall off. You be cuttin' off the blood flow."

"Oooh, Jimmy, the ship is so small and the sea is sooo big."

"I'm sure the captain knows what he is doing. He has done this a thousand times before."

When they took the time to explore their berths more closely, Bridie and Odette spent several minutes discussing the oil lantern in its frame on the wall in the small sitting room, which joined their two sleeping berths. The only light in sight.

"Seems a poor light for a first-class suite," Odette offered.

Bridie checked again in the two narrow rooms containing a sleeping berth in each.

"This is the only lantern. There is a small glass dome in each of our ceilings and look, there is one in this sitting room too." At that moment, Jimmy's familiar clatter on the door turned their attention to his arrival.

"What do you think of the electric lights, Miss Bridie?" he asked.

Before she had an opportunity to ask, "What electric lights," Jimmy flicked the switch in the wall near the door with one hand and pointed to the glass dome in the ceiling with the other.

"See," he crowed.

Bridie and Odette began to laugh. "How did you figure that out, Jimmy?"

"I must confess it was Topas who showed me how the lightin' worked. He said the power to run the lights comes from the engine room."

Bridie flicked the light on and off several times before Jimmy remembered to tell her of the other message from Topas.

"Topas also said not to flick the lights on and off repeatedly or it will kill the light."

"It would have been nice to have this system of lights at the manor." Odette turned the switch on in her sleeping cabin.

The days fell into a routine. Jimmy and Rosa were the first to rise. They ate with several other servants of the first-class passengers in a small room off the saloon dining room. All passengers received a small glass of lemon juice with their breakfast. When they returned, Bridie and Odette were beginning to stir. Jimmy always delivered a bucket of warm water for their morning ablutions.

Rosa dispensed her herbal potion to each of them to ward off any seasickness, and in so doing did not notice that she might be harbouring other reasons for having nausea in the morning. As the ship passed along the edge of the Bay of Biscay, the barometer began to drop, the wind squalls increased, the seas tossed restlessly beneath them, and at times broke over the bulwarks. The barometer readings fell further. The squalls developed into a tempest. The yardarms on the foremost mast almost kissed the waves as they barrelled down the deep troughs before water poured from the ship in torrents as it lifted on the next crest. The ship's hatches were battened down and all portholes were checked to be closed. Bridie and Odette clenched the arm-rests of the two settees bolted to the floor in their sitting room. Their bodies tossed back and forth like riders on the backs of wild horses. Following each flash of lightning, the thunder grumbled along outside until exploding like cannon fire. Along with the growl of the engines beneath them and the crash and clatter of the storm above, it felt as if their eardrums might burst. They looked up at the sound of the knock on the door. Jimmy's head appeared. He stood with his feet braced and one hand on the handrail outside the doorway. His other hand slapped the wall in search of the rail inside the suite.

"Are you ladies alright in here? Can I do anything for you?"

It was Odette who replied. "Jimmy, will you help me to my bunk? I think it will be safer for my baby if I lie down there with the rail up, rather than being thrown about while sitting here."

Placing his foot carefully with each jolt of the ship, Jimmy helped Odette into her cabin and onto her bunk. She lay on her side with her back to the bulkhead and a spare pillow held between her and the rail. She dragged the bedcover over her legs.

"Do you wish to lie down too, Miss. Bridie?"

Bridie glanced towards her cabin on the opposite side of the small sitting room but changed her mind.

"Will you help me to the chair in Odette's cabin? I will stay there near her until the weather settles."

Jimmy arranged Bridie comfortably on the chair and delivered a pillow from her own cabin to rest her head against.

"Do your vomit buckets need emptying?" he asked.

"Thanks to your Rosa and her herb mixture, no, we are spared that indignity," Bridie assured him.

At the sound of thudding feet on the deck above, and orders screamed through a speaking trumpet, their heads turned to the portholes, but whatever was happening on deck was not visible. In fact, nothing was visible through the glass but their reflections – with the night outside and the dim light inside the sitting room. Only at each strike of the lightning outside did the room fill with a brilliant flash.

"You better get on back to Rosa, Jimmy, she'll be getting worried," Bridie advised. "I am sure if there is anything we need to know, the stewards will keep us informed."

On the deck outside, the winds howled in fury. Pelting rain pummelled the seamen as they struggled to cut down the trysail which had been blown out of its gaskets. Between each flash of lightning, they worked by feel alone in the otherwise pitch-dark night full of impenetrable clouds, which obscured any hint of moon or starlight. Regular bellows of sound erupted from the foghorn.

The captain ordered a double watch as they inched along the main channel, steering almost blind.

Nineteen hours later the wind began to abate, somewhat reluctantly. Under the supervision of a steward, the lascars, who usually worked in the kitchen and saloons, began to deliver tea and biscuits to those passengers feeling able to eat.

Three days after they had waved goodbye to the shores of their homeland, the passengers lined the rails to welcome the sight of the Rock of Gibraltar. Cheers rang along the decks of the ship at the sight of the calm mirrored waters of the Mediterranean Sea.

Odette returned to the peace of her cabin where she retrieved the new journal given to her by the staff of Clawhaven as a farewell gift. She took up her pencil and began to write of her heartache in saying goodbye to the home of her childhood. She expressed her feelings of fear, confusion and anticipation, as they made their way to a new home in a new country.

Having been roused from their bunks, as the ship eased away from the Malta harbour, Jimmy and Rosa stood at the ship's rail enjoying the relative quiet of an early morning. According to Topas, the lascar who served their breakfast, the shadow of land in the distance creeping off to the north of them was the tip of Italy. Rosa leant back into the familiar comfort of Jimmy's chest.

"Jimmy, what would you say if I told you Mrs. Odette is not the only one going to have a child in Australia?"

Jimmy stepped back and spun Rosa about to face him. A grin as wide as the ship was long, spoke of his joy, his anxiety, his pride, and his concern.

"Are you tellin' me we be havin' our own little Australian? When?" He pulled her into the protection of his arms. "Are you sure?" he mumbled from within her hair wafting up into his face on the light breeze. "How far along?"

"I think it must be at least two months. I didn't realize I might have morning sickness. I assumed it was sea sickness and the ginger and herbal mixture dampened the effect." A frown sat upon her brow. "When should we tell the ladies?"

Jimmy hugged her closer. "Not for a wee while yet. Let's savour this ourselves. We've waited such a long time."

"Well, we had best return to our cabin because they'll be stirring shortly."

"Alright me love, but this is our secret for a bit yet."

"Yes, Jimmy, our secret." Rosa stretched up and planted a kiss on his cheek.

They arrived at Miss Bridie's suite just as she opened the door and looked out along the corridor.

"Good morning, Rosa, Jimmy. What is the matter with you two? You both look like the cat that got the cream."

Rosa and Jimmy's glances met; their eyes sparkled. It was Jimmy who answered. "'Tis nothin' Miss Bridie, only a beautiful morning outside. I have your hot water here. Will I take it in?"

"And I have your tea tray, Miss Bridie, will I put it on your little table?" Rosa followed Jimmy in and placed the tray gently on the table between the settees. "Is Mrs. Odette feeling better this morning?"

"Yes, thanks, Rosa," Odette called from her berth. "Did you and Jimmy put in a good night?"

"Yes, thanks," Rosa smiled as she bobbed her head on the way out.

"You will not forget the concert the captain has planned on the promenade deck later this morning? The children from the steerage class are looking forward to it so much."

"Oh, yes, Mrs. Odette, we wouldn't miss it for anything." Rosa turned back to answer. "I have been through all the masks in the props' box like you asked and spruced them up a bit. I am sure the little ones will appreciate all the work you and Miss Bridie have put in."

Bridie laughed. "It should all be a lot of fun."

Parents from the steerage class along with their children of all ages, blinked several times as they first arrived on the promenade deck. The men's and women's clothes were unironed but obviously brushed out, especially for the day. Most had their feet covered. The children of all sizes, dressed in almost a uniform array of browns and greys, with bare feet, watched agape at everything around them. Crew members guided them to where they were to gather. They sat on the deck in the shade of the taut tarpaulin high above their heads.

Bridie stood at a table behind the Broadwood piano which had been manhandled up from the saloon immediately after breakfast. She dipped into the props' box and retrieved, one by one, the freshly painted and repaired masks to be worn by the actors. Their purpose was to enable the audience to identify each character. Odette sat on the stool at the piano running through the music scores selected for the entertainment.

The captain arrived with a medium-sized ship's bell in his hand. The man, in his spotless uniform neat and ironed to perfection, stood tall at the side of the gathering. The polish on his shoes gleamed and his cap sat jauntily on his head. When his fingers tugged at the clapper of the bell, the clangs echoed out over the ocean. A hush fell over the chattering and shuffling spectators.

"Welcome everyone. I am sure the children here are all wishing for my introduction to be short and sweet, and that is what it will be. The passengers from the upper deck have generously given of their time to provide this amusement for the children – and I am sure for their parents also – to make a bright change in your day. May I introduce our pianist, Mrs. Treloar, and her aunt, Miss Mayford, who have organized this event? Please put your hands together in appreciation for all their efforts."

The captain stepped back and remained standing beside the lifeboat in its davit near the ship's rail. His eyes seldom left Miss Mayford's face. The woman intrigued him. A lady without a doubt, whose well-preserved figure in a dress designed to make the most of her curves, he found alluring. The softly tanned skin of her face and neck, and those deep blue eyes, a deeper blue than the bluest sea he had ever seen, drew his gaze. Beneath her bonnet, the dark curls shone when caught in the sunshine. He knew her age – he had checked in the ship's records – to be forty years and in the past week, he had never discovered a grey hair visible on her head.

As if she had read his thoughts at that moment, Bridie reached up, untied the ribbons of her bonnet, and placed it on the far corner of the table. She smiled over at Odette, whose fingers ran up and down the keyboard in a lively polka. The children, of their own volition, tapped the rhythm out on the deck.

Captain Ryan Aitkins felt his breath catch in his throat at the sight of Miss Mayford's uncovered head and the smile that dimpled her cheeks. He sucked air into a chest starving of oxygen when she spoke.

"Good morning, children. My name is Miss Mayford. Mrs. Treloar," Bridie's hand waved towards Odette, "and I hope to hear a lot of singing and laughter and cheers as we bring you songs and stories. We have several others here who will be helping you enjoy the morning and I will introduce them to you as we go along."

The children applauded again and some even whistled. A man's voice, obviously a parent, was heard to call from the back row of adults.

"Dopples Dawkins don't let me hear you whistling at a lady, or you won't sit down for a week."

This brought a great cheer and laughter from the other adults, as well as the children.

Bridie signalled to three young ladies from the first-class deck who had been sitting in the shade of the lifeboat. They came and stood at Bridie's side. Bridie introduced them each in turn.

"This is Miss Mary, this is Miss Peggy, and this is Miss Meg, they are going to sing a favourite nursery rhyme and when they have finished, I want you children," Bridie cast her arm around the deck taking in all the audience, "to sing the same nursery rhyme as loud as you can, to drown out the engine noise."

Mary started with Baa Baa Black Sheep. Her soprano voice rang out over the deck.

Baa Baa Black Sheep have you any wool?
Yes, sir, yes, sir, three bags full,
One for the master and one for the dame,
And one for the little boy who lives down the lane.

At the beginning of the last line, Mary's voice disappeared beneath the shouted voices of the children who knew the tune and the words so well.

Bridie grinned at Odette and said, "Can we do that again with the children this time?"

Captain Aitkins' heart pounded inside his chest at the sight of Bridie's grin. Guilt and anxiety filled the glance he cast around, even when the loud singing voices assured him it would be impossible for anyone else to hear his heartbeats.

Peggy stood waiting for the roar to quieten so she could sing her piece "A Hunting We Will Go"

Her voice was no match for the enthusiasm of the children and the piece was sung by them twice.

Bridie's gaze caught the wide smile and the crinkles at the corners of Captain Aitkins' eyes. She smiled. Her heart fluttered. She barely recognized the sensation. It had been a long time.

Meg took her place beside the piano – laughing. "Do you all know Hickory Dickory Dock?"

"Yes," returned the shouted cry.

Once again everyone on the deck sang with enthusiasm.

When peace returned to the deck and the flap of the shade-canvas stirred by the breeze was audible again, Bridie asked their guests, "Do you know the story of Little Red Riding Hood?"

"Yes!" the squeal burst along the deck.

Mary stood beside Bridie with a red cloak now thrown over her shoulders.

"Who is this?" Bridie called to the children.

"Red Riding Hood!" once again the shout threatened to blow out the bulwarks.

Jimmy grinned at Bridie as he arrived to stand beside Red Riding Hood with a wolf mask tied around his head.

"Who is this?" she called.

"The Big Bad Wolf!" the shout rang out.

Peggy joined the actors' line with an old gown over her clothes and a large pair of glasses on her face.

"Who is this?"

"Grandma!" The children began to stand to ensure their voices were heard.

Meg arrived wearing a man's coat over her clothes, a man's hat on her head and a small hatchet held over her shoulder.

"Who is this?"

"The woodcutter come to save Grandma and Red Riding Hood!" Feet pummelled the deck. The squeals lifted higher than the engine's smoke.

Bridie's voice was no match as she tried to reclaim order. Her glance beseeched the captain for help. He grinned in return. She felt the flutter again. Her smile turned to one of relief when he clanged the bell and the children settled down onto the deck.

Odette's music tripped along with Red Riding Hood, as she danced through the woods with the basket of goodies on her arm. Odette's left hand pounded the notes as the wolf approached. The audience squealed and tried to warn Red Riding Hood of the danger approaching.

"Nooooo!" they yelled when Grandma opened the door to her cottage, and the wolf stole her gown and glasses and locked her in the cupboard.

"The wolf, the wolf!" they squealed when Red Riding Hood sat beside the bed asking about the big teeth and big eyes of what she thought was her grandma.

"Hurry, hurry!" they called as Odette's fingers on the keyboard reflected the woodsman's approach.

"Chop off his head, chop off his head!" The yell rose in a cloud of voices as the wolf was put out of action.

Laughter, cheers and applause filled the air. "More, more, more!" the crowd called.

As Jimmy placed his mask back on the table, he mumbled to Bridie, "I think I want danger money to do that again."

"Go on, they loved you," she laughed.

Captain Aitkins did not miss the friendliness of Miss Mayford and the man he understood was her servant. *Could they?* The thought ran through his head. *Never, I will not believe that of so fine a lady.*

When Rosa ran up to stand by Jimmy, the glances passing between them convinced Ryan Aitken his suspicions were unfounded.

At last Bridie's voice began to make an impact on the noise of the people on deck.

"It is not too long and Christmas will be upon us. Would you like to join in with a few favourite Christmas Carols?" She nodded at Odette who played the introduction to Jingle Bells. After a little hesitant start, the crowd on deck stood and sang out.

Captain Aitkins' sent his gaze Bridie's way again when he heard her powerful soprano voice dancing above and around the notes of the general singers. Knowing this was something to which he might contribute, he walked over to stand beside her, adding his impressive bass to her lead.

The ship's decks rang to the melodies of Away in a Manger and Silent Night.

Bridie whispered in the captain's ear, "Do you know Charles King Harris's latest, "After the Ball?"

Ryan Aitkins nodded. Bridie walked over to talk to Odette at the piano and the music changed.

The audience fell silent as the voices of Miss Mayford and the ship's captain held them in awe, but on the last refrain the captain encouraged them to join in once again.

A voice called from the crowd, "Do you know Daisy Bell?"

Cheers and whistles split the air. Bridie turned to Odette who nodded her head and the music changed. The decks vibrated and not from the calm seas below their hull, but to the rhythm and pounding on the deck.

Eventually, it was Captain Aitkins who had to call time with the aid of his bell.

"Thank you, everyone, for your enthusiasm this morning, but now we had better prepare the ship for our arrival at Port Said this afternoon. In the meantime, you will find your mid-day meals ready for you. Can we have one last round of applause for Mrs. Treloar on the piano and Miss Mayford with her fine voice and a wonderful band of actors?"

Everyone left the deck still humming the tunes from the morning's repertoire.

Captain Aitkins spoke quietly to Bridie before he left to take up his duties.

"Do you think I could invite those who have entertained us here this morning, to my dinner table this evening?"

"I am sure they will be delighted, but the wolf has his wife with him, may she come too?"

"Of course." Ryan Aitkins left, pondering the feeling of relief at learning the man was married with his wife close at hand.

At the captain's table that evening, Ryan Aitkins met the actors from earlier in the day.

"Ah, so this is the wolf?" the captain laughed when he shook Jimmy Braydon's hand.

"I be a lamb in wolf's clothin' – you ask my little Rose." Jimmy brought his wife forward to be introduced.

"It's true, Captain, he's but a lamb."

Bridie sat on the captain's right with Odette at her side. Mary, Peggy and Meg sat on the opposite side of the table. Jimmy took the opposite table head with Rosa on his left beside Odette.

Bridie's breath almost choked her. Her appetite deserted her. She felt her colour rise every time she looked up to see the captain's eyes upon her. It seemed her intelligence refused to make an appearance. It was left mostly to Odette to speak on their behalf. The three young girls were on their best behaviour. The captain did not forget Jimmy and Rosa at the far end of the table.

"Can you tell me a little of yourself, Mr. Braydon?"

"Tis not much to be tellin', sir. I lived my life on a farm in Sussex. Horses always bein' my interest. I was twelve when mother hired me out as a groom to Miss Mayford there, who was only a slip of a lass at the time."

This brought a smile to Bridie's lips. "Oh, yes, and you arrived at Clawhaven Manor on a horse twice your height."

Jimmy chuckled. "I did. Flyer was his name. Brown horse and seventeen hands, he was."

"That day, I learnt every challenge can be overcome as I watched this midget scale the heights of a seventeen-hands-high horse." Polite mirth circled the table at Bridie's comment.

"I see you may not have so much difficulty these days in mounting the horse," the captain offered.

Jimmy nodded.

"You enjoy riding, Miss Mayford?" Ryan's gaze turned to his right.

"Oh, yes, my grandparents' estate was a productive farm with crops, cattle – dairy and beef, and horses. Later, when my niece joined us, riding was our favourite pastime."

Bridie blushed and directed her attention to the meal on her plate. The captain queried the girls about their backgrounds before turning to Odette.

"You are extremely skilled at the piano, Mrs. Treloar."

"Thank you, Captain, but I fear I will never be as skilled as Aunt Bridie nor our grandmother."

"You did not mention this, Miss Mayford."

As she pondered an answer to his question, the vision rose before her of David Lewis, sitting at the piano in his cottage on the cliff. She felt the tears pressing within her eyes. She could not speak. She offered a weak smile.

It was Jimmy who noticed Bridie's dilemma and spoke up.

"Captain, what about yourself, what brought you to the wheelhouse of a ship like this?"

Ryan Aitkins struggled for a moment to redirect his thoughts from Miss Mayford's strange reaction to his question and back to his guests.

"I don't think I had a chance to be anything else. My father and his father before him both captained ships. My father often raced his clipper around the Cape of Good Hope to Australia with all sails billowing to their limits. My brother swore if Father could have added another mast or two to his ship he would have." He smiled at the memory. "My brother is a captain on the sister ship to this one."

Bridie reclaimed her equanimity and threw a passing appreciative glance Jimmy's way.

When the dinner was finished, it was the captain who escorted everyone to their cabins. He placed a gentle hand on Bridie's elbow allowing Jimmy, Rosa and Odette to walk in front.

"I am sorry if I upset you earlier," he whispered.

Her blue eyes drowned in the grey eyes shining in the lights set in the walls along the corridor between the cabins.

"I am sorry, it was something that happened a long time ago, and I should have forgotten by now."

When Captain Ryan Aitkins returned to the ship's bridge curiosity hung in the air along with the aromas of a strange land.

The following morning, the passengers gathered to eat their breakfast in the saloon, where they found copies of the one-page ship's news sheet in a pile on the table. Voices lifted in question and concern when they read of the order for the passengers to remain on board while the crew loaded the ship's coal replenishments. Due to unrest on the harbour front, local workers refused to load the coal. For their safety, the passengers were to remain ship-bound. Musical entertainment was available for the first-class passengers in the saloon on the upper deck, but the lascars would not be available to wave the punkahs thus keeping the guests cool. They had been commandeered to assist with the coal loading.

A notice was given of the number of passengers from steerage class who had been admitted to the sick bay with measles and chicken pox.

"Those poor souls being locked in and unable to seek a cool breeze in this heat," Odette commented.

"As I understand it, the relatives are keeping vigil with hand fans," Jimmy always the font of the latest information updated the Mayford group. "At least they'll have an able body to stomp on any of the rats running rampant down in that part of the ship."

Everyone stared at Jimmy. Rosa nudged him in the ribs. Bridie rolled her eyes and Odette gasped before she hurried to divert everyone's attention away from Jimmy's unsolicited words.

"Did you read the small addition at the bottom of the page? A man has been admitted with cholera. The captain advises everyone to pay attention to personal hygiene, and to eat only the ship's food until further information is available." The rustle of news sheets rose from each table as everyone scrambled to the end of the page.

By late afternoon the coal was loaded, and their ship lay anchored in the bay awaiting its turn to enter the Suez Canal. The promise of dawn glowed on the horizon to reveal the narrow channel through which they passed. Once the scattered remains of the city were left behind, the sands spread out as far as the eye could see on either side of the waterway. The ship crept forward as they passed other vessels travelling in the opposite direction. When the ship entered the Gulf of Suez the next morning, the breeze lifted bringing with it fine granules of sand, which had everyone rushing back to their cabins to close portholes on the side of the prevailing wind.

A cheer rang throughout the decks when they moved out into the Red Sea. The breeze now held a degree of coolness, as it ruffled the waters. Having been on the ship's bridge for over twenty-four hours, Captain Aitken stumbled to his berth, stripped off his clothes and dropped onto his bunk. His last thought was of the deep blue eyes of Miss Bridie Mayford, and when he awoke six hours later the thought of her filled his head once more.

He lay still with the picture of Bridie Mayford in his mind, but the sense of his ship, its sounds, its movement, its heart, within his soul. He sighed and dragged his feet out and onto the floor. His body's first need was for a bath and a shave with breakfast not far behind.

"We'll not be leavin' the Red Sea 'til tomorrow mornin' and we'll be near Aden shortly after," Jimmy reported to Bridie and Odette when he brought in the warm water for their wash.

"Is that from your Lascar friend or the news sheet?"

"From the other fellow, Tindal, Mrs. Odette. He is always ahead of all other news." Jimmy opened the door and made his exit.

After they had eaten, Bridie and Odette walked several laps around the promenade deck.

"Right now, I feel like I could take the horses for a good canter along the beachfront back home."

Bridie looked over at Odette with a smile and whispered for only the two to hear.

"I think that might be rather difficult, and I am not talking about the fact we are a long way from home. Have you thought how you might climb aboard your horse?" Her glance fell to Odette's seventh month baby bulge.

Odette laughed, as she patted her unborn child with the hand not holding her parasol.

"It would be difficult, I agree."

"You will have to settle this morning for the lecture by our ship's doctor on *Healthy Travelling*."

"Or I could return to the cabin and write up my journal, Bridie."

"With the whole day to fill, I suggest you do both things."

"Do you think we are halfway there yet? Next time you are talking to Captain Aitkens will you ask him?"

"What makes you think I will be talking to the captain any sooner than you will be?"

Odette chuckled softly. "Maybe because I have seen the way he looks at you with those dreamy grey eyes. He has been busy on the bridge lately bringing the ship through the narrow canal and channels, but once we are out into the wide oceans, he will be popping up at your shoulder again, just you see."

"Nonsense, I do not know where you get your ideas from."

It was the same evening when the two met out on the promenade deck. Ryan Aitkens may have been busy on the bridge recently, but he had noticed Miss Bridie made a habit of taking a walk in the evenings, usually alone, before retiring to her cabin.

"Good evening, Miss Mayford."

Bridie felt the trip of her heartbeat and the rush of joy through her veins at the sound of his voice behind her. She struggled to bring her breathing under control.

"Good evening, Captain. It is such a pleasant night out." *Oh, dear me, how droll. What must he think of me?*

"It is that. Would you mind if I accompanied you on your evening stroll?"

"I would enjoy that very much." Her voice sounded breathless in her ears as if she had just run a mile. *Did I just gasp that out? Why am I all of a dither? Will he think I am too forward?* Her thoughts sent a flush over her face. Her gaze fell to the deck. It lifted again when he rested his hand under her elbow.

As they entered the shadow of the lifeboat, Ryan paused and Bridie turned into his waiting arms.

"Miss Mayford, please tell me you are feeling the same way I am feeling?"

To her chagrin, Bridie heard herself stutter. "C-C-Captain Aitkens, I am sorry, but I have led a rather sheltered life. However, I am not totally innocent. I know what love and desire are – or I did a long time ago. You will need to tell me what it is that you are feeling or I will not be able to answer your question. Oh, and please call me Bridie."

Ryan Aitkens' hand reached up and with his forefinger, he gentled an errant dark curl off her face and behind her ear.

"Bridie, I like that name."

Bridie smiled.

"I am a widower; I have been for the past two years. My wife and I had three children, two boys and a girl. They range from eighteen years to fifteen years of age. The two eldest, the boys, are at boarding school and our daughter is with my parents. I am not an inexperienced youth and yet I feel as though I am. My heart is pounding and I know I am rambling. From the moment I first saw you, I knew you were special."

"Captain, it seems we are of similar minds."

Blue eyes stared into grey eyes, reading the language of lovers in each.

"Bridie, I so much want to kiss you. I want to hold you tight and make passionate love to you, but it would not be appropriate to do so out here on the deck, even if we are hidden in the shadows."

A soft smile tweaked at Bridie's lips. "I would like that very much, Captain."

It was the captain's turn to smile. "Not unless you call me Ryan when we are alone together. Will you come to my cabin to drink a nightcap, and we will see what eventuates after that."

Bridie's smile widened. "Yes, Captain, … er … Ryan."

Bridie stepped into the captain's small sitting room which contained two chairs and a small table. A door led off to the right that she assumed led to his sleeping quarters. Through the open portholes facing the sea, the lights from the bridge nearby provided all the illumination they needed. As Ryan used his foot to shut the door behind him, Bridie slid into his arms and raised herself on tip-toe for his kiss. His lips felt soft and warm on hers. They felt hungry for love. She felt a revival of sensations she had not felt for twenty years. A groan escaped her lips. The thrill deep in her core filled her arms with the strength to draw his body closer. His hands fumbled with the buttons at the front of her bodice. Her fingers pushed him aside and released each one at speed. The dress caressed her skin as it slipped to the floor, where it settled around her feet. It was the captain's turn to groan. Bridie helped him with his buttons until they both stood naked and trembling.

"Captain, Ryan, please make love to me right now."

"Your wish is my command." Ryan's strong arms swept Bridie up. He carried her into his berth and lowered her onto the narrow bed. He sat on the edge of the bunk admiring her body. His fingers traced the outline of her curves. "You have the body of a woman half your age, Bridie Mayford. Just the sight of you sets me all a quiver."

Bridie smiled and admired him in return as he climbed over to lie upon her. Their kisses held as he entered her demanding body. Slowly at first, their bodies developed their own rhythm, until the sensations overwhelmed them both and their groans deepened. Eventually, contented sighs were all that was left.

Silence filled the cabin. The smell of seawater filled the room, drifting in on a gentle warm breeze through the open porthole. Ryan covered her face with nibbling kisses. Bridie held him close.

They both dozed for some time. Ryan kissed Bridie awake as the eleventh-hour ship's bells rang out.

"Wake up, my lovely lady. You may be able to idle your day away, but I must report to the bridge at four am. Come, my dear, and I will walk you home."

Bridie stole another kiss before she began to stir.

"Where are my clothes?"

"Wait here, my love, I think they are keeping mine company in the sitting room."

When they were both dressed and Bridie had wrangled with the tangles in her hair, they stepped out onto the deck. Ryan led them through the shadows towards Bridie's cabin, where they stole another embrace before she opened the door and entered. Odette's soft snuffle of sleep greeted her.

With her respectable nightdress in place, and her day dress hanging from the hook in the wall, Bridie stretched back against the pillow of her bunk and relived the night. The secret smile never left her lips. It entered Bridie's thoughts, just as she drifted off to sleep, that they never did get to drink a nightcap together.

≈

The heat was palpable as the ship anchored off Aden to await the agent's arrival with the mail to go on to Australia. After a twelve-hour delay, Captain Aitken's First Mate gave the order to up-anchor and set a course southeast to Batavia. No one complained when the breezes from off the Arabian Sea caressed the decks.

As the ship crossed the invisible line of the equator, the crew provided entertainment for the passengers. The expression on the face of the Ship's Mate indicated he had lost not won, as he did, the draw to see who was to wear the costume of King Neptune. The crew offered encouragement and noisy suggestions. During the enactment of imaginary life under the deep waters, the men rollicked around, before they captured King Neptune, the woeful Ship's Mate. Just before Neptune could be corralled into a cage with a multiple-armed octopus represented by the cabin boy with stuffed hessian bags rolled up as extra limbs, a second group arrived in the nick of time to rescue him – all to the delight of the children.

Ryan and Bridie's relationship deepened in the following days. Ryan's smile lit up his face, but dark rings appeared under his eyes. Odette began to worry about her aunt despite Bridie's reassurance that her frequent tiredness was probably nothing more than the result of being caged-up on the ship for so long.

"Please do not worry, Odette, I promise you I am not ill in any way."

Jimmy was not one to worry. He would rather seek out reasons for any strange phenomenon, and in this case, discovered the regular early morning returns of Bridie to her cabin on the arm of their captain. He had not seen such happiness on her countenance for a very long time; not since he caught her secretly returning from her liaisons with David Lewis, at least twenty years ago. When Odette shared her worries with him, Jimmy was in two minds as to what he should reveal. After his wife and now his expected infant, his loyalties would always belong to Bridie.

"Mrs. Odette, maybe Miss Bridie is just a little claustrophobic after such a long time on the ship. She is a healthy woman. I am sure there is nothing wrong with her," was all he found to mumble.

"Perhaps we should organize another concert for the children, Jimmy. She said the last concert gave her a lot of pleasure."

Jimmy nodded his head in reply, but his thoughts went a little differently. *Miss Bridie needs a little less pleasure I be thinkin'.*

It was Mrs. Beatson, a fellow first-class passenger, who organized another concert on the promenade deck. Odette agreed to play the piano accompaniments for the singers. Having years of experience sharpening up the talents of the vocalists at her local church choir, Mrs. Beatson now gathered many of the steerage-class children seeking out those with voices that might hold a tune. When they presented their repertoire to the ship's passengers and crew on the day before the vessel was due to make land at Batavia, the children gave a sterling performance. Bridie and Captain Ryan sang a medley of songs on the day. Few of the adults present missed the warm connection this pair shared, not only in their memorable voices but also on a personal level in the warmth of their shared gazes.

The ship was due to remain at the docks of Batavia for thirty-six hours. Immediately after an early breakfast on Wednesday, Captain Aitkens waved the explorers, with the Ship's Mate and three crew members as guides, on their way. It was the Mate's reward for being such a good sport at the equator crossing. Ryan and Bridie's eyes held for a long moment before she turned to walk with her friends down the ramp. When the small colourful drays, pulled by horses that plodded along with little interest in their surroundings, dropped the passengers in the centre of the city, the aromatic waves of food spices, smoke from small fires, concentrated human body odours and animal excreta, provided accompaniment to the wall of noise that assaulted the tourists' ears. The harsh and loud voices of the traders promoting their produce and hardware exploded above the heads of the crowds. It seemed no one spoke softly here. The Mayford group gaped as each item for sale was haggled over from the highest to the lowest prices without a pause. Odette found a dress length of light material in blended colours of the seas, the skies and the sands. It was Tindal, a Lascar crew member, who offered to help her make a purchase. When Bridie noticed Rosa looking through baby materials, she paused for thought. Tindal, once again, stepped up to assist with the negotiations. Bridie selected several souvenirs for their friends back home at the Clawhaven Estate. The contents of the basket carried over her arm soon lapped the sides of the plaited cane.

By eleven o'clock, with the sun creeping up on the zenith, the group of passengers was ready to retreat to the ship. Perspiration ran down their faces and stained the armpits of their clothing. Most women waved their fans vigorously. Several women almost fell into their transport in a faint. The moist heat suffocated and sapped their strength.

A shadow of doubt niggled at Odette who, being in her delicate condition, felt the discomfort of the high temperature more than most. She worried how she was going to cope if they found Australia to be of similar conditions.

Bridie spent the afternoon pondering how she was to put the question to Rosa and Jimmy regarding Rosa's interest in baby materials. Eventually, she decided it might be best to face the sensitive question head-on. She decided to take the easiest option and she spoke to Jimmy first.

She found Jimmy up on the top deck leaning over the rail watching the unceasing activities on the harbour.

"Hello, Miss Bridie, did you enjoy the trip to the markets this morning?"

"Yes, Jimmy, but it was something I would choose to experience in the middle of winter, next time."

"That is if they have a winter here," Jimmy laughed.

"Now, Jimmy, I hope you will not be upset if I ask a sensitive question of you."

"Anythin', Miss Bridie, you know that."

As Bridie hesitated over the wording of her question, it was Jimmy who suddenly guessed what might be coming.

"You know, don't you, Miss Bridie?"

"If you mean I know Rosa is in the family way, then I cannot say I know, but after seeing her with the baby materials this morning, I suspect. Is Rosa pregnant?"

"How about we go and ask Rosa herself?" As they approached the cabin door, Jimmy turned on his heel. "Rosa will still be able to do her work for you and Mrs. Odette, Miss Bridie. You won't be sackin' her or us, will you?"

"What do you take me for, Jimmy? Of course not. I guess you and I will have to step up a bit and help with the two new mothers."

Jimmy stopped off to collect Rosa while Bridie went next door to see if Odette was respectable enough to receive visitors.

When Rosa confirmed Bridie's suspicions, Odette was so pleased for Rosa and excited to know her own infant was going to have company in the new country.

"I doubt whether I will have my baby until three months or more after you, Mrs. Odette."

"You will be able to get some practice on my infant then." Odette stood up awkwardly and hugged Rosa as much as she was able with her near-term infant.

≈

When the ship exited the port of Batavia and swung around into the Indian Ocean heading in an easterly direction, everyone welcomed the cooler breezes coming off the waters.

Bridie only had a brief visit with Ryan on the first night out of Batavia.

"Most of the channels, where there are still many unmarked reefs from here across to Cape York and down the east coast of Australia to Brisbane, will demand most of my attention, my love. In the Torres Straits, the sands are known to shift about at the whim of the tides." His finger ran down the side of her face as he held her close. "Bridie, I don't want to say goodbye to you, you do realize that don't you?"

"I am hoping you will want to keep in touch."

"I have the name and address of your hotel written in my journal, and you will let me know as soon as you have your permanent residence, won't you?"

Bridie delivered her assent with a kiss.

"I'll have to devise ways to put a spanner in the engine, so we will need to stop over longer in Townsville each time I pass by."

Bridie snapped her head up. "You would not do that, would you? You are the captain."

He grinned at the sight of the horror written on her face. "Desperate measures and all that, Bridie my temptress." He kissed her. "No, I could not hurt my ship. She is my mistress after all."

Bridie took the scarf from her neck and slipped it around Ryan's neck pulling him closer.

"Will you keep my scarf like the knights did in the olden days?"

"I will treasure it with all my heart." Ryan gentled her head onto his neck for a moment until he stood straighter. "I have something for you too." He retrieved from his pocket a golden tie pin shaped like a ship's anchor enclosed inside a golden heart. He showed her how, at the touch of a hidden clip, the heart and anchor fell apart. He gave half, with the heart, to Bridie, and kept the second half, with the anchor, for himself.

"You are my heart, Bridie. I will be left with only an anchor and no heart. Hopefully, we meet frequently to join these two together."

Tears welled in Bridie's eyes. "If we met every minute of every day, it would not be too much for me."

Ryan kissed her long and hard. "For me too," he whispered.

The landmark named Castle Hill loomed over the municipality of Townsville like the large rocky face of some sleeping prehistoric monster. The skirts of its mane draped around its shoulders, once graced by a canopy of native trees, now lay almost denuded. Raw axe wounds stained with timber blood dried under the North Queensland summer sun. The large settlement lay in some disorder around the base like minions offering prayers to the monolith behind.

Magnetic Island, the site of the local quarantine station at its West Point, lay behind the ship. Several of the immigrants who had planned to disembark at Townsville were already being prepared to be transferred to the quarantine station, until the signs and symptoms of their recent infections resolved.

The Mayford group, along with many other passengers, stood at the ship's rail absorbing the first sight of their new home. Colourful parasols cast small pools of shadow over the pale faces. Bridie's gaze looked up towards the bridge of the ship where Captain Ryan Aitkens oversaw the activities in all sections of the vessel. A thin stream of dark smoke from the idling engines below drifted landwards. Ryan caught and returned her smile with a finger to the tip of his cap.

Due to no berth being immediately available at the wharf of Townsville, and with only the Mayford group of first-class passengers and forty of the steerage passengers, other than those already setting off to the quarantine station, due to disembark in Townsville, the captain arranged to have those passengers and their luggage, plus three bags of mail for the district, conveyed to the docks by the steam launches from the Townsville harbour.

Bridie could not decide how she felt. Relief at knowing her feet were to touch solid land within the next hour shifted a weight from her shoulders. But that weight transferred to her heart knowing she was not going to see or talk to Ryan again for a long time. She was not going to feel his arms about her, nor his lips drawing every ounce of love from her body. Her strong mind stamped down upon the faint shadow of fear which challenged her belief and trust that this was not just a ship-board romance – not that she knew a lot on the subject being a reader of more educational material.

She felt Odette's arm on her waist and smiled at her niece.

"A new life, a new country, a new start," Odette smiled a watery smile.

Bridie clasped her hand tightly. Just then Jimmy arrived with Rosa by his side. They placed the lighter luggage at their feet.

"We've checked both cabins and ensured nothing has been left behind, Miss Bridie." Rosa stared across towards the port, "Jimmy has spoken to Tindal and ensured all items of our luggage from the hold have been identified and will be sent on to the Queen's Hotel just as you requested."

"Thank you, Rosa. Now will you look out there? Our new home." Bridie's cast of her arm took in the splendour of the sight of Townsville guarded by Castle Hill.

CHAPTER ELEVEN

Arrivals

1896

The sailor guided the launch through the channel, beside the rock groyne, and alongside the wharf where, under Captain Aitken's instructions, he ensured the Mayford group were first to step out of the vessel and onto the ramp. Each of the travellers wobbled on their feet as they acclimatized themselves to solid land. A deckhand followed them up with the remaining hand luggage that Jimmy was unable to carry. The man led them to a rough-timbered building where they found the customs representative inside. Wooden chairs lined one side of the structure opposite the table where their papers were scrutinized.

"Welcome to Australia, ladies and gentleman," the man nodded at Jimmy, "if you wish to step outside, I think you will find a carriage waiting to deliver you to your accommodation – the Queen's Hotel, isn't it?"

"Yes, thank you," it was Bridie who replied. "And when can we expect the remainder of our luggage to arrive at the hotel?"

"Within the hour, I should think," the man smiled.

When the carriage pulled up at the Queen's Hotel, Bridie sighed.

"At least this looks like a tidy and well-maintained building, even if it is only of timber structure."

Odette pointed her finger, "Judging by the number of horses and buggies parked outside it must have a busy clientele."

"It is so close to the sea," Rosa's gaze flew from one carriage window to the other trying to take in everything new. "We will be able to walk along the water's edge."

"We may have to ask if that is a safe exercise, given crocodiles inhabit the north."

"Oh dear, it looks so peaceful."

Jimmy landed on the ground with a soft thud, having jumped from the roof of the vehicle. He opened the carriage door for the ladies.

"Welcome to your new home, Miss Bridie and Mrs. Odette."

"And to you, Jimmy, and Rosa also," Bridie confirmed. It entered Bridie's thoughts as she took in the surroundings, *Less than two weeks before Christmas. Will Odette have to deliver her child in this hotel?*

While Bridie and Odette went into the hotel's reception area, Rosa and Jimmy gathered their luggage together in the shade of the verandah. Laughter rang out from the drinkers inside the bar to their left.

"The ladies will not be happy if the bar gets too noisy," Rosa commented to her husband.

It was Odette who spoke from behind her. "The publican has placed us in rooms above the dining room which he assures us are very quiet."

"Are you feeling alright, Mrs. Odette, you are looking rather pale," a frown of concern lay on Rosa's brow.

"I cannot deny I am looking forward to putting my feet up as soon as we get to the room." Odette gave Rosa a long stare, "How are you coping with all this rushing about, Rosa?"

"I am fine thanks, Mrs. Odette. Unlike you, I do not have only a few weeks until my baby is due. Now let me help you up the stairs to find your room."

Bridie joined them, just as they were about to enter the foyer.

Rosa gasped as she entered. "Oh, Miss Bridie, this is beautiful." A polished timber sideboard on one wall reflected in the central gleaming silver flower vase resting on a patterned doily. A selection of fresh-cut flowers filled the foyer with sweet aromas. Pale floral covers on well-padded cushions on four comfortable-looking chairs welcomed all newcomers. Lace curtains danced at the opened doorways as the cool breeze drifted in from the waterfront outside. A thick green carpet hushed their footsteps on the staircase which hugged the wall on its way to the top floor. A solid polished timber balustrade protected the outer edge of the stairs.

"The porter will be here shortly to help you carry our luggage upstairs," Bridie told Jimmy, before turning to Odette and Rosa, "Ladies, shall we go and view our home-for-however-long?"

The three ladies climbed the stairs to the top floor, where the hallway went left and right at right angles, to separate the rooms facing the sea at the front and those rooms facing the back of the building.

Bridie stopped outside Suite 6AB, at the corner of the corridor. She sorted the keys in her hand and opened the door which led into a room with a bedroom opening on either side. White lace curtains, similar to those in the foyer downstairs, billowed in the sea breeze. She placed the folded newspaper she had been holding on the small table near the doorway. Keys jingled in Bridie's hand once again when she picked out another key that she handed to Rosa.

"This is for Room 6C. It is the double bedroom for you and Jimmy. It is directly opposite this room. Apparently, there is access to the front verandah just up from this room."

"Thank you, Miss Bridie, but I think I will help Mrs. Odette to lie down and rest for a bit first before I explore."

After eating her lunch from a tray of food sent up, Odette slept most of the afternoon away. Working as quietly as possible, Bridie and Rosa began to empty one of the large sea trunks, draping items for placement in Odette's room later, over the backs of the two settees and two individual comfortable chairs. After Rosa left to sort out her room, Bridie sat on the eastern verandah to enjoy her first newspaper in two months.

The still-blazing sun hung above the western horizon when Odette awoke with colour now returned to her cheeks and the lines of strain softening on her face.

"That bed is heaven after the ship's bunks. I feel so much better." Odette turned to Bridie, "Has anyone asked if we can walk along the seafront?"

"I'll pop my head in and ask Jimmy to do so right away. You are looking so much better than when we arrived."

Later, Jimmy's soft knock sounded, it was Odette who opened the door.

"You be lookin' more chipper, Mrs. Odette."

"Thank you, Jimmy, did you ask if it is safe to walk along the seafront?"

"Yes, I did. There be a pathway above the sand which goes quite a ways along the seafront. The locals call it, The Strand – the seafront that is. The publican says it's quite safe to walk there in daylight. He said he would not be inclined to do so in the dark."

"Good, there is just enough time for a short walk, before we will need to change for dinner. I am hoping to dislodge this sensation I have of still rocking up and down on board the ship."

Bridie ran the comb through Odette's wet hair while she sat near the window looking out at the morning sunlight reflecting off the sea. Both Bridie and Odette had savoured a morning tub bath washing

310

away the lingering hints of stale body odour mixed with the faint aroma of violets from frequently applied body powder.

"Will that be all?" the chambermaid asked as she waited at the door with the damp towels. "I have left a fresh commode pot and I will return later to clean the rooms."

With Odette settled, Bridie left to find the writing room mentioned by the maid earlier. It was only a short step along the corridor. The early morning sun streamed in across the verandah and through the doorway almost reaching the legs of the desk at which she sat with her stationery folder at the ready.

Her thoughts turned to Clawhaven Estate and all the friends she had left behind. A wave of homesickness washed over her for a moment, but the thought of her and Odette's heartache left behind dissolved it quickly. She decided to send a short note to Mr. Birmingham first, after all, it was thanks to him their travels had been so comfortable and free of unnecessary complications. As Bridie blotted the ink, her thoughts drifted to Captain Ryan Aitkens, a dreamy smile and a far-a-way gaze stared out over The Strand. If all goes to plan, he could very well be back at the port of Townsville within a week or two. It took a conscious effort to drag her thoughts back to the task at hand. The next letter was to Mr. Axel and Mary. Bridie knew Mary would be anxious for the news of Odette. Mary's motherly instinct for her early charge had never left her, even after the birth of her two boys. Bridie's next duty-bound letter must be to Mrs. Sanders and her husband, who now lived with the huge responsibility of looking after the manor.

During the following week, Bridie and Odette made calls upon both the local solicitor, Mr. Livingston, and the accountant, Mr. Stuart, to whom Mr Birmingham in Portsmouth had referred them. They were assured by Mr. Stuart that their finances were sound here and credit from the estate in Sussex would be arriving on a regular basis.

Mr. Livingstone spoke of a cyclone that had devasted many houses causing death to several citizens the previous January. Bridie and Odette's anxious glances met across the spartan office room.

"It is not as bad as it seems," Mr. Livingston reassured them, "Cyclones are not an everyday event here and when choosing a house, select a sound one with some protection. I will be more than happy to have my builder check out any you may take a liking to."

"Thank you, Mr. Livingston, we will be happy to take your advice."

The sound of muffled footsteps running up the staircase drifted into their room, where Bridie looked up from her reading to meet Odette's curious gaze.

"Sounds like someone is in a hurry."

A sharp rap at their door lifted Bridie from her chair. She opened the door to find Jimmy with his hair in disarray and his dark eyes aglow. He bent over to suck hot air into his lungs.

"Jimmy, what are you all in a pother over? Come on in."

"Miss Bridie, Mrs. Odette, I've just returned from a ride in the spring cart with Mr. Glennin', our publican. He showed me a place only several streets north o' here that I think you might be interested in." Jimmy gushed out his news. "It's not immediately on the waterfront, which's a good thing according to the man. He reckons some o' the buildin's on the front took a hidin' in the cyclone earlier this year. This place for sale has two blocks of land and the sea can be seen from the balcony o' the big house. On the block behind the big house is a smaller cottage where the owner's daughter lived with her husband and kids. They've all gone to live on a cattle farm, station, he called it, in the Gulf. That's northwest o' here, I understand."

Bridie interrupted as Jimmy paused to catch a breath.

"Jimmy, stop and gather your thoughts. Have a glass of water." Bridie lifted the lace cover with local shells attached to weigh the edges and prevent it from falling into the jug contents. She took up a spare glass and poured a drink. While he drank, Bridie picked up a sheet of blank paper and a pencil from the small writing desk in the corner. "Now can you sketch what you have seen?"

This time Jimmy spoke slowly as he drew a rough design of the large and small houses on adjacent blocks that he had visited.

"Mr. Glennin'll be happy to take you to look at the place when 'tis cooler if you want," Jimmy explained. "He knows the fellow who's sellin' the properties for the absent owner."

Bridie and Odette exchanged glances. "It would be lovely if we had our own home before the little one presents itself," Odette suggested.

"Maybe Jimmy and I should inspect the place with this Mr. Glenning today, and if I think it is promising, we can hire a hansom cab and all go for a trip tomorrow morning."

After cool fruit drinks in the mid-afternoon, Bridie and Jimmy retired to the latticed verandah on the lower floor and sat in the chairs amongst the hanging baskets and potted plants, which gave an illusion of cool surroundings. It was four o'clock when Mr. Glenning pulled up at the front of the hotel driving his horse and open carriage this time. He removed his hat to wipe the perspiration from his brow, as he walked in out of the sun. From where she sat, Bridie watched the medium-built man of wide girth and with sun-faded brown hair and moustache.

After the introductions were made, Mr. Glenning let Jimmy ride up front to steer the horse while he joined Miss Mayford in the carriage. On the short journey north of the Queen's Hotel, Mr. Glenning appraised Bridie of the town's history and pointed out landmarks they passed.

"The hospital is just up the back there."

They alighted from the carriage in a street shaded by a few scraggly trees, and one back from the waterfront. Mr. Glenning led them past the timber-built cottage set in a well-maintained garden which included fruit trees in bloom. A faint citrus aroma drifted on the sea breeze.

"This is the cottage," Mr. Glenning explained.

Worn hollows under each end of a child's see-saw told of numerous small feet. The seat had a great need for a coat of paint. A front porch shaded from the western sun by a huge tree in the yard invited them up the three steps and onto a verandah. Inside, a hallway led them past two bedrooms to their left and living areas to the right. A partially closed-in verandah on one corner provided another small bedroom. A solid table with chairs dominated the kitchen, which also included a clean stove, a bench with wash tubs, a cupboard for crockery and another for supplies. The outer walls all had panels of louvre windows which allowed breeze to flow in from all directions. A water tank stood at each of two corners of the house. Behind the cottage stood a shed and a stable large enough for two horses. A three-railed fence enclosed a small run. The outdoor toilet backed up behind the neighbour's, over the fence.

This block of land was adjacent to the big house on half its length and at right angles to it. Once again Bridie felt her spirits lift at the sight of another neat garden with lovely bushes and fruit trees which added a sense of coolness on a hot afternoon. It was only a short walk from the cottage to the big house. On their way over, they discovered a rough shelter for laundry purposes. It consisted of a roof and two walls and stood about ten yards from the big house. A well-used, dented, shiny, copper for boiling the clothes sat in an open brick frame beside a heap of timber for use in lighting the fire. An old smooth timber table sat in the middle of the shelter and three large wash tubs sat on a bench against the back wall.

The large, part-timber and part-masonry-built home, included a lower and an upper story, both surrounded by wide verandahs. It lay parallel to the sea and faced out onto a street running perpendicular to the waterfront. Mr. Glenning let them in through a back door, which opened directly into a spacious kitchen with an ample stove and large table. A sluice room to the left contained tools for cleaning a large house and a sluice sink to drain away the waste. Through the kitchen, a doorway to the right opened into a sizeable pantry. A bathroom on the opposite side of the pantry backed onto the verandah. Three water tanks outside were visible through the windows.

The lower floor also revealed four large rooms plus a storage room built in under the staircase. Bridie's mind immediately began to plan how she might utilize this area. Her first thoughts were for a dining room, a parlour, a library/office and maybe a music room cum drawing room. Her spirits began to lift further. *Of course, it must suit Odette's needs also,* she reminded herself.

Up a gracious staircase to the top floor, they found five large rooms each with tall double doors opening out onto the verandahs. A wide hallway led out to the verandah also. From here, she found herself at right angles to the sea and only one house from the front road. Bridie realised immediately, that the view from chairs on this verandah would take in a large area of sea and part of Magnetic Island.

"This house is well protected by the house in the front there, Miss Mayford. They lost part of their roof in the cyclone in January, but neither of these two houses sustained any damage at all."

315

Bridie tried not to let her enthusiasm show and walked back slowly through the rooms on the top floor. Her mind ticked off Odette's room, baby's room, my room and two spare rooms for visitors, maybe even a ship's captain.

"Mr. Glenning," Bridie turned to address their guide, "I can say I am feeling quite enthusiastic about these properties. Before I make any decision, I will contact my solicitor, Mr. Livingston. He has a builder he wishes to have view anything that I consider suitable to our needs. May I intrude upon your time to show him this property, at a time suitable to you both?"

"Of course, Miss Mayford. Just let me know. It will be no trouble." He began to turn around but touched his forehead. "Sorry, I nearly forgot to mention. If you do buy the properties, it will be suitable to move in when the papers are signed, and before the settlement date of property transfer if you wished."

"That is most helpful, particularly with Mrs. Treloar so close to her confinement date, thank you Mr. Glenning." Bridie followed the stout man down the stairs.

Later in the hotel dining room, only half of the twenty or so tables had been prepared. It was Jimmy who explained what he had learnt earlier.

"Mondays and Tuesdays are quiet nights for diners. Fridays and Saturdays get busy when the country folks come to town. There be people lined up in the parlour rooms waitin' for a vacant table on them days."

White unmarked and pressed damask tablecloths covered those tables for use. Glasses glittered beside the folded napery on which lay silver cutlery, that gleamed in the gas lighting from the lanterns set into the wall.

Rosa sat almost twitching with excitement but had been warned by her husband not to mention the houses. He knew from experience that Miss Bridie liked to ponder on ideas before committing to their implementation. The pair excused themselves after eating and left on their evening walk along The Strand and well away from the water.

Bridie and Odette followed the sound of music to one of the parlours, where a soiree was about to begin. Later when they sat in their room upstairs, Bridie related to Odette everything about the houses she had seen with Mr. Glenning in the afternoon.

"It sounds perfect, Bridie."

"Yes, I think so. It has nearly everything that we talked about. What I thought you might appreciate is the fact we can move in as soon as the papers are first signed."

"You mean we do not have to wait until the deeds have been officially transferred?"

"That is what Mr. Glenning said."

"Bridie are you saying my baby can be born in our own house?"

"Yes, I do hope so. Hopefully, we will be able to move in before Christmas."

"Goodness me, Christmas is just over a week away. There is no chance we can forget with the carollers out singing on the street each day."

"Perhaps I should order a hansom cab tomorrow morning, and we visit the place? If you like it, we can go from there directly to the solicitors. We will take Rosa with us to see the cottage. I want her to be happy too."

≈

Tuesday, only two full days before Christmas Eve, Rosa and Bridie, arrived back at the hotel hot and tired having spent most of the day at

Burns Philps making purchases of furniture and household items for the new accommodation and then making a detour on the way back to inspect again their new home.

"I'm perishing," Rosa complained when they stepped out of the hansom cab at the hotel.

"I am sure afternoon tea will be in progress. Let us venture into the dining room and see what is available." Bridie led the way.

Jimmy and two shop employees were at present delivering the items purchased to the big house and to the cottage. Rosa had left Jimmy in no doubt as to where each item was to be placed.

On Wednesday morning, December 23, 1896, Jimmy, with the help of a dray and horse for hire, plus a casual labourer recommended by Mr. Glenning on the payroll for the day, and the strategic placement of Rosa at the new residences, began to transfer their belongings to their new homes. Bridie remained at the hotel to ensure all the trunks in storage, and their lighter luggage were collected for delivery. Odette rested at the hotel offering suggestions where applicable.

Wednesday night, Bridie and Odette planned to spend their last night at the hotel. After dinner, Jimmy and Rosa were to walk back to take up residence in the cottage.

Husband and wife stood on the back verandah of their new home listening to the sea breeze blowing through the trees outside, the noises of wildlife in the garden at night, and from behind them the faint crash of the waves on the beachfront at high tide.

"Come, my busy bee, 'tis time we'd an early night. Whatever's not been done now can wait until first light. There be enough wood chopped to light the stove in the morning."

Rosa was wont to protest, "But Jimmy, all the groceries will need to be put into the cupboards."

"Tomorrow is another day and you, my love, need to rest. You have our little infant to take care of."

In the gloom of Christmas Eve morning, when the milkman stopped his horse and dray at Jimmy's call, he filled the large can in Jimmy's hands with milk and poured cream into Rosa's metal jug. The man had three large ice blocks remaining which were also purchased. Jimmy delivered these to the ice chest in the kitchen of the big house, where most of the cooking was to take place. Jimmy and Rosa were to eat in the big kitchen, while in the dining room with its large table freshly polished and now covered with a tablecloth from one of the trunks, Miss Bridie and Mrs. Odette and any guests if present, were to dine. The heat in the kitchen was not just from a mid-summer day in North Queensland, but radiation from the stove. Rosa already had bread baking in the oven and a pot of savoury stewing meat on one of the hot plates for use as contents for two meat pies, the pastry of which she thumped and rolled on a wooden board on the table.

Christmas Eve flew by in a swirl of chores. Jimmy sent Rosa to call the ladies downstairs when a man turned up with a gift from Mr. Glenning.

"This horse and open carriage are on loan until we can acquire one of our own," Jimmy repeated the message from the horseman who delivered the large grey horse and a simple open carriage sparkling clean.

"Wonderful, we will be able to attend the church in the morning for the Christmas service. I was so hoping not to miss that." Bridie smiled.

Bridie's slippered feet whispered around the corridor to Odette's room.

319

"Wake up, sleepy head. Merry Christmas. Welcome to our new home." Bridie moved a book and brush off the side table and placed upon it the silver serving tray holding a cup of hot tea and half a slice of fresh bread. "Rosa is already busy in the kitchen downstairs. You would think there were a dozen of us not just four, the way she is going."

Odette rubbed her eyes and pulled herself up. Bridie packed the pillows in behind her back.

"Bridie, did Rosa tell you about the lass looking for work as a housemaid? Mrs. Glenning recommended her. The girl will be around first thing Monday morning to talk to us."

"That is the same morning you have your appointment with the doctor at eleven."

"Yes, as if I am going to forget. Hopefully, he will recommend a good midwife."

"We have a lot to thank the Glenning family for. They have made our settling in a much easier process than it may have been." Bridie stood and made to leave. "Jimmy has brought a warm bucket of water up for my bath. I will be as quick as I can. He will bring up a second bucket for you after I have finished. We will need to make haste if we do not want to be late for church. I am not too sure how the locals might take that."

1897

Bridie bent to cut another of the green ferns growing on the eastern side of the house. She placed it on those already lying in the basket on her arm. As she stood up, the sound of laughter lifted her gaze to the tree branches above her head. A bird with a long beak raised to the sky greeted the day with a raucous sound of laughter. Bridie stood entranced.

At her shoulder, Ethel-May whispered, "Miss Mayford, my dad used to say it's lucky to hear the kookaburras laughing in this area. He says they laugh every morning further south, but not so much here."

Bridie paused until the serenade ceased. "Is that the bird's name, a kookaburra?"

"Yes, although many like to call it a laughing jackass."

"I can see why they would say that," Bridie smiled at the new housemaid. "And you say it is lucky to hear them?"

"That's what my dad used to say, Miss Mayford."

"Well then, you and I are going to have a lucky day, young Ethel-May."

Shortly after, with her basket overflowing with her cuttings, Bridie turned to go inside when the sound of a whistle sent her around the corner to her front gate to investigate. A postal delivery boy was about to slip a letter into her mailbox.

"Thank you, young lad, I will take that for you."

The not-so-young lad with his flaming-red hair sticking out from under the straw hat upon his head, and wearing long trousers with the knees worn thin, lifted his head.

"Are you Miss Bridie Mayford?"

"Yes, I am. Is that for me?"

"Yes, Miss, the lady at the Queen's Hotel said you were living here now."

"Thank you for taking the trouble," Bridie said as she reached out her hand. She took the slim envelope glancing down at the handwriting. Her heart pumped hard in her chest. She felt the sparkle in her eyes, but she restrained the threatening grin. She slipped the paper into her skirt pocket and, securing her basket on her elbow again, turned to enter the house. Rosa was heard from within the kitchen beating something in a bowl. Ethel-May was heard upstairs setting the bedrooms to rights, while Bridie guessed Odette rested on the upstairs verandah with her feet elevated.

Bridie slipped into the parlour and tore the letter open. Her fingers eased the one page out and unfolded it. Her first glance ran down the paper to the signature. Again, her heart skipped a beat before racing off at a gallop. Her finger traced the letters over the paper.

My dearest Bridie,
I hope to be at Townsville between Christmas and New Year. This will depend on the service at the various wharves we pass through, given it will be during the holiday period.
I will ask at the Queen's Hotel for your current residence if I have a chance to take time off on shore.
My love, I count the hours.
R.A.

Bridie could hardly breathe. Today was the first day of 1897. Her lover could be in her arms any day now. She almost ran up the stairs and into her room. She stopped at the mirror and stared at the lines deepening at the corners of her eyes. Her slim fingers took hold of a single white hair peeping through near her ear and pulled hard. The offending strand came away. Trembling fingers smoothed her hair back to the knot resting on the nape of her neck. Bridie took a step back examining her dress. Her hands ran down her body from the ruffles at her neck, over her still-firm breasts and down over the well-rounded curves of her hips. She sucked in a breath and bit her lip.

It was the day after New Year's Day when Jimmy knocked at the music room doorway where Bridie's hands flew over the keyboard in a Straus waltz.

"I found this fellow wandering around the backyard."

Bridie looked up. Her face drained of colour and then flooded with a bright pink flush. A weakness invaded her every limb. It felt as if her legs might not hold her upright.

"Captain Aitkens." A breathless rush from her lips. Bridie stood, supported by her hand on the piano frame. "Thank you, Jimmy," she spoke to Jimmy as he disappeared out through the doorway. In two strides, Captain Aitken reached Bridie's side and wrapped his arms around her.

"Bridie, is it really you? I was beginning to think you must have been just a figment of my imagination." His words were lost in a deep kiss of longing that stirred Bridie from her own haze of disbelief. Her warm lips responded in equal measure. They drew back to drink in the vision of each other again.

"How long do we have?" was all Bridie could think to say.

"I must be back on board by four o'clock tomorrow morning."

"You will stay with me until then?"

"I will need to leave at 03.00 hours if I am to be ready to report on deck at 04.00 hours." Ryan's fingers caressed Bridie's face.

"Such a short time. Perhaps I should book a trip back to England and then back here again so I can have all that time with you on your ship."

Ryan laughed. "Or we can take a stroll along the waterfront before it heats up too much."

"Heats up where – inside here, or the sun outside?" Bridie smiled – her eyes shone.

"I want to hear all about your adventures since we dropped you off here in Townsville only a few weeks ago."

"It seems like an age since I last saw you." Bridie took a firm hold of Ryan's arm and led him to the side door, taking up her parasol before exiting into the garden. The breeze off the waterfront helped cool the heat from the morning sun. She began to relate their experiences, stopping every few sentences to stare into his face in disbelief.

"I was sure you had only been a wonderful dream, and yet here you are – flesh and blood."

"Maybe tonight I can convince you our relationship is real."

"Maybe, I might take a lot of convincing, kind sir."

"I think you are a little minx, Bridie Mayford, but I do like your thoughts."

Later that night, as Ryan lay asleep beside her, Bridie's eyes refused to close despite the satisfaction of her sated body. It would be soon enough to sleep when her bed became a lonely recline once more. As the moonlight seeped into her room, her gaze wandered over his body with amazement and pleasure. All too soon the chime of the hall clock downstairs announced it was three o'clock.

"You're looking at me aren't you, my love." Ryan opened one eye. He smiled. "That will cost you a kiss." ·

"A penalty willingly given," Bridie's lips flittered across his face to be caught and held by Ryan's urgent kiss in return. She jumped apart, all of a sudden. "I can hear Jimmy hitching up the horse to the trap. Oh, Ryan, it is all too soon. I do not think I can bear to see you go." Her fingers traced his face, his chest and his arms. She rose to her knees and traced his legs and returned to that which had given her so much pleasure.

Ryan groaned. "Darling, as much as my body is telling you of my desire, my mind is telling me I must go. You will always be in my heart. Tell me you do believe this."

Bridie nodded her head as the tears fell to her naked chest. She kissed Ryan's hands as he slipped out of bed and began to dress.

≈

New Year's Day had been and gone these past two weeks when Odette woke feeling hot, restless and out of sorts. The discomfort of her stuffy nose due to the sense of claustrophobia caused by the netting over her bed was a small price to pay when it meant fewer biting mosquitoes. Moonbeams filtered into the room through the lace curtains at the open doorway onto the verandah. The sound of the waves on the beachfront was punctuated by the call of a noisy mopoke owl in the trees outside. In the distance, a faint baby's cry told of a parent's sleepless night. Odette felt a twinge in her abdomen and smiled at what she thought was a sympathy vote from her unborn infant. She rolled over and tried to support her enlarged abdomen with pillows. Dissatisfied still, Odette threw the sheets back and dragged her legs over the side of the bed. Her bladder demanded attention. She sank onto the commode just in time. When she was about to stand again, she felt another flood of fluid run away from her. She plopped down onto the pot. Another twinge ran through her belly.

Odette gasped when realization landed. *This will be the breaking waters the nurse mentioned.* Odette felt her heart begin to race. *My baby wants to make an appearance.* She hugged herself. She hugged her belly. Her heartbeat now pounded in her ears. All the instructions delivered by the midwife two days ago deserted her. *Dear me, what should I do first?*

Her head snapped up at the sound of Bridie's voice from the corridor.

"Are you alright there, Odette?"

"Please come in, Bridie, I think my time has arrived. Will you send Jimmy for Nurse Laffeter? Oooooh." Odette placed one hand on her belly and the other over her mouth.

"Of course, dear, should I help you back into the bed first?"

"No thanks, I feel the need to move about." Holding onto the edge of the bed, Odette padded back and forth. At the sight of her always-so-calm and efficient aunt shuffling backwards and forwards, unsure where to go first – to support Odette or to call the nurse – Odette gave a short burst of laughter. "I am fine here, Bridie. The nurse did warn us that being the first, this baby was not going to pop out immediately."

Bridie ran over and hugged her niece. "I will go and wake Jimmy this very moment, just the same."

No sooner had Bridie disappeared down the staircase, than Odette felt the urge to call her back when a wave of fear almost overwhelmed her. A sharper pain stole her breath away and snapped her forward to hold tight to the bedpost. She snatched at a short sharp gasp of air, then another and another until the pain eased. She heard Bridie's footsteps running up the stairs.

"Jimmy has taken the horse to fetch the nurse. Rosa is downstairs stirring up the coals in the stove to boil the water. Now, before we get you back into bed, I will spread out the rubber sheet the nurse left and tidy your bed again."

"Will you fetch me a clean nightie too, please? I think this one is soiled." Odette reached over, closed the lid of the commode and sat upon the chair. After a wash in the bowl with water from the ewer on the wash table, Odette changed into a clean nightie. She told her aunt, "I will not get back into the bed just yet. Please take my arm and walk with me around the room?" Odette sucked the air into her lungs again, when another contraction triggered a streak of pain through her abdomen. She rubbed at the burning pain in her lower back.

"Are you sure you should be walking around right now?"

"No, but it is what my body is telling me it wants."

It seemed an age, but it was less than half an hour, when the sound of Nurse Lafferty resting her bicycle against the hitching rail under the window, drifted up to the two anxious women. Along with the first light of dawn, the nurse swept into the room. She placed her bag on the chair tucked away in the corner.

"I see you have the wanders, Mrs. Treloar. That is quite usual. Can I ask you to climb back onto the bed for a moment and I will examine you to see how far your baby has advanced? When did the pains first start?"

Odette did as the nurse instructed, but her eyes pleaded with Bridie not to leave her. Bridie pulled a chair closer and sat at Odette's left side.

Odette paused to think. "About one and a half hours ago, maybe longer."

"Well, it is only early hours yet. As I mentioned when I visited the other day, the first baby can often take quite a while." After her examination, Nurse Lafferty sat up straight with a thoughtful expression on her face. She patted Odette's knee and smiled down at her worried expression, "On the other hand, you may be one of the lucky ones whose baby does not want to mess about."

A soft knock sounded on the door. Rosa called, "Miss Bridie, can I bring anyone a cup of tea?"

"Ask Rosa to bring me a cool drink of water, thanks Bridie," Odette asked. Not forgetting her manners, even under these circumstances, she looked over at the nurse. "Can we offer you a cup of tea, Nurse Lafferty?"

"Thank you, I would appreciate that. Might we have a couple of warm towels to place on Mrs. Treloar's abdomen? Let us stir the infant along a little."

Odette heard Bridie give the order to Rosa, just as another wave of pain threatened to tear her body apart, or that is what Odette

327

thought it felt like. Tears trickled down her cheeks. Odette bit down upon her bottom lip. She groaned. Rosa's footsteps were heard on the staircase.

The following hours passed in a red haze of pain and disorientation for Odette. When short periods of clarity returned, worry for her baby became uppermost in her mind.

"Is my baby safe, Nurse?" was her frequent cry.

"Everything is going a treat, Mrs. Treloar," the nurse assured Odette.

Nurse Lafferty gulped the second cup of tea delivered by the wide-eyed Rosa as fast as the heat of it allowed without burning her tongue. She watched the progress of her patient's increasingly frequent contractions. A slither of concern ran through her mind at the realization this might be a rather fast birthing. Even though she knew there were blessings in having a fast birth, she also had the experience to know this is not always a good thing. After placing the cup on the escritoire against the wall, she returned her attention to Odette settling her back to be examined again.

"This baby is in a hurry, by the looks of things. You are almost fully dilated already." The nurse placed another towel at the end of the bed, and two cord clamps, a pair of scissors and a length of twine. She washed her hands in the bowl of hot water waiting on the small table and poured a dash of Spirits of Methylate over them before waving them to evaporate in the air. "Have we a cot to put the baby in when he or she arrives?"

Bridie walked over and undraped a piece of furniture near the escritoire to reveal a wooden cradle holding a thick mattress covered with a clean sheet and a small rug. No sooner was the cradle revealed than Odette groaned a long heart-felt groan.

"Can you send for more warm towels please, Miss Mayford?" The nurse returned her attention to Odette. "Don't push just yet, Mrs. Treloar. I will tell you when. Just concentrate on taking quick, shallow breaths."

Odette had no time to answer the nurse's instructions before a short sharp cry escaped her lips. She bit down on a low extended groan.

Once again, the nurse lifted the sheet and bent to examine Odette's progress.

"Yes, now on the next contraction, I want you to push until I say stop."

Odette reached again for Bridie's hand. Her gaze searched her aunt's face.

"You won't leave me will you, Bridie?"

"No, Odette, I will stay right here."

Odette's eyes widened; she gasped when the next contraction hit. She responded with all her strength. It seemed as if Odette was not going to pause for a breath when the nurse called, "Stop now. Soft breathing again. Your baby is just about to enter the world." Nurse Lafferty ran her fingers around the top of the child's head and neck. "When you and baby are ready let's get this job done." The moist and slippery baby slithered out into the capable hands of the nurse. Her loud cry filled the room before the infant had stopped its forward progress. "You have a fine and very impatient daughter, Mrs. Treloar." The nurse took up the warm towel on the end of the bed and wrapped the infant.

"Odette, can I have my hands back," Bridie said with a very wobbly laugh. "You have a baby girl and I have a … what – a grandniece – you are a clever pair."

Tears leaked from Odette's eyes as the nurse placed her baby onto her chest. An overwhelming wave of sorrow at the absence of Peter washed over her. Odette gasped as she struggled to contain the urge to burst out into deep, noisy sobs. Odette's trembling fingers stroked her daughter's cheek. She used the corner of the towel to wipe the little face. Bridie's eyes were not dry either where she sat at the side of the bed gazing in utter amazement.

Nurse Lafferty clamped, tied and cut the cord once pulsations ceased. She turned to wash her hands and asked Bridie, "Can we pack more pillows behind Mrs. Treloar to prop her more upright? This will help gravitation remove the afterbirth. This can take anything up to one hour."

Bridie and the nurse assisted Odette into the new position with her baby in her arms. The nurse tidied the bed linen.

"If you offer the nipple to her, Mrs. Treloar, the stimulation may hurry the process along a little."

Within the suggested hour, Odette had delivered the placenta, freshened up in the bowl of warm water brought up to the room by Bridie herself, and redressed in a fresh nightie. Disbelief filled her eyes as she sat in the comfortable chair just out of the sunshine beaming through the verandah doors, with her baby in her arms. Rosa stripped the soiled linen rolling it into a ball for delivery to the laundry shed where their new housemaid, young Ethel-May waited for the delivery with a tub of warm soapy water.

At the sound of the baby's cry, Jimmy looked up from grooming the newly acquired brown gelding in the stables. He jumped high and kicked his heels, lay down his brush and hurried to the big house where Rosa stood staring up the staircase. Jimmy wrapped his arms around his wife and swung her about.

"Your turn next, my love. It didn't seem too bad. It was all over in a couple of hours."

Rosa punched him lightly on the shoulder.

"Ouch, what was that for?" Jimmy rubbed his arm.

"Not too bad, how would you know? When did you ever give birth to a baby?"

"I've delivered a lot." His voice held a ton of hurt.

"Animal births are a lot different to humans, my man. So be ready to offer lots of sympathy to me when our time comes." Rosa grinned.

Over the following months, Odette found herself filled with love and happiness at the sight of her developing infant. For hours she sat staring at the sleeping Florence's features seeking some sign of Peter hidden therein. It was blonde not brown hair lying like soft down upon her head. The baby's eyes were changing to a soft grey – unlike her own violet eyes. She tried to recall Peter's grey eyes when he looked deep into her own eyes after they made love at the manor. This in turn set her off in a sobbing episode. She yearned for what should have been.

As the heat of summer eased, Odette and Bridie walked miles along the waterfront taking it in turns to push the perambulator ahead of themselves.

"Are we agreed then," Bridie asked one day in early June, "we will buy another pram like this one for Rosa when she has her baby?"

"Yes, Bridie, I told Jimmy not to go buying one himself. Rosa will find it a godsend walking from the cottage to the big house and back each day."

"It will not be long now."

"Rosa thinks about two weeks."

Rosa placed the last of the breakfast dishes into the sink when her waters broke. Miss Bridie and Mrs. Odette were out walking baby Florence in the perambulator along the waterfront. Was Ethel-May upstairs collecting the laundry or had she gone out to the washhouse?

There was only one person she really wanted with her right at this moment.

"Jimmy!"

She stirred the stew on the stove and ensured the coals damped down a little before she started to make her way to her cottage.

"Jimmy!" she called again.

The sound of his pounding footsteps heralded his arrival from the house next door.

"Did you call, my little Rose?"

"Aaaah," Rosa groaned as a cramp almost pulled her to her knees.

"Oh, gawd, it's time." Not knowing what else to say, Jimmy stated the obvious. "What should I do?"

"Get me into my bed," Rosa gasped through the discomfort.

Once into a clean nightgown, Rosa decided she wanted to sit near the window. She instructed Jimmy on where and how to place the rubber sheet left by Nurse Lafferty the previous week.

"Should I get the nurse yet? Should I find Miss Bridie? Should I get towels? Maybe I should get a pot of water on the stove to heat up?"

"It's unlikely I will be as lucky as Mrs. Odette and get this over and done with in a hurry. Ma always said her babies took forever to be born." Rosa stood and stretched upwards triggering another cramp to wash over her. She groaned again. "Light our stove and put the water on to heat. Then you had best let the nurse know. When you have done that, you come right back here and stay with me."

Relief filled the wide grin on Jimmy's face when he returned to find Miss Bridie sitting with Rosa. He knew everything would be fine now.

"You're here then, Jimmy, can you sit with Rosa, while I go and check the stew on the stove in the big house."

"You won't be long, will you, Miss Bridie?"

Bridie and Rosa shared glances and laughed.

"No, Jimmy, I will not be too long. Anyway, the nurse will be here any moment now."

"Won't be soon enough for me."

Rosa almost jumped up from her chair. "For you? Forget you, what about me and the baby?"

"Y-y-yes, yes, of course, I mean that too."

At that moment, they both heard the bike squeaking past the front door.

"I'll just go and oil the nurse's bike chain, my love. She'll be right in."

"Coward," Rosa mumbled as the back of her husband disappeared out through the bedroom door.

Bridie and the nurse kept Rosa company inside, while she berated the absent Jimmy, called for her absent mother, and begged for her baby to be born.

Outside, Jimmy hurried between asking Mrs. Odette what could he do for her, relating all his worries to his new horse, and creating jobs that must be done that very day. He did remember to pop back into his kitchen regularly to check on the fire in the stove and the water heating in the big pot.

Between feeding her five-month-old baby Florence, Odette supervised Ethel-May as she prepared the cups of tea and sandwiches for Bridie and the nurse. When the night was falling without any imminent sign of a new birth, Jimmy was almost beside himself with worry.

"Each baby will come in its own time, Jimmy. There is no need to worry. I have every faith in the nurse." Odette strived to calm the father-to-be. She had Ethel-May offer stew to everyone, but little was eaten. She added more water to the pot and set it aside on the stove until the morning. She kept the fire flickering in the firebox.

"Have you got more wood chopped outside, Jimmy?" Odette asked, "Maybe you can fill the wood bins in both kitchens."

The town around them quietened and the moon rose high in the sky. Odette and Jimmy dozed in comfortable chairs on the back verandah of the big house within the thin wisps of drifting smoke from the slow-burning manure heap which deterred those mosquitoes that persisted even in the winter months. It had been hours since Odette had given Florence her last feed for the night and sent Ethel-May to bed in the maid's small room near the staircase. Jimmy's snuffled snores joined the chorus of other nocturnal animals in the garden. Odette watched the unwavering lantern in the cottage, she felt anxiety stir her own thoughts. *Rosa has been a long time. Please God keep her and her baby safe.* She felt herself nodding off.

Both sleepers in the chairs lifted as one when the bellow of a baby echoed across the backyard.

"I bet it's a boy," Jimmy laughed in relief. "Rosa said all boys were born bellowing like bullocks."

"Did she also add, that all boys like to do things in their own time?" Odette sighed with relief.

"Not yet, but I bet she will next time I talk to her."

"I'll go over and see all is well and if Rosa is ready to see you, will I, Jimmy?"

"I'd be grateful if you'd do that, Mrs. Odette."

Jimmy paced across the front verandah of his cottage, while Odette went in to see what was happening. It was Bridie who came out to speak to Jimmy.

"Saints above, can you be tellin' me, is Rosa alright, Miss Bridie?"

"Rosa is fine now. You have a baby boy – a big baby boy, who was in no hurry to come into this world. Both are doing well. Come, I will take you in."

"I said it was a boy when I heard the first cry. Rosa's going to give me a good tongue-lashing, isn't she?"

"I think not. She is very happy with her son."

Rosa burst into tears when Jimmy sat by her side. She reached over and took his roughened hand and placed it upon the smooth down on their baby's head resting at her breast. Bridie and Odette exchanged glances when Jimmy's eyes sparkled with moisture. Never had they seen Jimmy shed a tear. They smiled and tip-toed outside.

The household attended church on the morning when Florence Mayford Treloar aged seven months, and James Taylor Braydon aged six weeks, were christened.

As so often happens in households where infants are present, routines at the big house changed during the following years. Rosa and Jimmy now had Sundays off unless it was raining or the mornings extremely hot, at which times, Jimmy prepared the horse and carriage to drive Bridie and Odette to the church. On milder days, it was a lovely walk to the church and the baby was always soothed by the movement of the perambulator. The voices of the choir inside teased a smile onto the baby's face.

Ethel-May looked after the kitchen duties on a Sunday, before enjoying her Mondays off work. The new laundress, Ruthie, washed the clothes on a Monday and tidied the bedrooms. Ruthie's chores on a Tuesday morning included heating the Pott's irons on the stove before she pressed the creases from those items requiring such attention. Each Tuesday afternoon she babysat the two little ones: Florence now two-and-a-half years and James Braydon who, at two years, followed Florence as close as any shadow. Bridie and Odette visited the town where they usually enjoyed afternoon tea at either the Queen's or the Lowth's Hotel dining rooms.

It was on one of these afternoons as Jimmy steered the horse into the driveway, the animal shied violently. A large snake followed closely by the neighbour's dog raced between the equine's legs. The near side wheel lifted and the vehicle threatened to overturn. Jimmy threw himself from his driving seat and onto the horse's back. He hauled on the reins while filling the horse's ears with quiet, soothing, if not delicate, words.

Odette squealed. Bridie threw her arms about her niece and bit down on what could only be termed a sailor's curse. Shopping bags bounced to the carriage floor, some emptying the contents on the way.

Quiet had not settled, when their neighbour, Mr. Rankin, rushed into Jimmy's front yard in pursuit of both dog and snake. A long-handled shovel waved dangerously above his head. Once more the horse threatened to break the traces and Jimmy resorted again to his soft talking.

"Sorry, Jimmy, sorry, Misses," Mr. Rankin called, but he did not pause in his endeavour.

The black and white dog and the neighbour prowled up and down at the site where the snake had vanished within the red lilies growing near the fence line. Once the horse settled, and Jimmy removed the ladies from the carriage, he walked over to ask what all the fuss was about.

At that moment, the dog pounced. The shovel blade landed at the back of the snake's head and an inch in front of the dog's nose.

"Bloody snakes," Mr. Rankin cursed. He looked up to see his audience. "Sorry, ladies. The last thing you want is a snake in the same yard as those little children of yours," He paused for only a second, "or yourself. One bite and you can say, 'Goodbye world'."

He reached down and patted the dog's rump sticking up in the air. "Good dog." The dog reluctantly stepped away from the writhing reptile. The arm holding the shovel lifted and flashed down with a resounding thud to sever the snake's head. Mr. Rankin bent and picked up the snake by the tail. In its dying throes, the snake's body wriggled spasmodically. "I'll just take these to the burner. I don't give the snake to the dog, particularly the head. The head will most likely be still full of poison."

Within a week, Jimmy was tasked with fencing the two properties containing the cottage and the Big House with a dog-proof fence not necessarily to keep out the neighbour's dog, but to keep inside their own dog, which Mr. Rankin had promised them, when available. Mr. Rankin promised Jimmy the pup would be a trained snake killer before it was released into his care.

CHAPTER TWELVE

Bristol Channel – Britain.

March 1899

A moody March sunlight reflected off the waters of the outer Bristol Channel. A strong breeze filled the sails of the ketch sending the vessel skimming across the waves. Michael Aitkens, at eighteen years of age, looked up to the skies and delivered a yell of pure enjoyment. Today he skippered his father's ketch under Ryan Aitken's watchful eye. Michael knew his father had been pleased with his efforts.

Up near the bow of the vessel, his brother Aiden, worked with his father to sort out the spare ropes and canvas sails.

"Mike is going to be absolutely unbearable for weeks." Aiden's bottom lip drooped. 'He will never stop crowing at me, you do realise this, Father?"

"There are advantages in being the youngest sometimes, but not always I'm afraid, Aiden. Just remember, when you are his age, you will have the same opportunity. Just keep up your studies in the meantime." Ryan shut the locker and took his son's arm, "Come on, let's give you a go on the helm, and send Michael to check the other locker."

Michael showed no animosity in surrendering the helm to his younger brother. He moved towards the bow with alacrity leaving Aiden with the tiller in his hand and his chest swelling with pride.

Ryan grinned at them both, but something triggered a rush of fear through his nerve endings. He sniffed the air and looked up at the sky. Very little had changed, but Ryan's experienced eye took in the dark streak of cloud spreading rapidly. He noted the change in the wind direction and knew things could turn nasty in moments, but he did not realize just how quickly the sea would turn upside down. His shout reached Michael just under the mainsail at mid-ships.

"Lifejackets!" As Ryan relieved Aiden at the helm, he was pleased to see Michael had already pre-empted his call. The lad pulled on a jacket and passed the other two up to his brother. Aiden secured his and passed the bigger one on to his father who had little time to tie it in place, when out of nowhere a tremendous swirl of wind almost tore the wooden tiller from his hand. He clung on tightly. His body bent almost double. The rogue squall ripped the mainsail, as a child in a tantrum might tear a strip of paper. The heavy timber boom flew wild. Metal bolts snapped like match sticks before flying through the air like shrapnel. Before Ryan could warn Michael, the timber caught his son a solid whack across the head and like a large tattered cricket ball, Michael spun overboard and into the angry sea. Blood spurted across the deck. Now, attached to only a scrap of sail, the boom landed in the sea beside the boy.

Ryan was torn. He wanted to dive in and retrieve his eldest, but the sight of his younger son cowering against the cabin, grey eyes wide with fear and hands white with the effort of gripping the rail, held Ryan back. The last Ryan saw of his elder son was the movement of an arm as it reached weakly over the boom. As far as he could see, Michael's life jacket was still in place. He sighed a sigh of partial relief. His son was alive and holding onto the boom.

Out of nowhere it seemed, another rogue wave and wind-swirl lifted the vessel above the water and slammed it down into a trough with the bow pointing to the bottom of the ocean. Ryan gripped the

339

tiller with all his might. It felt as if it might snap at any moment. He reassured himself this was a strong vessel and well-built. It had been declared unsinkable, but then after his years on the sea, he knew nothing was unsinkable if the conditions were right, and these were the strangest of circumstances that he had ever experienced. He searched for Aiden near the cabin but the lad was hidden by the sea water as it poured over the decks like a waterfall in flood. Ryan struggled to maintain his own position. Rain burst down upon them almost blinding him.

Ryan felt something wrap itself tight about his leg almost dragging his feet out from under him. Only allowing himself a split second to glance down, relief flowed through him like the rush of the wind around his ears, when he found Aiden clinging to his thigh. Not able to risk taking one hand from the tiller, he used his elbow to push the boy between his legs, and by shuffling his feet he clamped him into place without lifting his foot from the deck. The following wave lifted over the top of the vessel. The ship's timbers groaned and grated above the sound of the screaming winds. With a twitch of the ketch's stern, father and son were tossed off the vessel like a novice horseman may be tossed from a recalcitrant horse. Ryan's one arm clenched around his younger son, while his other sought protection from whatever was ahead in the roiling waters.

Down, down, down, father and son dived through the depths. Ryan used his one arm and his legs to twist them around and force his way back up – at least he thought it was upwards. Neither felt the weight of the ketch as its stern slammed down upon them, dragging them unresisting to the depths of the sea.

Half a mile away, onboard the coastguard cutter 102A, Captain Benson stood jammed in against the cabin with the telescope, while his helmsman struggled to maintain control of the vessel. He had been watching the ketch when the storm blew in from nowhere. He knew Captain Aitkens well and had sailed on his boat on several occasions. He swore when he saw the older boy collected by the boom and dumped into the sea. He watched in horror as Ryan and the younger lad disappeared overboard and the ship followed them stern-first into the waters. He scanned the area inch by inch seeking to find any sign of life of the captain and the boy, but all that rose from the depths was debris of the ketch like kindling firewood. He scanned out wide and targeted the boom and part-sail once again.

Benson called to the helmsman, "Keep it just idling slowly and head towards the boom and sail floating about fifty yards to the west of the main debris. A boy was holding on to the boom."

He directed the telescope back to the heavier accumulation of debris. As if on the call from an unseen director the wind and rain stopped. Only a slight breeze remained. The waters settled to a choppy surface. Every few seconds his scope returned to the boom and the sight of a body draped across its length. The cutter edged in slowly until they idled beside the floating spar.

"Hold it there," Benson called to his helmsman, then turned and yelled, "Deckies!" Three burly lads arrived on the double. "Can you put a harness on the lad and get him on board? Be careful, he took an awful whack to the head."

Wearing his life jacket and taking a spare lifebelt with him, one deckie sank into the water near Michael and placed a harness about his torso. He could not help but notice the nasty split scalp above the boy's right eye. *How can this boy still be alive?* he thought, then smiled with relief when the lad coughed and struggled for air. The deckies hauled the lad and their mate up and into the coastguard vessel.

While his crew took the wounded lad below for treatment, Captain Benson continued to search the surface for the remnants of his friend and the other son. For an hour they remained, but with the failing light and the badly wounded survivor on board, the decision was made to mark the area and turn for home.

CHAPTER THIRTEEN

House of Mourning

September 1899

Odette looked up from where she played with Florence, her daughter of two years and eight months. A small frown flittered across her brow. It worried Odette, the way Bridie read every word in every paper they had delivered to their front door – especially the infrequent ones from the United Kingdom. *Even Grandpa Wellington never became so engrossed with the news, be it local or world.* The memory flashed across her thoughts.

"Bridie, do you realize it is the middle of September and it is such a beautiful spring day? The weather will warm up soon and it will be too hot to walk anywhere in a matter of weeks. Will we take Florence for another walk through the Botanical Gardens?"

"There is an article in this paper right here," Bridie folded the newspaper in half and began to read aloud the report on the plans for the expansion of the Townsville Botanical Gardens due to begin in the rapidly approaching twentieth century. When she finished reading, she put the paper down, looked over at Odette and sighed. "If you wish, dear."

Odette smiled, but her anxiety for Bridie, who wore sadness like a favourite cape these last few weeks, churned inside her. This was so out of character for Bridie and Odette had her suspicions as to why. During the past two years, Captain Ryan Aitken had made consistent, if not regular visits, when his ship called into the port of Townsville.

Sometimes it may have been weeks between the arrival of his letters and then several arrived at once sending Bridie into raptures. It had been at least seven months since Ryan's last visit and at least three months since the arrival of any correspondence. In these recent weeks, Bridie's smile was a rare event and usually only stirred by Florence's antics.

"Maybe, by the time we return home from the Gardens, the mailman will have delivered half a dozen letters from your captain, which have been held up in some inefficient mail depot in some foreign country."

"Hmmm," Bridie's attention was now directed to her reading of an English paper. "Oh, just a moment, there is something here about the Bristol Channel. Let me read this and then I will fetch my hat."

When Odette next looked up, she noticed the pallor of her aunt's face. The deep gasp from Bridie's open mouth brought Odette to her feet.

"What is the matter?"

Bridie's trembling hand pointed to the paper. She struggled to pronounce the words stuck in her throat. Tears fell from her eyes.

Odette eventually understood the words Bridie tried to enunciate. "Ryan has been killed."

Odette dropped onto the seat beside Bridie and wrapped her arms around her shoulders.

"There must be some mistake."

"No, it is quite clear." Bridie began to précis the report. "Captain Ryan Aitkens and his two sons Michael and Aiden, were in a ketch sailing outside the Bristol Channel when a freak storm sank the vessel with the captain and his two sons." Bridie's tragic eyes looked up to explain to Odette, "Ryan's two boys are named Michael and Aiden. Ryan often takes them sailing when he is home for any length of time. According to this report, only the older son Michael, has survived."

Bridie drew another deep breath. "The coastguard was in the area at the time and witnessed the event, but it all happened so fast there was nothing they could do. It was they who retrieved the older boy and brought him back to shore. According to this report, there has been no sign of Ryan or his younger son." Bridie's voice faded away to nothing. The paper tore as Bridie's fingers fumbled to find the date of the report. "This was back in March of this year." A wail filled the room. "I cannot believe it. Ryan has been dead these past six or seven months. I should have known. Why didn't I feel it inside me?"

The small child sitting on the floor with her dolls looked up in consternation at the sight of her mother and Auntie Bridie sobbing in each other's arms.

"I am cursed, Odette. I have dragged you all out here to escape my curse, and now I find I have brought the curse along with me. I cannot escape my father's curse."

"Hush, Bridie, it is not like you to talk such nonsense. If you are cursed, then I am cursed too. Remember it was my tragedy that triggered our travel plans."

Rosa found Jimmy under the carriage in the shed, banging on something with his hammer.

"Jimmy, Jimmy, please come out from under there, right this minute."

"Just a tick, my love."

"No ticks, Jimmy, I need you out here, right now."

Jimmy slithered out and stood up trying to brush his back with his hands to remove the dirt on his shirt. Rosa spun him around and took over the dusty chore.

"Both Miss Bridie and Mrs. Odette are sobbing something terrible in the music room. I have no idea what is wrong. Newspapers are lying all over the settee."

Dust scattered in every direction as Jimmy ran his hands through his hair. He turned and took Rosa by the shoulders.

"There can only be one thing that might set Miss Bridie off like this. Something that concerns her Captain Aitkens."

"Should we say anything?"

"No, let them be for a while to gather their wits. Maybe a cup of tea might help, though."

"I'll bring Florence outside with me, then."

"Good idea."

By the time Rosa prepared the tea tray, the violent sobbing had settled to a few sniffles. She lay the tray upon the table and retreated, gathering Florence up as she went.

Odette threw her a grateful smile.

1900

The big house remained in mourning for many months. Odette suggested Bridie talk to their minister, but her aunt showed no interest. It had been almost twelve months since Bridie learnt of Ryan's demise. Each morning when she awoke, Bridie hoped she would find it had all been a terrible nightmare. When a small parcel arrived in August 1900, having been sent from a Mr. Michael Aitkens from Bristol in England, Odette was in two minds whether she should give it to Bridie or not.

Odette knew Bridie would be furious if she thought her mail had been withheld. She waited until after dinner when they were alone together.

'This arrived for you earlier today."

Bridie took the small package examining the addresses on the front and the back. She registered immediately it had been sent from the hand of Ryan's elder son. She sat staring at it on her lap for some time before she began to open the wrapping. A sheet of writing paper had been rolled around a small jewel box.

May 1900

Dear Miss Mayford

I am not sure if you have been informed of the death of my father when out sailing in March 1899. It is only recently that I found the courage to look through Father's office, and I found his journal in which he has spoken of you in glowing terms.

Reading his entries, I understand he had plans to emigrate to Australia once Aiden, my younger brother, and I had forged our futures. He planned to ask you to marry him.

I found the wedding band he had for you, along with half of a tie-clip, of which I understand you have the other half. My father's instructions accompanied these items. In the event of his passing, they were to be forwarded on to you.

With condolences

Michael Aitkens.

Bridie had no more tears left. She passed the note over to Odette and sat unmoving staring at the little box on her lap. She removed the wide gold band and slipped it onto the ring finger of her right hand.

CHAPTER FOURTEEN

Federation

1901

Odette cast an anxious gaze Bridie's way, as they descended the staircase together. It bothered her somewhat to see her aunt still dressed in severe black without a hint of colour. Her parasols now lay in the store cupboard, replaced by a plain black umbrella. The only adornment she wore was Ryan's band of gold on her right third finger. A small dose of self-righteousness rationalized her concern. It had been nearly two years since Captain Ryan Aitkens had drowned.

Odette sighed and consoled herself with the thought that at least she had succeeded in convincing Bridie it would be seen to be unpatriotic if they did not show up at the celebrations for the Commonwealth Federation Day today, the first day of the first month of 1901.

Outside, Jimmy took a last swipe with his cloth over the seats and floor before he handed the ladies into the carriage. Rosa stood at the front of her cottage with Florence, almost four years of age, in her arms. Her son James, three and a half years of age, played with a pet frog on the verandah steps. Rosa and Florence waved enthusiastically as the carriage trundled out onto the roadway. James barely lifted his head. He did not like it when his father went anywhere without him.

As they approached the town, the traffic slowed and the crowds began to close ranks.

"I think, Jimmy, you had better set us down here while you find somewhere to leave the horse and carriage."

"It is alright, Mrs. Odette, I have arranged with Mr. Turnbull at the stock feed place to keep us a parking space." It was only another street on when Jimmy turned the horse and carriage into the back entrance of the Stock and Station Agents.

"We have to make our way to the corner of Denham and Flinders Street, ladies," Jimmy guided them along a shortcut track.

On the street corner, a temporary stage seating many dignitaries had been set up beside the flag pole. The noise of the snappy tunes played by the band members, all dressed in their whites, drowned the voices of hundreds of the population here today to see the raising of the Federation Flag over Townsville.

"It is a shame the decision has not been made by those responsible, on what our Australian Flag will finally look like, but I have to admit it will be good to see the Union Jack waving in the breeze of Townsville until then," Bridie's voice was barely heard above the music and the din of so many people.

Only a spattering of parasols was seen in the crowds, as many women had chosen the shade of the more substantial black umbrellas on this hot summer day. Their colourful dresses brightened the bustling street. Straw boater hats adorned the heads of many of the men, some in dark suits, some in white, and many in just dark trousers and white shirts, with maybe a few wearing a dark waistcoat.

When a hush fell upon the crowd at the end of a musical score, the Mayor stood and began speaking from his notes.

Jimmy sighed, "I hope he doesn't go on forever. We'll all be meltin' soon."

Odette nudged his elbow and grinned up at him.

Eventually, the man ran out of puff and words. The deputy began to hoist the flag. As the red, white and blue Union Jack lifted on the breeze, the crowd sang God Save the Queen.

As the people began to disperse, the trio made their way along Flinders Street visiting and supporting several stalls run by their favourite charities. Odette stopped, when a man she recognized as a member of the school council which Bridie and she attended, spoke at her side.

"It was a good day for it don't you think, Mrs. Treloar?"

"Yes indeed, sir, thank heavens the rain has held off. That would have put a dampener on things."

"Will we see you at the next meeting? That will be on the first week after school resumes."

"Yes, of course, if possible."

"It will be a pleasure to see you then, good day, Mrs. Treloar."

Odette looked up and found Bridie and Jimmy had left her behind. Thank heavens Jimmy was a head taller than most of the men around her. She hurried as best she could to catch up.

"Thank you very much for deserting me," she grumbled at Bridie's side.

Bridie's smile pleased Odette – not because she was being teased for being caught by the most obstinate man on the school council – but because it was a natural smile. It seemed ages since Bridie's beautiful smile lit up their lives.

1903

"I think, Rosa, it is nearly time you began to put your feet up more. Christmas may have been too much for you. Perhaps we need to have Ethel-May take over more of the cooking until you have had that little one – and for a few months after too."

Rosa ran her hand around her swollen abdomen. "Thank you, Mrs. Odette, it is this heat more than anything that seems to have taken its toll on me. I am sure this must be the hottest summer we have ever had."

Odette laughed and gave the pot of stew on the stove a stir with the ladle.

"You say that every summer, Rosa."

"This time I mean it. You mark my words; it is going to be a summer to remember."

On the last day of January 1903, Rosa delivered twins: a baby girl, who Jimmy and she named Evelyn, and a boy, they named Charles.

When Odette and Bridie came to visit, all Rosa was able to repeat again and again was, "I thought my body was finished with having babies, but now it hands me two at once."

"No wonder you were so large and feeling the heat, my dear. Twins will be good because Odette and I will not need to share the cuddles. We now have one each," Bridie smiled, "and don't you worry about a thing in the big house. Odette is having a wonderful time practising her few cooking skills on Ethel-May's day off. Florence and I are practising our survival skills."

'Bridie, you are so ungrateful." Odette admonished her aunt. Rosa laughed.

Florence and James paid a scant greeting to the infants. They found more interesting entertainment in their bicycles – Christmas gifts to them each from Bridie and Odette. Jimmy had been offered one of his own to ride when supervising the children travelling to school, but he snubbed the idea.

"I have a horse in the stable there, Miss Bridie, what other mode of travel would I ever want? I will ride bareback beside Miss Florence and young James on their bicycles. Think of the time it will save hitching up the buggy. The school is not too far from home."

Only five weeks later, on the night of the 8th March 1903, Odette woke Bridie with a hand on her shoulder.

"Bridie, are you awake?"

"I am now. What is wrong?"

"Everything is so hot and still. There is not a breath of air coming off the sea. I am in a lather of perspiration. I swear my nerve ends are all on edge."

Bridie lay quiet listening for the usual sound of the night sea breeze rustling the bushes outside her window. Only a silence greeted her. She threw back the sheet.

"Are the verandah doors open?"

Both women made their way out to the verandah and stood peering towards the sea.

"I will not be surprised if we are in for a storm. This sort of heat cannot go on. Something must break." Odette offered.

"It certainly has that feel about it." At that moment, the hall clock chimed four o'clock. "Let us go down and put the kettle on for a cup of tea."

When they opened the kitchen door to find someone on their knees resetting the fire in the stove, both women jumped back in alarm.

"Good morning, ladies, did the heat get you up too?"

"Oh, Jimmy, you near scared me half to death," Odette gasped. "Are Rosa and the babies alright?"

"Yes, both babies were fretful during the night. They're all asleep now." Jimmy had the wood burning nicely and stood upright, before pulling the kettle over the heat. "I think we be lookin' at a storm with this kind of heat. In fact, if we be home at Clawhaven Estate, I know

352

Mr. Axel would be tellin' us all to batten down, before the heavens opened up and gave us hell, er ... sorry ... gave us what for."

Bridie smiled at Jimmy's slip of the tongue as she offered, "Jimmy, do you think you should bring the family into the big house, in case it is a bad storm?"

"That's a solid little cottage we have there, Miss. If I were you, I'd close off the upstairs rooms and huddle in downstairs when the rain hits."

"There was hardly a cloud in the sky when we looked out fifteen minutes ago," Odette intervened, "I don't think we are going to be lucky enough to get rain."

By the middle of the day, Odette discovered how wrong her prediction had been. The fury of the wind vented upon the town. At first, it hit from a southerly direction sending whipping gusts of winds along the streets collecting weapons of galvanized iron sheets, tree branches and any unsecured debris of houses. The wind whistled along the verandahs of the big house sending pot plants spinning off into the tall hedges around the yard. Doors and windows rattled, threatening to bend and snap at any moment. Salt spray, picked up on the gale force winds, smudged the glass windows. Rain pelted down upon the roof. Normal conversation was out of the question. A long, drawn-out screech of iron and the crack of breaking timber followed by Odette's squeal sent Bridie, holding firmly to Florence's hand, running up the staircase to discover the reason for her call.

"Look, on the hedge," Odette's pointing hand trembled. "That is part of the roof of our front neighbour's house." Florence ran to place her arms around her mother's waist. Odette looked down at her six-year-old daughter. "It is a dreadful storm, my pet, but we are safe inside here." Odette was tempted to cross her fingers. "I think we had better take Jimmy's advice and stay downstairs."

"Oh, good heavens, how are Rosa and Jimmy out there?" Bridie went racing back down the staircase on her way to the back door. Peering through the glass circle in the top half of the door, she found it impossible to see as far as the cottage, but she was able to define the shed and everything seemed in place. "The poor horses, what must they be thinking?" She spoke to herself, but Odette with Florence had followed on her heels.

"One thing we can be sure of, Jimmy will have done a good job of checking the buildings this morning. He will have them as safe as is humanly possible."

"This storm is beyond normal, Odette. I have never seen the like of it before."

"How long is this storm going to last, Aunt Bridie?" Florence asked hesitantly.

"Sweetheart, I do not know. What I do know is that we are in a big safe house, which has solid foundations, and we have nothing to fear." This time it was Bridie who found her fingers crossed. She shook her head at her fear. "Now, how about we get out the chess set and try to divert our minds?"

The two women, with Florence an ardent onlooker, played chess. When they found their minds returning to the noise of the wind-swept rains on the side of the house, they practised all their choir songs planned for the competition at the Eisteddfod in a few weeks. Knowing how the wet weather tended to interfere with a piano's tuning, it was left covered with a heavy blanket. Bridie's fine-tuned musical ear started them off with the keynotes.

It was mid-afternoon before the rain eased to intermittent showers. The noises around the big house quietened to the slow rattle of something loose on the upper verandah. Gusts settled to a light breeze. Bridie, Odette and Florence made tentative steps outside to assess the damage. Their yard was covered in small and large branches of bushes and trees interspersed with debris from sites further up and down the street. The front hedge lay squashed under the neighbour's partial roof.

They stepped carefully towards Jimmy's house. At the shed, they heard the horses stomping their feet and snorting. Every now and then Jimmy's voice calmed them. As their three heads poked over the half door, Bridie called, "Is everything alright in there, Jimmy?"

"All good here. How be you at the big house?"

"Nothing that cannot be fixed with a rake and a broom and a strong arm. How are Rosa and the children?"

"A bit shaken up, but they be all safe."

At that moment, the neighbour's voice was heard calling, "You okay there, Jimmy?"

Jimmy opened the stable door and stepped outside. "Yes thanks, Jack. What about you and the family?"

"We're good – only had a little damage." He noticed the women standing nearby. "Sorry to interrupt, Missus, glad to see you are safe."

"And you, Mr. Rankin, and Mrs. Rankin," it was Odette who replied before Jack Rankin went on to speak.

"The word is that one of the hospital wards has completely collapsed. What's left of the hospital buildings is not much better. The police and army are on site now. They're calling for everyone available to help. There're patients trapped, I understand. I came to see if you'll come down with me to help, Jimmy."

Jimmy looked over at Bridie who gave an imperceptible nod of her head.

"I'll just pop in and let the wife know where I be goin'." Jimmy ran to the cottage to tell Rosa.

The men were moving at a fast walk through the gateway, when Bridie called, "If there is anything we women can do, let us know, Mr. Rankin."

"Thank you, Missus, I'll tell whoever is in charge you've offered."

When the photos of the extent of the damage at Townsville began to appear in the local papers, everyone who had survived, gave thanks. Church services were held to pray for those lost on the day. Money was raised for the families they left behind and contributions were made for the rebuilding of the Townsville Hospital.

1907

When the three walked out of the cinema at dusk, Flinders Street sparkled with the glowing circles of the recently added gas lighting. Jimmy grinned to himself as he listened to his almost-ten-year-old son James sprout all his knowledge on the gas street lighting. Jimmy knew full well this was the boy's strategy of payback to his friend Florence Treloar, whose constant instruction on movie productions stole much of the magic of the film inside the theatre.

Jimmy's smile disappeared, as his mind drifted back to the health of his four-year-old twins. Over the past week, with little respite, Rosa nursed them as they struggled to breathe during the terrifying bouts of whooping cough. She rubbed their small chests with her herbal remedies and walked the floor day and night. Ethel-May had taken up Rosa's chores at the big house. Ruthie worked extra days and added housemaid chores to her laundry duties.

"What's that stick in your hand for, James?"

"It's not a stick – well, it is a stick, but it's my fishing rod. Dad is taking me fishing for my birthday today. He said, now I'm ten, I'm old enough to be taken fishing."

"Oh, great, where is my rod, then?"

A pink flush infused Florence's face, when James, her loyal friend and best mate, laughed at her.

"Girls don't go fishing at this creek, Flo. Only us men go fishing at this creek."

At that moment, Jimmy came down the steps with a rod of his own and a crib box with sandwiches wrapped in newspaper. In a small sugar bag, he carried a sharpened pocket knife, spare bent pins fine string and a packet of worms dug from the garden. A water canteen hung on a strap around his neck. He was taken aback when Flo accosted him at the bottom of the steps.

"Mr. Braydon, James said I am not going fishing with you today."

"Miss Flo, girls do not go fishing at this creek. Only the men go fishing there."

Flo's flush turned a bright red. Disbelief filled her eyes. She stamped her foot.

"Mr. Braydon, you are a servant here and I am telling you, you are to take me fishing."

The breath left Jimmy's body. He had never been spoken to in such a manner. He sucked the air back into his lungs. He spoke through clenched teeth.

"Miss Flo, I am not and have never been anyone's servant. I work for people who I like and respect, but never will I work for someone who thinks of me as just a servant. NO, I will not invite you to come fishing with me today or ever."

Tears squirted from the blue eyes. Her blond hair streamed out behind her as she ran back to the big house. Somewhere on the way, a little commonsense seeped into her thoughts. She realized there would be little sympathy for her if she reported her poor behaviour to either her mother or her Aunt Bridie. *Everybody hates me,* she thought as she threw herself onto her bed.

At the airless narrow tidal creek, the water began to rush in leaving a narrow strip of mud between the channel and the native trees that hung over the water to meet almost halfway, providing dappled shade for the numerous men and some youngsters with their simple wooden rods and hook lines. Once Jimmy had shown his son how to bait the hook and hang it in the water, Jimmy stood back to lean against one of the trees. The memory of the scene back at the cottage poisoned his earlier enthusiasm for fishing. He felt sick in the stomach knowing he must tell Miss Bridie and Mrs. Odette what had happened.

Jimmy need not have worried. Back at the big house, a long-faced Florence threw herself into Odette's lap. Her sobs increased.

"Take care child, you nearly had this crochet hook in your eye. What has you in such a pother?"

"Nothing."

"Nothing then is it? You have taken to sobbing your heart out over nothing?"

"Nobody loves me."

"Why would you say that, child?"

"James and his father have gone fishing and did not take me."

"I should think not. Girls do not go fishing, Florence. It is not lady-like to be grubbing around with dirty mud and fish."

"I don't want to be a lady. I just want to do what James does. We do everything together, all the time, and now he has just left me behind."

Bridie arrived in the room having been over at the cottage discussing the coming week's menus with Rosa. She had found Rosa quite upset and though unwilling to say anything at first, did eventually reveal Florence's abominable behaviour earlier in the morning.

Odette stroked her daughter's long blond hair across her lap. Bridie took a pencil and paper from the table and wrote a short note, which she held in front of her niece's eyes, and out of sight of Florence's vision.

FLO RUDE TO JIMMY THIS AM.

Odette's lips formed a silent ooooh.

Bridie retrieved her note and squashed it in her hand. "I'll make a cup of tea," she called as she disappeared towards the kitchen.

Odette waited until the sobs subsided and Florence sat up before she asked her question.

"What did Mr. Braydon say?"

Florence bit her bottom lip. "He said, no. He said ladies don't go fishing at the creek."

"Quite right of him too. Is that all you said?"

Florence's lips pouted. Odette knew the child's reluctance to answer spoke volumes. She waited.

"I said he had to do what I ordered," Florence admitted reluctantly.

Odette knew full well this had to be a watered-down version of the event but decided not to press the point further for the moment.

"Do you think that was a polite thing to say?"

Florence had the grace to cast her eyes downward. "No."

"I must admit to feeling ashamed to think my daughter would be so rude to a good friend. What did Mr. Braydon do then?"

"James and his father left me behind."

"And so they should, don't you think?"

"B-b-but, James and I do everything together. I wanted to go fishing with him."

"Florence, you are not a baby anymore. You are over ten years of age. It is time you realized boys and girls are very different. There are things boys can do that girls cannot do and things girls can do that boys cannot do. You cannot go fishing in the muddy creek with the men and the boys. This does not mean you and James cannot be firm friends."

Florence lay her head back down upon her mother's knees but turned away from her mother's knowing gaze. Her guilt burnt in her belly.

"Mother, I was rude to Mr. Braydon."

If Odette was asked, she could not have explained the relief she felt in hearing her daughter confess her error of judgement, even though she retained a niggle of doubt that this might not have been all of the poor behaviour.

"What do you think you should do for Mr. Braydon?"

"I will write him a note of apology."

"I think that would be appreciated."

1910

"Come in, Jimmy, come in, James," Odette invited the Braydon men into the big house. "Miss Bridie is waiting in the library for you. Go on through. I will follow in a moment." Odette turned to make a hasty retreat to where she knew her daughter was most likely sitting quietly on the verandah outside the office-come-library hoping to glean information on this meeting.

"Florence, I am disappointed in you. You know very well it is impolite to listen in to private conversations." Odette pointed her arm towards the other side of the house where Florence was supposed to be practising on the piano. "Go, and don't let me hear anything but your music."

Florence rose with a sigh. She threw her blonde plaits over her shoulders.

"I just wanted to know what James has done wrong."

"As far as I am aware, James has done nothing wrong."

"Then why have he and his father been summoned to Aunt Bridie's presence?"

"That, Miss Nosey, is none of your business."

Once the flow of the musical scales drifted over from the east side of the house, Odette left to join the other three at the meeting.

With Odette seated, Bridie opened the discussion.

"Jimmy, I wanted you both here to discuss James's future studies."

James went to speak, but Bridie's raised hand halted his words before they were formulated.

"James, we promised your father that we would fund the education of his children in return for your parents having emigrated to this country with us thirteen years ago. Mrs. Treloar and I both agree this is a small price to pay for the loyalty of his and your mother's service."

It was Odette who spoke when Bridie stopped to take a breath. "As we understand it, James, your grades at school have been exemplary throughout junior school and now you will want to use this opportunity to push forward to a career that will solidify your future – maybe law or accountancy perhaps."

From where James sat on the settee beside his father facing Miss Mayford and Mrs. Treloar, he felt the three pairs of adult eyes boring into him. He opened his mouth to speak but the words stuck in his throat. He swallowed and tried again.

"Please, Miss Mayford and Mrs. Treloar, don't think I am being ungrateful because I really do appreciate this opportunity you offer me, but I do not wish to do any more book-learning work. I want to do what I always wanted to do. I want to work with horses like my father did when he was my age." James turned to face his father directly. "I'm sorry, Dad, but I want to finish school at the end of this year. I already have a job as a station hand on a place outside Cloncurry."

Confusion, disappointment and even pride struggled for the upper hand in Jimmy Braydon's expressions.

"James, this is a chance of a lifetime. Do you not wish to think on it a bit more?"

"Thank you both again," James turned back to Bridie and Odette, "this is not a recent flash-in-the-pan decision. It is something I have planned for since my father first sat me on a horse."

Bridie smiled a warm smile. Her thoughts sped back to the first day she watched a skinny, knee-high, Jimmy Braydon slithering up the legs of his seventeen-hands-high brown horse named Flyer.

"I first met your dad with the horse he called Flyer. He was an amazing horseman, James. It is not too hard to see why you have entertained this desire for such a long time. If at any time you need assistance, I do hope you will not forget we are always here to help any offspring of Jimmy and Rosa Braydon."

Jimmy laid a gentle hand on his son's shoulder. He turned to Bridie and Odette.

"Thank you so very much for this wonderful offer. I know, whatever James takes on, he'll give it his all. I'm very proud of him."

"As are we," Bridie and Odette said in unison.

When James walked through the back garden, while his father remained to speak to Miss Bridie about some work she wanted doing, he felt himself dragged unceremoniously into the jasmine bush near the stables.

"What was that all about, what have you done wrong, James?"

"Flo, let go of my collar, you nearly strangled me." Once released, James complained with every brush of his hands to smooth his collar. "For once, Flo, this has nothing to do with you. It is none of your business."

"Cuttlefish, everything you and I do is the business of the other. We are best friends, aren't we?"

"Mates don't half strangle their mates. If you want to know Miss Busybody, Miss Mayford offered to pay my fees to go to secondary school."

"Oh, how wonderful. We will still be going to school together."

"Well, no, Flo, I told you I have a job to go to on a property outside Cloncurry."

"You cannot do that. I will never see you from one Christmas to the next."

"I hadn't thought of that – sounds peaceful."

Flo placed her two hands on James's chest and shoved hard before turning and going back to the big house.

"Men …," she muttered.

$$\approx$$

Florence found it hard to believe just how fast the time flew by. One day she and James raced their bicycles hell-for-leather home from the last day of the school year, and the next she stood with Mr. and Mrs. Braydon and the twins as they waved goodbye to James when he boarded the west-bound train to Cloncurry. At the sight of tears on Mrs. Braydon's cheeks, Florence's control deserted her. Tears washed down her face.

"Why did James have to go away, Mrs. Braydon?" she struggled not to sob.

Rosa's arm slipped around Florence's shoulders. "James is a big boy now, Miss Florence. He wants to go out and make his own way in the world."

"But… but…," Florence retained some self-control and did not repeat what was inside her head. *He should have waited for me. We could have got married and gone away together.*

Rosa smiled a sad and knowing smile. "One day you will find a young man of your own class, Miss Florence, and then you will begin your life."

When a week later, Florence's mournful face continued to greet her mother and aunt at the meal tables Odette was at a loss. She sent a silent appeal to Bridie hoping for inspiration. Bridie raised her eyebrows in an unspoken, *Why me?* In sheer desperation, she threw a question across the table.

"Florence, have you noticed the motor cars on the streets lately? I thought we might go to town and visit the car display shop. Will you keep me company?"

Florence looked across the table at her aunt. To both Bridie's and Odette's surprise, a soft chuckle filled the room.

"Aunt Bridie, can you see our Mr. Braydon sitting at the steering wheel of one of those machines? I have heard him go on a treat about how they will never replace the horse and buggy. They make too much noise and they smell – in his opinion."

Odette and Bridie laughed out loud with relief, if not at the imagining of their Mr. Braydon

.

CHAPTER FIFTEEN

World at War

1914-1918

Newspapers lay scattered across the settee, as Bridie searched for every entry related to the declaration of war and all the following reports.

"We knew war hovered on the horizon, but one always hoped it might be avoided," she spoke to her niece.

"I worry for our friends in the old country. They must be terrified. Poor Mary Axel, she will be worried sick for her boys," Odette looked up from the musical score she was examining. "Rosa's sisters' children will be old enough to be called up too. All I can say is thank goodness we are so far away from it all."

"I think we will be drawn into the conflict if it escalates further. Australia is part of the Commonwealth, after all. They are already sending troops to Thursday Island to protect the north here." Bridie folded the paper roughly and opened the local Bulletin. After scanning the first page she looked up at her niece. "Oh, Odette, we must go to this."

"What is that?"

"The Queens Hotel is holding a concert to raise money for the war effort. They are looking for anyone interested who may contribute towards the entertainment. Donations will be accepted at the supper to follow." Bridie lowered the paper to her lap. "If you accompanied me on the piano, I could sing something."

"Yes, of course. I will contact the church choir and see if they are going to do anything."

"Perhaps we should ask Florence if she will play a solo, or maybe the two of you could present a duet?"

"I will talk to her when she comes home from school," Odette looked up to the clock, "in an hour."

For three weeks, Bridie, Odette and Florence spent every spare moment available in the music room preparing their acts for the fund-raising concert. Florence refused to perform on her own, but she did agree to play a piano duet with her mother and sing another duet with her aunt.

One night, as Florence prepared for bed, she asked her mother, "Will James have to go away to war?"

Odette's hand trembled as she brushed out the crinkles in the blond hair after undoing Florence's plaits.

After a long pause Odette answered, "He is only seventeen just yet, and at this stage, they are only taking the men aged nineteen to thirty-eight years old. Let us hope it never reaches a point when they need to drop those ages."

"I hope so too. I will absolutely die if he is sent off to war."

"Florence, my darling, please don't think like that." Odette bit down on the warnings she wanted to issue to her offspring about becoming too fond of this young man with whom she had grown up. "What we can do in the here and now is to help raise money for the war effort to ensure our troops have all they need to fight the enemy."

The concert was well attended and the applause after each item on the program threatened to lift the roof from the hall. Laughter and merriment filled the night as the audience made their way to the Queen's Hotel, a short walk up the street, where supper was to be served.

Mr. Glenning and his wife made their way through the parlour rooms greeting their guests.

"Miss Mayford, how lovely to see you and the family again. We did enjoy your performance tonight. Miss Florence, you were wonderful."

Bridie looked up from where they sat at a small table and thanked their host. She turned towards a sudden movement and a sharp sound of surprise from a distinguished-looking gentleman sitting at a neighbouring table. Their gazes met. Bridie's mind raced back through time, struggling to register if she knew this man with sparkling brown eyes, who sat with an attractive smile directed her way. After Mr. and Mrs. Glenning moved on to another group of guests, the stranger, with the sensual smile and the neat grey hair, moved to stand at the table beside her.

"Miss Mayford, I believe. Would that be Miss Mayford of," he paused, "now what was the name of your grandparent's home?" His smile almost turned to a grin, "Clawhaven Manor, I think."

Bridie stared vacantly at him, while her mind raced.

He chuckled, "I am hurt. You once turned down my proposal and now you do not even remember me?" He reached out a hand. "Miss Mayford of the Mayford family shipping company, I am thinking. Never to be told what she is to do, no less. I am Stewart Cruickshank."

The cogs of Bridie's brain slipped into place. She laughed. "Stewart Cruickshank, of course I remember you." Bridie reached out her hand to meet that of Stewart Cruickshank, who bent and kissed her fingers in a display of old-time good manners. Bridie's eyes took in the tall, slim body which still angled down to narrow hips. The laughter lines at the edges of his eyes were deeper and other lines now reached over his face and hands, she noticed. He was doing nicely for a man of – once more she sent her brain into overdrive

367

searching for data – *I am fifty-eight years of age so he must be at least another five years older.* Her eyes approved the vision in front of her.

"Lovely to meet you again. Is your wife here tonight, Edith, if my memory serves me correctly?"

"I knew when we met you had a sharp mind. I took your advice that night and listened to your brother's ideas. And no, we lost Edith three years ago, I'm afraid. She was a good woman and gave me three sons and two daughters. Two of those sons now have sons who are hell-bent on joining up to this debacle the Kaiser has instigated."

"Oh, dear, that must be a worry." Bridie did not wait for an answer. "Will you pull up a chair? May I introduce my niece, Odette, George's daughter, and her daughter, Florence."

Odette and Florence contributed little to the conversation, as Bridie and Stewart returned to their reminiscing.

"I did take up a partnership with your father, Bridie. He and George were easy to work with, but when Edward," Stewart turned to Odette, "that will be your brother, I believe, became more active in the company, I fell out with the family and left to set up my own shipping company here in Australia."

People were beginning to depart. Bridie realized the night was over. She felt saddened to have to say goodbye.

"Will you be in Townsville tomorrow night?" she asked before she even thought about it. "Would you like to join us for dinner?"

Stewart accepted the invitation with alacrity and the group stood up and made their way outside. "Can I offer you a lift home?" Stewart asked.

"Thank you, no, we have our man here with the buggy. Goodnight then, Mr. Cruickshank, you have the address, we will see you about 7.30 tomorrow evening."

Stewart laughed. "My pleasure."

Later as Bridie prepared for bed, she stood in front of the mirror, her long cotton nightie thrown carelessly on the bed. Soft hands ran down over her skin. A smile lifted her lips. Despite a little sag here and there, her body retained its shape, despite her age. She twisted to the left and then to the right. She felt goosebumps rising due to a cool draft through her open window. Another shiver fluttered inside her belly at the thought of what might happen.

It was arranged for Ethel-May to sleep over in the big house the following night to help with the serving of the meal and the clearing up later. As the conversation drifted around the table, Bridie found it impossible not to send frequent glances in Stewart's direction. After dinner with the three ladies, Stewart requested a repeat of their performance the previous evening.

When the evening drew to a close, Bridie walked out to see their guest settled on his horse. With the moonlight at his back, Stewart looked down into Bridie's sparkling eyes.

"Bridie, I have to go south again tomorrow for business, but on my return would you accompany me to the new movie theatre here in town?"

Bridie admonished herself silently at the pattering of her heartbeat inside her chest. Her breath caught in her throat and she managed a soft, "That would be lovely, thank you, Stewart."

Having waved Stewart on his way, Bridie walked into the house. Her feet threatened to swing into a slow and sensuous waltz. A gentle smile turned into soft laughter. It seemed her feet did not touch the floor as she glided up the staircase. *For heaven's sake, woman, you are not a young girl anymore. You are old enough to be a grandmother, even perhaps, a great-grandmother.* But commonsense had no place on this night.

It was three months later, on the first day of May, when Bridie and Stewart consummated their relationship. Having been invited to stay in the big house when he had cause to remain overnight in Townsville, Stewart was shown into his room by Bridie, who, with a mischievous grin to cover her pounding heart, pointed to the connecting doorway leading into her room.

Stewart drew her into a tight embrace. "I only hope my lovely that this old body is still capable of stirring a woman such as yourself to pleasure." He placed his lips over hers.

When Bridie was able to draw breath she responded, "My body is telling me that you will have no problem at all."

Bridie was very satisfied to discover later, as they lay on top of the sheets with the caress of Stewart's sensuous fingers and soft kisses trailing over her body, she felt her inner core spin out of control. She bit her lip to silence the threatened cry of pleasure. Her prophesy had been correct, but just to be sure, like butterfly wings, she explored his splendid body until his arousal brought them both to an encore.

Stewart fell back on the pillows and sighed. "Woman you are going to kill me. I am not as young as I once was, remember."

"You do very well – for an old man. I will give you five minutes of breathing space." Bridie giggled as she threw herself upon him.

Extracts From Odette's Journal 1914:

Since the declaration of war, Bridie and I, with the help of Florence, have worked to raise funds for the war effort. Mr and Mrs Glenning from the Queens Hotel held a concert, earlier in the year, which proved very successful.

War News Headlines 1914:

Too few reports feeding back from the battle fronts deliver us good news. A horrendous thing called trench warfare has been employed in Europe.

1915

Rosa swished the dust from the broom down her front steps, when she heard the noise of the new motorized bus pulling up at their front gate. She smelt the fumes of the engine. Rosa looked out to the road just in time to see a young man waving his hand to the driver. She sucked in her breath. She recognized the gait of her elder son walking into the yard.

"Jimmy, Jimmy," Rosa called for her husband, as she ran down the steps. "Come quickly, it's James, he's just off the bus." Dust rose from under her feet when Rosa stopped in her tracks. A horrible thought crossed her mind. There was only one reason James had returned from the job he loved at Cloncurry. Only last week, Rosa read in the newspaper of the recent changes to the enrolment ages. Hastily she put the smile back on her face. *James is a man now. I must support him in his decision.* How easy it is to think these things, but already her heart weighed heavily in her chest.

Her instinct had been correct. James explained how he was back to enrol in the Royal Australian Navy.

In a voice forced through the clamped fingers of anxiety around his throat, Jimmy asked, "Why the Navy, son?"

"Remember, you said your grandfather was in the Navy, Dad?"

"Yes, he was." Jimmy pondered for a moment on how his great-grandparents must have felt at the time of their son's leaving. *Did their world feel as though it was collapsing around their heads?*

371

"Yes, James, he joined the Royal Navy, when he was not much older than you, I think. Gran often told us of how the crew called him The Gull because he flitted around the sails like a seagull." Jimmy felt his voice fading as the memories flooded in.

Rosa met Jimmy's gaze across the table on which were scattered the teapot, sugar bowl and three cups. Her hand reached across to take that of her husband. Rosa knew that as bad as she felt at losing her son to the war, Jimmy was going to feel worse still. Rosa understood it had been difficult for her husband while James worked in Cloncurry. Every day he felt the absence of the shadow, their son, at his heels.

"I guess you haven't told Miss Florence yet, son?"

James's glance dropped to the table in front of him. He fiddled with the cup.

"Not yet, Dad, I think it will take more courage to tell Flo than it will to sign up for the war."

Rosa swallowed her fear and sorrow. She stood up from the table to walk around and lay a hand on her elder son's shoulder.

"I think it'll be best if you tell her as soon as you can. She'll need some time to get used to the idea."

When James was able to get Florence on her own, near the stables, he did not miss the pallor that fell over the beautiful honeyed tan of her skin when he explained. He was surprised when she did not protest. In fact, he had to admit a little hurt.

"I am not surprised, James. I have been expecting this ever since I read the changes to the enlistment conditions in the paper."

A week later, the railway platform was crowded as a large group of local lads lined up to board the train taking them to Brisbane, where they were to begin their training.

The platform reverberated with the popular melodies of the day. *Australia Will Be There* and *Keep the Home Fires Burning* were presented by the members of the town band dressed in their smart clothes and playing their shiny instruments.

Florence Treloar stood between her aunt and her mother with her back straight, but her gaze lowered to the platform. James's parents were nearby. Desolation was written on Flo's face. Even though she had pinched her cheeks mercilessly to stir up a touch of colour, her efforts had failed miserably. She politely held her hand out to touch that of James before he joined the line which snaked off down to the other end of the platform. Nausea rose in her throat. This was a nightmare. Her heart sagged with the weight of a rock inside her chest. James was two men away from the entry to the carriage when Florence could not contain herself a moment more. She sprinted across the platform to swoop James into her arms and pressed a heavy kiss on his cheek. James's eyes opened wide. He struggled to believe what was happening. He drew back in surprise, before he wrapped his arms around Flo in return, and kissed her soundly on the lips. The line of men went berserk with cheers and catcalls. Florence's face flushed scarlet. She turned and ran to hide at the back of the crowd. Tears ran down her cheeks, deep sobs caught in her throat. It was James who found her. He took the crushed handkerchief from his pocket and wiped away the tears.

"Hush, little Flo. You know I must do this. Please tell me you understand."

Florence's sobs settled enough to speak. "Yes, James, I know, but the knowing does nothing to ease the pain." She reached up around her neck and unclasped the chain of her pendant. "Please carry this with you at all times, James. Hopefully, the love I give with it will bring you home safe."

James took the pendant and placed it in his top pocket and buttoned it down.

"Now come, my little Miss, I must go, or they'll lock me up in the clink before I even get to where we are going." He took her soft hand in his own tanned and roughened fingers. James led Florence back to the family and resumed his place in the line wending its way to board the train.

Odette walked into the dining room to find Bridie opening the windows further, to entice a little breeze inside.

"Where is Florence, she is seldom late for a meal?"

Bridie smiled a soft knowing smile. "Perhaps she does not feel like eating this evening. Saying goodbye to James this afternoon has left her very much at a loss. War is an unpredictable monster. We can never be sure our loved ones will return."

"Oh, dear, of course. I will need to talk to her about her behaviour at the railway station this afternoon. I was holding off to give her a chance to settle down a little first."

"There were many people there saying goodbye to loved ones. I am sure they barely noticed Florence's actions." Bridie pulled out her chair and sat. "Florence is smart enough to know she could have behaved with a little more decorum, but sometimes good manners go out of the window when heartache engulfs the soul." Odette looked up ready to speak, but Bridie interrupted. "Odette, my dearest, we have both known the devastating sorrow at the loss of a loved one. If you leave Flo alone for a little while, she might come to you, ready to talk."

During the following weeks, Florence felt as though each foot weighed a ton. With her school days at an end, she taught music classes to the junior school students two days a week. One day of the week, she played the piano with the town choir. The rest of the days were her own and she found they dragged so slowly she wanted to scream. Some days she begged Rosa to show her how to cook. But every day, when she was at home, her ear was always cocked to the sound of the mail delivery boy.

Her first letter from James did not come via her mailbox. Creased and stained with dirty finger marks, it had been slipped into an envelope that arrived for Rosa and Jimmy.

Rosa passed her letter across to Florence to read.

Dear Mum, Dad, Evie and Charlie
Me and the fellows had a good trip on the train and are now learning how not to fall off a ship, peel spuds, wash floors and salute. I understand the next thing we are to learn is how to march back and forth around all the obstacles on the deck of a ship. After that, we get to learn to carry ammunition to and from Bertha the big gun on the deck. Incorporated in that lesson will be one on how to load Bertha again, without falling overboard or sending ourselves off with the round of shot. Meanwhile, all of this is being done while we are firmly attached to the shoreline.
Send my kind regards to the family in the big house.
Enclosed is a note to Flo – please explain that I have only the one envelope until I can find more.
Hoping everyone is well. Your son, James.

"He sounds contented, Mrs. Braydon. You must miss him too."

"Yes, Miss Florence, we do, but he is a man now and must do what a man must do." Rosa rested a sympathetic hand on Florence's shoulder and she passed across the letter from her son marked for Flo.

Florence's blue eyes sparkled and soft laughter curved her lips, as she slipped up to her room and closed the door gently.

Dear Flo

All the new chums in my group have met the expectations of the brass who have worked so hard to ensure we pass the muster. We will be shipped out within the week, so we are told, but not to where or how. Maybe they might toss us out to paddle a canoe down the river.

Your letter arrived saying you are thinking about going to do your nursing training. I cannot imagine your mother permitting such a thing but I give you full credit for the ambition.

Sorry, I had to put this into my parent's envelope. Will get some more tomorrow on our half-day in town.

Kindest regards

James

Her heart ached. The wording at the end of the letter left her anxious. *Am I worth only his kindest regards?* This preyed on her mind more and more each day. Flo's shoulders sagged despite her mother's continual reminders to stand straight. Odette fretted over her daughter's lack of appetite.

"I am at a loss," Odette turned to Bridie for advice.

"Our Florence believes James has gone to his death and who knows, she may very well be correct. You and I have both lost the men we loved. Can you not remember how it felt to know Peter's smile would not light up your day again? How you ached for the touch of his hand in your own? Let Flo mourn and, in the meantime, we will pray every day for James's life to be spared."

After reading the news report on the transfer of the quarantine station from Magnetic Island to the mainland at Pallarenda and of the trained nurses assigned to work there, Florence's mind turned another corner.

Florence was to remember the night of the 1st of August 1915 for years to come. It was the first time she had ever defied her mother. The light of the lamp flickered in the breeze cooling the late winter night. An owl hooted softly in the trees outside the parlour room. Odette looked up from the balaclava she was knitting for the troops fighting in the colder regions when Florence spoke.

"Mother, I must speak with you."

"Of course, Florence, what is on your mind?"

Florence's gaze dropped to her lap. She paused to collect her breath and calm the pounding in her chest.

Odette felt a cold shiver run along her spine as she watched the fine fingers on her daughter's hands twisting around each other.

"Mother, I wish to commence training as a nurse." The words came out in a rush.

Odette sucked in a tortured breath. She cast her gaze around the room. *Where is Bridie when I need her?*

"We only need to read the newspapers to see our young men are dropping like flies on the battlefront. There will be a great need for nurses both there and at home."

Odette's mind swirled. "Florence, you are little more than a girl. They need mature women to carry out the duties of a nurse."

"I am old enough to begin training here at the Townsville Hospital. Yes, they are recommending mature nurses for near the battle fronts."

Odette attempted to swallow the lump in her throat. "But, Florence, there are many ways to contribute to the welfare of our soldiers without putting your health and reputation at risk."

"Mother, it is only common sense that the nurses' training will include how to care for one's own health. As for reputations, I am sure it is only a few bad apples that have dragged down the reputations of many good nurses. It is the individual's responsibility to maintain dignity and to hold one's head high."

"Flo, I am sorry, but you will learn in life that a lady does not have to do anything wrong. It is how the world thinks her character has been sullied. Nurses are all very well to have around when you are sick, but many have come from very dubious backgrounds."

"I will either go nursing here at the Townsville Hospital close to home and family, or I will join the army nurses to serve my country that way," Florence looked boldly into her mother's anxious eyes. She bit her lip and breathed slowly.

Odette spluttered. "War is a man's business."

"The fighting is, Mother, I agree, but who will care for the wounded men?" Florence watched her mother struggle with her thoughts. "Our boys are being wounded and we will need many nurses before this war is over."

Odette strived to hold back her tears. "Florence, you are a sweet and gentle person. The duties that a nurse must perform on the male patients are not ladylike and will harden a young lady's personality. A nurse sees too much. They must do things a young lady should never have to do." Odette's hand reached out to beseech her daughter's understanding. She felt her mind slipping into a sinkhole. "Besides, it would be wrong for you to take the wage of someone who needs it more than you. We employ people. We work with charities to support the community; we do not take the jobs of the needy."

Florence coughed back a snort of impatience. "If it's my wage you are worried about, I will donate every penny to charity." She drew air into her depleted lungs. "Donating money is good, Mother, but I want to offer more."

Odette accompanied her daughter to the interview with the matron. She had intended to put her point of view across in no uncertain terms, but when the first question was fired directly at Florence who blinked at the sudden onslaught, Odette sat quiet and listened. Florence sat taller and looked the lady in the eyes. Odette felt pride fill her heart as this young girl, her daughter, spoke from her soul.

"Matron, many of my friends from my school have left to risk their lives for our country in the war effort. The first thing I asked myself was, 'What can I do?' After reading up on the wars and their aftermath, I am sure many soldiers will need medical and nursing care long after the war is over. I felt the least I can do is learn how I may help these valiant men."

Having gained the matron's approval for Florence to spend her one day off a week at home with her mother and aunt, Odette gave her consent for Florence to begin her nurse training.

Jimmy packed Florence's valise into the buggy and assisted Florence up into her seat. As they travelled the short distance to the hospital, he dug into his top pocket and removed a folded scrap of paper.

"This is the last note we received from James. It was posted after they left the Australian shores."

"Oh, Mr. Braydon, I pray for him every night and every morning."

"As do we, lass, as do we." Jimmy reached over and patted her hand.

With her heart thudding in her chest, Florence spread the crumpled paper out and strained to read the written words in the fading light of day.

Dear Mum, Dad, Evie and Charlie
Sorry, I had planned on getting this letter away before we departed the Australian shore but now it will go within the mailbag for sending when our vessel arrives in a port somewhere.

There is little I am allowed to say within our letters for security reasons but I find the shore to our left has familiar details. And the saltwater we bathe in is quite warm.

My offsider, Max, has been as sick as a dog since we left the harbour. I gave him a ginger bulb to chew on – one of those you gave me, Mum, and it has done wonders for him. So far, I have not been bothered by the ailment, but we have been warned we have not seen a rough sea yet.

Hope you are all well.

Kind regards to those at the big house.

Your son, James

Slowly Florence folded the note and passed it back to Jimmy Braydon.

"Now, when do you have to begin work?" He asked as he tucked it back into his pocket.

"First thing in the morning. It may take me a day or two to get used to waking early. The shifts are twelve hours a day with one day off a week. I think I might collect my bike so I can ride home on my day off."

"It will be no bother to collect you and deliver you back, Miss Florence. It is a wonderful thing you be doin'."

The home matron escorted Florence to the room she was to share with another nurse.

"You will need to be quiet. Nurse Browning will be sleeping. She worked the twelve-hour night shift last night and will do the same tonight."

"Of course."

Once Florence thanked the home matron for showing her the way and explaining where the meals would be available, she opened the door softly and crept inside. Soft snores rose from the sleeper on the bed to the left of the window. Florence set her case gently on the floor. She stood at the window near her bed and stared out into the dusk seeing in her mind's eye the sight of James Braydon as he climbed onto the train.

Tears trickled down her cheeks. *God keep him safe.* She whispered her oft-repeated prayer.

Somewhere in the distance, she heard a gong announcing dinner according to what the home matron had told her. She went to move towards the door when the voice of her roommate halted her.

"Hello, my name is Gabe Browning but my friends call me Brownie. Was that the dinner bell I heard?" She mumbled.

"Yes, I think so," Florence agreed with a nervous smile.

"If you wait a minute, I'll meet you outside in the hall and show you the way down. I will need to go on duty right after I eat." Brownie's voice regained some strength as she took up her bath towel and made her way to the washroom.

The first twelve months of Florence's training passed in a nightmare of exhaustion, an unending rattle of shocks to the nervous system and stimulation of the brain to absorb the matron's lectures. Episodes of laughter and tears shared with fellow students were treasured along with the free tickets provided by the movie cinema downtown. Flo found the one day a week at home with her mother, Aunt Bridie and the Braydon family contributed to the maintenance of her sanity.

On her first day, Florence learnt a senior member of the staff had resigned to join the army nurses at the battlefront. A rush of fear and excitement flowed through her veins. Did she have the stamina and courage to do such a thing? She bit her lip when the thought of James in danger followed behind her doubt.

Rosa provided Florence with a special cream that made some inroads on the dry and rough skin of her hands after washing dishes, floors, patients, furniture, bed pans and soiled linen. Florence found it reduced much excoriation and discomfort. Her friends heard via the gossip grapevine, the usual means of communication amongst nurses, that next year they were to have their junior nurse rotation in the operating theatre, where one added washing bloody sponges, bloody instruments, surgeon gloves and bloodied gowns to the soap and water usage, and the list of ways to convert the skin of their hands into dry raw meat. If the older students' advice was anything to go by, there was no fear of seeing any gaping surgical wounds, as the junior nurse never entered the sterile operating room. They were there to receive and resolve its excretions only.

At night, when the lights were extinguished and she lay listening to Brownie's relaxed breathing, Florence's thoughts drifted to her imagination of where James might be and what he might be doing. Her fingers caressed the increasing number of his letters stored inside her pillowcase. With a final prayer for his safekeeping, fatigue carried her away to the land of dreams.

Extracts From Odette's Journal 1915:

Young James Braydon has enlisted in the Australian Navy. Jimmy and Rosa are both very proud, but every day is a torment when the mail is delivered.

Florence began nursing training at the Townsville Hospital this year. I believe she wants to take a more active role in caring for the sick and wounded. I worry for her though. It is a demanding chore.

Christmas 1915 was filled with laughter and tears. Bridie organized our choir group to present a musical concert for the patients, staff and their families at the hospital on the afternoon of Christmas Eve. After an hour of performing in the dining room at the nurses' quarters, we walked down the stairs to the main building to sing our selection on the verandahs outside the wards for the enjoyment of the immobile patients.

On Christmas morning, the neighbour and Jimmy visited Mr Rankin's farmer-friend to collect three hampers of food which they delivered to the hospital for staff and patients on our behalf.

War News Headlines 1915:

Unbelievable numbers of men from both sides are being wounded and killed. As far as I understand it, there seems to be no end to a conflict that seems to achieve so little. War is a terrible thing. Will we ever see peace again? Bridie believes young James Braydon is on a cruiser protecting the northern straits.

1916

Lavender dresses covered with fresh white starched aprons filled the small waiting area near the hospital office. All the uncomfortable starched white cuffs and collars were buttoned up correctly and not left agape as happened sometimes when the matron was unlikely to be prowling an area. Nurses of all levels remained in silence without any thought for a relaxed chat. They all stood – it was a cardinal sin for a nurse to be seen sitting when wearing the uniform in public. Through the slats on the verandah, the clear skies shone down on a cool morning in late July. The birds in the tree near the entrance path chattered in the branches, oblivious to the seriousness of the day for those inside. Sighs and nervous glances filled the space, while nurses waited for the results of the annual examinations to be posted on the bulletin board.

The light breakfast consumed by Florence an hour earlier, stirred around like a rough sea in her stomach. She was nearing the end of her first year, and her examination results would indicate whether she was to progress to a second-year nurse or choke on her pride. Never had her school examinations generated such a dither.

After eleven months of conditioning, the junior nurses stepped back to allow those more senior to absorb the contents of the notice when tacked to the board.

"I don't think I can bear to look," Brownie whispered to Florence.

Florence struggled to swallow with a mouth as dry as the Simpson Desert. She tried to boost her friend's confidence despite her own misgivings.

"Brownie, if you fail there will be little hope for the rest of us." Florence reached over and held her friend's hand.

Squeals erupted from close to the notice board. One senior nurse was seen to walk away with her head bowed, tears running down her cheeks.

Neither Brownie nor Florence had reached the notice board, when a second-year who they both enjoyed working with, passed them with a satisfied grin on her face.

"I passed; I cannot believe it, but I passed." She nodded cheerfully at the two junior nurses. "Oh, and so did you pair. Your names are up there too."

Florence bit down on her lips. Her eyes threatened to leak tears of joy. She turned and hugged her friend who jumped up and down with glee.

"We are here for another year." A grin lit up her face.

Florence's joy for the day did not end there. The lady from the office approached her from behind and tapped her on the shoulder.

"Nurse Treloar, I think this letter belongs to you. With the envelope crumpled, it was hard to decipher your name on the front."

At first glance, Florence recognized the writing immediately.

"Thank you." This time the tears of joy would not be deterred. She disappeared to her favourite hiding spot behind the array of equipment in the store room. Trembling hands tore the paper open.

Dear Flo

We are still patrolling in warm waters. It is not unlike mustering cattle, but on water. Whereas with mustering one has miles and miles of bare landscape around you in which to find the blighters trying to hide away, we patrol miles and miles of empty sea searching for a different kind of blighter to bring into line.

Hopefully, when we return to a shore, somewhere, there will be mail waiting for me. I am interested to know how the nursing training is going.

I always carry your pendant in my top pocket.

Wishing you all the best

Kindest regards to you and the family from James

Once again, a flicker of hurt burnt inside Florence at the words, 'Kindest regards.' She desired much more. Her fingers traced James's message referring to her pendant. She felt the pain soften.

If Florence found her pride a problem with her raised status as a second-year nurse, it was short-lived. She discovered the washing soap still wore down the skin on her hands, but the theory work became more interesting with lessons on treatments for various ailments and the simple medicines required.

Her friend Brownie seldom ran short of witty sayings to lift the spirits on a trying day.

"I swear if I had a ha'penny for every poultice I applied today, I'd be on my way to becoming a millionaire," Brownie said on more than one occasion, as she shut the door to their room and threw herself onto her bed while massaging the heat-dried skin on her hands.

"Try this cream," Florence offered some of Rosa's hand cream mixture.

Brownie dipped her finger into the jar and spread a thin smear over her hands.

"This is heaven, Flo, where did you get it?"

"A friend makes it up for me. I will ask her to make some for you too."

"You have an interesting array of friends, don't you?"

"Friends of the family, Brownie."

After an extended shift, running to everyone's commands in the operating theatre, Florence dragged her feet up the steps with only the thought of her bed on her mind. At the nurses' quarters, when the Home Matron handed her an envelope with James's familiar handwriting on the front, her exhaustion fell away like leaves from the trees in the autumn months. Her smile lifted. Her feet tripped lightly up the stairs.

Dear Flo

We have been out of contact for some months lately and I have only just read your three letters written from your room at the hospital.

I am pleased to hear you are enjoying your work despite the attending exhaustion. Thank goodness you get to go home on your day off. Your mother would be devastated if she did not have you home at least one day a week – I think Miss Mayford might be a tad upset also.

I know from my Mum's letters that my dad gets such a thrill from taking the buggy up there to collect you and deliver you back the next day. They are very proud of you too. Charlie and Evie have a blazing row each time to see which one gets to travel with you.

I have been transferred to a new ship. It is the sister ship of the one I was on. As before, we are out mustering on the sea still in warm waters.
Think of me often as I think of you.
Fondest regards, James.

Florence stole several moments alone to hold her letter close. Tears trembled on her eyelashes at the thought of her James so far away.

Extracts From Odette's Journal 1916:
Florence continues with her nursing. She looks so tired sometimes. I do worry, but she will not give in. She has passed her examinations. I am sure Peter would be so proud of her. With her grey eyes and some of her facial expressions, she brings her father right into the room with me.

Christmas 1916 at the hospital was a repetition of 1915. According to what Florence has told me, many of the patient faces have changed. Most were healed and discharged, but others never made it through their illness. These thoughts place a dampener on the nurses' spirits until they remember they must stay upbeat for the morale of other patients and the younger staff. The nurses have added and lost some of their numbers also. Another of their senior staff transferred to join the army. After the choir finished their renditions, the staff and patients enjoyed lunch from the hampers of food Bridie had Jimmy deliver to the kitchen.

War News Headlines 1916:
The Battle of Gallipoli, where the Allied troops hoped to defeat the Ottoman Empire, developed into a prolonged misery of unproductive trench warfare. The Allies only reclaimed some honour

by keeping enemy troops unavailable for other battles, and in their brilliant retreat during December 1915 and into January 1916.

The Battle of Verdun in which the French Army repelled the German offensive has, after ten months, produced nearly a million men killed or wounded. The world holds its breath. Never has it seen such destruction as this war with its modern weapons of artillery, tanks and even airplanes.

During the encounter between the British and German battleships in the first half of the year, Britain lost two ships but sent the Germans running.

The Battle of the Somme in the latter half of the year became what is described as a deadlocked battle of attrition.

Reports arrived telling of the successful Russian offensive led by Aleksei Brusilov.

When will this end?

1917

Of Florence and Brownie, it was the latter who made her way into her second term of Operating Theatre work first. At the time, Florence worked in the surgical ward. They spoke briefly at those times when Brownie delivered a patient to the ward after an operation. There were nights when Brownie's bed remained unslept in, while she covered an emergency in the operating room. It was not unusual for her to work around the clock. When Florence returned to her room each day, she knew by the depth of her roommate's snores, the level of Brownie's exhaustion.

During Florence's theatre stint, she learnt what it was to stumble down the three flights of stairs from the nurses' quarters to the hospital theatre in the dead of night, while the world around her slept.

On frequent occasions, she struggled to shrug off the thick sludge of weariness suffocating her brain and to recover her senses.

Rosa and Florence stood in front of the stove at the big house. Rosa stirred a savoury meat dish to be added to the pastry she had pounded into submission on the large wooden board. Florence stirred the creamy white mixture in another pot, which she had prepared herself, under Rosa's guidance.

"There will be enough for two big jars there, Miss Florence, one for you and one for your friend Miss Browning. Hopefully, that will keep both your hands looking soft again."

"Thanks, Mrs. Braydon. This cream is so soothing." Florence looked over to where Rosa now emptied the meat into the base of the pie pastry and dropped the pastry lid on top. "Have you heard anything from James lately, Mrs. Braydon?"

"Yes, my dear, I have the last letter in my pocket here to show you. He always sends his regard to the big house so I always give his letters to Miss Bridie and Mrs Odette to read. I think they like that very much." With her meat pie constructed, Rosa dug her hand into her pocket. She dragged out the crushed envelope and handed it to her pupil at the stove.

Florence removed her cream from the heat. She opened the letter addressed to Mr. and Mrs. Braydon spreading it out smoothly on the table top.

Dear Mum, Dad, Evie and Charlie
Gossip on board the ship is that our sojourn in this area is almost over and we will be moving to warm waters on the other side of the planet soon – at least before Christmas 1917. But then if I had a penny for every snippet of gossip that floats around this ship, I'd be living on Toff's Hill. I'll believe it when we cross the equator.

You did not say if you received the last two letters I wrote, but then it will be no surprise if they are still finding their way home.

We had races to climb the mast last week. Awful glad the weather was calm. I feel sympathy for those sailors who had to do so regularly in the good old sailing days. We get to run a mile a day round and round in circles over the ship. The powers-that-be say we don't need an exercise room because if we do need more exercise, they will increase the number of drills we have carrying the ammo up and down to and from the decks.

Hoping to be in dock in the next few weeks to catch up on more mail. Hope everyone is well.

Kind regards to you all and those in the big house.

"James seems to be out of the worst of the fighting, Mrs. Braydon. You must feel some comfort in that."

"Yes, Miss Florence, not a day goes by that I don't thank God for the small mercy."

On their return from a pleasant evening walk along that waterfront not commandeered by the army and their numerous defence barriers, Bridie and Odette entered the house through the back doorway.

"I must go and lie down," Odette announced as she climbed the staircase.

Bridie picked up the mail left on the table by Rosa earlier. Her smile widened and her eyes twinkled as she opened the envelope with Stewart's familiar handwriting. A sadness sobered her thoughts when she read of his anxiety at the posting of his eldest son to the European theatre of war. Her sadness deepened when she read of how he did not see his way clear to return to the north in the immediate future. A chill ran over her skin filling her heart with dread. She admonished herself. *What, are you now believing in ghosts, werewolves and fortune tellers, woman?* For weeks to come the feeling of dread frequently caught her unawares.

≈

After a particularly trying day in the ward, Florence's legs felt like they were not going to drag her up the three flights of stairs to the nurses' quarters. When she stepped through the front doorway and found a letter for her on the table near the home matron's office, her spirits soared. Her legs took the stairs to her room three at a time.

"I hope I cannot hear the plod of feet running up the stairs," the voice of the Home Matron halted Florence's hasty progress.

My Dear Flo

I enjoyed reading the four letters I received from you the other day. We are now approaching the regular overseas holiday area of the lords and ladies of England. I cannot say any more about our position. The temperature is quite pleasant given summer is turning into autumn over here.

Your mention of the work you do in the operating theatre leaves me amazed. Who would have thought you were able to cope with such sights? I thought I knew you well – we were best friends as you reminded me on many occasions but you can still surprise me.

Hope this finds you well and safe

Thinking of you always James.

Florence's fingers traced the last line. A soft smile sparkled in her eyes.

Extracts From Odette's Journal 1917:

Christmas 1917 Florence and I felt the absence of Bridie very much. For several weeks, Bridie has been feeling poorly. The doctor diagnosed hypertension and ordered her to rest. A morning of traipsing around the hospital singing carols was out of the question.

Matron kindly allowed Florence the time out to accompany me and the choir in providing entertainment for the patients and staff.

Once again, on my instruction this time, Jimmy collected the three hampers from the local farmer and delivered them to the hospital for the Christmas lunches.

War News Headlines 1917:

Every day, during the horrors of the Battle at Passchendaele in the Third Ypres Campaign, a constant flow of wounded Allied troops was transported across the waters to the makeshift hospitals on Britain's mainland. Many either did not survive or were declared unfit – to await transport back to their homes. Others were patched up and returned to the dreaded front lines, where the trenches often filled with rain and mud to add to the torture of our men.

1918

After a subdued introduction to the New Year, Odette watched Bridie's health deteriorate markedly. Ethel-May now lived in the little room near the staircase downstairs at the big house. Her workload increased to take in much of the care of Bridie. With the matron's permission, Florence returned home as often as her nursing shifts permitted.

The sun was barely over the horizon on her day off when Florence's bicycle clattered against the wall of the shed. Her first port of call was to Aunt Bridie's bedroom. She found her great-aunt had slipped away in the night. She recognized the signs and was convinced her aunt had suffered a massive Cerebrovascular Accident. She felt the tsunami wave of sorrow inundate her heart and begin to spread throughout her body. Her legs trembled. She bit down on the scream of denial that fought its way up through her throat. Only a groan of despair emerged into the warm morning air of January as her training took over without invitation.

"Oh, Aunt Bridie, what am I going to do without you? What are any of us going to do without you?" Her knees gave away. She collapsed onto the chair by the bed. Florence took one cold hand into her own. She could not have told anyone what time had passed until she was drawn out of her grief by the voice at her side.

"Miss Florence, is Miss Bridie …," Ethel-May's voice refused to produce the word needed. "I have a cup of tea for her." Words which may have sounded silly to some, but Florence recognized the denial in Ethel-May's words.

Tears welled in Florence's eyes as she answered.

"Yes, Ethel-May, Aunt Bridie is dead. I am sorry. Will you go down and let Rosa and Jimmy know? I will tidy up here and tell my mother shortly." As Ethel-May ran from the room, Florence's calm deserted her too. She sobbed until there seemed not a tear left to fall. While she pulled herself together, she tidied the unresponsive body and, with a final brush to her aunt's hair and a gentle kiss to her forehead, Florence pulled up the covers to beneath Bridie's chin. The carpet runner muffled her slow footsteps around to her mother's room. Odette, already dressed for the morning, opened the door instantly.

"Oh, Florence, you startled me. You are home early today."

Florence wrapped her arms around her mother and held her tight.

"Mother, I have been here for a little while. I am sorry, but Aunt Bridie has passed away in the night."

Odette pulled herself back out of Florence's arms. Her head swung side to side refusing to believe her daughter's words.

"How are you so sure? What has killed her?"

"It seems to me she has had a severe stroke, Mother."

"This cannot be true. Bridie is like a mother to me. She is the only mother I have known. I cannot lose her too. You must be mistaken." The horror in the depths of Odette's violet eyes revealed that she knew Florence was not mistaken.

"I will go down shortly and ask Jimmy to call the doctor." Florence reached out to take her mother's hand. "Come, I will go with you to say goodbye."

In a whirl of numbness and disbelief, the weeks passed. Florence was grateful to have her work which kept her mind otherwise occupied. Each time she was able to leave her responsibilities at the hospital and return home, it broke her heart to see her mother's sorrow.

A letter from James held her together.

My dearest Flo

I cannot believe it is 1918 and we are still locked in battle with our enemy after nearly four years. How much punishment can the men take? We are reasonably safe where we are now with only the occasional skirmish, but it makes my blood run cold to hear of what is happening to our countrymen in Europe.

The captain has had all the crew taking turns learning to swim in the sea with a lifeboat crew to guard and encourage us. Most of the Aussies are proving to be veritable fish, but there is a contingent of Englishmen with us who swim like stones – straight to the bottom.

It was wonderful news to hear both Evie and Charlie have taken up the offer from Miss Mayford and Mrs. Treloar to cover their secondary school fees. Who knows just where their studies might take them?

There's the whistle to call us to work.

Flo, you cannot believe just how much the thought of you keeps me sane.

Missing you terribly and hoping to see you soon, James.

Florence's finger traced the last words repeatedly. "Oh, James, please come home safe," she whispered.

It was left to Odette to answer the letter addressed to Bridie, which arrived from Stewart Cruickshank. As she sealed the notice of Bridie's death inside the letter of condolence, Odette allowed the acceptance of the loss of her aunt to overwhelm the resistance within her.

When in the latter months of 1918 the newspapers reported the exciting news of the anticipation of war's end to the home front, neither Florence nor the Braydon family received any news of the damage to the cruisers The Huon and The Yarra while working in the Mediterranean Sea. The family waited in excited expectation for the news of James's impending arrival home.

It was several weeks after peace had been declared when Jimmy received the dreaded black-banded envelope.

"I am truly sorry, Mr. Braydon," the mailman offered.

Jimmy felt his legs give away. He leant back on the mailbox. *Is this some perverse joke? The war is over. My son is somewhere on his way home.* He heard Rosa's call and heard her running feet.

"Jimmy, Jimmy, what's happened? What's wrong?" Her arms wrapped around her husband's shoulders. Tears streamed down her cheeks before the letter had been read. She had seen the black band on the envelope. Jimmy pulled himself upright.

"Now don't get in a pother, Rosa. This must be a mistake. The war is over. This is some dastardly error on someone's part."

As she clung to Jimmy, Rosa hushed into a total silence for several minutes and then in a very quiet voice, she responded.

"Jimmy, you know I sometimes have the visions like my grandmother. I am sure this is not some mistake. Our James is gone." She led Jimmy by the hand into their cottage.

As they sat at the kitchen table, Jimmy tore the envelope open.

Dear Mr. and Mrs. Braydon
It is with great regret I must inform you that your son Able Seaman James Braydon died at 7 am on the 11th of November 1918 after having caught the disease The Spanish Influenza while we were at port for repairs at Genoa.
James Braydon has performed his duties with diligence during his service in the Royal Australian Navy. He is sadly missed.

Neither Jimmy nor Rosa could read any further. They struggled to understand what they had done to deserve to have their son die like this on the very morning that peace was declared. It was beyond believable.

Extracts From Odette's Journal 1918:
The loss of Bridie earlier this year followed by the loss of James Braydon to Spanish Flu, while waiting to be sent home after the war eventually came to an end, has left a huge gap in all our lives. With Florence working all the hours that God gives at the hospital, where many wounded returned soldiers begin to fill the wards, it is Rosa and I who have become confidantes in our sorrow.

Christmas 1918. It is hard to think of Christmas without Bridie, but we must give thanks for the end of the terrible war that took so many. The choir, devoid of us three Mayford women, delivered the carols at the hospital where I believe, the feelings swayed from great excitement at the recent announcement of the end of the war and great sorrow at the loss of so many countrymen.

Three hampers were delivered to the hospital on behalf of myself and Florence.

The Braydon family strived to maintain some spirit for the benefit of the twins. Rosa and Jimmy struggle with their loss.

Florence stayed with me during Christmas Day but left on her bicycle for the night duty at the hospital at 5 pm.

Weariness fills my soul after the innumerable arguments Florence and I engage in about the continuance of her nursing training. I believe her place is at home now, with Bridie gone. Florence's response – her nursing diverts her sorrows from herself to other people's problems. Without it, she would not cope. I worry at the signs of her exhaustion.

War News Headlines 1918:

The allies took a severe hiding in the Somme River Basin, but they regrouped and the enemy was eventually halted. In the spring advances made by the enemy, the allies struggled. The arrival of the US Army helped save the day. At Marne River, the enemy was repelled. The allies' hope lifted. In the following month at Amiens, the allied troops again offered a significant blow to the enemy morale. In the Battle of Meuse-Argonne in France, the fresh American troops alongside the French delivered a massive blow to the enemy. The Commonwealth troops struck a decisive victory in Cambrai in Northern France.

The Ottoman Empire sought a peace settlement on the 30th October 1918 having been overcome by the Egyptian Expeditionary Forces under Lieutenant-General Sir Edmund Allenby.

It was during the Battle of Mons, the troops learnt that Germany had agreed to an armistice at 11 am on the 11th day of November 1918. When the word filtered through to the battle fronts, the news was received in a disbelieving silence, before gradually the exhausted minds accepted this was real.

CHAPTER SIXTEEN

Things Come in Threes

1919 - 1920

With a heavy heart and aching feet, Florence concentrated on her work and her studies to push the deep ache of James's loss from her mind. She felt the last months approaching her final examinations seemed to fly past like the silent charge of an eagle upon its prey. After finishing her twelve-hour shifts, she tried to focus her bloodshot eyes on her nursing books, but sleep quickly washed over her before a page was turned. When at home on her day off, guilt ate away at her, as she watched her mother make little effort to overcome her sorrow at the loss of Bridie. Odette seemed to be fading away in front of Florence's eyes. It seemed seldom Odette laughed these days. Never had she touched the piano in Florence's presence during that time.

Florence spoke to Rosa and Jimmy who confirmed what she witnessed herself.

"Do you think she is sickening for something?" Florence asked Rosa.

"Miss Florence, you are the nurse, dear, but I think it is possible. She only eats enough to feed a sparrow."

"Mrs. Odette has always been as strong as an ox, even though you would never think it to look at her. She just needs a bit of time to get over the loss of Miss Bridie," Jimmy assured Florence.

"How often does she go to the choir meetings?"

Jimmy threw Rosa a furtive look before answering. "I must be tellin' you the truth, Miss Florence. Your mother has been to neither the choir nor any of her fund-raisin' activities for a long time. The only thing she goes out for is to attend church on a Sunday. The minister turns up here once a week to talk with her."

During the last weeks as a trainee, Florence's inner self swung like a pendulum. If she passed her examinations, she would be a trained nurse. The pendulum swung back – what if she read the examination questions wrongly? She found herself praying earnestly. Another sway of the pendulum tugged the smile at the corner of her lips. The questions were to her liking. The pendulum oscillation moved again to dwell on her concerns for her mother. This worry became a well of despair. *If only Mother would allow me to call the doctor,* Florence often repeated softly to herself.

At her end-of-training interview, Florence walked out of the Matron's office struggling to breathe. She carried in her hands the veil to identify her as a trained nurse, in her head she carried the words of praise for her efforts, and assurance that she had a position at the hospital if she wished.

"Sister Treloar, I have to admit that when you first commenced your training, I held a little apprehension at how a privileged woman like yourself might cope under these difficult conditions." The matron smiled. Florence was to remember that smile – maybe the first time she had seen the matron smile. "I had been reading the works of Florence Nightingale at the time. She was a woman with a privileged and educated background who suffered conditions a hundred times worse than anyone here would ever do. She changed the conditions around herself to improve the survival of so many soldiers who were dying of diseases such as typhus, typhoid, dysentery, and the like before they died of their wounds." The matron's smile flashed again.

"Congratulations." The Matron went on to discuss Florence's future employment at the Townsville Hospital.

At that time, there was little reason why she would refuse the offer.

Several months later, the doctor arrived having been summoned by Odette via a note delivered by Jimmy. Florence arrived home on her day off to meet the man just about to leave.

"Good morning, Doctor, is everything alright here?" Florence stepped back to leave room for the elderly gentleman to exit with his bag in his hand.

"Good morning to you too, Nurse ... er no ... Sister Treloar now, isn't it? Your mother asked me to call. If you have time now, I really would like to talk to you."

"Of course, please come back in. May I get you a cup of tea?"

Florence was pleased to see Rosa in the kitchen when she popped her head through the door.

"Rosa, is there a chance of a cup of tea for the Doctor?"

"Just coming up, Miss Florence."

The nurse and the doctor sat at the large dining room table drinking tea and eating fresh scones with jam. Florence noticed the weariness in the faded blue eyes. Exhaustion lines lay deep in the elderly medic's face.

"So, what are the plans now for your future, Sister? Will you continue at the Townsville Hospital or have you other ideas?"

"I will stay at the hospital here, I think. The men are coming back from the front in droves and many will need nursing care for some time, as you will have seen, no doubt, yourself."

"Yes, the side effects of a war go on for generations to come, I think."

"Please, doctor, tell me, do you think my mother's malaise and lack of appetite is a by-product of the loss of Aunt Bridie, or is there something more serious we are looking at here?"

"Sister, or may I call you Miss Florence, seeing as we are not at the hospital now?"

"Florence is quite alright, Doctor."

"Miss Florence, I must be honest with you, I think your mother's condition is something more serious than simple malaise and depression. I have taken several blood samples that I will look at in the office. I fear she may have an abdominal growth which is quite advanced."

"Oh, dear, this is my fault. I have given all my time to the hospital and not looked after my mother properly."

"That is enough of that. You could have been here every minute of every day and, unless your mother wanted to reveal her suspicions, you would not have known any earlier. From what I gather she has gone to great lengths not to reveal her condition. I think this has been bothering her since before her aunt died."

"Are you saying there is nothing we can do?"

"I am saying that, yes."

Florence felt the tears trembling on her eyelids. She struggled to hide her feelings.

"I will need to talk to Matron. I shall not work at the hospital for the time being. We will nurse my mother here in our home." Florence battled with each word to sound it out.

"I shall keep in touch," the doctor patted Florence's hand.

After she waved goodbye to the kindly man, Florence turned to go inside. She paused to pull on her nurse facade and bury her own feelings deep inside. As she climbed the steps on her way to her mother's bedroom, her mind planned the care of her mother but her heart wept hidden tears.

Odette sat out of bed on a comfortable chair near the open doorway from where she watched the unending wavelets of the sea rolling onto the shore.

"Hello, my dear, the doctor took a while to leave. Can I presume he had a chat with you?"

"Yes, Mother, he did."

A silence lay between them for some time. "How many people have died in the world since those waves first started washing onto this shore, do you think?" Odette eventually spoke.

Florence swallowed her sorrow. "Quite a lot, I should imagine."

"Darling, I am sorry this has happened right now. You have had to cope with the loss of Aunt Bridie and then your best friend overseas, and if the doctor is correct, I shall not be too far behind."

"Mother, I shall be here to care for you every day. You may go on for quite some time. Please do not think of leaving just yet."

Florence chose to tell Rosa and Jimmy the news of Odette's failing health before Evelyn returned home from work at her new position at the local solicitor's office. Charles was away at the university in Brisbane studying medicine and would not be back until later in the year.

Florence was not surprised to see Jimmy and Rosa's sorrow when told of Odette's prognosis. They sat at the kitchen table inside the big house. Rosa rose from her seat and pulled the kettle over the heat on the stove to make a fresh pot of tea – her panacea for all situations.

"I will not be going back to the hospital while Mother is unwell. I wish to nurse her myself. Rosa, will you ask Ethel-May if she is willing to stay here at the big house indefinitely?"

Rosa nodded her head in affirmation, as she rinsed the teapot out with the hot water and added the tea leaves, before filling it from the bubbling kettle.

"Do you think that little room near the staircase is adequate for Ethel-May?" Florence asked another question.

Rosa moved across to the china cupboard and set out the cups and saucers. She placed a tin of biscuits on the table beside them.

"I think you will find Ethel-May is very happy in her little room, Miss Florence. It is far more than she ever had at her home."

Florence nibbled a biscuit in politeness to Rosa for having baked them. Her gaze fell to her cup rather than her audience.

"If," she shook her head and went on, "when mother passes on, I want you both to know that the family offer to pay for Charles's education will continue." Florence sucked in her breath and taking the handkerchief from her sleeve, she wiped the tears falling from her eyes.

Jimmy nodded his head. A tear splashed his cheek. "Thank you, Miss Florence, it is very much appreciated. The lad has always done well at his lessons."

As Florence walked back up the stairs, she gulped at her sorrow. It seemed as if her world had collapsed around her. *What have I done to deserve this?* But her selfish thoughts were quickly discarded when she remembered the many families, who had lost multiple loved ones in the recent war.

Thinking of the war, she pondered in disbelief when she realized it was over twelve months since James had died, and nearly two years since her Aunt Bridie had passed on. Now, in a matter of weeks, the New Year of 1920 would take away her mother.

Pausing at Odette's door, Florence stood tall and wiped away her tears. Her cheeks ached as she placed a smile firmly in place.

Florence often wondered at her mother's last words, before she succumbed to her illness. Odette's dull violet eyes opened wide, she drew in a noisy breath and opened her mouth to speak. Her words shuffled out. Florence bent her head – straining to hear.

"Peter, why did you not listen? I told you to take Sanders. Oh, Peter, Peter, I loved you so much. Every day has been a struggle without you in it."

Odette's voice faded away into nothing. She did not speak again before her death.

PART FOUR

FLORENCE TRELOAR

CHAPTER SEVENTEEN

The Visitor

1921

The whisper of their shoes and the hush of the soft voices came to an end, as Florence Treloar finished doing the second ward round of the night with the senior night nurse on the Woman's Ward. Her sharp ears caught the "Boinggg!" of the Emergency Bell. Slim strong legs whisked her along the verandah and across to the Casualty Room. The familiar outline of the police uniform worn by Officer Rawlins brought a smile to her face.

"We have got to stop meeting like this, Officer. Twice in one night is making a meal of things, don't you think?"

"Sorry, Sister Treloar, it is Mr. Manning again."

"Oh, dear, what has the poor man done to himself this time?"

"The usual – screaming curses down upon the Recruitment Office for taking his two boys away and not bringing them home. Only thing is, this time he began bashing his head and face against the brick wall. He's in a bit of a mess."

Florence made her way to where a regular patient of the emergency room sat on a wooden form beside a second policeman. Blood trickled from Mr. Manning's face and scalp wounds onto an already muddy and bloody shirt.

"Good night, Mr. Manning, you have got yourself in a right fix this time, haven't you?" Florence assisted the man to lift his head. She examined the damage revealed by the feeble light on the wall.

407

"You will need a few stitches in the laceration there on your cheek." She used a hand under his elbow to guide him into the dressing room. With the help of the two policemen, they soon had Mr. Manning lying flat on a rubber protector covering the surgical table. Florence drew a white cotton sheet up to his chest.

"Will you two men keep an eye on Mr. Manning for me, while I get everything I'll be needing."

"Certainly, Miss," answered the younger man whose blushing face failed to be hidden in the poor lighting.

The rattling wheels of the white-painted trolley proceeded her back into the room. A clean cloth covered a surgical tray on the top shelf and a bowl of soapy water with a washcloth sat upon the lower shelf. She took a kidney tray holding a medicine glass containing a liberal dose of sedation. Florence spoke to her patient, before touching the damaged skin.

"Mr. Manning, are you going to drink this medicine for me?"

Without further ado, the man raised himself on one elbow and reached out for the small glass. He tossed the fluid down his gullet. Florence resettled Mr. Manning and asked Officer Rawlins to hold a lantern to improve the lighting. She began to bathe the wounds. A sigh slipped out into the room, after she had cleared away the dirt and blood clots.

"I'm going to have to put in a couple of internal stitches to hold this together before I add the skin sutures, I'm afraid, Mr. Manning."

Florence removed the cover from the suture tray, washed her hands, and addressed her skills to the task. When the younger policeman wobbled over to a stool against the wall, Florence and Officer Rawlins exchanged amused glances.

A Tincture of Benz Co dressing was applied to the suture line on the scalp. Iodine soon decorated broken skin on the remainder of Mr. Manning's head and face.

"Now please, Mr. Manning, I want you to go straight to bed when the policemen take you home. Will you do that for me?"

"For you, Sister, I'll do anything." The patient's gravelly voice replied.

Officer Rawlins whispered aside to Florence, as he walked towards the door.

"What man wouldn't?"

Florence smiled.

By the time Florence had cleaned up the dressing room, boiled the instruments and washed the blood from the sheets, it was time to make a final round of the hospital before sitting down to complete her night reports, ready for handover to the day sister when she arrived at 6 o'clock.

A slight breeze carried a hint of salt from the nearby sea. The sun felt warm upon her face. Florence crunched up her eyes and on aching legs dragged herself outside, where she offered up thanks to the heavens for sending Jimmy Braydon with the horse and spring cart to collect her from work. The distance to her home may be less than two miles, but it seemed like an unending trek at the end of a long night shift.

"Who is that at our front door, Mr. Braydon?" Florence asked when her eyes caught sight of the tall man standing unmoving, with one hand resting on a walking stick and the other hand raised as if ready to knock.

"Can't say I recognize him, Miss Florence. Do you want me to see what he wants?"

"No, you've got enough on your plate today, thanks Mr. Braydon. You unhitch the horse and get your breakfast. I'll speak to this chappy if you drop me off here at the front gate."

The visitor turned at the clatter of the horse's feet. He stood with his back to the door and stared at Florence as she descended from the spring cart. The look of amazement or was it surprise which filled the man's face, intrigued Florence. She endeavoured not to stare back. Try as she might, she could not recall having ever known the gentleman before.

"May I help you, sir?" She took in the dark beret pulled down to partially cover the knotted scar on the side of his face and head where part of an earlobe appeared to be missing. The stranger lifted the beret from his head and balled it in his hands. Florence noticed long strands of grey hair had been dragged from the other side of his head and over the scar. The hair had been secured within a knotted leather strip at the back of his head.

"You are the spitting image of her … of my Detta," The warm voice spoke quietly.

Florence stood stock still.

The man went on, "I was thinking I was on a wild goose chase, but I can see I'm not. You are Detta Mayford's ... er ... Treloar's daughter, I'll bet my life on it."

Florence gasped. Her breath snagged in her throat. She gave a sharp cough. Her arms wrapped around her body as if warding off a chill breeze. This time she did not bother to disguise her prolonged stare at her visitor.

"I'm sorry, you have the advantage over me, sir. Should I know you?"

"Please, I am not here to frighten you. My name is Peter Treloar. You may like to read this letter from Mr. Livingstone Junior, your solicitor here in Townsville. It will go some way to easing your concerns." Peter Treloar handed over a thick brown envelope to the young lady in front of him.

As Florence stared at the familiar writing on the front of the brown envelope, Mr. Treloar spoke again.

"Mr. Livingstone did not reveal anything about you until he had checked out my references. He did employ me as a handyman and housed me in a room in his shed while I waited for Mr. Birmingham's communication to arrive from England. Mr. Birmingham was Bridie's solicitor in Portsmouth." Peter Treloar did not miss the softening of Florence's expression as her fine fingers caressed the writing on the envelope. In his work as a veterinarian over the years, his patients, the animals, could not tell him their problems which meant Peter became an attentive observer. "I'll just wait out here in the garden while you take the time to read that, shall I?"

Florence lifted her eyes sharply. "Sorry, no, Mr. Treloar, I don't think you need to wait out here. Please, join me on the verandah where you can sit down. Have you eaten this morning? I'll ask Ethel-May to bring us our breakfast and a cup of tea."

After they both ate a bowl of porridge, Florence read the epistle and the many documents attached. She drank her tea. She looked up to pour them both a second cup while she read some, and scanned others, of the papers again. Tears began to fall over her smooth pale cheeks.

"Please, child, I'm sorry. I did not want to make you sad," Peter stuttered.

Her watery smile reassured him. "These are not tears of sadness, Mr. Treloar, well maybe a little when I think of all I have missed out on. I am sad that my mother passed on without ever learning all that happened to you. I am sad that you both missed out on the happiness you deserved. They are also tears of joy. Joy to finally learn about my father." A sharp breath drowned in tears almost choked her. She coughed and sipped at her now cold tea. She reached over and lay her hand over Peter's hand noticing as she did so, the scars patterned there and up his arm to disappear under his rolled-up sleeve. "I will fetch us another pot of tea and I want you to tell me your story."

"Perhaps that should wait until tomorrow, lass. I understand you have been working the night shift at the hospital."

"Peter, may I call you Peter, or could I call you, Father – my eyes will not close until I hear it all. I am not on duty tonight. I only do relief duties nowadays, so I have plenty of time to catch up."

"You may call me Peter if you wish, but one day, I hope calling me 'Father' will come naturally to you."

"Thank you, Father, before you start, may I suggest we retire to the parlour which is usually much cooler in the mornings. This verandah will be steaming hot very shortly."

Florence and Peter Treloar settled into the comfortable lounge chairs. Peter's head rested back upon the padding and his eyelids drooped to half-mast. Florence worried he may be going to sleep, but then his lips began to move. His warm voice vibrated with emotion as he spoke Odette's name. Florence sat spellbound as her father related the story of her parents' short time together.

The first time I met your mother was in a barn at Clawhaven Estate. It stank with the blood and fear of a young mare in the throes of delivering her first foal. I lifted my head and wiped the muck from my cheeks and turned at the sound of a soft voice close by.

"Will Sunshine be alright, Mr. Treloar? Will her foal live?"

The sight of her beauty in such drab surroundings stole the words from my tongue. Automatically my hands massaged the chest of the new-born foal. I removed the mucous from its mouth. The Colonel's voice came from my left.

"Now, lass, please stand back out of the way. What will your Aunt Bridie say if you arrive back at the manor covered in filth?"

My gaze flicked back to the vision standing at my right shoulder when her laughter rang out like the tinkle of an angel's bell. I stumbled to rise out of the way of the foal slipping and sliding on the wet, dirt floor, seeking its mother now struggling up from the bed of straw.

"You can release the mare, Mr. Axel, and every one step back. She may not like us too near her baby," I called to the farm manager before guiding Miss Odette away to the perimeter of the barn without touching her with my hands and arms dripping with mess from the birthing.

I found it difficult to focus on my work. The silent, pale-faced Miss Odette watched my every move as I wiped my hands on the bagging kept for that purpose. Errant strands of blond hair peeped out from under the dark scarf over Miss Odette's head. Her small hands held her dark skirts above the top of the durable work boots she wore. On more than one occasion my glance met her blue-eyed gaze.

"Come, young Odette, we need to be getting back. It will be breakfast time shortly and the veterinary man will need to be washing up now." Colonel Wellington's voice sounded in my ear as if coming from afar. The angel called Miss Odette turned with a last look, which pierced right through to my heart setting its beat pounding like the hooves of a thoroughbred horse.

Three months later, I met Miss Odette formally in the Clawhaven Cliff Village, when she and Miss Bridie Mayford attended the Sunday service in the company of my landlady, Mrs. Carrington. Miss Odette's downcast eyes caught my glance on more than one occasion. I drew a sharp breath and smiled gently at the sight of a pink flush blossoming across her cheeks. My hands felt damp; my chest ached with the racing heart inside.

413

The year was 1892. A glorious year. Our love grew in our long walks across the fields, in our time on the beach digging sandcastles and paddling our feet in the cool waters. On most occasions, Miss Bridie accompanied us. At other times, it was just Odette and myself. She did not mind at all when I began to call her Detta.

I wiped her tears when Detta told me of her early childhood locked in the west wing of the London house. I hugged her close when she revealed her awe at discovering the world outside. We smiled together when my Detta shared her gratitude for her Aunt Bridie's rescue and her great grandparents' welcome to their home on the Clawhaven Estate. Tears streamed down my cheeks on hearing of Detta's fear of the Mayford family and the power they held over her. Detta told me of her terror if our friendship were discovered and reported back to London. My heart clenched, as I listened to the warning in Detta's story of her Aunt Bridie's fiancé found dead on the beach.

I promised Detta that we would be married the moment she turned twenty-one. Her warnings I took seriously. In the following weeks, I found myself observing my surroundings more, as I moved from one farm to another – forever alert for strangers who may be intent on doing me harm.

Peter sat up in his chair in the comfortable residence of what was once his deceased wife's Australian home. He sucked in a noisy gasp, as the enormity of their misfortune in never finding each other again overwhelmed him. A shudder ran through his body.

Peter looked up and told Florence, "A letter arrived from Detta's father, George. He forewarned his sister Miss Bridie, of Detta's brother Edward's plan to force Detta to marry a man of his choice."

Peter relaxed back in his chair. After several minutes a smile smoothed the frown and softened the face.

"You have never seen such a kerfuffle at the manor several days after my Detta turned twenty-one and Bridie's great plan for our wedding was put into action. By this time, Bridie had given me permission to call her 'Bridie' rather than 'Miss Bridie'."

I often slept in a spare room at the manor when I was not on call at the veterinary office. I was usually the first to rise. On the morning of the 9th of April 1896, it was the Thursday after Easter, Bridie met me on the staircase of the manor fully dressed in her day clothes and with her hair pinned up tidily.

'Good morning, Peter,' she said with a smile. 'Now remember, you can let nothing delay you this afternoon.'

'Yes, you did mention it last night, Bridie. You did not say why exactly.'

Bridie's smile turned into a chuckle. 'Tonight, we have the Rector from the local church coming to dinner. He is going to marry you and Odette.'

'I thought you said you were going to ask him to marry us?'

'Well, I am going to give him an incentive he cannot refuse.'

'You are going to bribe him, then.'

Bridie patted my hand. 'Now, Peter, you do not need to worry. You and Odette will be married before the night is over.' Bridie turned to look me in the eye. 'You do want to marry Odette, do you not?'

'More than anything in this world, Bridie.'

A smile sparkled in Peter's eyes now wide open as he looked across at Florence.

"Bridie was one of the wisest and most determined people I knew. She knew how to make things happen."

Florence did not want to break the spell within the room. She sat quietly and waited until Peter took up his story again.

The minister looked nervous when he first arrived – as a schoolboy might do when up to some mischief. Bridie soon had his blood flowing with a heady dram of the best Scottish whiskey, before she led us into the dining room.

Bridie sat at the head of the table with the Reverend Andrews on her right. Detta pressed into my side on Bridie's left. Bridie shamelessly offered to finance the man's current project of a new church hall. Once the man got started on his hobby horse, it seemed as if he was never going to stop. Bridie rolled her eyes at Detta and me.

When Bridie explained to the Rector what was expected of him in return for her largesse, the man became distinctly nervous. He tried everything he could to wriggle out of marrying Detta and me, but Bridie was not going to let her fish slip off the hook.

The band of gold I had kept to place on my Detta's hand nearly burnt a hole in my pocket. I admit that I was a little befuddled by the operation of the night but grateful for its completion.

As we lay together in our marriage bed, Detta reminded me that we had not entirely escaped the clutches of Edward. We whispered in the darkness until the dawn light rose over the trees along the beachfront.

Florence watched the closed eyes flickering and the muscles of Peter's cheeks twitch as he relived his memories. His hand rubbed furiously at the scar where only a partial ear remained.

Within a week, when I returned to the Clawhaven stables after work, Rosa Braydon the cook, passed me a note from Bridie. I had to strain my eyes in the fading light to read her words. Detta's brother Edward had arrived and Bridie wanted me to hide in the secret underground tunnel which went from the manor to the forest. I was tempted to ignore her instructions. I stank and dripped with sweat after a hard day's work. I wanted to soak in a tub of soapy water. Hiding behind a woman's skirt did not come easily to me. I was more inclined to brazen things out with the ogre called Edward Mayford. Then the vision of Detta's tears, when she spoke of his threats, directed my thoughts to what was best for Detta. I turned from the stable and made my way to the forest near the tunnel entrance.

No sooner had I closed the first silent door into the tunnel, than the chill on the air almost froze the sweat on my clothes. I arrived at the office spy hole in time to witness the entry of Edward and a burly hard-faced man, into the room on the other side of the hidden panel. Bridie and Detta sat at the office desk to receive them.

Once again, my instinct to protect my Detta almost ruined the night for everyone. I bit down upon my impatience and listened. Just when it seemed I must emerge and save the women, Jimmy Braydon and Sanders exploded into the room and overpowered the interlopers. The last I saw was the backs of the villains being dragged away.

I was reminded again that Bridie always made detailed plans.

It was only a day or two later, when the letter arrived for me from my brother in the Cumberland area, telling of our mother's failing health. I felt torn. I wanted so much to see my mother one last time, but I did not want to leave Detta and Bridie on their own while those two villains might be in the area.

That night we had our first argument. Detta insisted I take this opportunity to see my mother.

'A mother is very special,' she said. 'I never had a mother to care for me. My great-grandparents and Bridie offered me so much love, but I still feel I missed out on not having the love of a mother. You have been lucky to have done so. Go to her, Peter, and say goodbye.

Only, you must do one thing. Take one of the men with you for protection.'

I argued that I would be much happier knowing every man on the estate was here at Clawhaven to protect her and Bridie.

Our warm tears mingled, as we held each other tight in the darkened doorway of the silent kitchen.

"I will be back as soon as I can, my love, my Detta."

'My love, my love, Peter, take care. Oh, please take care. Sanders has your horse ready in the stable. He is to travel with you – at least as far as London. I will be happier if you travel together all the way.'

Detta's arms unravelled from around my waist. I held and kissed her fingers for some moments.

"Now close and bolt the door, my love, and say your prayers for me." I laid my lips over hers once more. "Until I return, my darling Detta."

My heart weighed heavy in my chest as Sanders and I made our way to the railway junction, where we were to meet the train going to London. A haversack with a change of clothes and sandwiches pressed upon me by Detta hung over my shoulder and across my chest to rest at my left hip. A canteen of water hung across my chest to rest upon my right hip. Sanders sat his grey horse whistling a quiet tune, which left me free to ponder the choice I made. Again, I asked myself was I doing the right thing in going?

The soft music ceased. As if he had read my thoughts, Sanders advised. "Leave it, son. They will be fine back at the manor. Miss Bridie's people will die to protect her and Mrs. Odette."

It was Sanders who found Edward and the man he called Hammers on the train heading to London. We decided the pair must have been returning to London from Portsmouth. When the train came to a stop at the feebly lit station, we watched as Mayford and Hammers made a hasty exit to the street outside. Sanders insisted on waiting until everyone else had left the train except the guard. As best we could, we examined the people on the platform, before stepping down from the train. From the street, we caught a hansom cab which dropped us at another station where the trains travelled to and from the north.

With our eyes alert, we walked the length and breadth of this platform. We examined the faces of every person waiting there.

"Sanders, it seems obvious Mayford will not be travelling north today. I cannot see any reason to drag you away from Clawhaven on a wasted trip to the border."

"Miss Bridie insisted I tried to convince you otherwise."

"Consider yourself insisted," I grinned.

We shook hands before I purchased my ticket and climbed aboard a carriage.

People filled every seat. A few stood in the corridors between the seats when the train pulled out of the station on its journey north. I dozed as my body rocked with the swaying carriage and the mumbled voices of the passengers buzzed inside my head. Even at the many stops, where passengers shuffled and shoved their way to the exits, I barely raised my head.

The late afternoon sun streamed through the windows and brought me to full consciousness. Many of the seats were vacant. Through the window, I recognized the approach to the town of Preston. I rose to go for a walk along the corridor and stretch my legs. Before I reached the door at the end of the carriage, I felt each arm grabbed in a vice-like grip. Two men rushed me through the doorway and onto the platform outside the carriage. Three men in such a small area made for a tight squeeze. Before I had time to realize what was happening, I felt myself being forced over the small gate at the side of the train.

A hand stronger than my own, wrenched my grasping fingers loose from my hold on the steel rail. The wash of the wind past my ears deafened me. I knew my earlier lack of attention was going to be the death of me. My last thoughts were of Detta.

"Forgive me, Detta, forgive me, my love. I should have listened. You were right."

Peter stood. He limped across the room to stand against the windowsill. He peered out into the garden. Tears sparkled on his eyelids. He swallowed, searching for moisture on his tongue.

Florence watched in silence not wanting to break the magic of her parents' story brought to life. She now understood her mother's last words. Her mind swirled with visions of these people and places her father spoke of. People and places of which her mother and Aunt Bridie never mentioned.

Peter brushed the tears aside with a scarred hand. He limped back to his chair.

"Over the following years, nothing delighted Irina more than to listen to her grandson, the family storyteller, relate the story of my survival. This tale was told at every gypsy family gathering." Peter mumbled as he settled into the chair. "I believe the story became almost a legend amongst the gypsy families over the years."

A haze of smoke caged by the tree foliage hung above the caravans of the gypsy family circled at the central fireplace. Suspended from a tripod, the contents of the large steel pot warmed over glowing coals. An intermittent flame rose from the heat. Its light flickered over the campsite.

Alexei and his lad were heard returning from checking their traps. They were late. Michail commented on how much noise they seemed to be making. Alexei led the horse hauling the dray right up to the edge of the circle.

When everyone saw the size of the body lying in the tray of the dray, gasps swirled around the group.

"That's a big rabbit you have there, Alexei?" some wit called.

Alexei ignored the comments. "Irina – Mudraya Zkenschchina – wisewoman, this man needs your help."

The wide, dark eyes of Alexi's son shone in the firelight. "We saw two men push this fellow off the London train."

Irina stood up from where she sat on the steps of the mobile dwelling with a railing at the red front door. She leant heavily on her walking stick. She called four names, and four strong men jumped to do her bidding.

The men carried the unconscious man inside and lay him stretched out upon the spare bunk. While Irina watched, a middle-aged woman removed the stranger's clothing and looked aghast at the wounds.

"Irina, how are we to repair this damage?" Marfa turned to her companion.

The voice of the fragile lady sitting on the other bunk covered with a blanket of many colours, trembled when she spoke.

"The torn flesh on his arms and legs can easily be sewn together, but repairing the large flap of skin with part of the ear lobe missing will be another thing altogether. We cannot be sure what bones may be broken, either." Irina sat deep in thought. "I wonder where the remainder of that ear is?"

"Feeding the fish or crabs by now I should imagine." Marfa's thoughts were more on the task ahead of her.

Irina rose from her bed and reached up to the cupboard above. Her long, knobbly fingers drew out a large jar filled with a greenish-grey, grainy paste.

"Here, Marfa, put a good handful of this in a bowl of warm water and wash his body thoroughly. This will help fight any infection."

Irina sat dozing, while Marfa sponged the man's body, taking extra care around the open wounds. Irina's head rested upon her hands folded over the top of her polished, solid walking stick. The caravan creaked when Marfa went outside to dispose of the bloody water. Irina aroused herself. She took up her sewing box and sorted through her needles and threads. While Marfa threaded the needles under Irina's guidance, the older woman took up the scissors to cut the end of the stitches when in place.

Marfa placed many smaller sutures under the edges of the flap of flesh and the part of the earlobe. Taking up the large needle and stronger thread she placed intermittent stitches over the upper edges of this wound. The woman stood and stretched her body for several moments, before taking up more thread and the needle. She continued to pull together the simple wounds on the shoulders, the arms, and the legs of the still-silent man on the bed. Only his stertorous breathing assured the women he was alive.

A gypsy man peered through the open doorway.

"Irina, can I talk to you a minute?"

"Of course, Mikhail, come in," Irina invited the leader of the family into her home.

"I think it might be wise to make a move at daybreak tomorrow. There will be people looking for this man in the days to come."

"A good plan, Mikhail," she sighed, a sigh of resignation. "No doubt the gypsies will get the blame for the man's injuries if it is the coppers. If it is those who did the deed checking up on the success of their efforts, they will not look favourably on witnesses to their deeds." Irina reached over and snipped another thread. "It is nearly time we thought about moving north. It will be summer before we know it and farms will be looking for workers. I will travel in my van with this poor man. Will you ask one of the others to lead my horse?"

"Of course, Irina." Mikhail turned from Irina back to Marfa, his wife. "Are you finished here, Zhena? Will you come and get your meal?"

"Yes, Muzh, I'll just clean up this mess for Irina before I leave."

Irina poured a tin cup with water and took a spoon out of a drawer of the cupboard. Drop by drop she poured a little fluid into the man's mouth.

A fresh breeze cut along the maze of tracks through the Lake District. Six draught horses plodded along the road each pulling one of the six caravans, all of which creaked and rattled their way to the field on the outskirts of the town where gypsy families had camped during the summer months for more years than many could count.

Inside the wagon with the red door, the semi-comatose body of the man rocked with the sway of the vehicle. Occasional grunts of complaint were heard by the old lady sitting on the couch behind the table. Each time the wagon stopped; she shuffled back to check on the man's condition. Often, she sighed in disbelief to find the poor fellow still alive.

Over the weeks, the days lengthened. Men left early for work – where they could find any in the town. Others took a horse and a dray out to find wood to sell to the townsfolk, who began to stock up their supplies for the winter to follow. The eyelids of the guest behind the red door fluttered. He coughed and groaned. Irina or Marfa dressed the healing wounds.

One day he struggled to raise himself but found his left side too painful. He shuffled to his right side and used his right arm and shoulder to lift himself a little from the pillow. He attempted to speak, but the words did not form. He sipped water from a cup offered by a gentle hand.

"Where am I?" He tried his vocal cords again.

"You are with Mikhail's gypsy family."

"How did I get here?"

"My grandson and his father saw two men push you from a passing train near our encampment. You were lucky to have landed mostly in the water and missed a lot of the rocks at the edge of the stream. My son dragged you out and brought you back to our camp. They saved your life. What is your name?"

The man sipped more water before attempting to talk again. As he went to answer Irina's question, she watched the wall of surprise and horror fill the man's expression.

"I don't know – I don't know who I am. Who am I?" He struggled to rise again, but pain ripped through his body. It dropped him back onto the bed. His eyes closed.

Irina stroked his forehead. "Never mind, lad, I will name you Pyotr. You look like a Pyotr to me."

Over the summer, the man Irina named Pyotr regained his physical strength. Irina knitted the man a soft cap which he pulled over the large scar and the remaining piece of his left ear. The hair on his head grew except over the scars. It turned grey almost overnight which gave him the appearance of a man much older than he really was. Irina showed him how to drag it across his head to camouflage the scars.

As Peter reclined on the comfortable chair over twenty years later in a parlour thousands of miles away, his left foot twitched and work-hardened hands trembled as they rested on his lap. Peter roused himself from his trance of memories. He rubbed at his face and smoothed his hair over the scar before sighing deeply and resting his head back.

"Florence, for the next twenty-three years I remembered most of what happened to me once I regained consciousness, but nothing of my life before Alexei and his son pulled me out of the stream. I lived my life with the gypsies until the beginning of the Great War."

Tears trickled from Florence's eyes as Peter took up the tale of his life with the gypsies.

By the beginning of autumn, my body had recovered enough to assist with the lighter chores around the campsite. My obvious knowledge in the handling and treating of the animals surprised not only myself but the gypsy family also.

"Either you have been trained in this kind of work or you have a lot of the gypsy magic in you," Irina laughed.

Both day and night, my mind gnawed at this persistent loss of memory. Deep inside me, I knew there was something urgent I should be doing, but I had no idea what it could be. What really bothered me was that I had no idea who had wanted me dead or why.

Mikhail and Irina spoke to me one evening as the family sat around the fire eating their meal.

"Pyotr, have you thought about the men who tried to kill you? One would have to assume they are from somewhere within the southern part of England?"

"Yes, Mikhail, often I ponder on this. It worries me a lot."

"In a few weeks, when the weather cools, we will look to be moving south where the winter is not so harsh. Will you consider coming with us?"

I sat quietly for a long time. Obviously, this was the most sensible thing to do, but there was something inside me screaming to go somewhere or to do something.

"Can I think on it for a day or two? Something is holding me back and I don't know what it is."

Irina rose from her chair and with Mikhail's help hobbled up the steps and into her wagon.

"Come with me, Pyotr. I want you to try something for me."

Irina sat me at her table. She took down a mug and a small medicine bottle. After pouring a small draught of the dark solution, she eased herself into the seat opposite me. Irina said I was to drink her brew and then she was going to hypnotize me. I drank the offered potion.

I do not remember going to sleep, but Irina told me later of my responses.

"Pyotr, you sank into a state of deep relaxation easily, and I asked you questions about your past, but your mind blocked me at every turn. The only thing you said was the word, 'Detta.' What might 'Detta' mean, Pytor? Was it a person's name or a place, do you think?"

All I could do was stare blankly back at her.

While the weather still held any warmth, I accompanied the gypsies on their travels through the northern districts. The pastures responded to the warm weather and light showers of rain. The gypsies set up camp on traditional lands along the remains of Hadrian's wall on the border with Scotland, not too far from the village of Whitehaven. Work was available for the men on the local farms and some at the harbour. My senses tingled from the moment we first set up camp in this district. I felt a sense of comfort, of belonging, in the area. I wandered around the town and the harbour. I climbed the foothills of the mountains. Flaccid muscles regained their strength and began to bulge. My body recovered, but my mind remained confused and anxious. An anxiety I did not understand.

Peter sat up in his chair. He looked over at Florence whose gaze had not left his face.

"You must be tired by now, lass. Why don't you have your sleep and we resume this later?"

426

At that moment, Ethel-May entered the room with a tray loaded with sandwiches and freshly juiced oranges.

"It is past noon, Miss Florence. I thought it was time you and Mr. Treloar ate your lunch."

Florence smiled her gratitude. "We will eat in the dining room thanks, Ethel-May." She indicated to Peter to follow her next door.

"Father, I understand this must have been about 1896 going on 1897 when all this happened. I was born in January 1897 – not long after my mother and Aunt Bridie arrived in Australia."

Peter's warm smile filled the room. "Yes, my child, that will be so."

After they had eaten, Peter asked Florence. "Is there somewhere I can lay my head for an hour or two? I think you too need to sleep. Perhaps I should return tomorrow and finish the story."

"Father, I very much want you to stay in this house. I will show you to your room." Florence reached across the table to lay her hand on her father's fingers.

As they walked up the staircase to the bedrooms, Florence promised to take her father out to meet Jimmy Braydon and his wife Rosa, later in the day – when she awoke.

"You might remember them from England. They came over here with Aunt Bridie and my mother."

"Yes, I knew Jimmy quite well. Not so much Rosa, but I tasted some wonderful meals she cooked. Now my child you need sleep."

"I promise I will sleep all afternoon knowing you are not going to disappear on me again."

Peter lay back on the pillow and closed his eyes, but sleep eluded him. His heart pounded knowing he lay so close to where his Detta had slept for years. His heart ached at the thought that he had only missed talking to her one more time, by a matter of months.

He listened to the hall clock strike two o'clock in the afternoon. Peter rose and made his way quietly down the stairs. At the kitchen, he paused to speak briefly with Ethel-May who pointed him in the direction of Jimmy Braydon's residence.

"Just go out the back door, sir, and follow the worn path past the shed and the stables. You'll come right onto the cottage."

"Thank you, Ethel-May."

Peter followed the well-trimmed path that led around the side of a shed, from which he heard the banging of a hammer and the sound of a mild curse.

"Is that you, Jimmy Braydon?" Peter called.

Wiping his hands with a rag cloth, Jimmy appeared from the shadows within, to stand staring at his visitor.

"Ethel-May said 'twas a Mr. Treloar who had arrived. Cannot say I believed her, but looking at you, I can see you are indeed Peter Treloar – the Clawhaven Estate vet. Looks like you have been in the wars."

"Yes, I have, but not the Great War – these scars were delivered long before that."

"Are you here to stay?"

"If Florence will have her old man around, then yes."

"There will be plenty of time then, to learn about every scar you have to offer. Now come on over to the cottage and meet Rosa, my wife. You remember Rosa from the manor?"

That evening while Peter and Florence ate dinner together, Peter regaled her with the reunion he and Jimmy Braydon had enjoyed together during the afternoon, while she slept.

"Jimmy took me over to my previous lodgings to collect my belongings."

A pleasant sea breeze drifted in through the parlour windows along with the streaming beams of a full moon. Florence and Peter returned to the chairs of their choice. Peter sat back sipping his cup of hot, black tea. He placed the cup on the small table and rested back to collect his train of thought.

"I travelled with Irina and her family for nearly eighteen years – until the war started. Against all the advice of my gypsy friends, I applied to enlist with the cavalry, but I was refused acceptance based on my previous injuries. Thanks to several officers who had witnessed my skill with horses, word spread as far as the cavalry ranks. The army had me attached to the breeding program of the horses for the cavalry, as a civilian. I discovered I was thrilled at the birth of every foal, but it broke my heart knowing what their future held for them."

Florence poured them both another cup of tea from the fresh pot delivered by Ethel-May. She watched fascinated as the expressions of happiness, sadness, regret and loss flickered across her father's face.

"When did your memory return, Father?" Florence asked tentatively.

"It was after the war's end. Things in Britain were all at sixes and sevens. I remained working at a northern estate breaking in the horses, while Irina and her family travelled their roads further south during the colder months. Late 1919, I had a tumble riding in a steeplechase for my employer." Peter's gaze stared off into another world. He drew a deep and noisy breath.

I rode low in the saddle on the horse called 'Lightning.' The cap on my head held the hair in place revealing little of my old scars. I concentrated on the sound of the pounding of my mount's hooves followed by the silence as they lifted over each jump. On my left, I sensed rather than saw, my mate Skeeter. We were always fierce competitors on the race track but close companions in everyday life. When Skeeter's horse shied at something at the water-jump and leapt sideways into 'Lightning,' I had no chance. I was dislodged from the saddle. My head clipped the rail and I tumbled into the water face down. I was told much later that Skeeter landed on his feet just in front of me. He looked back to see me unmoving with my head under the water. Several horses had hauled up on the far side of the jump. Some had galloped wide around the jump. Skeeter hurried back and dragged me to safety.

Officials, including the race-track veterinarian, ran onto the track. One man signalled for the Red Cross driver to head over with his dray."

Peter squirmed in his chair. "That was when I regained my past," He stared at his daughter still trying to come to terms with all he had missed out on.

I coughed and spluttered as consciousness crept up on me.

"Where the hell am I? What the hell happened?"

I heard someone calling nearby. "Do we have to shoot that horse, Vet man?"

I thought they were talking to me and answered in a voice few could have heard.

"Don't shoot the horse."

As they stretchered me onto the ambulance dray, the track veterinarian walked over and shook my hand.

"I agree with you. There is no need to shoot the horse." The man stared hard at me. "Don't I know you from somewhere?"

But I must have drifted back into unconsciousness again.

Florence became worried when her father ceased to talk. She watched him closely. He appeared to be in deep thought. She sat silent until he explained, "It was others who related the story of my stay in the hospital and who helped me put my life back on track."

In the hospital, the doctor examined his new patient. He turned to the nurse at his side.

"This man has been battered about. I don't think the war can be blamed; these scars are much older."

"There are two men outside asking to see our patient. They may shed some light onto his history."

After the introduction of Doctor Berryman to Skeeter and the track veterinarian whose name was Gorden Wheeler, the medical man learnt the patient had suffered memory loss since the infliction of the old wounds. The patient had no idea of his past, it seemed. Gordon Wheeler swore he had trained at the University in London with this man. He knew him as Peter Treloar. As far as he recalled, Peter was from the north here somewhere.

At that moment, the patient opened his eyes and groaned. "Bloody hell that's one headache."

"Good morning, sir. Can you tell me your name?"

"Florence, I will never forget the feeling of confusion in my head at that moment. My mind shuffled two names and histories inside my skull at the same time. I wanted to close my eyes and forget everything. But then a vision of a young woman's face haloed by blond curls held my attention."

"I ... er ... I..." Confusion must have been written all over my face. "I think I am Gypsy Pyotr, but I think I have another name." I closed my eyes and breathed deeply. My hands rubbed at my head as if

hoping the pain in the scars would answer my question. Like an early beam of daybreak, awareness crept in. "Yes, I am Peter Treloar, a veterinarian in Sussex. I was attacked. I cannot remember how or why." My hands shifted to rub at my eyes. "I'm sorry, I'm exhausted." I shut my eyes and as I drifted off to sleep, I heard the words of my friends.

"Will he be alright, Doctor?"

"I'd better stay here with him in case whoever wanted him dead finds him," Skeeter offered to guard me.

"I'll see if I can find his family," Gordon Wheeler offered.

During the following week, my memory returned in dribs and drabs. The vision of my beautiful Detta consumed me. I worried for her safety. Commonsense told me the chances of things being the same, after more than twenty years, were slim to nothing. Skeeter remained by my side, as much as his work allowed. Gordon returned with news of my family only fifty miles away. He offered to visit them and tell them the news. I willingly agreed to this knowing that as soon as I was released, I had to return south and learn what had happened to Bridie Mayford and my wife, my love, my Detta."

"Peter, my lad, I won't let you go back to where you were so viciously attacked without me coming with you," Skeeter vowed.

"Skeeter, you've got work here. Who's going to recognize me now?" The pair of us sat in the warm morning sunshine at the back of the hospital grounds. Things looked like becoming heated when Gordon, the veterinarian arrived.

"I hope you pair aren't about to get into a blue here?"

"No, Gordon, I just have to talk a bit of sense into this boyo." I laughed. "What are you doing here? I thought you'd be working today."

"I came to see you. Have you remembered anything else from twenty years ago?"

I stalled. I had in fact remembered lots of things. I remembered Bridie and Detta's determined belief that Detta's father and brother were ambitious and dangerous men. I felt vulnerable and unsure of whom I might trust.

Gordon's excitement could not be contained a moment longer.

"I have learnt that a Peter Treloar was secretly married in 1896 to the daughter of the shipping magnate, George Mayford. His bride lived at Clawhaven Estate with her aunt, Bridgette Mayford. The Clawhaven Cliff villagers were only too willing to tell the stories of George Mayford and his son Edward, an evil pair by all accounts who killed the young girl's new husband. Some even claimed that the aunt believed her father Douglas, had killed her fiancé years before. Fearing both these men, Bridgette Mayford and Odette Mayford Treloar emigrated to the other side of the world. Some say to France, others claim South Africa and some claim Australia even."

I was pleased to hear that my recollections matched Gordon's findings.

Gordon took a deep breath and continued, "About nine or ten years ago, the Mayford shipping company went into a decline. Some say Edward Mayford, was drowned at sea. Others say he escaped to Europe to avoid his creditors."

After my visitors left, I lay quietly on the bed. With a sheet of paper and a pencil borrowed from the nurse, I wrote a short note to my family explaining my disappearance and my anxiety about finding my wife. When the doctor discharged me in the morning, as promised, I planned to head south. I felt good. My head had cleared and the pain only occurred infrequently.

433

After a slow journey on horseback, nearly a week had passed when I stood in the shadows of the manor forest not far from the old crypt. Dew sparkled on the grass in the early morning dawn. All seemed quiet over at the manor house. The sounds of cattle at the dairy bellowing to be milked broke the silence of the new day. I led the horse deeper into the trees. After the hobbles were tied in place, I used a lead to secure the animal to a tree branch.

When I pushed it open, the crypt door screeched like a banshee. I sucked in a sharp breath and froze. It appeared no one paid attention to lubricating things like old Colonel Wellington and Bridie used to. My gaze took in the undisturbed dust layer on the floor. I strained to shut the door as quietly as possible. My feet led me to the familiar angel with the hinged arm. The statue only made a slight scrape as the secret passage opened.

Having spent one night hiding in this tunnel over twenty years previously, I was not surprised to see the familiar tinderbox and candles (not so new these ones) on the ledge. Light filtered in through the grill high in the stone wall. I paused. Disappointment dragged at my heart. I felt sure Detta would have left a note of some kind here for me. What if there had not been time to walk the tunnel? Maybe she left a message at the other end of the underground passage where it exited into the office? With little hope, I lit a candle and made my way down the steps and into the tunnel proper. At the bottom of the steps, I paused again and drew a deep breath. Hopelessness almost overwhelmed me. Was I on a wild goose chase?

The tunnel seemed longer and darker than I remembered. I tried to buoy up my spirits with visions in my mind of my beautiful Detta. The steps seemed to come at me suddenly. I almost stumbled. Just as I was about to curse, I remembered that I must not make any noise at this point. Noises inside the tunnel could be heard inside the office, faint though they may be.

My heart soared at the sight of a large brown envelope sitting on the ledge and leaning against the wall. I brought the candle closer. My name printed in ink across the front brought tears to my eyes and a rush to my heart. Dust fell from the paper as I took it up. I froze at the sound of muffled voices coming from nearby – the office, I presumed. I raised the candle and swung my gaze around the small space – searching for something more. Oh, my darling Detta, thank you for this note.

Unwilling to leave the place so close to where we had been so happy, I forced myself to turn and I began the return journey back to the crypt and out to my horse. I held the envelope close to my heart. My future lay here in her words.

The music of the rippling brook, the chittering of the birds in the trees above and the munching of my horse nearby broke the silence. I tore open the envelope and smoothed the letter on my thigh. As if afraid to read the words, I felt unable to recall my gaze from the sparkle of the sunlight on the water.   With a conscious effort, I dragged my focus to the page. My heart jumped in my chest at her first words.

My dearest Peter,
I fear something dreadful has happened to you.
Why did you go off to visit your parents without taking Sanders with you all the way?
I know your love for me is all-encompassing, just as my love is for you.
I believe you would never have stayed away so long unless something or someone had prevented your return. I am convinced my brother has harmed you. Just as Aunt Bridie is convinced her lover David Lewis fell foul of Douglas Mayford.
I pray night and day for your safe return.

Aunt Bridie and I must leave Clawhaven tonight for our own safety. Bridie has completed all the legal arrangements for the maintenance of Clawhaven and for our emigration to Australia.

Our solicitors are Mr Birmingham & Sons in Portsmouth whom we will keep in contact with, and who will send you on to us if you escape from whatever dangers have befallen you.

I am sure you will know to look in the tunnel for this message from me if you are able to return.

The ocean over which we must sail will swell with my tears.

My heart, my darling, I beg you to follow if you possibly can.

Heartbroken until we meet again. Your one true love Odette (Detta).

Tears streamed down Peter's face. His hands trembled. Florence rose from her seat and wrapped her arms around his shoulders.

"How cruel they were – Bridie and Odette's family." Florence lifted her head. Her eyes opened wide as another thought registered. "Oh, I guess they are – were – my family too."

Florence kissed Peter's tears away. "That is enough for today. You will stay here and keep me company, won't you, Father? My mother would never forgive me if I did not make this your home too."

THE END

Meanings of Russian words used

Pyotr — Man's name.

Mudraya Zkenschchina — Wisewoman.
Pronounced 'Moodraya Shjenshina'.

Zhena — Wife.   Pronounced Shjena.

Muzh — Husband.   Pronounced 'maush'.

≈

CAST OF CHARACTERS:

Blue Seas House London:

Douglas Mayford — Head of Mayford Shipping. Wife Athena.
Issue: George – Max – Toby – Bridgette.

George Mayford — wife Beatrice.
Issue: Edward – Odette.

Staff at Blue Seas:

Alec Bacon Dowd — Secretary to Douglas Mayford.

Evans — Butler.

Larkins – Housekeeper.

Ally — Beatrice's maid.

Clawhaven Cliff Manor:

Colonel William Wellington & wife Anna:
Maternal grandparents of Bridie and Odette.

Bridgette (Bridie) Mayford: Daughter of Douglas.
Grandchild of the Wellingtons.

Odette Mayford: Daughter of George Mayford.
Great-grandchild of the Wellingtons.

Staff at Clawhaven Cliff Manor & Estate:

Housekeepers	Mrs. Coburn / Mrs. Dempsey / Mrs. Sanders.
Cooks	Mrs. Ogilvie / Rosa Dempsey.
Nannys	Granville to Bridie. /Mary to Odette.
Jimmy Braydon	Groom/Gardener/Handyman from 1873.
Bernie Axel	Farm Manager.
Sanders	Horseman.
Donald Turner	Village veterinarian. Wife Josephine.
Peter Treloar	Village veterinarian.
Tutor Bacon	Tutor for Bridie then village school master.

OTHERS

Mr. & Mrs. Featherstone	At Clawhaven Cliff Post Office.
David Lewis	Organist at Village church.
Stewart Cruickshank	Shipping investor.
Gladys Berrington	Long-time friend of Anna Wellington.
Captain Ryan Aitkens	Captain on ship to Australia.
Doctor Rains	Local doctor.
Local policemen	Graham, Rogers, Stone.
Inspector Davies	CID London.
Accountants	Portsmouth – Mr. Langford.
	Townsville – Mr. Stuart.
Solicitors	Portsmouth – Mr. Birmingham.
	Townsville – Mr. Livingstone & Son.
Mr. Glenning	Publican Townsville.

www.ingramcontent.com/pod-product-compliance
Lightning Source LLC
Chambersburg PA
CBHW060814120726
47909CB00006B/1922